...Sufficient...

G. Lloyd Helm

ISBN: 978-1-62420-530-9

Editor: Sherry Derr-Wille
Cover: Designs by Ms G

Printed in the United States of America

Dedication

This book, like all my other work, is dedicated to Michele, who believed.

"Take therefore no thought for the morrow: for the morrow shall take thought for the things of itself. Sufficient unto the day is the evil thereof."

Matthew 6:34

King James translation of the Holy Bible

I

The grinding whir of the cement mixer was a sound Stephen heard in his sleep. He had been shoveling sand and cement into one all summer so the grind was with him like tinnitus, as was the feel of the shovel handle in his hand. Henry Hardtwick, for whom the Hardtwick Christian Academy was named, called it an idiot stick and Stephen was inclined to agree. Hard to argue with a man who had dreamed of a Christian school then grubbed that school out of the dry brown hills of southern California one shovelful at a time.

Stephen Mitchell, tall, toward skinny, sun-bleached brown hair, tanned face and bare upper body tossed the shovel down into the sand pile and pulled a bucket of water out of the fifty-five-gallon drum that served as a reservoir. He dumped the water into the mouth of the mixer then watched for a moment as it thinned the mortar turning inside. After a moment he dipped another half a bucket out of the reservoir and poured it in slowly and studied the mixture as it thinned.

Thinned. The word made him smile because it made him think of Bill Thinning, a friend from college, a friend he had never expected to see again when he left the town of Mason, Tennessee last spring. Stephen finished his freshman year and decided he'd had enough. There had been good things in school, and he learned a lot, but there were plenty of bad things, too—death, betrayal, protests, heartache. He had left Mason College with intention of joining the Marines like his father had during WWII. It seemed a good plan since the draft was looming over him as it was over every male above the age of eighteen. He qualified for an IIS student deferment but keeping up with his studies was remarkably difficult. He ended up on probation after the first quarter, which made the draft blow a chilly wind on his neck so he decided to beat the system and enlist. Besides, the adventure of it seemed tantalizing. It was like joining the Foreign Legion in a slap-dasher novel.

Stephen thought his life was all arranged when he presented his paperwork to the recruiter to begin the process of examinations physical and mental. Even the Marines, always presented as jarheads who didn't give a damn if you could read or write so long as you could learn to shoot a rifle and make it through boot camp. It wasn't so. The Marines liked young college people.

Stephen took a battery of tests that reminded him of the SATs and ACTs he took before entry into Mason College. While waiting to go into the room for testing he listened to several of the young men waiting with him. They all were dreading the tests and wondering if they were going to be able to pass them. Stephen thought there was no pass or fail in these tests. They were evaluation/placement tests to decide whether you were going to be a rifleman, a radio operator or whatever. In the end they weren't hard, but a couple of the questions gave him pause. Questions about scars or identifying marks on one's body made him remember what his friend Leonard, who had been a door gunner on a chopper in Vietnam, told him about picking up bodies and pieces of bodies that had to be identified by scars or tattoos or birth marks.

Stephen finished the written tests without much trouble, then went off to the physical part of the entrance exam. He expected a "warm body" physical and that was what he got at first. A dozen young men lined up mother naked, carrying brown folders were asked to bend, stretch, open wide, breathe deep and stand still as doctors, or more probably PAs, went down the line clapping stethoscopes to chests. *Make sure the recruit has a heartbeat.* Stephen thought and grinned to himself.

When the PA got to Stephen he did as he had done to the man before, clapped scope to chest. "Deep breath," the PA said.

The stethoscope was still rather clammy warm from all the

previous chests. Stephen took a slow deep breath as he had seen the others do. The PA listened to his heart a moment longer then asked, "You have some kind of heart problem, boy?"

Stephen remembered Southern cops calling him "boy" as they included him among his black friends though he was white, and it made him flinch.

Stephen blinked at the man for a moment then said, "No, sir."

"No shortness of breath, fainting, pain or tightness in your chest?"

"No, sir. I mean, I get out of breath if I run a while, but no more than anyone else I don't think. My stomach feels kinda funny, but I figure my breakfast didn't land right."

"Okay," the PA said. He turned and stripped a piece of paper off a pad lying on the table beside him. He held out the piece of paper to Stephen, who took it. "Put this with your papers and take yourself right through that door." He pointed at a door with a fuzzed glass window on top.

"Yes, sir," Stephen said and stood still.

"Now would be a good time, boy," the PA said.

"Oh, yes sir," Stephen said and pulled out of line, taking the few steps to the half glass door and stepped through it. The room was like a waiting room with bent pipe and plastic cushion couches. There was a slide open window which had a desk inside it. Room and desk were empty. Another half glass door was to the left of the desk. Now separated from the other naked recruits he felt exposed and moved the Brown folder to block the view of his "Meat and Veg," as his father called it.

A balding older man in a white lab coat with a stethoscope draped around his neck stepped through the door bedside the desk. "Right this way, young man."

Stephen did as he was told and stepped through the door.

The doctor pulled a wide strip of paper from a roll at the head of an examination table to cover it.

"Have a seat on the table," the doctor said, and again Stephen did as he was told, laying the brown folder beside him.

The doctor put the stethoscope in his ears and pressed the listening part against Stephen's chest. This one was not pre-warmed like the other one had been. This one was icy cold and it made Stephen pull a short breath and wonder if the thing had been kept in the fridge.

"Slow deep breath, please." Stephen drew in air and let it out slowly.

The doctor moved the stethoscope a little and said, "Deep breath again and hold it."

Stephen did as he was told.

After a moment the doctor said, "Okay." He picked up the folder, opened it, examined the papers for a moment, then settled the folder on the table again. He wrote something on one of the sheets, closed the folder then offered his hand which Stephen, though puzzled, took. "Congratulations, young man."

Still confused, Stephen said, "For what, sir?"

"You just dodged the draft legally."

Stephen frowned. "I wasn't trying to dodge the draft, sir. I enlisted in the Marines."

"Well, you just dis-enlisted. You have a heart murmur that makes you what they used to call 4F."

"But..." Stephen began to protest.

"I'd go to your own doctor and have it checked out. Might be nothing at all, just a slightly crooked valve, but it might be something serious that needs treatment."

And it was done. All his plans collapsed and he was left with nowhere to go. He did go to see Doctor Quixon who gave him an electro-cardiogram and found nothing at all wrong. Stephen went back to the Marines to tell them Quixon found nothing.

The sergeant at the desk just shrugged. "If the doc says no, you're cleared." Stephen was stunned. He took the papers and went home.

He spent a couple of days sitting in front of the TV not watching it, just trying to absorb and digest what just happened. At last his father said, "You're gonna have to do something, Steve. Can't just sit here like a lump."

"I guess, Pop, but I don't know. I guess I could go back to school or something."

"Not for a couple of months."

"Yeah. Maybe I'll just go back to Hardtwick. I'm sure they are looking for people."

His father didn't look all that pleased about the idea, but he said, "That would be okay. Give you some time to sort yourself out."

"I guess so."

So, he reacquainted himself with the operation of an idiot stick and the formulas for concrete and mortar.

Stephen watched the cement mixer barrel go around for a bit longer, thinking he wanted a cigarette. He had taken up smoking at school and now wished he had not. He had the habit, but it was not good to exercise the habit at work so he smoked only before or after. He suffered the craving during the day.

Dave Wilton, for whom the mortar was being mixed, stepped up. He was dressed in khaki pants and shirt with a dirty Dodgers baseball cap on his head. "Earth to Steve," he said.

Stephen looked up at Dave. A couple of years before Dave would have been Mr. Wilton to him, since Wilton was a teacher at Hardtwick during the school year, but when they worked together at grubbing Hardtwick out of the hills he became Dave.

"Batch is ready. Where's the wheelbarrow?"

"Still up there. I'll get it after lunch."

"Lunch time already? Morning just disappeared."

"If you say so. Let's eat."

Stephen looked into the mixer again then took the bucket, and poured a splash more water into it. "That oughta hold it till we get back" he said taking his T-shirt from where it was hanging on the fence. He pulled it on.

The two walked down the covered walk way toward the break room. It was the teacher's lounge during the school year. Now all the people working used it for a lunch-break room because of the

5

two soda machines and the fridge. Stephen dusted himself as he walked. A cloud of gray cement dust puffed every time he brushed his hand over his pants. They didn't look much better for the effort.

Inside the break room there were several people seated around the tables in various stages of lunch. Stephen glanced around not really noticing who was there until his eyes landed on Sherry Kinert. Seeing her sitting alone at a table made him smile. He went to the fridge, took out his bag lunch, bought a Pepsi from one of the soda machines and went to Sherry's table.

"Hi Steve," she said.

"Hi. You got paint on your nose."

She wiped at it with the back of her hand. "Guess I got as much on me as I got on the wall."

Stephen grinned. He and Sherry were good friends who'd painted many walls together. They'd had some precious hours together before he went off to Tennessee last year, but not this summer. Everything had been too confused, too shaken up. Stephen didn't want to bring Sherry into his troubles. He had too many good memories of her.

"You're getting ready to head for Tennessee again?" she asked.

"I reckon," he answered.

"You don't sound too sure."

"I'm not. I didn't expect to be going back, but apparently the Lord had other plans for me so I'm off to Mason College again."

Dave who had been listening said with a small laugh. "That's the way it goes. You wanna make God laugh, tell him your plans."

"Yeah, I guess that's true," Stephen agreed.

"When are you leaving?" Sherry asked.

"You trying to get rid of me or something?"

"No, just curious."

She smiled and Stephen felt the smile in his guts, and lower.

"Tuesday morning next week I'm eastbound on the big silver bird."

Sherry blinked at him a couple of times and actually looked

sad that he was leaving. "Will you write me?" she asked.

"Maybe. If I have time. If you'll write me back. Nothing more discouraging than writing letters and not getting any back."

"I'll answer any that you send."

"Okay. Fine. Maybe I'll write you a story or something."

This sounded like an idle boast, but in fact wasn't. Since Dr. Marchant told him he had some talent as a writer he had been fooling around with some stories and even some poetry. Still he never referred to it except jokingly. He had started keeping a journal, burning up the pages with all the craziness concerning his heart and the Marines.

They sat side by side quietly eating, not quite touching, but only an inch from it. They looked at one another in quick glances and smiles.

Dave got up when his sandwich was through. "Okay, you two. Knock it off. Time to go back to work. I need Mud!"

Stephen glanced up at him. "Ugh, need wheelbarrow. Bring Barrow, I give you Mud."

Dave raised his right hand like a cigar-store Indian and said, "Ugh. Chief-Mud-in-the-mixer."

Stephen laughed. "You better watch out. My Apache ancestors take offense at being mocked and they might just scalp you."

Dave lifted his Dodgers cap to show he was balding. "Not much to worry about." He laughed, and went out.

Stephen stood up to follow him. He glanced back at Sherry and was caught by the memory of kissing her in the dark as they looked over the city lights when parked on Mulholland Drive. The memory made him want to lean over to kiss her again right now, but he didn't.

The afternoon went on as had the morning, except hotter. Stephen tended the mixer and when called for, brought a load of bricks to the upper level where Dave was working. He was putting brick caps on a hollow stone edging that ran along the sidewalk.

After he offloaded the bricks, Stephen stood for a moment

catching his breath and looked around the campus. He'd worked at Hardtwick since he was fourteen and could point at several of the buildings where he had carpentered, cemented, roofed or painted. He was very much a part of the place, not just a graduate. Blood, Sweat, and Tears. The school taught him the three R's but also Scripture which ultimately made him go off to college with the idea of becoming a minister. His Mason experience left that plan in rags. There was just too much in the faith he could not believe, and too much in science which could not be refuted, so he was slowly restructuring his own belief system. Every day as he wrote in his journal he cut away at the unbelievable, stitching in reality as he went. He found he was more and more amazed by the power of God. This was not the piddled, jealous little God he had been taught at Hardtwick or in church. The Creator of the universe was much bigger and more powerful than anything these people could believe in.

Dave looked at the remains of the wheelbarrow of mortar, the one that had been mixing at lunch. The barrow was near empty. He looked at his watch and said, "I think we're done for today Steve. I'll finish this course and put the last of the mud down the hollow stones. "

"Okay. I'll go clean out the mixer and head for home."

"This it for you?"

"Yeah, I guess so, Dave. I'll use the weekend and Monday to finish packing and say my goodbyes. I'm gone Tuesday morning."

Dave stood and offered Stephen his hand. "Great working with you, Steve."

"Thanks, Dave. I was just thinking we've put an awful lot of work into this place."

"True enough," Dave said grinning. "Dug a lotta ditches."

Stephen laughed too, remembering when Henry Hardtwick handed him a shovel and said, "See if this fits your hands."

"See you at church Sunday?" Dave asked.

"Yeah, probably," Stephen said turning away.

Half hour later Stephen slid into the driver's seat of the black Rambler sedan and pushed in the cigarette lighter. He thought of the Rambler as *his* though it belonged to his family. He stuck a Marlboro between his lips and drove out of the parking lot. As he was reaching the street the lighter popped out and he lit the cigarette, drawing in a long breath of smoke. He now regretted having ever started smoking, but he didn't have enough will to quit cold turkey. He was smoking far less now than when he left Mason, but he would have liked to quit altogether.

And the thought was gone. Replaced by thoughts of Sherry Kinert. *Wonder if I should ask her out before I go?* he thought, then discarded the idea. Her folks were still strict even though she was in college now, so it would probably have taken an act of Congress to get their permission. Besides he didn't want to let go of the money that would be involved in a date. He thought of the paycheck in his wallet and wished it were fatter, but since it wasn't, he was going to have to be squeeze-nickel about it. He was going to have to wash dishes once again. He didn't look forward to the miserable steamy dish room Still it was better than the boring library work he started out with. It was also farther away from Cathy Powell. He still had scars from his dealings with Cathy Powell and the Baptist Student Union. Thoughts of her made his stomach sour, as did thoughts of Mary Ann Younger.

Stephen had thought never to see either of them again when he left Mason last Spring. but now he was going back. He remembered the grip of Mary Ann's legs around his waist. He rather looked forward to feeling it again, but there was a certain pinch of guilt involved in the memory.

He left those thoughts when he went into the bank to deposit his check. The account was nothing like as fat as it had been last year. Last year he'd managed to pay the whole year's tuition and most of the books from his savings, but this time he was going to have to rely more on his folks. He was not happy about that. There had been a huge blowout when Stephen ended up on academic probation at the end of the first quarter, but he had been able to say

It was my money! Not yours that was lost, when his mother wailed about the loss. This time he wouldn't have that club to use if the need appeared again.

At home he hollered, "I'm home," as he came through the door and went directly to the shower, dropping his cement-dusty clothes in the laundry room.

Showered and combed Stephen pulled on gym shorts and T-shirt then walked out the front door with cigarettes in hand. He went to the back bumper of the Rambler which was parked in the drive way, sat down and lit a cigarette. His folks knew he smoked, but he still tried not to smoke in the house, a habit he'd picked up from his father.

"Hey Steve," Leonard Turros, who was walking by, shouted. Turros was a Latino, dark tanned with curly black hair and black eyes. He looked tough, and was. It was odd to see him walking.

"Hey Len. Where's your car? What's up?"

"Phil has it." Philip was Leonard's younger brother. "He had to go down to Burbank."

"What for?"

"Looking for a job. Place over there looking for a machinist trainee. Thought he might get it, maybe get into an apprentice program."

"They let him do that being draft age? I figure they wouldn't let him start if he was likely to be pulled out by Uncle Sugar."

"If he can get into the program, he can get a deferment."

Stephen nodded. Leonard had been drafted, done his time and gotten out around last Christmas. He tried mightily to make Stephen understand how bad Vietnam was. When he heard Stephen enlisted in the Marines he came around and threatened to punch Stephen in the nose, for being stupid. "Are you fuckin' crazy, you stupid *cabron*? You could get killed over there!"

"You didn't," Stephen had countered.

"Pure luck. And I wasn't a Marine. They are all bullet-catching crazy motherfuckers. I thought you had more brains than balls."

When that came out of Len's mouth Stephen started to laugh and after a moment Leonard began laughing with him, shaking his head. "You gonna get killed over there. Pinche Loco Gringo."

When news of Stephen being 4F got out Leonard came to see Stephen again, even going so far as to knock on the door and ask for him which almost never happened. "God was looking out for you, *cabron*." he told Stephen.

"Bullshit. I was all ready to go when He kicked the props out from under me."

Leonard lifted an eye brow. "I don't know what use God has for a crazy-ass gringo like you, but you'll be more useful alive than dead." He offered his hand and after a moment Stephen shook it. "Maybe so," he said. "Maybe so."

Now they sat quietly and smoked. "When you leaving?" Leonard asked.

"Tuesday morning."

"Wish I could get outta here."

"And go where?"

"I don't know," he sighed. "That's the trouble. I don't know. Maybe to Mexico or something. I could always get a job smuggling pot."

Stephen looked at his friend, not quite sure if the other was joking. He knew Leonard and Phil smoked pot some, but he didn't think they smoked heavily enough to want to get into smuggling the stuff. "That could get you killed for sure, Len," he said.

"Yeah, I guess. Still, better than sitting here."

Better than sitting here, Stephen thought. *Better Mason than Vietnam, I guess.*

Leonard dropped the butt of his cigarette and ground it out under his foot. "You wanna go get a beer?" Stephen wasn't technically legal to drink yet but Leonard was. A few times he went into the store at the corner and brought out a six pack of Mexicali. It was cheap and tasted all right. Stephen was not much of a beer drinker, but he enjoyed sitting in the back parking lot of the store sharing a drink with his friends.

"Naw, I better not. Mom almost has dinner ready so I better not."

Leonard stood up from the car bumper. "*Adios, cabron*," he said and turned to go.

"See ya, *pachuco*."

II

Uncle Paul, a Cumberland Minister, Aunt Esther, and their two daughters were waiting at the gate when Stephen got off the plane, and he was glad to see them. He could have caught the Greyhound bus at the terminal just a little way from the airport, but it would have been a hassle with the monstrous bag he had brought, not to mention the guitar case and small carry-on bag.

Paul and Esther waved when they spotted him. Paul was a head shorter than Stephen with dishwater-blond hair and gold-rimmed glasses. He always seemed to have a smile on his face. He and Aunt Esther offered Stephen a place to hide out if school got too much for him and he had taken them up on their offer a couple of times. Esther looked so much like Stephen's mother they might have been twins, except Esther had hair a couple of shades lighter than her husband's, while Stephen's mother's hair was black.

"Better than riding the train?" Paul said with a laugh, remembering last year when Stephen came into the Memphis train station.

"It's quicker and cheaper, but the scenery isn't as good."

"You're so tan!" Aunt Esther said. "I almost didn't recognize you."

"Worked outdoors all summer. Better than going to the beach."

As they walked to the baggage claim Aunt Esther, looking anxious, asked, "Did they feed you on the plane?"

"Yes, ma'am, they fed us lunch."

Esther looked a bit crestfallen. "Guess you aren't hungry

then."

Stephen knew from the look she'd prepared a nice lunch for him, and he ruined it by eating on the plane. "Oh, I can always eat," he said.

"Wonderful. I have ham, deviled eggs and potato salad all ready."

"Picnic lunch," he said.

"Except it'll be in the dining room at home," Paul said with a wide smile as they reached the luggage carousel.

"I probably won't need half the stuff I brought," he said hefting the suitcase, which was just below the weight limit, off the roundabout. "I remembered freezing my California behind off last winter so I brought some heavier clothes this time."

"The trouble isn't so much the cold," Esther said watching Paul pick up the battered cardboard guitar case. "Doesn't get that cold in Memphis, but the damp just burns into you." She shivered at the thought of it.

"It's worse up at Mason. Not the humidity, but the snow. It's a good deal higher there than Memphis," Paul said.

They threw the suitcase and the guitar case on a rent-a-cart and pushed them out to the car. By the time they actually got into the car they were all sweat drenched in the September heat and humidity. Paul cranked up the air conditioner.

As they drove, making chitchat and talking about family, Stephen looked out the windows. Memphis was a beautiful city. He had always liked Memphis from the time he was little when his folks brought him to visit his grandmother, aunts, and uncles. But those were kid things, going to the Overton Park Zoo and seeing the Fourth of July fireworks over Mud Island. Now there were some grown-up things he liked. Old Memphis, the blues cafés on Beale Street. The city was well kept, and clean, at least in the parts of it he had seen. Stephen also remembered there were some things he didn't like about Memphis.

The city had been King Cotton for years before the civil war and consequently King Slave at the same time. Stephen never

14

considered that much as a child, but his year at Mason brought those things to the top of his mind. His black roommate and the black friends he made reminded him how human beings were once sold like cattle in the slave markets of the south, especially in Memphis. He never thought much of the segregation that was Memphis when he was a child. *White only* drinking fountains, bus station restrooms, and waiting rooms were just something of daily course. It came home to him forcefully when he and his black friends were pulled over by a Memphis cop simply because there was a white boy riding with a car load of young black men. That stop cost him a beating because the cop didn't like his attitude about being stopped. He learned with a bloody nose and black eyes that so far as the cops were concerned no one in Charlie Horse's car had any rights. Stephen and the others were lucky the cops were only out to "hooraw" some "niggers," not lock them up. After the intimidation and beating they were released, but suddenly the reality of segregation was brought home to Stephen. He now remembered what segregation was. It was supposed to be illegal since 1963 but there were still *white only* signs in public places

As Stephen, his aunt and uncle drove toward home, Stephen noticed there seemed to be a larger police presence than he remembered.

"Sure are a lot of cop cars out," he said.

"Yeah, they've started making like an occupying army since there has been so much civil rights agitation," Paul said.

"Here in Memphis?"

"Not exactly here in Memphis, but all over the place. Even riots up north stirs up the mess down here."

Stephen remembered the riots in LA. They had been far away from home, but there had been lots of talk about them at Hardtwick. Lunch time became a debate society several times and things got quite heated. At first Stephen tried to be an advocate for the rioters. "They can't get anyone to listen being civilized like Dr. King, so they finally just boil over into riots."

"Bah, King is just a communist agitator. He goes out and

stirs up the coloreds till they riot," was an opinion Stephen heard often from several of the white conservatives working at Hardtwick. He was shouted down several times without anyone listening to his reasoning so he finally gave up trying to talk to these ignoramuses who had no idea what it was like to be black in a white society.

Paul said, "There is some talk about the garbage collectors going on strike, but I don't know if it is gonna happen or not."

"They have plenty of reason," Aunt Esther said. "They are paid almost nothing."

They rode along quietly for a time, until Stephen asked, "How are things at school? They were pretty tense after Robert and them were murdered."

"Still are," Paul said. "There has been a KKK presence on campus forever, but they seem to have gotten stronger. Mason has always been a pretty liberal school, but over the summer with the increase of student body there seems to be a greater divide than ever before. There are a couple of groups that are not actually KKK but they lean that way pretty hard. Kappas have started being kinda nasty, or rather nastier. They were always exclusively white, but they were less noisy about it. Now they have gotten in trouble for active harassment of some black students."

Again, they rode in silence for a few moments when aunt Esther decided to change the subject completely. "I had the feeling at the end of last year that you might not be coming back, Steve."

"I actually hadn't intended to. I intended to enlist in the Marines, but stuff happened."

"Stuff?" Paul asked.

Stephen didn't really want to talk about this, but clearly, he was going to have to. He thought he'd managed to leave Tennessee without anyone knowing what he had on his mind but apparently, he had been wrong.

"I didn't pass the physical. They said I had a heart murmur and wouldn't take me."

"Heart murmur?" Aunt Esther asked, concern in her voice.

"Yes. It's nonsense. I went to the doctor afterward to have it checked out. He gave me an EKG, and stress tests, all kinds of stuff and he didn't find anything at all. But when I went back to the Marines to show them, they wouldn't change their minds. Wouldn't even let me take another physical to check it out."

"Well, with all the ongoing craziness in Vietnam you're probably better off," Paul said, relief clear in his voice. "They just decided to send several thousand more American troops over there."

That twisted Stephen's guts a little. He had been ready to go to Vietnam if that was where the Marines sent him. He really had no opinion of the right or wrongness of the American involvement in the war, but now he was more bothered by it. One moment he thought the U.S. was right, then the Vietnamese government would do something that just seemed tyrannical and he would doubt the rightness of American involvement. He often wondered at the commitment of the Buddhist Monks who were burning themselves in protest.

The rest of the ride was more chitchat about family which Stephen mostly enriched with grunts of yes and no. In his mind memories of school rolled over and over. Especially memories of Cathy Powell. With thoughts of her his stomach soured. He didn't know if she was still going to be in school or not. He hoped not, but *that's not the kind of luck I'm having here lately.* One way or another Stephen decided he was going to stay away from the Baptist Student Union. With that came the thought of Mary Ann Younger, and the tingling below his belt buckle, the thickening of his maleness. Mary Ann was a BSU faithful so there probably wouldn't be any avoiding the place if he was to have anything further to do with her. He wished he could just cut her off but he couldn't do that. There was too much between them.

At Paul and Esther's house, Paul asked, "You need your suitcase for tonight?"

"Naw. I got my toothbrush and clean underwear in my carry-on. No need to handle the others. I assume we are going up to Mason tomorrow morning?"

Paul nodded.

"You really don't have to drive me up there, Paul. I can catch the bus, no trouble at all," Stephen said.

Paul laughed. "With that suitcase? I'm not so sure Greyhound would carry you. I'm surprised the plane let it on."

Stephen laughed. "It did take two sky caps and a stewardess to move it to the luggage belt."

The meal Esther had prepared was as delicious as Stephen knew it would be, and though he was not terribly hungry he ate enough to convince his aunt he was starving. The evening was spent in quiet conversation in front of the television, and when it was over Stephen fell into the bed more exhausted than if he had worked a full day mixing mud.

~ * ~

The morning was much cooler and much drier. Drawing the sweet air into his lungs made Stephen feel as though he might be all right with coming back to school, but that feeling lasted only until the car radio news mentioned there had been a battle at some Marine outpost along the DMZ.

"You might have been in that," Paul said, with a twist in his voice.

"You sound like my friend Len Turros."

"Not a fan of the war, is he?"

"No. He got drafted right out of high school and did a year in Vietnam. He doesn't have anything good to say about it. Gave me down the road when he found out I tried to enlist. I thought he was gonna punch my face in. Come to think about it, I have a couple of friends here at Mason that are pretty anti-Vietnam. Jimmy Brodski hates it. He got shot in the rear end over there, and Brad Stringer, one of the dorm monitors in Lorring Hall last year, he used to have nightmares about it."

"Wars always seem to have consequences that were unlooked for when they started."

"I guess. Not just war either."

"Yeah, that's true."

"I don't know, Paul. I'm confused."

"You and the whole rest of the U.S. Welcome to the second half of the twentieth century. About all we can do about it is trust God and keep moving forward."

Stephen wasn't surprised by what Paul said. He was, after all, a minister.

After a few minutes of silence, Stephen said, "How can you stay so sunny all the time? I mean you're in the middle of this mess with the war, the race wars and all, but you stay sane."

"Maybe it isn't sanity?" Paul said. "If everyone around you is running around in a panic but you are keeping your head, maybe you just don't know how bad the situation really is."

"Come on, I'm serious. I mean the whole world seems to be coming apart. It doesn't look like trusting God is necessarily the way to go. It sure hasn't worked out for me."

Paul glanced over at Stephen. "Yeah, things haven't gone according to plan for you, have they, Steve?"

"For sure."

"That's part of trusting God. You have to just mark all your plans *Subject to Change Without Notice.*"

"But..."

"The Muslims say *Inshalla.* Means God willing. That's the way Christians need to live as well. We are in God's hands like it or not, so you might as well give in to it. I mean, remember when Saul met Jesus on the Damascus Road? Jesus said *Saul, Saul, why do you kick against the pricks?* Saul had to be blinded and left helpless before he got the idea. I know it's hard, but if you want to make your life simpler just give in to it. The Lord is gonna do what the Lord is gonna do so relax."

"How do we ever gain anything? We can't make plans?"

"Sure, make all the plans you want, and move forward as though they are gonna happen. Sometimes they do, but don't be surprised if they don't. You have to be ready to land on your feet, no matter what."

As they passed the Mason bus station, Stephen remembered walking with hundreds of people up this same road. State Trooper cars and armed men had blocked the road then.

Paul said, "You wanna drop your stuff off at the dorm or go on to Morton and Jean's?"

"I guess Uncle Morton's. I don't even know which dorm I'm supposed to go to."

"Well you'll probably go to Lorring Home. That's the upperclassmen's dorm, but if there are too many you may wind up back in Lorring Hall. They are talking about building a new dorm since we have so many students from up north."

Stephen thought of all the students from New Jersey and New York who had come to Mason because of the war. IIS deferments were fairly easy to get if you had been accepted at a college or university but the colleges in the northeast were expensive and filled up fast so Mason got all the overflow. It was good for the students and good for the school, mostly. The glut of students had caused classes to be jammed and dorm space to be at a premium.

"I may have to sleep on the porch or something," Stephen said, with a laugh.

"Naw, you can always stay with Morton and Jean. Their kids won't mind."

The very thought of staying with Uncle Morton, called the Pope because he was head of the Philosophy and Theology departments, sent a shudder through him. He liked Morton well enough, but there was something about living with *Dr. Connors* that was less than appealing.

They bumped over the railroad tracks at the edge of town and Stephen remembered how the State Trooper cars had blocked the road there.

Mason. It was a town right out of Flannery O'Conner. The central square, which would have been the courthouse square had Mason been the county seat, was a small park with crisscross sidewalks lined with benches where loafers sat whittling small sticks from larger sticks. Consequently, there was a constant layer of shavings under foot at the benches. Last spring the benches had been moved out for a gathering to honor Robert Gillium and three other black students, all friends of Stephen's, who had been killed in the fire when the Mason KKK threw a fire bomb into the African Methodist Episcopal church.

Now Town Square Park was back to the way it had been with a few loafers sitting in the warm afternoon watching the traffic, such as it was, pass. Everything looked about the same as last year, but Stephen was not seeing it with the same eyes. Too much had changed in his life to see Mason with the same naïve wonder and sense of adventure he had seen last year.

As they passed the drugstore, Stephen saw Jimmy Brodski step out onto the sidewalk. He waved and hollered hello which made Brodski look up and raise his hand in answer though he might not have recognized where the greeting came from. Stephen was glad to see Brodski. Jimmy had helped him with some dreadful life moments last year. Death and betrayal, separation and lost love.

In a few moments they left "downtown" Mason behind and got out into the suburbs. The houses were most all variations on a theme. Clean two-story brick structures with well-trimmed green lawns and trees. Many were faux-plantation with columned veranda front porches. That was Dr. Connors' house. It had not changed much since last year. Paul turned up into the driveway, blocking the car already parked there.

Apparently, Paul and Stephen had been expected, because when they climbed out of the car, Aunt Jean was waiting at the door for them.

"Hello, Steve. My, you are so tan!" Aunt Jean said with a welcoming smile.

"Yes, ma'am." Stephen said with an answering smile. He liked his Aunt Jean. "Everyone thinks I spent the summer at the beach, but I didn't. I worked outdoors all summer. Sun's as hot in the San Fernando Valley as in Santa Monica."

"Hotter, I imagine," Uncle Morton said coming up behind his wife.

Stephen again thought how much his Uncle looked like the cartoon Clyde Crashcup with his pointed nose and brush of a moustache. Stephen was once more glad Connors didn't wear a white lab coat. The resemblance would have been so much that Stephen could not have contained his laughter,

"Yes, sir," Stephen replied. "The Valley is pretty close to desert so it gets hot."

"Well, come on in, let's get you some iced tea," Jean said doing her best Scarlet O'Hara imitation and grabbing his upper arm. "My, my, you are hard as stone."

Stephen had to smile again. For the first time since waiting for his name to be called at LAX he felt himself relaxing a little. They all went into the living room and the men sat down. Jean disappeared into the kitchen.

"You timed it pretty well again, Steve," Uncle Morton said.

"Sir?"

"Got here just in time for the pre-class mixer, just like last year. You'll get a chance to meet all the new professors."

"New professors?"

"Yes. We have a couple of new ones. Dr. Scripps is going to be the new head of the Music Department."

"Name like Scripps he oughta be a science professor," Paul said.

"Oceanography," Stephen agreed.

Jean came out of the kitchen carrying a tray with glasses of iced tea on it, followed by Connie Washington, whose coal-black complexion was made darker by her usual white work clothes and white apron.

Stephen stood and stepped around the coffee table with his hand out to Connie, but she would have none of it. She threw her arms around Stephen and gave him a big hug. The top of her head went just under his chin. He had first thought Connie was the Connors' maid, but had been set straight by his aunt. Connie Washington was a businesswoman extraordinaire. She was the head chef at Mason, but she also owned a catering company that served

22

occasions throughout the county. She was catering the Connors' mixer that evening and this evening. Stephen had worked for Connie in the Mason Cafeteria last year, and he stood beside her when the Sherriff came to report her son had been killed in the AME church bombing. He marched beside her from the burned remains of that church to the square in Mason in honor of her son and the others who gave their lives in the fight for civil rights.

After Connie let him go, she said, "You gonna come wash dishes for me again this year Steve?"

"I hope so. Depends on whether the work-ships are still open."

"I'll make sure you got a job, if I have to hire you myself." She laughed. That was not an idle boast either.

"What's for dinner, Ms. Connie?" Stephen asked.

"Pulled pork, slaw, potato salad, and pinto beans."

"Sounds like I got here just in time."

"I gotta get back to it," Connie said. "I'll see ya later." She turned and was gone with her usual quick efficiency.

Guests began arriving in the next half hour. The doorbell would ring and Aunt Jean would answer. Stephen was amazed at how she seemed to make everyone who came to the party feel like they were the most special guest. She was Southern hospitality at its finest.

All the usual guests came through. Professors of history, philosophy, sociology, psychology, language, science. Doctor Connors was a man of influence in the college and in the Cumberland denomination so everyone on the Mason College faculty wanted to stay in his good graces.

Stephen greeted all the professors, some of whom had been his teachers last year, but many were new. Mostly he didn't remember their names after they were introduced, but one new one stuck in his memory, Dr. Scripps, the new director of the Music Department. He was a she which Stephen hadn't expected from the slight description he had been given. She was quite handsome with sun-streaked brown hair, brown eyes and a bright smile. She was much younger than he would have thought to be the head of a department. Of course, the Music Department at Mason was not huge.

"I understand that you have a pretty good voice, Mr. Mitchell," Scripps said.

Stephen shrugged. "I guess. I've been singing in choirs since I was in elementary school."

"You play guitar?"

Now Stephen was more than a little interested. How did this stranger know so much about him? "Well yes, sorta. Not like classical, I don't read music, but I know how to play a lot of modern folk rock. Lots of Simon and Garfunkel. Some of the softer Beatles."

"By ear?"

"Yes, ma'am."

"Are you going to take some music this year?"

"Yes, ma'am. There are a couple of mandatory classes I have to take to get my degree. Music Appreciation and like that."

"Choir?"

"It's not required, but I probably will. I like choral music."

"I heard you were singing with the Baptist Student Union Choir a good deal last year. Will you again this year?"

Stephen smiled. The memory of the BSU was not particularly happy. It contained remembrances of lost love, betrayal and death that he did not particularly want to recall. Again, he wondered how this woman could know, or care, so much about a college sophomore. "I thought about it," he said, "but singing with the BSU got me on probation after my first quarter so I had to cut back after Christmas."

"That won't be a problem this time. My choir will not do much traveling. We'll have regular hours, and you'll get credits from it."

Stephen smiled again. "That being the case I probably will, depending on what else is on my plate."

"Good," Dr. Scripps said, nodding.

The ring of the doorbell barely registered on Stephen but he turned a little and saw Aunt Jean welcoming Dr. Marchant.

Stephen was unreasonable buoyed up by seeing him. Marchant, compact with red-brown hair, squinty eyes and gold-rimmed glasses, was the professor who told Stephen he had some talent in writing. Because of that Stephen began keeping a journal, writing some poetry, and even some short stories.

"Excuse me, Dr. Scripps," he said.

"We'll talk more later," she said to his retreating back.

Stephen approached Dr. Marchant with his hand extended and the other man took it. "Stephen, how good to see you! I was under the impression you wouldn't be coming back this year."

"There seems to be a lot of that going around, and I truly didn't expect to come back, but *stuff* happened and here I am again."

"Well, I am glad. I hope the *'stuff'* was not too painful or tragic, but I am glad it brought you back all the same. Have you been writing?"

"Yes sir, some. I started a journal."

Marchant laughed. "You know what Mark Twain said about journals?"

"No sir, I don't."

"He said, 'If you wish to inflict a heartless and malignant punishment upon a young person, pledge him to keep a journal a year.'" Marchant laughed again.

Stephen smiled at that. "Hasn't been that difficult for me yet. If it gets that way, I may have to give it up."

"Whatever works for you. There have been other authors who have written diaries that became famous, so if you are comfortable with it, then keep going. Are you writing anything otherwise?"

"Some. I've written some short stories and some poetry—not very good in either department, I think."

"Not a problem. Most writers start out bad, but get better with practice. I'd rather like to have a look at them."

The flattery of that simple request made Stephen's heart swell, but having grown a little cynical with all that happened he tamped it down. He remembered how his first thought last year when he met Marchant was that the man was an obvious homosexual. There had been many of Stephen's friends, Bill Thinning for one, who had teased him to the effect of Dr. Marchant only wanting to get into Stephen's pants. The thought again crossed Stephen's mind, but it was pushed farther back by Marchant's stated admiration and desire to see more of Stephen's work.

"You going to be in any of my classes this quarter?" Marchant asked.

"I don't know yet. I'll have to talk to..." he almost said, *I'll have to talk to the Pope,* but changed it to "Uncle Morton first. He's my advisor."

"Still thinking about the ministry?" Marchant asked.

Stephen remembered Marchant had not been wonderfully happy about Stephen's announcement of his theological intentions. It didn't really matter much to Stephen now. He had thought of changing his fields of study from fine arts to something else but he couldn't think of anything else that interested him so, he decided to just go ahead with his pre-ministry fine arts to see what happened.

"Well, sir, the thought is still at the back of my mind but some of that *stuff* I mentioned earlier has made me question my choices a little. "

Marchant smiled. "It's fine not to know yet. You are still a young man with lots of life ahead of you. I hope to see you in one of my classes."

"I probably will be. Always gotta have more English."

"Indeed." Marchant looked around at the party.

There were professors standing and sitting with iced tea glasses and little plates of appetizers. Stephen noticed that eyes kept turning toward the dining room, where dinner was set out buffet-style. Wonderful smells of roasted meat drifted around the gathering, drawing attention away from the conversational buzz.

"Smells like dinner may be ready any moment," Stephen

said, drawing in a deep breath.

He had no more than noticed his hunger when Connie, still looking cool and efficient, stepped from the kitchen and said, "Dinner is served."

III

The Mason campus didn't look much different than it had when Stephen left it last June. He saw it from a little different angle this time. His room was in the upperclassmen's dorm as had been predicted. Lorring Home was very much like Lorring Hall had been. Old semi-Georgian brick, two two-story sections with shared bathroom facilities and a communal TV room between the towers. The major difference between the two was the dorm mother. Lorring Hall's mother had been Tillie Eleanor who seldom came down her stairs into the dorm proper. Lorring Home's mother was much different. Maxine Brigman was twice the size of Mrs. Eleanor and much hardier in her dealings with her charges. She introduced herself as Ma Brigman. She was good natured and easy to get along with so long as her charges maintained a minimum amount of civility, but she brooked no crap from anyone. She had a mallet of the kind usually used to tap old-time beer barrels. It was rumored Ma Brigman once owned a Georgia Road house and Stephen never doubted it for a moment. Her accent was thick and Georgia sweet.

"Well, Mr. Mitchell, I do have one room. It isn't a good one. It is an upstairs corner room."

"That's all right with me. My room at Lorring Hall was an upstairs corner room."

She still looked unconvinced. "It has three windows and they are all drafty."

"I can deal with drafty, if I have someplace to sleep out of the rain," Stephen said.

"Well, there is," she hesitated enough to make it clear there was something else.

"Mrs. Brigman, I don't care if it has mice or termites or anything. I need a room."

"You're Dr. Connors' nephew, aren't you?"

Stephen wondered if his connection to the Pope was going to help him or hurt him. "Yes, ma'am," he said.

She let out a long breath and said with obvious distaste, "The room is up in the section where several negro students have rooms." She pronounced negro, "nigra."

Stephen blinked several times in confusion at that. Mason had been an integrated campus last year with students of all colors mixed everywhere. His roommate had been black. Stephen learned a lot from Robert. They became friends and Stephen had cried real tears when Robert was killed. "Um, so what? That makes no difference to me. I have lots of friends in the Black Student Union."

Now it was the dorm mother's turn to blink. She was surprised and not particularly happy to hear that Stephen was a member of what she considered a radical negro organization. "Nor to me," she said, but there was the sound of a lie in her mouth. "There has been some trouble about mixing the races here."

A suspicion crept into Stephen's mind. *She never sold a drink to a black man in her bar I'll bet,* but rather than say that he asked, "There are lots of Kappas in this dorm, aren't there?"

Ma Brigman nodded. "Quite a few."

"I'm not one of them. Can I please have the room?"

"All right, then."

"Do I have a roommate?"

"Not yet. Is that going to be a problem?"

"No. I'll take whatever comes."

Brigman looked him up and down thoughtfully. "Very well, whoever comes next."

Stephen's room was basically the same as his Lorring Hall room. A corner room with double windows facing west on one side and a single window facing north. Two twin beds, heads against the east wall, reading lights centered above them, a long desk with a shelf above it, all made of Formica-covered plywood and pipe legs set beneath the west-facing double window. This time, rather than looking out on the quad, Stephen's room looked out onto the street that ran past the Student Center and the Little White House where Jimmy Brodski had lived the last part of last year. The other end of that road was where the Baptist Student Union stood. Stephen didn't want to think about the BSU. There were too many painful memories connected with it. Cathy Powell and her betrayal, Ethan Patrick's suicide, and Mary Ann Younger. He dreaded meeting her again, but even as he dreaded the meeting his maleness was aroused with memory of where he and Mary Ann left off last year. Stephen had made no effort to keep in contact with Mary Ann. He thought to never see her again, but that was going to be unavoidable now if she was back in school.

Stephen left the door standing open in hopes of seeing some of this year's dorm mates. He threw his huge bag onto the bed in the corner and leaned his guitar case against the wall beneath the north window, thinking how Ma Brigman said the windows were drafty. *Might make it hard to keep my feet warm,* he thought. *If it leaks like Ma said.* He shrugged and kept unpacking

He was unloading his suit case when Ma Brigman knocked gently on the open door.

Stephen turned from his unpacking and said, "Yes, ma'am?" There was someone standing behind her but she was wide enough to fill the door so that he couldn't see who it was. "Please come on in."

She stepped in and to the side to let the fellow behind her step in.

"You have a roommate, Mr. Mitchell. This is Mr. Andrew Bankuski."

Bankuski stood a little shorter than Stephen's six foot two inches. He was heavy set but not fat. His shoulders were thick and his hands large. His hair was stiff, wavy, dishwater blond barely controlled by whatever grooming cream he used. His eyes were blue behind thick black-rimmed glasses.

Stephen stepped away from his bed and stuck out his hand. The guy took it and they did the one-pump shake of strangers meeting for the first time. "Call me Drew," the other said.

"I'm Stephen, but I answer to Steve or Hey You," Stephen said with a grin.

Bankuski answered with a smile, but seemed a little puzzled at the joke.

Uh oh, Stephen thought. *Either this guy has no sense of humor or he's a little slow on the uptake.* He glanced at the suitcase in Bankuski's hand and said, "I just dumped my stuff on this bed, but I really got no preference. You can have this one if you want it."

"No, no, this one is fine."

"Gentlemen, you can come down to the supply closet to pick up your linens. You missed the orientation yesterday."

"It's okay, Mrs. Brigman," Stephen said. "I got the orientation last year over at Lorring Hall. I assume it is about the same here as there."

"Yep. Clean linen once a week, clean blanket once a month. You can get an extra blanket if you need one. You can supply your own sheets if you want but you'll have to do your own wash."

"Yes, ma'am," Stephen said.

Drew just nodded.

"Dorm monitors are Brad Stringer and Bill Hartly."

"Same guys as last year," Stephen said.

"They are upperclassmen. They room together on the ground floor. Any problems go to them first. If it needs more than they can handle they will take it up with me."

"Yes, ma'am."

"If either of you want to make room changes, you'll have to clear it with them and they will clear it with me."

Stephen and Bankuski looked at one another, rather obviously measuring each other.

Ma Brigman turned and walked out without another word leaving the door open as she had found it.

Stephen said, "Welcome to Mason College. Where you

from?"

"New Jersey."

Stephen turned back to his unpacking and Bankuski threw his suitcase on the other bed. He began unpacking too. "You were here last year?"

"Yeah."

"Where you from? You don't sound like Tennessee."

"Good ear. I'm from California."

"Geez, that's even farther away than New Jersey."

"Little bit, but I got some connection to the Cumberland Church so I got connection to the college. The Pope is my uncle."

"The Pope? I thought this was a protestant school?"

Stephen laughed. "It is. The Pope is my uncle, Dr. Morton Connors. They call him the Pope because he is head of the Religion and Philosophy Department."

"Oh, okay."

"You'll meet him when you get your Bible class assignment. He teaches a lot of them."

"I'm a math major. I don't think I will get a bible class."

"Oh, I'm pretty sure you will, unless you took one as a freshman. You don't graduate from Mason without at least one Bible class."

"I'm Catholic."

"Doesn't matter. It isn't a religion class, more like Bible as literature. There's some comparative religion classes too, but they are mostly electives."

"Oh. Well, I guess it won't hurt me any. "

Stephen glanced over at Bankuski and thought, *Maybe he does have some sense of humor after all.* "Probably won't try to convert you, but you gotta watch out for the Baptists, they'll try sure as shit." He laughed.

"Baptists?"

"Yeah, from the Baptist Student Union..." Stephen hooked a thumb toward the north window "...down there at the end of the block." Suddenly the lightness went out of him as memory of last year washed over him. "I used to hang out there some." He looked back at the half empty suit case and stopped talking.

After a little silence Bankuski said, "It sorta seemed like Mrs. Brigman didn't really want to let me room with you. How come? Is it because I'm from New Jersey?"

"That's probably the only reason she let you in. She didn't want to let me in because this is the ghetto up here."

"Ghetto?"

"Lot of black guys up here in this tower. Brigman is a pretty dyed-in-the-wool segregationist. I had to be kinda nasty to make her let me have the room."

"So, what does that have to do with me being from New Jersey?"

"She thought since you were a 'damn Yankee' you wouldn't mind being up here among the niggers."

Bankuski's eyebrows went up at the word "niggers."

"Sorry about that," Stephen said. "I don't usually use that word, but I learned from a guy last year that if you want attention all you gotta do is whip out the N-word. I personally have a lot of friends among the Black Student Union. I'm probably the only white guy in Mason, or maybe in Tennessee that ever got stopped by the cops for 'Driving while Black'."

Bankuski frowned. "Driving while black?"

"It's a kind of a bitter joke. The cops will pull a black driver over just to give them grief. Last year at Thanksgiving I bummed a ride to Memphis with Charlie Horse and some other black guys. Memphis cops pulled us over for no reason at all. The other guys knew the drill and cooperated by putting their hands on the car and not objecting while the cops searched them, but, being a stupid white boy, I assumed I had rights and said so. Cop put me face down on the sidewalk, damn near busted my nose."

"Really?" Bankuski said with a little awe and a little disbelief in his voice.

"The guys warned me not to mouth off, but I'm a little thick headed so I almost got us all arrested."

"Arrested?"

"For driving while black. Turned out that the cop just wanted to hooraw a carload of niggers. He didn't want to waste his time doing paperwork on the eve of Thanksgiving. He was satisfied with bloodying my nose, so he let us go."

"You hadn't done anything wrong? Not broken the speed limit or anything?"

"Nope. I know it is hard to believe. Was hard for me to believe too until I got schooled by my roomie Bob Gillium." Stephen's voice broke a little at Robert's name. "Way different here than what you're used to I'm sure. It was for me even though my family is all from back here in the south."

Bankuski went back to his unpacking.

A clatter in the hall made both of them look up and out the door to see two black men unlocking the door of the room across the hall.

"Hey Charlie. What's up?" Stephen shouted.

Charlie Horse was compact and well-built with close-cut hair and deep chocolate skin.

Both men turned and Charlie, a bright smile lighting up his dark face. "Stevie! What you doing up here in the Ghetto?"

"Ma Brigman figure out this is where I belong." Stephen went forward, hand extended. Charlie, generally called Charlie Horse, took it and shook then turned the handshake into the upright brotherhood clasp.

Stephen broke the clasp and extended his hand to the other man. "How you doing, Snatch?"

Leroy Parker put his head down and shook it in disgust, but extended his hand. He was tall and skinny with glasses, and a square-cut Afro. Charlie and Stephen both laughed.

Bankuski had followed Stephen to the door and now stuck out his hand to Charlie Horse as well. "Drew Bankuski," he said.

Charlie examined Bankuski with a quick look then cautiously took the extended hand. He made no effort to go to the brotherhood clasp. Bankuski extended his hand to Parker as well.

34

Parker took the hand with the same quick examination Charlie had given.

"You from New Jersey?" Charlie asked.

"Yeah, Elizabeth."

Stephen said, "You can ask Charlie about driving while black, Drew. He was driving."

Charlie looked a question at Stephen then up to Bankuski.

"I told him about us getting stopped in Memphis last Thanksgiving. I think he didn't quite believe me that we weren't doing anything when the fuzz pulled us over."

Charlie nodded, "Your roomy didn't have the sense to keep his flap shut so he got bounced. We almost spent Thanksgiving in jail." He laughed, but there was an edge to it that even Bankuski could hear.

"I thought Stan was gonna kill me when we got going again."

"Wasn't for Robert, he might have," Charlie laughed again.

"Yeah. I don't know if I ever thanked him for that."

"Yeah. Poor Robert."

"A Civil Rights soldier to the end."

Charlie and Parker nodded. "Well, anyway. You ready for classes to start?"

"I guess. I still gotta go get a job, but Ms. Connie said I could wash dishes for her so I guess that's covered."

"I'm gonna be doing grounds again," Charlie said.

"Speaking of which, I gotta get back to my unpacking and get down to the registrar," Stephen said.

"Okay. We'll see ya later," Charlie said and finished unlocking his door. He and Parker went in and left the door open.

"Seem like nice guys," Bankuski said returning to his suitcase. "How come you called him Snatch?"

Stephen burst out laughing. "Parker is a real lady's man, though I don't see why. He's about a skinny piece of bone, but he has a hundred girlfriends so a lot of the guys started calling him Snatch 'cause he was always with some girl. Everyone thought he was probably porking them all so *Snatch*. I made the mistake of referring to him as Snatch in Dr. Garret's sociology class. Just about caused a riot. Doc Garret is a kind of an older lady so she didn't get it, but most everybody else in class did. They all laughed. We didn't get much sociology done the rest of the period. Snatch, Leroy, has never forgiven me."

Stephen took the last of his clothes and a small clock radio out of the suitcase. He hung the shirts in the closet, and placed the clock radio on the shelf above the desk and plugged it in. "Not much on the radio around here. There's an FM station, but this thing doesn't get FM. If the weather is right, we can get WLS from Chicago. Most of the time we can get WSM, and WMCA Memphis. The alarm works." He tossed the bag into the closet beneath his side of the hanging rod. "If you need more room, just shove my stuff over."

"Okay," Bankuski said.

"I'm gone," Stephen said and headed out the door.

Walking down the steps from the dorm Stephen looked left and right. The campus was small, with only a few buildings, but it didn't feel cramped. To Stephen it felt familiar, homey. It was a feeling he hadn't had since the Marines turned him down. That had jarred him out of his comfortable rut of thinking his life was planned and moving forward.

The women's dorm was to the left. It was a modernistic building with a wide veranda all around it and lots of glass. The downstairs lobby where men were welcome was a glass box that ran from the center of the building to the side closest to Lorring Home. Glancing over, Stephen saw there was a lot of activity in the lobby but he didn't let it deter him from his mission. Across a wide grass lawn was the cafeteria where he would probably be washing dishes in the next day or so. Dead center between the women's dorm and the cafeteria was a fountain that was universally called "The Horse Trough." It was a white stone oblong tank with a pipe that squirted straight up in the center. It was covered with fine mesh chicken wire in a desperate attempt to keep various fraternity pledges from tossing a bottle of dishwashing liquid soap into it. Last year some pledges had gotten creative and tossed in the soap along with some green food coloring. It created waves and clouds of green suds that kept Mr. Miller's ground crew dipping, washing and scrapping for a couple of days. Stephen remembered it and laughed. The wire was probably not going to work and it certainly didn't fit with the simple lines the fountain was meant to evoke.

Next to the cafeteria was the theater arts building. Mason was not exactly a theater school but there was a very active theater group that presented stage plays at least once a quarter.

Stephen stepped off the Lorring Home porch, turned right and headed up the sidewalk at the edge of the quad toward the administration building, which was on the right. In front of him was the math and science building. Beside it was the history and English building where Dr. Marchant had his office.

Across from the admin building was the social sciences' building. The campus chapel where a daily Vespers service was held every night was upstairs. The first part of last year Stephen had attended Vespers nearly every day, but as more and more questions as to his path in life arose his attendance flagged.

A gentle breeze moved through the elm trees, which guarded the quad and the entry porches for most of the buildings. The weather was not so hot and sticky today. *Maybe the fall is setting in,* Stephen thought. He looked forward to the cool weather, and even the snow that might come.

Up the porch steps between the two stone benches and through the double door he went. Across the stair landing and down the stairs to the basement where the registrar and the work-ship office was. Stephen noticed how the place smelled. It smelled of books and ink and chalk and paper, with a heavy back pinch of tobacco smoke. *The smell of scholarship*, he thought and laughed. He turned left at the bottom of the stairs remembering it was where he had first bashed into Cathy Powell. His balls pulled up at that thought. It passed quickly as he went on through the door of the registrar's office.

"Mister Mitchell," the school secretary Mrs. Hartnet greeted him. "You're running a little behind, aren't you?"

"Yes, ma'am. Stuff happened and I didn't get out of California as fast as I should have."

"Looks like what happened was spending time on the beach," she said with a smile.

Stephen's eye brows drew down, missing her meaning, then remembering how people commented on his tan, but he didn't try to explain to her.

Susan Hartnet was of indeterminate age, above thirty but probably not fifty, heavy set with limp brown hair and mud-colored eyes. She always seemed jolly though. *I guess you'd have to be to deal with all the students she deals with, especially this time of year,* Stephen thought. "I need my work papers, Mrs. Hartnet," he said.

She turned back to the pigeon-holed shelf behind her and began looking. After a few moments she stopped, turned and picked up a ring binder from another shelf, put it on the counter, and flipped it open. She ran her finger down a list of names then said, "You don't seem to be on the work-ship list this quarter, Mr. Mitchell."

"I was afraid of that. Miss Connie said I could wash dishes for her no matter what."

"Ah ha. Well, hold on just a moment." She picked up the telephone, dialed and waited a moment. Stephen heard the other phone pick up and someone say, "Hello," but that was the last he could understand from that end. On this end, Mrs. Hartnet said, "I have Mr. Mitchell here and he says you promised him a job, Miss Connie, but I don't have him on my list." She listened a moment and said "Oh, I see. Well that's all right then. I'll put him on the list now." She listened again. "Oh, that's all right, Miss Connie. Just a first of the quarter snag. I've dealt with a thousand of them so far this week. No problem. Bye, bye." She hung up the phone.

Mrs. Hartnet penciled Stephen's name in a blank space near where it should have been alphabetically and drew a little carat pointing to its proper location. "There we are. All fixed. Report to the cafeteria to pick up your hours."

"Yes, ma'am. Thank you. Sorry I caused a problem."

"Nothing to it," she said.

Stephen turned and found himself in the arms of Mary Ann Younger, the one person he'd hoped to avoid for at least a little while longer. She was dressed in her usual modest, almost uniform style of white blouse and knee-length blue skirt. Her blonde hair was a little longer than it had been and her eyes seemed a little bluer for some reason.

"Oh Steve, I am so glad to see you!" she said and put her arms around him, crushing herself hard against him. She turned her face up to be kissed.

He felt his maleness react to her pressure and he remembered, appearance notwithstanding, Mary Ann was a wonderfully warm sexual being.

From somewhere deep in his memory the Mamas and Papas' song "I saw Her Again Last Night" began to play with all its regrets and shame, but remembering too, "What can I do? I'm lonely too."

Stephen bent down and kissed her, slow and deep.

Mrs. Hartnet cleared her throat and brought Mary Ann and Stephen back to where they were.

"Sorry, Mrs. Hartnet," Stephen said.

"That's all right Mr. Mitchell, Miss Younger. Such meetings are, um, heartwarming, but don't really belong in the registrar's office," she said with a chuckle.

"Yes, ma'am," Stephen said dis-embracing himself from Mary Ann's arms. He took her hand and they went out. They sat down on one of the benches on the porch beside the entrance to the admin building. She was clinging to his arm as though she would never let go.

Stephen was completely torn about Mary Ann. He first met her through the Baptist Student Union, but hadn't thought of her as a sexual being at first. He'd helped her to the doctor when her arm got broken at the celebration/funeral for his roommate Robert and the others. Perhaps that was where his awareness of her had really begun, but not until Cathy Powell had ripped his heart out did he begin to think of Mary Ann as more than just a female friend.

He was more than a little bitter about how Cathy Powell treated him and disgusted with the happenings at the BSU. Mix in that Mary Ann was a Baptist girl who was not one anyone would ever think of hitting on. Not that she was ugly, but she was a little heavy and quite plain. Those were the reasons Stephen hit on her. She was low-hanging fruit. Added to that was a factor he only half knew about. He knew her father had been ill. He didn't know her father had died which left her more vulnerable. The first night, after they made love, she told him about her father. Stephen felt bad about that—about the whole escapade. After the deed was done, he felt guilty, but the guilt was buffered by the afterglow of sexual satisfaction. He held her as she cried and tried to comfort her. That night was the beginning of an ongoing love affair. Though Stephen was sure Mary Ann had been a virgin, she was now a sexually hungry young woman and Stephen was her meat.

"When I didn't hear from you all summer, I was so afraid that you weren't coming back," Mary Ann said.

Stephen drew in a deep breath and let it out slowly. "I actually wasn't coming back. I thought I was done with Mason, but apparently God had other plans, and here I am."

"You didn't want to see me again?" she released his arm and hung her head.

"Not like you make it sound. I just felt like everything I needed here was finished. That doesn't sound right either, but I felt I needed to go. I don't know how to explain it."

Mary Ann grabbed his arm again and scooted over tight against him. "It's all right, Steve. I don't care why you weren't coming back. I just care that you *are* back." She turned her face up for another kiss and with a small hesitation, he obliged her.

When they broke from the kiss Stephen noticed someone coming up the steps. It was Cathy Powell. She looked into his eyes and smiled at the two of them. The smile went through Stephen's heart like a stiletto. He hoped the pain didn't show and just for camouflage's sake he turned and kissed Mary Ann again.

IV

The Campus got busier and seemed more crowded in the next few days. Classes were to begin the following Monday so all the students were running around with class schedules and catalogues and books. Stephen ran into more old friends as he went along. He had seen Jim Brodski coming out of the drugstore downtown earlier, but had not talked to him yet. He had not seen Bill Thinning and didn't know if Thinning was back.

There was a tension about the campus that was different from last year. There had been a sort of ongoing racial tension then because Mason was an integrated school. It had integrated without being forced, unlike other Tennessee schools, but that didn't mean there had been no difficulty. Stephen's Uncle Morton, the Pope, and his family had been threatened because they allowed the first black student at Mason to stay in their home while he found more permanent quarters. There had been bomb threats and even an actual shooting through the Connors' window, but things calmed down when John Gillium found a roommate and moved into Lorring Hall. There was still a bit of difficulty there with some white students who didn't want to integrate, but after a little shaking up and sorting out that calmed down and school went on. It hadn't dawned on Stephen that the famous John was Robert's elder brother until Reverend John Gillium came to officiate at the gathering honoring the students who had died in the AME Church fire last year.

This year was different. Though the campus had been integrated for several years the anti-integration sentiment had ramped up and things like Ma Brigman's actively segregating

Lorring Home began happening.

When Stephen ran into Bill Thinning in the Student Union, they bought Cokes and sat down to catch up. Thinning hadn't changed much. His dirty-blond hair was a little longer and he still looked strong with his wide shoulders. They lit cigarettes, adding to the already thick blue layer of tobacco smoke that seemed to always hang in the air of the Student Union. Stephen mentioned the racial tension that seemed more prevalent on campus.

Thinning said, "Yeah, seems like we are all of sudden marching backward."

"I don't understand why the administration is allowing things like the segregation in Lorring Home," Stephen said.

"They wouldn't have if they had been paying attention. Brigman just started doing it on her own. She says it is to keep peace in the dorm, and that might be part of it cause the Kappas are getting militant. "

Stephen had seen several "Kappas" as he went about the campus. They all wore red baseball caps with large capital Ks front and center.

"Kappas. Who are these assholes? I don't remember them from last year. They aren't really the Ku Kluxers, are they?"

"They're the Ku Klux Klan, writ collegiate. They can't actually own up to it so they just use the single K for Kappa and call themselves a fraternity. They were here, but they were real low profile. This year they elected a new president." Thinning took a drag on his cigarette for effect. "Elgin Fester."

"Oh shit," Stephen said, remembering. Elgin Fester was a Mississippi bigot who moved out of the part of Lorring Hall where Stephen and Robert roomed because he "wasn't gonna live with no niggers." Later, after Robert was killed Fester came back up to the second floor to gloat. That had been too much for Thinning who jumped on Fester, gave him a bloody nose, and almost knocked him down the stairs. He probably would have done worse if Stephen and a couple of others had not grabbed Thinning until Fester could beat a hasty retreat.

"Yeah," Thinning continued. "When they elected Fester all of a sudden, they went from low profile to militant. They go down the straight KKK line. They hate blacks, Jews, Catholics, and race traitors like us."

"Hum," Stephen said, grinning. "Never thought of myself as a race traitor."

"Something else to put on your resume," Thinning said nodding. "Speakin' of which, I kinda figured you weren't coming back. I thought you'd be in the service or something."

"Ya know, I thought I had gotten out of here without anyone knowing my plans. I'm not sure I really knew them myself, but everybody seems to have known."

Thinning sipped his Coke and said, "It ain't like you're all that hard to read, Stevie."

"Yeah, well, as the saying goes, *shit happens*. Marines didn't want me, so here I am again."

"Didja go to the Army? I bet they would'a taken ya."

"No. I had my head set on the Marines, and them not wanting me just sorta took the heart out of me. Besides, I might still get drafted, can't ever tell."

"I don't think you will. Once the Marines turn you down, I think you're away clean." Stephen shrugged. "It's in God's hands, or so I'm told. I'll go if I have to, but," he shrugged again. "Have you been watching what's happening over there?"

Thinning nodded. "Yeah, it's pretty awful. I'm not so sure we're really winning like Johnson keeps saying."

"Does seem like an awful lot of American soldiers are dying, but the VC keep coming."

Stephen glanced up and saw Jim Brodski just coming in. "Hey Jimmy," he called. "Got any Old Crow?"

Brodski, longish brown crew cut, scruffy three-day beard, a little heavier, but still true to his Polish roots, ambled over to the table grinning. "I might have a pint somewhere, but you gonna have to start buying your own."

"Can't afford it. I'm just a lowly dishwasher," Stephen said, sticking out his hand. Brodski shook it and turned to offer his hand to Thinning who gripped it.

Brodski pulled a pack of Chesterfield cigarettes from his shirt pocket and lit up, putting the burned match in the overflowing ashtray in the middle of the table. "So how you doin', Steve? Other than being thirsty, I mean?"

"Doing all right, I reckon. I'm back here at beautiful, beautiful Mason College. The Seat of Higher Education."

Brodski laughed. "Yeah, Buddy. That's us, the ass end of education."

"How are you doing? How's it going with Billy Jo?" Brodski had been in love with her forever, even though she was married to Ethan Patrick, who had been the director of the BSU.

Brodski shook his head. "She still won't talk to me. She's the new director of the BSU and doesn't want me around."

"Damn. I'm sorry to hear that, Jimmy. I thought maybe you being away would let her cool down and maybe get over Ethan, but I guess not, huh?"

"I'm still hoping. I go into the BSU once in a while, but I don't hang around. They gave my old room away so I got no reason really."

"You back at the Little White House?" Stephen asked.

Brodski nodded. "Me and Dennis are back rooming together. Where you at?"

"Lorring Home. Up in the Ghetto," Stephen answered.

"How 'bout you, Thinning?"

Thinning was looking down at the ash tray, as though he were ashamed at how full it was. "I'm in the other ghetto, with the Kappas."

Stephen's mouth fell open. "No shit?" he said. "How'd you get over there?"

Thinning smiled ruefully. "Right color face."

"Yeah, but did Ma Brigman know you're anti-segregation?"

"I told her I didn't want to be around any Kappas, but she did it anyhow."

Bill Thinning's father had carried him to his first civil rights demonstration when he was just a baby, and he had been involved in the Civil Rights Movement ever since. He had walked with Dr. King across the Edmund Pettus bridge at Selma.

"So, are you rooming with a Kappa?" Brodski asked.

"No, and I'm not really up in the tower with 'em. I'm on the first floor down by the TV room. My roomie is a New Jersey guy name of Calistari. He doesn't really know what's going on."

"Lots of New Jersey people around." Brodski said.

"More than double what were here last year I heard," Thinning said.

"It's the draft," Brodski said. "Mason will pretty well take anybody who can pay, and that gets 'em an IIS so all the draftable guys in Jersey are coming down here."

"My roomie is one. He's a Pollock like you, Jimmy, name of Bankuski."

"Here, here, let's watch those racial epithets," Brodski said, grinning.

"Time for me to leave before the fight breaks out," Thinning said, standing up. "Besides which I find myself weighed down with all this money in my pocket, so I gotta go buy some books to relieve myself of the burden."

Stephen said, with a rueful grin, "Yeah, me too. See ya later Bill,"

"Later," Thinning answered and turned away.

"That is gonna be trouble sure as shit," Brodski said looking after Thinning.

"Yeah, one of those Kappa assholes are gonna say something stupid and Thinning is gonna answer him back or pop him one and it'll be off to the races."

"Off to the races because of the races," Brodski said.

Stephen shook his head at the joke. "That was really bad, Jimmy, really bad, and with that," he stood, "I'm off to relieve myself of my own burdensome money."

Brodski crushed out his Chesterfield and stood. "I'm in the

same room as last year. Come around for a drink."

"Will do, bud. See ya later."

Stephen's first class, eight o'clock Monday morning, was English Lit with Dr. Marchant. It was a mixed blessing. He hated having to get up early to go wash dishes before going to class, but the class was with Dr. Marchant, which almost made up for the stacks of morning dishes.

Stephen picked a desk toward the front, but not right in front. He didn't want to be "teacher's pet," but he did want to be up front enough for Dr. Marchant to see him.

"'Lo Mitchell," Elgin Fester, wearing his red ball cap said, plopping himself into the desk behind Stephen.

"Fester," Stephen answered.

"I heard you were living up among the niggers," Fester said.

Stephen was saved from having to find some kind of answer by Dr. Marchant coming into the room. "Good morning, class. I'm going to send a sign-in sheet around." He looked over the students. The room was near full. "I think I know most of your names, but please forgive me if my mind skips." He looked down at his desk then moved to hand the sign-in sheet to Drew Bankuski who was sitting in the left front desk. "Mr. Bankuski, isn't it?"

"Yes, it is."

"If you will simply print your name and pass the sheet back, thank you."

Marchant went back to his desk, shuffled his notes then looked up. "Will you gentlemen please remove your hats?"

Stephen looked around to see that there were four more Kappas in the class besides Fester. Those four took off their hats with no thought of it.

Fester blinked then slowly removed his cap as though it pained him to do so. Stephen could almost feel the heat of Fester's boil behind him.

"We are going to be studying pre-Shakespearian English poetry including Geoffrey Chaucer's *Canterbury Tales*. We will read them in their original middle English. Unfortunately, we won't

46

read all of them, but only what is contained in this book." He held up the thick blue lit book. "If you do not have one of these, get one. The Student Union has them new and used. They are expensive. If you have financial difficulties please come and see me after class. I have a few to loan. Now then, please open your books to the Chaucer section and follow along as I read."

Stephen opened his book.

Marchant said, "If you do not yet have a book, please share with a neighbor who does."

He drew in a large breath and began.

The words hardly sounded like English at all. There was an almost Germanic tone to them. Stephen tried to follow along in his book, but was lost in only a few lines.

Marchant made the poetry flow and, in a few moments, Stephen didn't care if he was lost. Marchant's voice was a smooth soothing baritone that sounded more like song than speech.

Class time flew by and when Marchant closed the book and passed his eyes over the class he said, "Well, well, no one asleep? That is fine. I will expect you to have read through what I just read for you and into the next section for Wednesday's class. Now, one more thing. The Mason Poetry Round table will hold its first meeting at eight o'clock tonight in the administration building conference room." He smiled a crooked smile and looked right at Stephen. "If you have pretensions to poetry please come and meet your brothers and sisters."

The bell rang and everyone was on their feet. Elgin Fester jammed his cap back onto his head, muttering. Stephen couldn't quite understand what he was saying except the words, "Fuckin' queer."

Stephen's next class was US History. Dr. Kathleen Parker. Stephen had been in another of her classes last year and he liked her. Tall, southern, with a short back-swept hairstyle sprinkled with gray. He had enjoyed her world history class and looked forward to this new class.

Stephen went toward the front, but not as close as with Dr.

Marchant. Noticing how many red hats were in the class room, he took a desk away from most of them, sitting between Drew Bankuski and Bill Thinning. "Hey guys, what's up?" he said as he sat. Both mumbled some answer close to "nothin' much."

"You seen how many Kappas are around?" Stephen asked.

"Yeah," Thinning said. "I'm seeing 'em in my nightmares."

"How come?" Bankuski asked.

"They are KKK in red hats instead of white hoods," Thinning said.

"Oh," said Bankuski.

"You guys know each other?" Stephen asked.

"Naw," Thinning said. Bankuski just shook his head.

"Well, Drew, this is my friend and fellow conspirator Bill Thinning. Bill, this is my roomie Drew Bankuski."

They nodded at one another. "Watch out for him, Drew," Thinning said with a bitter grin. "He's about half Baptist and they're dangerous."

"How's that?" Bankuski said.

"They have beautiful women, like her," Thinning said as Cathy Powell came into the room. She drew every male eye in the class.

"Wow," Bankuski breathed.

"That's Stevie's ex," Thinning went on.

Bankuski looked at his roomie with a new respect and once more said, "Wow."

"She is a dick straightener," Thinning said. "Bait for the BSU, and if you get pulled in you may never get out."

"I got out," Stephen protested.

"Not without scars."

"True enough," Stephen said.

Dr. Parker came in and went to the desk. A lectern stood beside it and she put a stack of papers upon it. She glanced over the class then said, "Please sign your names on the sign-in sheet that is going around. I will mark you absent if your name is not on the sheet."

Stephen looked around wondering if she would say something about the still-hatted Kappas but she didn't. She went right into her lecture and the red caps stayed put.

After class, out in the hallway, they watched the red hats disperse. Stephen said, "Dr. Marchant made them all take off their hats. Pissed Fester off something awful."

"I'm not surprised. Fester wears a cap so the point on top of his head doesn't show," Thinning said.

Bankuski laughed and Stephen smiled.

"They are getting worse and worse," Thinning said.

Stephen said, "Just be a little careful about stirring 'em up, Bill. Fester doesn't like you much after last year. He's liable to get some of his boys to come and try to even the score."

Stephen glanced at his watch. "I gotta go wash dishes. See you guys later."

As he walked across campus toward the cafeteria Cathy Powell stole into his mind. He had been deeply in love with her, until he caught her giving a blow job to David Hall. That image still haunted him partly because he had considered her pure, and partly because she had never allowed him any sexual play other than an open-mouthed kiss. Truth be told he still had a burned place in his heart with Cathy's name on it. Shaking his head to himself he thought, *Bill's right, she really is a dick straightener.*

Walking up the porch steps to the cafeteria door he almost ran over Mary Ann. She grabbed his arm to keep from being knocked over. "Where you going in such a hurry?" she asked.

"Lunch, then dishes," he said. It sounded short to him and he didn't mean it to be.

"It's a little early for lunch."

"Call it brunch then. I didn't have breakfast."

"I'll come and sit with you so you don't have to eat alone."

"That's okay, I don't mind eating alone. Got dishes already stacked up waiting for me in the dish room." Again, he felt he was being short with her and he didn't want to do that. He liked Mary Ann and God knew she was the best lover he ever had—well, the only real lover he ever had.

"I don't mind that you have to eat fast. I'll just sit and watch."

Stephen laughed. "Like watching pigs at the trough, right?"

Mary Ann giggled. "No."

Stephen said, "I gotta warn you, I'm not in a much social mood at the moment."

"Why not?"

Cathy passed through his mind again, but he said, "Red hats. Damn Kappas are all over the place and they worry me."

Mary Ann stretched up on her toes and kissed his cheek. "I'll try to take your mind off them while you eat."

Stephen looked into her smiling blue eyes and gave in. "Okay, come on."

"You need a shave," she said.

He rubbed his hand over his chin and said, "Guess so."

Inside Mary Ann said, "I'll get a table."

Stephen nodded and started down the line. There was beef stew, chicken, mashed potatoes and gravy, other things. He chose the readymade cheeseburger, some fries, and a glass of iced tea. He had his meal ticket punched, went out to the dining hall and looked around for Mary Ann. Spotting her on the right-side line of tables by the windows with a view of the horse trough, he headed toward her, but she wasn't alone. Another BSU girl whose name Stephen couldn't remember sat with her. She had been in the choir with him, and she had been in the BSU when Ethan Patrick shot himself. Then it came to him. Laura. Her name was Laura Pettibone. Her hair was light brown and curly, framing her face in an unflattering way. She wore square tortoiseshell glasses which did not help her looks at all.

Stephen set his tray on the table and pulled out a chair. "You two ganging up on me?" he asked with only a half joking edge.

"Just wanted to invite you over to the BSU open house tonight," Laura said.

"Can't do it," he answered.

"Why not?" Mary Ann asked sounding a little hurt.

"Poetry," he answered. "Marchant's Poetry Roundtable is meeting tonight and I need to be there."

"You a poet?" Laura asked.

Stephen shrugged. "Doc said, *Pretentions toward poetry,* and that pretty well says it. "

"You could come over later," Mary Ann said, with a certain look in her eyes.

The look caused his loins to stir a little. "Why should I do that?"

Mary Ann shrugged.

"Naw, I don't think so," he said and took a bite of the cheeseburger. It was dry. He followed it with a French fry which was more like a stick than a potato slice. He reached for the catsup bottle and poured some on the potatoes.

"Billy Jo said she would like to see you," Laura said. "She's trying to pull a choir together again."

"Definitely not," Stephen said. "Damn Baptist choir almost got me thrown out of school last time so no, I have other fish to fry." He took another bite of the dry cheeseburger and dropped it back on the plate, then scooted his chair back. "I gotta go wash dishes," he said and stood up.

"You didn't eat much lunch," Mary Ann said.

"Waste of a punch. Connie must not be in the kitchen. Her hamburgers are way better than this." He picked up the iced tea, slugged it down, then picked up the tray and headed toward the dish room window to shove it through. Gary Mamoni, a New Jersey guy who had been with Stephen in the dish room last year took the tray, slid the plate off, emptied it down the garbage chute and stacked it. The tray went into another pile. The stacks were not huge but Mamoni was alone so the stacks were not getting much shorter.

"I'll be in to help you in a minute, Mamoni." Stephen said.

"I'm outta here," the other answered. "I got Biology at noon."

"Okay," Stephen said.

He turned to find Mary Ann standing right behind him. She

pressed herself against him and got the reaction Stephen assumed she was after. He put his arms around her waist then slid his hands down onto her bottom for a quick squeeze. She broke away.

"Stephen," she scolded. "Everybody will see!"

He looked over her shoulder at the almost empty dining hall and said, "Screw 'em. Let 'em look." He bent forward and kissed her.

"Come over to the BSU later tonight and maybe there'll be more?"

"For a Baptist girl you are evil," he said with a grin.

"I'll see you tonight," she said and turned away from him.

"Maybe. The BSU has a lot of bad memories for me."

She turned back for a moment then said, "Please?"

Stephen shrugged. "Maybe."

She smiled and turned away.

He watched her for a moment then turned to go in the kitchen door.

V

Stephen climbed the stairs in the admin building heading for the conference room, carrying some of his poetry. He passed a group of night class students standing outside a classroom door on their midway break. As usual the tobacco smoke was thick around them. Focused so hard on his destination he didn't notice who was in the group until someone said, "Hey Hollywood, you going to that queer's poetry thing?"

Stephen stopped and turned back. It was Fester, still wearing his red cap. There were several more Kappas standing with him. *They always seem to be in gangs,* Stephen thought. He had no answer for Fester so he turned on his heel and headed on down the hall. Fester said something to the other red hats that Stephen didn't hear. They all laughed which made Stephen flush but he didn't turn around, just kept walking.

Inside the conference room there were a couple of large round tables. A half dozen students were there, some of whom Stephen knew, and others he did not. One who he recognized almost made him turn and walk back toward the knot of Kappas. Cathy Powell. She was dressed in a straight blue skirt and a peach-colored blouse with a tie in front, looking every inch *the dick straightener* Bill Thinning had tagged her. She looked him up and down when he came in and took a step toward him, changed her mind, and stayed where she was. Stephen swallowed hard looking at her, but decided to stay.

He recognized a couple of other people as staff on the Mason *Brick,* the school newspaper. All were milling around obviously not knowing what was required of them since Dr. Marchant was not yet present.

There was an ashtray on the table and several people were smoking so Stephen lit up as well. *Gonna have to watch this,* he thought, purposely keeping his thoughts away from Cathy by keeping his hands busy. *Damn cigarettes are expensive.* He thought, *Wonder if I can start rolling my own?* He had watched his father roll his own smokes for years. Velvet tobacco and OCB papers. *I think I could do that.* He took a drag off the Marlboro in his hand and thought, *I oughta just quit.*

Dr. Marchant came in and fanned his hand in front of his face. "If you are going to smoke in here, please open a window." He walked across the room, and raised one of the casement windows. He fanned some papers in his other hand trying to encourage the tobacco fog out the window, but didn't seem to have much luck with it.

"Sit down please, everyone," Marchant said and took his own command, sitting at the largest round table.

Everyone found seats and Marchant began, "This is going to be more organizational meeting than anything else. It is my intention to gather student-authored material, poetry and short prose, and produce an anthology of Mason student work. I will need some of you to function as first readers and eventually as editors. That will probably fall to you folks from the *Brick*, Miss Phillips, and you, Mr. Allen." He indicated the two who were sitting together. Miss Phillips was a skinny red head with long straight hair. Allen looked to be a grinder, dark-brown crew cut, worried face, thick glasses. The way those two looked at one another Stephen was convinced they were a couple.

"There are no requirements for this organization. No homework or readings, but to remain active you will have to write. I don't care what you write, but there must be some creative work. Probably, the majority of content for the anthology will come from this group, but we will open the offer to all who wish to contribute, and membership in this round table will be no guarantee of publication. It is my intention to gather material through this first quarter. We will sort and decide on content after Christmas and hopefully bring out the book by middle of the spring quarter."

"How will you gather material, Dr. Marchant?" asked a blond girl Stephen didn't know.

"I will have a box set up outside my office to receive contributions. I will remind all my classes weekly and I have asked the other English professors to do the same."

"That could pull in a lot of stuff, Dr. Marchant," a man Stephen thought was an upper classman said. There was something a little feminine and prancey about him which made Stephen wonder if he was homosexual. That idea made him uncomfortable. He had pretty well gotten over the discomfort with Marchant's homosexuality, but it still bothered him a little that he liked Marchant.

"It could indeed, Mr. Davis. I am hoping it will. The more we have to choose from the more likely we are to have some worthy pieces."

"Is the book going to be the sole focus of the round table?" the blond girl asked.

"No," Marchant said. "I hesitated to do this as it has potential for ill feeling, but I decided to go ahead to do reading critiques as well. The author/poet will read his or her own work and the other members will *carefully* critique it. There will be no simply saying 'It's lousy.' If indeed it is lousy, or magnificent the critic must be prepared to say why—to defend his position, as it were. It will help the writer to improve and help all to sharpen their critical thinking and reading skills."

He looked around the table. Everyone seemed to be thinking hard, perhaps considering whether or not to continue. "Seven of you. Seems auspicious. I look to have pieces from all of you within the next week," he said and stood up. "Any other questions?" he asked and waited a moment. There were no questions forthcoming so he said, "That is all for tonight. Thank you all for coming. We will meet here again next Monday. Bring something to read." He gathered his papers nodded to the group and left.

Stephen glanced at his watch. Eight thirty. *Maybe I could sneak over to the BSU and get Mary Ann out of there,* he thought. It had been a long time since he had felt her legs around him, and it was a nice warm night. The Methodist church cemetery was nice and dark. Almost before he knew it, he was on his feet, gathering his papers.

In the hall Stephen looked toward the stairway by which he entered. There was no knot of people there now, but Stephen turned the other way to go down the back stairs out onto the street behind the admin building. He turned right and started ambling toward the BSU, still not quite sure he wanted to go there, Mary Ann notwithstanding, but his feet seemed to know so he kept walking.

"You going to the welcome party?" Cathy Powell said, startling him.

He looked over at her in the fading light.

"Just to say hi to a couple people. Billy Jo maybe."

"She's re-forming the choir."

"So I heard, but I won't be in it."

"Why not?" she asked.

Her shoulder brushed Stephen's and he moved a little away.

"Lot of things. Too much time for one thing. Landed me on probation winter quarter last year."

"Is that all?" she asked and her shoulder brushed his arm again.

Stephen looked over at her. She was close enough to smell her perfume and that aroma went directly to his loins. Her face was tilted up a little. Had he been so inclined he could have kissed her with just a slight bend of his neck. He could taste her kisses in memory. They made him weak in the knees, until he remembered the pain.

"You and Hall still an item?" he asked.

Stephen felt the electricity of the question jump from his shoulder to Cathy's. She moved away from him because of it.

"No," she said.

"Good. I figured he was gonna jump out from behind a bush and kick my ass again." Stephen said.

"I'm sorry about that. I'm sorry about all of it, Stephen. I really am."

"So you've said." They walked along another step or two before he said, "I had it coming mostly. I was real nasty to you in the library that time, but I was hurt. Still, hurt or not I shouldn't have come after you like that."

"I am so sorry. It was all my fault, the library and all of it."

Stephen looked over at her. Her face was still angelic. Her eyes could swallow a man like bottomless pools. "Okay, okay," he said. "You're sorry, I'm sorry, David Hall's sorry, whole damn world is sorry, but I am not gonna come back to the BSU Choir."

They arrived at the gate in the white picket fence leading into the yard of the BSU. It was almost dark now. The light from the TV porch was blazing and the TV was on though there was no one watching. The low roar of people talking over music came from the big room that used to be the dining room and was now the meeting room.

Stephen opened the picket gate to let Cathy precede him. Her hips swayed gently and it made him swallow hard to watch her climb the two steps to the screen door onto the TV porch.

The meeting room was crowded, and a radio played in the back ground. Apparently, everyone who had ever been associated with the BSU had come to this party. Stephen, being slightly taller than most of the room, looked over their heads seeking Mary Ann. He did not see her and thought, *Maybe she didn't come since I told her I wasn't going to.* David Hall was there, as was Harley James. That one surprised Stephen. The only reason Harley James had ever hung around the BSU was to be close to Ethan and with him gone ...

The two large armchairs that used to be in the room were gone. The one where Ethan had been sitting when he shot himself was so bloodstained it could not be used again and the other was so much like its mate no one could look at it without experiencing the horror of that day again so it was moved out as well.

Laura Pettibone was there, as were several others he recognized, but whose names he didn't remember.

"Steve!" Billy Jo Patrick said, pushing through people to reach him.

She was as cute as he remembered, short, reddish-blonde hair cut boy short, an infectious smile, and a yellow sun dress that would have been more appropriate for spring. "Glad you could make it." Her voice and accent were Tennessee sweet.

Stephen smiled back at her. "Quite a crowd," he said

"The whole choir," she said. "Gonna start the Sunday rounds again in a couple of weeks."

Stephen wondered how many churches would want them back after all that happened last year, but he said nothing about it, not wanting to bring up the painful subject or seem to volunteer for this year's rounds.

"There's food and punch in the kitchen, if you can get to it," Billy Jo said.

Stephen smiled at her. He always liked Billy Jo though he considered her a fool for believing she could change Ethan—make him overcome his homosexual cravings. She was pretty and infectiously happy most of the time so he liked her. Jimmy Brodski liked her too, and Stephen half expected to find him hanging around this party to be near her, but he wasn't there.

"Is Mary Ann around?" Stephen asked.

"I don't know," Billy Jo said. "I thought I saw her earlier."

"Okay, I'll go check in the kitchen."

"I'll see you later," Billy Jo said. "We're gonna organize the choir a little and maybe sing some after a while."

Stephen nodded but did not tell her he was not going to be around for that. He pushed through several people who were between him and the kitchen door and felt like he had been squeezed out like tooth paste when he got into the kitchen. Glancing out the back door which lead onto the back porch he saw Mary Ann standing with a paper cup in her hand, talking to an oriental girl he remembered. Her name was Linda something. He stepped to the screen and said through it, "So here's where you're hiding."

Mary Ann turned to squint through the screen. "Oh, you did come. I thought you said you weren't."

"The round table didn't last as long as I expected so, here I am," he said opening his arms like he was about to take a bow. Ignoring the Linda girl, he said, "Could we get out of here now, before Billy Jo starts with the choir stuff?"

Mary Ann looked at Linda then said with sort of teasing twist, "Sorry Linda, my man wants to go, so I'm gonna go. We'll talk some more later."

Stephen pushed the screen door open and held it so Linda could come in, then stepped through onto the porch. He took Mary Ann's hand and started leading her down the back steps. She bridled a bit, slugged down the rest of her punch and set the empty cup on the porch rail. "Where we off to in such a hurry?" she asked.

"Methodist Cemetery," he answered her shortly.

She stopped and pulled Stephen to a stop. "Kinda presumptuous, aren't you? I mean you didn't as much as write me a letter all summer, then you expect me to go to the cemetery with you?"

He turned back and pulled her into his arms, sliding his hands down her back onto her bottom, pulling her tight against his already growing erection. "Didn't you just say I was your man?" He bent to kiss her.

Mary Ann's behind flexed as she pushed herself against him, giving the lie to her resistance. When he broke from the kiss, she stroked her hand over his cheek. "You still didn't shave," she said

"Sorry," Stephen said, and let go of her. She took his hand and they began walking toward Church Street where the Methodist church was located.

A first quarter moon was rising, but not giving much light as they threaded their way through the headstones toward the back corner of the grave yard. In the far back corner, there was a natural hiding place for lovers. The Danjo plot. They were a wealthy family in the town of Mason and their name was to be found in many places, but the only one Stephen was interested in was the one in the Methodist Cemetery. The headstone was a family headstone, four feet wide and a foot thick. The center of the curve in the stone's top was just a little below Stephen's waist which made it the perfect height. There were cypress trees planted around the cemetery and in the back corner those trees intermingled so it was like a wall.

Stephen pushed Mary Ann against the headstone and kissed her hungrily. She at first held back, surprised by the violence of it, but after a moment she relaxed into his arms. After a few seconds Stephen leaned back pressing his loins against hers and began unbuttoning her blouse. With each button he leaned in, kissed her until her bra was exposed. He pushed it up and leaned down to kiss and suckle her nipples.

"Oh Steve," she whispered as her nipples grew erect.

After some minutes of attention to her breasts Stephen stooped and lifted the hem of her skirt up to her waist then lifted her a little so she sat on top of the stone. The flesh of her legs was silky smooth and reflected the dim silver of the moon and stars. She opened her legs enough so he could see her white cotton panty crotch. He bent over and kissed a path up the insides of her thighs, stroking his fingers after the kisses. Toward her panty crotch the scent of her was so rich he had to move up to kiss her mouth again or risk cumming in his pants. After a few more kisses Steve put his thumbs into the waistband of her panties and began pulling them down. She lifted her bottom enough so he could remove them, and let them fall to the ground. He undid his belt buckle, unbuttoned his Levis, pulling the rubber from the watch pocket, and let his Levis and underwear fall to the ground around his ankles. He handed the little square packet to her. "Open that," he said.

Mary Ann took it and began to tear the top open, but was distracted when Stephen stroked her womanhood with his finger then inserted two fingers into her. He found her wet and fully ready for him. He took the rubber from her, removed it from the packet and unrolled it onto his straining penis, moved himself up to start the insertion. He put his arms around Mary Ann to brace and hold her. Her legs came up and her ankles locked around his waist.

Stephen began driving himself into her, slowly at first, but then with more and more force. Mary Ann began moaning with each thrust and the sound made Stephen drive harder.

As he climaxed, mind gone, concentrating only on the feeling, he breathed in deeply and whispered, "Cathy."

Mary Ann didn't seem to notice the whisper, being caught up in her own climax, and Stephen was relieved about that. He continued to thrust for a moment after his climax until he felt Mary Ann relaxing. She squeezed her arms and legs tight around him, kissed him and whispered, "I love you, Stephen."

Stephen answered her kiss with a kiss and a final thrust, but not with an "I love you" of his own.

Afterward they dressed and walked silently hand in hand to the women's dorm. Stephen brought her into the dorm lobby, kissed her and asked, "You okay?"

Mary Ann tightened her embrace squeezing him against her, turning her head to lie against his chest. "I can hear your heart," she said.

"Is it murmuring?" he asked.

She looked up at him, puzzled.

"Nothing," he said. "That is a joke so inside I'm the only one that gets it." He broke from her embrace. "Good night." He turned away and headed out the door.

Stephen went back around the building to the street and turned left intending to go in the back door of Lorring Home. The evening was still in his head, and not the good part of it—well, sort of the good part of it.

He could not believe that, at the moment of climax Cathy came into his mind, and worse, came out of his mouth. *You'd think when you were making love, you'd be concentrating on the one you were with,* he thought. That was problematic as well. He had first seduced Mary Ann more out of bitterness than anything else. To show himself and Cathy he didn't need her any more than she needed him. He never expected to actually make love to Mary Ann, but the stars had been perfectly aligned so it came to pass. Afterward, she became attached. They continued to make love the rest of the spring quarter, but when Stephen went home for the summer, never intending to return, he thought it was over. Now it was simmering again.

Stephen liked Mary Ann. She was sweet, nice, and kind. He did not want to hurt her, but he was obviously still smitten with Cathy, and Mary Ann whispered she loved him. *Oh Lord, what am I gonna do,* he prayed.

As he passed the Student Union, he saw Jimmy Brodski sitting with Dennis Grant, his roommate. There were the remains of a meal and coffee cups. Stephen turned in and went to sit with them. He lit up a Marlboro and let the first puff drift out.

Brodski, half joking, said, "You look troubled, my brother. Anything Dr. Crow could help with?"

"I don't know, Jimmy. I could use a drink I guess, but that's not really why I'm here."

"You kinda got that Cathy Powell look about you," Brodski said accusingly. "But I know it can't be that, cause you are smart enough to stay away from her. Right?"

"I try, Jimmy, but she follows me like a bloodhound on a scent. I went to the Poetry Round table tonight and there she was. I didn't know she wrote anything besides school papers, but there she was. She followed me out."

"Out? To where?"

Stephen looked down, ashamed of himself. "To the BSU."

"Aw, Steve, you're supposed to stay away from over there. It's a trap and Cathy is the bait."

"Yeah, yeah I know, I know, but Mary Ann was over there," he stopped and let that sink in for a moment, "and I needed her."

Brodski shook his head. "She's another bit of bait in the trap. All those girls are."

"I saw Billy Jo over there," Stephen said trying to pull the spot light off himself. It worked.

"How is she? How'd she look?" Brodski asked. "Did she say anything about me?"

"She looked great, cute and sweet as usual. Wearing a bright yellow dress. I really kinda expected you to be hanging around over there too. I mean, it was a big party. You could have probably blended in enough to not be noticed."

Brodski realizing what just happened shook his head, "I don't think she is ever gonna come around so I'm gonna quit trying. She's like the apple in the monkey trap. Long as the monkey keeps trying to hang on to it, he can't get his fist out of the hole. If he lets go, he can pull his hand out and run away. I'm about tired of being the monkey. If she wants me, she knows where I am."

"I hear ya," Dennis said, with a slight chuckle and a twist in his voice. "I don't necessarily believe ya, but I hear ya."

"Cynic," Brodski said.

"Un-smitten cynic," he said, standing. "I got pages to read for tomorrow. Good night, you poor tragic souls." He turned and went out.

"I got pages to read, too," Brodski said, standing.

"Yeah. Me too. See ya later."

Stephen walked out of the Student Union and down to the dorm. He climbed up the steps and went into the TV lounge. There were several men watching some show, among them Bill Thinning. Stephen slid in beside Thinning, who winced as Stephen bumped him. "What up, bud?" Stephen asked.

"Me and my mouth. Fester made some crack about Dr. King and I took a swing at him."

"That's certainly Dr. King's way." Stephen said with a sarcastic twist. "Violence and destruction."

"I know, I know, but Fester is just such an asshole."

"He is that. Did ya hit him at least?"

"Yeah, knocked him down. The red hats were all over me. They would have probably beaten me to death if Ma Brigman hadn't heard the noise and come out."

"You gotta watch that shit, Bill. Damn Kappas are always in

a gang. Just keep your mouth shut and yourself to yourself. Avoid conflict."

"We can't let these bastards bully us like this," Thinning said. "Something has to be done."

"Yeah, I guess. I'm just hoping they will do something really stupid and get booted off campus."

"Don't hold yer breath. Status Quo is the way we go."

VI

A warm autumn rain was falling as Stephen walked to his music class. Choir. He didn't mind the rain. As a Southern California boy, he had learned to cherish the rain since there was so little of it most of the time, so he enjoyed it when he could. He would have gone out in swim trunks and tee shirt but that wouldn't have been acceptable for class so wearing Levis and a collared button-up shirt, he walked under an umbrella.

All music classes were held in the old Church of Christ which had been converted to a music building. It had five practice rooms with pianos in them and three that were empty. The main sanctuary had been split up into a band/orchestra room and a choir room. There were two straight class rooms for study of music. These had sound systems for music appreciation as well.

Stephen stepped onto the porch and closed the umbrella. He shook it, put it point down beside perhaps ten more umbrellas leaning against the wall beside the door, and went in.

There were a dozen or more students already in the choir room. Most were seated in the old pews, already in their separate sections. Dr. Scripps was standing in the conductor's position with a black music stand before her. She looked up at Stephen and said, "Tenor, right?"

"Yes, ma'am."

"Wonderful, another tenor. We always need more tenors. Pick up a folder from the table over there and join your section, Mr. Mitchell."

Stephen did as he was told, sliding in at the end of the row of tenors beside Snatch Parker. Parker looked anxious when he saw Stephen and Stephen grinned wickedly. "How ya doing—Leroy?"

Parker let out his breath. "Doing' fine Stevie. Doing fine."

Dr. Scripps was shuffling music on her stand so Stephen took the moment to look over the choir. It was a mix of white and black, men and women. There was a young black man seated at the piano, shuffling music. Cathy Powell, Mary Ann Younger, David Hall, Laura Pettibone and Billy Jo Patrick were all there. Stephen's eyes lit on long blonde hair he thought he recognized. She turned enough to show him he was right. It was Janice Reed from the Poetry Round Table. She was enough to make coming to choir worth the trouble. Others Stephen recognized from around the campus were there as well, but he didn't notice them much. He did notice that there weren't any Kappas in the group, or at least none with red hats on.

"Good morning, choir," Dr. Scripps began. "I am not going to take time to audition anyone here. This is an elective so I assume you can all sing or you would not have signed up." She smiled. "I have a pretty good ear so if there are any clinkers, I can pick them out, so if you are here on a whim you might find yourself failing in a class that is usually an easy A."

The class all laughed and Scripps let it go on for a moment before saying, "It is my intention to present at least one Choir Concert each quarter. More if we can learn the music fast enough. It is also my intention to put together a small competition choir to compete with UT Martin, Austin Pea, UT Jackson and others. This will be an acapella group. There will also be some smaller groups, quartets, sextets, and octets, in competition. I will open a Greek competition that will happen in the spring. Any Fraternity or Sorority who wishes to put together a group can compete." She looked over the group to see if there were any questions or problems and finding none she said. "Very well. Open your folders." After a moment's hesitation she said, "Oh, for those of you who don't know, this is Mr. Trist accompanying us on the piano."

Trist looked from his music, lifted a hand then went back to looking at his music with his hands set to begin.

"Give us a C chord, Alan," Scripps said.

Trist nodded and hit the chord.

"Good. Now, one at a time." She pointed her baton at the bass section and when the piano hit the low end of the chord, they sang the single note. "Remember that note," she said, then repeated the procedure with each section. "All right, all together now." She raised her baton and brought it down. All parts sang and the blend seemed to please her. "Not bad. So, let us begin."

Trist played the intro to the first piece and they were off.

The hour flew by for Stephen. It was always that way for him with music. He had decided long ago that music was magic, and it was always with him. He woke every morning with a song in his mind, usually some pop song off the radio, but sometimes more classical music he had learned in music classes. He often thought he would love to make a life of singing and playing, but couldn't see himself as a rock star. Instead, he listened and learned from the radio. He knew most every one of Simon and Garfunkel's songs, and could play most of them. He was also a Beatles fan and could play some of their music. They were more electric than he could manage on his old flat top Silver Tone acoustic, so he mostly just listened.

Stephen said his "see ya laters" to Parker and the other tenors, gathered his music and put the folder back on the table per instruction.

It was still raining outside so Stephen grabbed his umbrella and opened it.

"Need a ride, Steve?" Mary Ann asked him.

"We got room," Billy Jo said.

"Naw. I love the rain. I got an umbrella."

"Oh, okay," Mary Ann said, clearly disappointed.

"Sounded pretty good in there, didn't we?" Billy Jo said looking at him.

"Yeah, not bad," he said. "See ya later," and he started down the steps.

"First rehearsal for the BSU choir is tonight," Billy Jo said.

Stephen ignored her and kept walking.

Between the warm rain and the music Stephen was feeling good. Then he thought of the dish room toward which he was headed. It probably wouldn't be too bad yet. Leftovers from breakfast. Lunch service was just beginning so he figured he'd grab some lunch, go to work for an hour or maybe two, before going to sociology, depending on who was in the dish room with him. Such thoughts tamped down his good feeling some, but didn't entirely put it to rout.

He left his umbrella on the porch among the others as he had at the music building and went in. The smell of food made him realize that he hadn't had anything but coffee at breakfast so he opted for the plate lunch, a ham slice with a pineapple ring, green beans, and potato salad, with a slice of fruit pie for dessert. He carried his tray out into the dining hall and looked around.

There seemed to be an abundance of red hats over by the windows, and Stephen wanted nothing to do with them.

Charlie Horse and Snatch were sitting at a table on the far-left side against the wall so he headed over that way.

"How'd you get here so fast, Snatch?" he asked, grinning. He sat down beside Charlie,

"I got a new car, Stevie. No more walking in the rain for Leroy."

"I like walking in the rain." Stephen said.

"Just wait until it stops being rain and turns into sleet. You'll be begging for a ride," Charlie Horse said with a smile.

"Yeah, maybe so, but till then I'll just make like Gene Kelly dancing along."

"Poetry with the queer, dancin', and niggers. You just barely human, ain't ya, Hollywood?" Elgin Fester sneered, coming up to the table.

"Why don't you just leave it alone, Fester? I am not causing you any grief. Just leave me alone."

"Naw, ain't gonna do that, but I ain't here to talk to you right now anyway. I'm here to warn this nigger," he pushed Snatch's shoulder, "to stop eye-ballin' white girls."

Snatch looked up with a stony gaze, but said nothing.

"You ain't even gonna deny it?" Fester said.

"Why should he deny it, Fester? You're probably making it up to cause trouble," Stephen said.

"Stay outa this, nigger lover," Fester said.

Stephen popped to his feet, ready to fight. Charlie Horse came up beside him, but much slower. "Stevie, there's ten more Kappas over there, and sure as hell you throw a punch, they gonna be on you like stink on shit."

Stephen saw that Charlie was right. He remembered Bill Thinning's experience and so took a deep, calming breath. "I'm gonna ask you one more time, Fester. Leave us alone. Let us eat lunch in peace."

Fester studied Stephen for a long time before turning back to Snatch. "You remember what I said, nigger. Keep them eyes to yourself."

Snatch's face remained immobile. He did not say anything, and he never took his eyes off Fester.

After another moment Fester walked on, taking his tray to the dish room window. Stephen and Charlie sat down and Charlie began eating his lunch again. Stephen looked at his plate and decided he had lost his appetite. "How can you eat after that?" he asked.

Charlie shrugged. "I been dealing with white assholes alla my life. If I let it bother me, I'd be skinny as Leroy."

Snatch broke into a laugh, his stony resistance gone.

Stephen drank his iced tea. "We gotta do something about this. Can't let these bastards threaten us like this. Mason is integrated and liberal arts. These bastards need to get over themselves."

"Don't stir up trouble, Stevie," Snatch said. "Just keep a low profile and let it roll off ya."

"I reckon, but it galls the shit out of me that they can get away with it."

"Fester do seem to be gunning for you," Charlie said.

"After I saved his useless life last year. I should have just let Thinning beat him to death."

"That kind of regret isn't worth having, Stevie," Charlie Horse said. "What's past and gone is past and gone. Let it go."

"Yeah, I guess," Stephen said, toying with his mashed potatoes. He took a bite then threw the fork down. "I'll see you guys later," he said and stood up.

He shoved his tray through the window and Gary Mamoni pulled it in. Stephen went in the kitchen door, put on his rubber apron and went into the dish room.

"You want me to take over dragging, Mamoni?" he asked.

"Naw, I got this. I'm out in ten minutes anyhow. You can start racking and running."

"Am I gonna be in here alone?" Stephen asked.

"Big Julie is on the schedule. He'll probably be in."

Almost before the echo of Mamoni's words were gone from the room Jules Ryan came in. He was shorter than Steve with a mop of shining black hair to go with his piercing black eyes. Stephen thought he must have had Gypsy blood in him or maybe Italian.

"Hey Jules, how's it going?"

"Not so bad," he said and stepped to the stretch of counter where the empty racks were waiting. He pulled one over and began loading plates. Stephen had already loaded a rack and run it into the washer. When the cycle finished, he opened the exit door and pulled the hot clean dishes out, but his mind was not on his work.

We have to do something about these damned Kappas, he thought. *Maybe I'll go talk to the Pope.* He discarded the idea. *What could Uncle Morton do about this that he wouldn't already be doing? Maybe go to the Dean, for all the good that would do.* Dean Wesley was a small bald-headed academic. He taught New Testament Greek and some Bible studies, but he didn't look like the kind of guy that would be able to do anything against the concerted efforts of Elgin Fester and the Kappas. Then he remembered the

Pope had been head of a disciplinary committee of some kind last year. With a mental shrug he thought, *Maybe I will go talk to him. Gotta start somewhere.*

Stephen cut out from his dish duty ten minutes early and headed for the Pope's office, getting there just in time to find Uncle Morton locking his door.

Dr. Connors turned and said, "Steve, I'm sorry. I'm on my way to class. Is this important?"

"Yes and no," Stephen said, feeling foolish for thinking the Pope could help him. "Nothing that won't wait a little, I guess."

"If it will wait until Sunday evening, you can come to dinner."

Mason's cafeteria did not feed its students on Sunday evening, so the kitchen staff could get a little time off. There was a large Sunday lunch like most southern families and many of the students took extra at lunch, wrapped it in napkins and ate the leftovers at the Sunday evening meals. Others went to Dairy Queen or Tasty Freeze for hamburgers or down to the diner at Main Street where it crossed the county road. Last year Stephen had gotten a loaf of bread, some sandwich meat and a small package of American cheese slices to make sandwiches most Sundays, but it was still early in the first quarter so the Pope felt obliged to ask him over for Sunday evening dinner.

"Your Aunt Jean told me to ask you."

"Okay, sounds good."

"All right then. See you about six Sunday evening. Bring your roomie along," Morton said.

"I'll ask him but I don't know if he'll come along. He's a Jersey guy."

"What, don't they eat in Jersey?" The Pope laughed.

"I guess they do, but you being 'Dr. Connors,' he may be a little skittish."

Connors laughed. "Tell him I don't bite and I won't give him a test or anything."

Stephen answered with a smile. "Okay I'll ask him, but don't be surprised if it is just me."

"I'll tell Jean to be prepared either way," he said and turned away.

Stephen did ask Bankuski and to his surprise the other said, "Is the food good?"

"Yes. Probably be cold fried chicken and stuff, but Aunt Jean's a good cook."

"Then I'll come along. Never turn down a free meal."

"My sentiments exactly," Stephen said.

"Besides, it never hurts to get in good with the faculty."

"I guess."

~ * ~

The dinner was just as Stephen expected. Aunt Jean was her usual charming self and the food was good. Drew started out a little shy, but loosened up as the evening went along. Table conversation was general with a little gentle probing into Bankuski's life. He told them he was from Elizabeth, NJ, and had come to Mason for the same reason all the other Jersey kids had. The school had a good reputation and though it was a "private" school, its costs were lower than any of the private schools in New Jersey much less the big schools like Rutgers or Princeton.

"I applied to Princeton and got accepted," he said, "but the cost was going to be astronomical and I couldn't pull it off. I applied for some scholarships, but there are lots of math geniuses that got those. I'm good in math, but not Einstein good so I did a year in community college. There was no degree program and it looked like the Army was getting more out of the school than I was so, here I am."

"Welcome," Aunt Jean said.

"How do you like us so far?" Uncle Morton asked.

Bankuski hesitated a moment then said, "It's fine. It's good."

"But...?" Morton asked with his questioning tone.

"No, no but really. I'm just a little uncomfortable with all the

Protestant education that is folded into the classes, and there isn't a Catholic church anywhere close."

Uncle Morton nodded. "There's actually a Roman service downtown every Sunday. A priest comes from Jackson and serves a Mass in the room above Heshman's drug store. Mason rents the room from Heshman for a little of nothing. It isn't a cathedral, but it does present a proper Mass for all you Romans."

Bankuski visibly brightened. "I didn't know that. Great. What time, if I may ask?"

"He does a nine o'clock service, usually. More at different times around the holidays and up toward Easter. You can find out all about that from Father Murphy," Uncle Morton said.

Aunt Jean said, "You'd expect him to have an Irish brogue with a name like Murphy, but he's from Mississippi and sounds it."

Bankuski laughed.

They ate and drank silently for a few moments. "Your tan's fading, Stephen," Aunt Jean said.

"Yes, ma'am. I don't mind. My shovel handle calluses are softening up, too." He smiled.

"Dishpan hands?" Aunt Jean asked.

Stephen smiled at that. "I guess so, though we don't actually have any dishpans in the cafeteria. I'd hate to think how much work it would be if we had to wash dishes by hand."

"You'd probably have permanently pruney fingers," Bankuski said, grinning.

Aunt Jean stood. "I have cherry pie and ice cream for dessert," she said.

"Yum!" Stephen said, "I love cherry pie."

"And ice cream," Bankuski added.

"Good. I'll be right back," she said, and headed for the kitchen.

"You said something about wanting to talk to me?" Uncle Morton said.

"Yes, sir," Stephen said. "About the Kappas."

Connors took a deep breath and let it out. "What have they

done now?"

"Beyond being just generally obnoxious, they are picking on people. Ganging up on them. Bill Thinning got a beating the other day, and the day I met you at your office, they threatened Leroy Parker."

"What happened?" Connors asked.

"Elgin Fester made some kind of racial crack and Thinning took a swing at him. Didn't get far. A mess of red hats came out of the woodwork and beat hell out of him. He said they would have probably killed him if Ma Brigman hadn't heard the noise and come out into the hall. Leroy, Charles and I were just sitting in the lunch room when Fester came up all insulting to me and threatening to Leroy."

"Threatening?"

"Yeah. Said he was warning Leroy to quit looking at white girls or there would be bad consequences."

"Is that all?" Connors asked

"Not exactly. I popped up to defend myself, but Charles grabbed me and pointed out that the place was full of Kappas who would probably kill me if I took a swing at their president, so nothing further happened. Still, the threat was implied."

Connors thought a moment just as Aunt Jean brought in the pie and ice cream. There was thoughtful silence while all took their first tastes.

"How about you, Drew, have you seen any of this kind of trouble?"

Bankuski swallowed the mouthful of pie he had and said, "Not like Steve was talking about, but I did see a couple of them harassing a negro girl in my English class. I didn't think much of it. One of them did ask if I was 'One of them New Jersey Catholics?' in a kind of nasty way. I didn't think much about that either. I know that lots of local people weren't happy about all the New Jersey people coming down here."

"Ma Brigman is contributing to all this by dividing the dorm into white and black sections," Stephen said.

Aunt Jean frowned. "I had heard she was doing that, but I couldn't believe it."

"She says it's to keep peace in the dorm, and it may be, but I think there's more to it than that. I mean she's Georgia to the bone and I'd bet my last nickel she's for segregation. Keepin' the niggers in their place."

Aunt and Uncle Connors both looked shocked at the N-word. Stephen mentally thanked Bill Thinning for explaining the power of it to him.

The four ate pie for a little before the Pope said, "I have been hearing some of the professors talk about how these Kappas refuse to take their hats off in class until they are told to do so."

"They get nasty about it. Dr. Marchant made them uncover and Fester was just fit to be tied. Called him all kinds of names under his breath," Stephen said. "Fester uses my going to Dr. Marchant's Poetry Round Table as a dig. Calls me," Stephen thought better of going any further with that. "well, calls me insulting names."

"Sticks and stones, Steve," his aunt said.

"I guess, but the insult is to Dr. Marchant, too, and I hate that."

Uncle Morton pushed his plate away. "I'll talk to the Dean about this and look into it more. I don't know that there is anything we can really do about it so long as they don't do something really stupid. "

"The segregated dorm..." Aunt Jean began.

"Is wrong and illegal, I'll grant, but at this point I believe we are better off not poking the bear. If we made a big shake up and everyone had to move that might start more trouble than we already have. I will talk to the housing committee and put a stop to Brigman doing it anymore, but that's about all I can do right now."

~ * ~

A couple of weeks passed. Kappas were still all over, but they seemed to be less obnoxious than before. *Maybe I'm just getting used to them,* Stephen thought, then discarded the idea. They were still there and Elgin Fester still made nasty remarks to Stephen, but the red hats now took off their caps in every class without being told.

As Stephen ran up the admin building stairs heading for the Poetry Round Table, Fester and three of his henchmen stepped from the crowd on mid-class break, blocking his way. Stephen's guts tightened. He started considering who to hit first, but decided to try to talk before kneeing Fester in the balls.

"What are you doing, Fester? Get out of my way."

"I'm betting this is your fault, yours and the faggot's," he sneered.

"Whose fault about what?" Stephen said, feeling his right thigh muscle tighten for the attack.

"Greek committee put us on probation. Said if they get any more reports we caused trouble on campus we'd be off campus. I'm betting you and your faggy friends are behind it, maybe the niggers. Maybe all of y'all."

"Or maybe everybody at Mason finally got sick of y'all prancing around like red roosters," Stephen said, staring right into Fester's eyes. "Come to think of it, those red hats do kinda look like coxcombs. Now let me by."

There was a second when Stephen thought he had taken it too far—that he was going to have to throw down with these assholes, but the seconds passed till Fester and his boys stepped aside. Stephen didn't hesitate. He took off at a fast walk that kept trying to turn into a run, but he wouldn't let it.

Inside the conference room with the door firmly shut he began shaking and sweating with the adrenal reaction.

Dr. Marchant was already present and when he looked over at Stephen, he said, "Are you all right, Mr. Mitchell? You look ill."

Stephen swallowed hard to keep his supper in place and said, "I'm okay. Just ran up the stairs on a full stomach."

Marchant looked him up and down and didn't push it any farther, though Stephen could see the professor didn't believe him. It didn't matter. Maybe the trouble was over. Kappas were on probation and he hadn't had to fight. All was well.

VII

The weather began to turn in October. The days grew shorter. Indian Summer began. Warm pleasant days and frosty nights that made trips to the Danjo plot first uncomfortable, then impossible. Stephen was both depressed and happy about that. He missed the sex, the taste of her mouth, but he did not miss her constant nagging about his coming back to the BSU Choir. He used that nagging to ease his conscience about making love to her, but not loving her. The equation did not quite work out, but it did help some.

Toward the end of October, the problem came to a head. "I am not going back over there, Mary Ann," he said firmly, walking to class, hands in pockets against the cold. She had come out of nowhere to grab his arm.

"Why not? You like to sing, and you're already singing in the School Choir."

"I get credit for that. Besides which, I told you I don't have time for Baptists anymore. I don't like what they preach and I don't like the way they act toward people who aren't Baptists."

"But you like fucking me," she said bitterly.

Stephen stopped walking and looked at Mary Ann. Those were words he seldom heard come out of her mouth except in the throes of passion. "Yes, I do like fucking you, but not enough to put up with all the shit you and your Baptist friends pump out."

Mary Ann looked as though he had slapped her. "Well, maybe we'll just have to put an end to the fucking if you don't wanna be a Baptist," she said, her eyes blazing.

"That's up to you," he said, "I am not ever gonna join the choir again. If I have any choice about it, I'll never set foot in another Baptist church." He pulled his arm loose from her grasp and started to walk away.

"But Steve, I love you," she said with an accusatory plea in her voice.

Stephen remembered saying something like that to Cathy Powell when she betrayed him, He half hated himself for breaking Mary Ann's heart now, but he didn't love her. She had been a steady piece of ass, and that was all. He turned back to her now and said, "I'm sorry about that, Mary Ann. I really am, but I don't love you."

Tears suddenly came into her eyes. Stephen was already feeling bad enough so he turned and walked off leaving her crying in the middle of the sidewalk.

Stephen felt like hammered shit through the whole class. Even Bill Thinning's irreverent joking couldn't bring him out of it. At last the class was over and though he had another right behind it he decided to cut that class and go get some extra hours in the dish room. Not that he loved the dish room all that much, but he felt like banging some things around and maybe even breaking something. He was glad to see that Mary Ann was not waiting for him outside the admin building. He could almost picture her still standing in the middle of the sidewalk crying and waiting on him to come back to her. *Yeah, you're a real prize that anyone would wait on you for anything,* he thought.

Stephen climbed up the stairs to the Ghetto Tower to relieve himself of his load of books. He unlocked the door and pushed it open. He had mail.

The mail delivery system was lousy. There was talk of putting post office boxes in each of the dorms, or of opening a post office in the basement of the admin building. It was just talk. As it was, mail was delivered by "The Mail Man," whose duty was shared by everyone in the dorm. Ma Brigman had a list of the inhabitants of Lorring Home and once a week, on Sunday, she would choose a name from that list. The chosen would be named Mail Man for the week. The real U.S. Post office sorted and delivered bags of mail to each dorm each day and, between classes, the Mail Man would sort through the stack of mail and deliver it by sliding it under the door. If the mail was too large to fit under the door a card with the word MAIL would be slipped under and the addressee would know that he had to go to Ma Brigman's room to pick up the package.

Inefficient as it was, it was made worse by the segregation in Lorring Home. The white Kappas did not want to deliver mail to the Ghetto Tower, the black students didn't want to go into the Kappa tower, but that was the system, like it or not. Ma Brigman made sure the Mail Man, black or white, made his deliveries.

Stephen stooped and picked up the letter. He had received mail from his mother and even from Mike, his brother, but he didn't recognize the handwriting on this one. He glanced at the return address. Kinert, it said, and the name didn't register with him at first. Kinert, Kinert, Kinert—Sherry! The knowledge finally bored through all the mephitis in his mind and it was like a sudden fresh breeze blowing away the stench. He threw his books onto the desk, ripped the end off the envelope and tapped the letter out. It was just one page folded in three and that took some of the joy out of getting it, but when he unfolded in and saw "Dear Steve," at the top he felt better again.

It was not sloppy or even all that personal. Written on white three-hole notebook paper, in a small neat hand, it was rather chiding,

Dear Steve,

It has been months since you left and I have not heard a word from you. I had a feeling your promise to write was a cookie promise, but just to make sure we were on the same wavelength, I am writing you this letter to keep my part of the bargain.

The rest was all about school—she was going to Valley State—weather, church gossip. Didn't matter. Stephen read it through, went back to the top and read it through again, all the way down through the "Love Sherry" signature. After the second reading, he lifted the letter to his nose and sniffed, fancying that he could smell Sherry's perfume on it, but decided at last that it was his wishful imagination.

Dish room, class, everything else was forgotten. He sat down at the desk and pulled out a yellow legal pad. Without conscious thought, he wrote:

Dear Sherry,
I promised to write, but I have been way busy, between classes and work I forgot, but I promised to answer if you wrote so here we go—

He didn't intend to make the letter romantic so he stuck to the weather, classes, and the Poetry Round Table, even including a short poem about the twinkling lights from Mulholland Drive. Dr. Marchant had said it was good. "A little teen angst, but not bad, Mr. Mitchell. Submit it to the anthology." Stephen was proud of it. It wasn't really romantic, but implied that it was about when he and Sherry were looking at the lights together.

He ended the letter with, "Okay, I did my part. Your turn now." He hesitated at the signature. *Should I sign it Love, or Your Friend, or Sincerely?* and finally signed it "Love." *After all, she signed it Love, and I do love her, sorta.* He addressed the envelope, gave it a lick, put a stamp on it and went to bed, but Sherry kept running through his mind, until he did something to relieve himself of the memory.

~ * ~

Between avoiding Fester, the red hats and watching out not to run into Mary Ann, Stephen began to feel like a man on the run. Of course, he saw both Fester and Mary Ann in classes, but he didn't have to talk with either of them. He even avoided looking at Mary Ann as much as he could because anytime his eyes landed on her she was looking at him with sad, cow eyes and that made him feel bad. It also made him horny. Looking at her made memories of the adventures on the Danjo headstone float to the surface. His mouth would dry and his groin warm and he would mentally kick himself for not simply playing her along for a bit longer. The Danjo plot was no longer an option. As Halloween passed and Thanksgiving came into view the weather turned colder. Nights were frosty and days, even the clear ones, were chilly.

"You coming to my house for Thanksgiving?" the Pope asked him.

"I don't think so, Uncle Morton. I got a letter from Uncle Paul asking if I was gonna come down to Memphis to help him serve Thanksgiving dinner like last year, and I think I'll do that."

"How about your roomie? Is he going home?"

Truth be told Stephen had not thought about what Bankuski was going to do. "I don't know, Uncle Morton. As I think about it, I doubt if he has money for plane fare and even if he did it wouldn't be much of a trip. I mean we only have about a week off."

"Six days," his uncle said.

After a few moments of thought Stephen said, "I may get back to you on that Thanksgiving dinner. I'm pretty sure Drew would come with me to your house, but I don't know if he's up for a trip to Memphis. How about I let you know after I talk to him?"

"Fine," Connors said.

"I'll let you know in a couple of days," Stephen said.

It turned out to be a moot question. "Fr. Murphy and some of the people from his parish in Jackson are going to do a big Thanksgiving dinner for college students over in Jackson," Bankuski said.

"Well okay. That's good. Geez you are just covered up with invites, ain't cha? The Pope and my uncle Paul in Memphis and—the other Pope, I guess, since it was the priest."

Bankuski shrugged. "It's because of my magnetic personality."

"Yeah, right," Stephen said sarcastically. "I'll tell the Pope.

But seriously, if that other falls through, let me know. No one should spend Thanksgiving alone."

Bankuski turned serious as well when he said, "Thanks, Steve. I was kinda wondering before."

Stephen passed the information to Uncle Morton next class period. "Paul coming to get you?" he asked.

"Naw. I'm just gonna ride the bus. I guess he'll bring me back Sunday afternoon."

~ * ~

Tuesday afternoon after sociology, Stephen threw a change of underwear and socks, his shaving kit, and the Robert Heinlein book he was reading into his carry on, walked down to the crossroads and caught the late afternoon bus for Memphis. It was a local which did not make him happy, *but at least I don't have to worry about driving while black this year,* he thought with a small laugh. He felt bad for making light of the problem. It had cost him two black eyes last Thanksgiving. He took off his jacket, threw it into the overhead and plopped himself down about half way back against the window. The Greyhound was almost empty. The air was stale with old tobacco smoke. Stephen leaned his shoulder against the window. There was an ashtray built into the fold-down arm between the two bus seats so he pulled out his cigarettes and lit one.

With each stop the bus filled a little more. The seat beside him stayed empty though and he wondered why. *Maybe because I'm smoking,* he thought, *or maybe I just look surly.* It didn't really bother him. It made him remember Jackie Bookman.

Stephen had met Jackie Bookman on the train his first trip to Mason. It was both a sexy and a painful memory. He saw Jackie and her girlfriends talking and looking at boys on the train. One of the boys ended up fucking Jackie in the aisle of the darkened observation car. Stephen, hidden by the darkness heard the whole thing. He heard Jackie cry when her paramour left and didn't come back. It made him feel like shit. He wanted to go to the girl and comfort her, but he hadn't. Stephen had said nothing. The two lovers had not known he was there in the dark and he got out of the observation car as soon as possible. He saw Jackie the next day and she didn't look any the worse for wear though he knew she was.

They met in the club car where Stephen bought his first pack of cigarettes and talked several times on the remaining trip. She was going to Memphis which was her home, then on to the University of Tennessee at Jackson. When they parted in Memphis, Stephen squeezed her bum though they had done nothing at all sexual on the train ride. The squeeze had gotten a strange look from her, but nothing more. He really never expected to see her again.

At the end of the school year when he was riding this same bus to catch a flight from Memphis to California, he had run into her again. She remembered and at the end she offered up her bum to be squeezed again. Stephen blushed as he remembered but he acted on the invitation. Jackie invited him to come with her, but he was on his way home thinking he would never come back so he didn't go with her.

The Greyhound pulled into Jackson. Night had pretty well closed in. There were several people waiting for it and Stephen studied the crowd with thoughts of Jackie Bookman still running through his head but he didn't see anyone he recognized and thought, *That was really stupid, Stevie. What did you expect?* He closed his eyes and leaned his head against the window. Not long now until he would be with—

"Is this seat taken?" a melodic female voice asked.

Stephen opened his eyes. A lovely dark-haired collegian with a small suitcase in her hand stood, her blue eyes focused on him.

"No, no. It isn't."

She seemed somehow familiar.

"May I?" she asked, her voice alto and honey sweet with southern drawl.

"Please," he answered her.

She smiled and stretched up to put her suitcase on the shelf above the seats. She was dressed in forest green pants and a flowered blouse. The pants were the form-fitting kind and they fit fine. Stephen found himself all but licking his chops as he watched.

As the bus pulled out, she half-sat, half-fell into the seat beside him, the flowery aroma of her perfume overcoming the stale air of the bus. She stuck out her hand and said, "Hi, I'm Jackie Bookman."

Stephen almost choked. He took her hand and said, "Weren't you blonde before?"

Jackie's eyebrows drew down in puzzlement. "How'd you know that? Do I know you?"

"Mike Mitchell's brother," he said, with a laugh, then added, "Steve Mitchell. We met on the train a lifetime ago."

"Steve!" she said as though she really did recognize him. She scooted over, hugged his neck and kissed his cheek. The bouquet of her perfume wafted over him.

"I was just thinking about you," he said. "Remembering the last time we met."

Jackie wiggled her bottom in the seat with a wicked smile. "I remember. I thought you were going away and not coming back."

"I thought I kept that to myself, but everybody seemed to think that."

"Was I wrong?"

"No. But stuff happened, I ended up back here," he said with a shrug in his tone.

"Well good! You on your way to California for Thanksgiving?"

Maybe she really does remember me, he thought. "No, too far. Just going to my uncle's here in Memphis."

"Could you come home with me for Thanksgiving?" she said. "As I remember we had an almost date set up for the next time we met."

Stephen smiled at the memory then hung his head. "Sorry Jackie, but the fates aren't gonna be that nice. I promised to help my uncle serve Thanksgiving to a bunch of lonely college students who can't go home, and I can't back out of that."

"Oh, too bad," she said and sounding as though she meant it. "Where is this dinner?"

"West Side Cumberland Church. My uncle is the preacher over there—Hey, why don't you come over there for dinner?" Then it dawned on him how dumb that invitation was. She was going home to family dinner.

"Maybe I will," she said. "At least for dessert or something."

"That would be great," Stephen said. "Last year we had a big crowd, and Paul isn't the kind of preacher that'll take the opportunity to preach at the drop of a hat. He'll do a Thanksgiving grace and let it go at that, so you don't have to worry about being assaulted with the Gospel."

Jackie gave him a questioning look but let it go. "What time?" she asked.

"We started serving about one but kept at it until like five. People come and go."

"Maybe I'll be over early to help. We don't usually eat until suppertime, so I can help you serve then we can go home for dinner."

Stephen blinked at that, not knowing how Paul and Esther would react to that but he said, "Sounds good. Two Thanksgivings."

She laughed, lifted the fold-down arm with the ash tray and scooted over against him. She stayed scooted over, holding on to Stephen's arm for the rest of the ride.

Paul, dressed in a trench coat, was standing on the curb when the Greyhound pulled in. Stephen, holding Jackie's hand and carrying both his bag and hers said, "Paul, this is Jackie Bookman. She goes to UT Jackson and she wants to help us serve Thursday, then take me home to meet her folks for late dinner."

Paul lifted an eyebrow at the phrasing.

"If it's all right with you, sir," Jackie said.

Paul who was almost always smiling looked over the two of them with a questioning gaze and said, "Fine with me. We can always use more help. This thing started out small, but it has gotten much larger as time has gone on."

"We'll serve till the evening, Uncle Paul, I promise."

"Yes, sir, till the evening," Jackie said.

"Fine. Fine. Can we drop you somewhere Miss—" he hesitated because of not knowing the name.

"Bookman," Jackie said.

"Ah, yes. Can we drop you somewhere, Miss Bookman?"

"No, thanks, my mom will be here pretty soon." She turned to Stephen, leaned forward and kissed him lightly. "I'll see you Thursday morning, Steve."

She took her suitcase from him and turned away. In a moment she raised her other hand and waved at someone, then hurried away in that direction.

"My, my, my," Paul said as they watched her meet a woman beneath a streetlight at the other end of the bus station. "Where did you meet her?"

Stephen looked at his uncle and shook his head. "It's a long-involved story, Paul. Let's go, I'll tell ya in the car."

When they arrived at Paul and Esther's house, they were still discussing Jackie Bookman and Esther asked, "Who is Jackie Bookman?" So, Stephen had to go through the same story again.

"I don't know," Stephen said after telling his aunt the story, "Just sorta seems like God, or the fates, are throwing us together. We have met by chance so many times—on the train, then on the bus, now on the bus again.

Paul nodded. "Of course, it could be because you are often traveling the same route at about the same time."

"Yeah, I guess, but you know."

"Ain't so romantical that way, huh?" Aunt Esther said.

Stephen flushed. "Sounds kinda silly when you say it like that."

Paul grinned, and said, "There is probably a lesson in it somewhere, but I don't see it at the moment."

"Maybe."

"All I know is I'm getting two servers for the price of one."

"Other than romantic bus meetings, how is school going?"

Esther asked.

"All right, I guess. I mean, my grades are okay this time. Probably won't be on probation next quarter."

"Well, that's good," she said.

"There is a lot more tension on campus this year though. Maybe I didn't notice it so much last year cause I was too dumb to recognize it, but there seems to be more racial trouble this year. Fights, near fights, harassment. Most of the black women students have taken to traveling in pairs, there has been so much noise from the Kappas."

"Noise?"

"They're everywhere and they are trying to bring back segregation on campus. They are like the mobs that tried to block the doors at Little Rock High School."

"Really?" Esther asked.

"Well not quite since they can't really block up classrooms, but if there are several of them in a class, they gang up outside the classroom doors before and after. Put the evil eye on anyone they disapprove of. That finally got them put on probation, that and refusing to remove their red hats in class. They really raised a stink about that. Said others were not removing their caps either, but the Greek committee put the kybosh on that by saying everyone would remove their hats during class meetings. Kappas didn't like that so they leave them on until the professor actually comes into the room and clap them back on the instant the bell rings."

"What happened with them? They have been a fraternity on campus for a long time. Everybody knows they are really KKK but they have always been more low profile," Paul said.

"They elected a new president. Elgin Fester. He's a Mississippi Kluxer that made no bones about it last year so they elected him president this year. He was one of the ones that cheered when Robert Gillium and the others got killed last year."

"Lord have mercy," Esther said. "Isn't it enough that the country is at war in Vietnam? Do we have to be in the middle of a civil war here at home as well?"

"We humans," Paul began. "Our days are few and full of trouble, most all brought on by our own stupidity."

Stephen turned his eyes to his uncle and was not at all surprised to see that Paul's perpetual smile was gone.

The following morning, Wednesday, Paul and Stephen went to the church hall after breakfast. They swept the place, set up four rows of long tables and wiped them down, then set out a hundred folding chairs. At last they stood looking at the hall.

"Now all we need are bodies," Stephen said.

"Yep. This thing gets bigger every year," Uncle Paul said. "Thanks for coming down again Steve."

"You are more than welcome," Stephen answered. "Good to get away from Mason for a while."

"I understand. There's a remarkable amount of pressure on college students, especially now, and especially at Mason. Between Vietnam, integration, classes and working, your plate is pretty full."

"I guess."

In the afternoon several ladies from the church showed up and began cooking preparations. Stephen found himself standing around watching and trying to stay out of the way.

Paul said, "I guess we've done all we can until tomorrow. Let's get out of here," and they did. They went home and Stephen found that the little bit of work had tired him out, so he went to the bedroom, and lay down with his Heinlein book. He was asleep in moments and didn't wake until Aunt Esther called dinner time.

"Are you okay, Steve?" his aunt asked. "You sure slept a long time."

"I'm all right. Just really tired. Guess Paul was right. Lot of pressure on me, but down here with you guys it all seems to be off and I can relax."

"Hope you can sleep tonight?" Paul said.

"Yeah, I probably can. I don't usually have trouble sleeping."

He was wrong. When bedtime came, he started to read and fell asleep easily, but he started to dream, and not peaceful, cloudy dreams. Horrifying, dangerous dreams wherein he had to fight to stay alive. He woke with a start, hoping the dreams were gone. He turned on his light and read a bit more before falling asleep again. This time the dreams were not fighting, but haunting. Robert came into his dream. He didn't say anything that Stephen could remember, but he stood as in a doorway, staring at Stephen. The sound of police sirens came into the dream. He found himself facing the police who had stopped the car. It was not a replay of last year's "driving while black" incident. This time he was alone and though he tried to explain he was just a server they handcuffed him and threw him into the back of their cruiser.

When Paul knocked on his door, Stephen came awake with a yelp. Paul opened the door and asked, "You okay?"

Stephen blinked and rubbed his eyes. "Yeah, Yeah. Just a dream."

"Breakfast is ready. You ready to work?"

"Yes, sir, I guess," he said, but wasn't really sure.

After breakfast he jumped in the shower and made sure his face was shaved extra smooth for Jackie.

The aromas were thick and delicious when they reached the church kitchen. Roast turkey, country ham, greens with bacon, mashed potatoes with gravy, sweet potatoes with cinnamon, and pumpkin pie. There was also old-fashioned Brunswick stew complete with short pieces of corn on the cob and squirrel meat. Pinto beans. Iced tea, both sweet and bitter, and lemonade finished out the service line.

The dishes were stacked at the beginning of the serving line just like the cafeteria at Mason, with silverware wrapped in a napkin and drinks at the end.

Stephen felt himself looking anxiously for Jackie Bookman, but somehow doubt she would be there kept picking at him. He was almost convinced his doubts were right when they started serving at noon and she was still absent.

"Looks like your friend isn't gonna help after all," Paul said.

Stephen shrugged. "Ah well," he said, looking toward the

G. Lloyd Helm

entrance just in time to see Jackie coming in. She wore another pair of form-fitting dark-green pants and a lighter green blouse that made his breath catch. She waved as she stepped in and came around the end of the line. "Where do you want me?" she said.

"Better get an apron from over there," Paul said. "Then you can stand right here by Steve."

"Okay, good," she said, sounding chipper as a mockingbird. She went to get the apron and was back in a moment.

Stephen served a big spoon of mashed potatoes and poured gravy over them and handed them down to Jackie who put a spoon of dressing and gravy. Each person she served got a hearty "Happy Thanksgiving."

A young lady with creamy chocolate skin stepped up. Stephen thought he recognized her from last year. There were several black students mixed into the crowd this year. "You're looking better this year," she said to Stephen.

Stephen grinned. "Yeah, I guess. I rode the bus this year."

The young lady smiled and moved on, getting her dressing and gravy then moving on down the line.

"What happened last year?" Jackie asked.

"I had black eyes and a swollen nose."

"How come?"

"I had a disagreement with a couple of Memphis cops. Almost got arrested," he said lightly.

Jackie's chirpy mood seemed to suddenly darken. "What happened?" she asked.

The line had grown much longer so he said, "I'll tell ya later," and kept dishing.

In a couple of hours, the line slowed down and Stephen and Jackie took a break. They got glasses of iced tea and sat down across from one another.

"So how did you get beat up?" Jackie said.

"Driving while black," he said.

Jackie's eyebrows pulled down questioningly, so Stephen explained about being stopped.

91

"Why on earth were you in the car with a bunch of nigras?" she asked.

Stephen looked at her, and blinked, remembering Bill Thinning's answer about why he used the word *nigger*.

"They were my friends. One of 'em was my roommate. They were going to Memphis and I needed a ride."

"But—" Jackie began

Stephen cut her off. "The Ku Klux Klan killed my roommate Robert a couple of months later."

Jackie didn't go on with whatever she had been about to say, then said, "I remember that."

"I dreamed about Robert last night," Stephen said, suddenly finding a catch in his voice so couldn't go on.

Jackie looked at him and saw the tears forming in his eyes. She reached across the table and took his hand. After a moment she said, "Well, I hope you don't bear any grudges."

Stephen looked a question at her. "My daddy's a Memphis policeman," she said.

Oh shit, Stephen thought.

VIII

When they went back to serving Stephen found that the food didn't smell as wonderful as it had before. Dread was a bad odor at the back of his mind. He seriously thought about making an excuse of not feeling well, but decided Robert would never forgive him if he chickened out. *That's probably why he came to me in my dreams last night,* Stephen thought. *Warning me, and daring me, like he used to do.*

When there were no more students to be served around five PM, Jackie untied Stephen's apron and took off her own. She smiled that heart melting smile at him and said, "Come on," leading him by the hand.

"We're going, Paul, unless you still need us." Stephen said

"Naw, I think we got the rest. We'll come back and finish the clean up tomorrow. Have fun."

Stephen wondered if Paul was being a smart ass, but said, "Don't know when I'll be home."

"No problem. We'll leave the door unlocked."

Stephen let Jackie lead him to the car where she opened the door for him and closed it again after he got in. He tried to relax on the drive from the church to Jackie's house, but the drive wasn't very long. Anyway, he didn't think that a drive clear back to LA would have been long enough. He felt as though he were walking into a cage of a hungry tigers, and for some reason the aphorism came into his mind. *When riding a tiger, it is easy to get on, but getting off without getting bitten is a little tougher.*

Jackie drove into the part of Memphis called Sherwood

Forest. All the streets were named after characters in the Robin Hood stories. Her house was on Little John Lane. The irony of a cop living in a place named for a famous thief was not lost on Stephen, but he said nothing about it.

The house was very much like a thousand others in Memphis, very like his grandmother's house. Red brick façade with white trim and green lawn, rather brown now because of the cold. The drip of acid into Stephen's stomach was not helped by the black jockey hitching post standing beside the front walk. *Just be polite and keep your mouth shut,* he thought. *Eat some turkey and keep your mouth shut.*

Jackie pulled the car through the driveway gate toward the garage and they got out. She grabbed Stephen's hand and lead the way up the back steps through the glass outer door that was steamed up from the heat of the kitchen.

"We're here," she announced as the door banged shut behind them.

A woman, a handsome matron, and looking very June Cleaver in her frilled apron over her flowery dress, came into the kitchen. "Hello children," she said in a honey-sweet Memphis accent. "Y'all are just in time. Go on in say hello to your father Jacquelyn, then come back and help me carry some of this to the table."

"I can help with that too, Mrs. Bookman," Stephen said.

"Why, of course not. You are a guest, and you must call me Estelle, or Stella."

Stephen felt himself relaxing a bit. "Yes, ma'am, Ms. Estelle. I'm Stephen, or Steve," he said. She had not extended her hand so he did not either.

Jackie lead him by the hand through the kitchen door into the dining room, then on through to the living room. The TV was on playing some football game. "Daddy, this is Steve Mitchell," she said.

The man stood, and stuck out his hand, and Stephen took it. "Mr. Mitchell. Glad to meet you," he said.

94

He was a little shorter than Stephen, slightly paunchy with gray hair and bushy grey eye brows. He was dressed in a sport coat, slacks, and a tie which made Stephen feel decidedly under dressed. *He doesn't look like a badge-heavy asshole.* Stephen thought, taking the extended hand.

"Sir," Stephen said, adding "I'm just Steve to my friends."

"And this is my little brother Johnny," Jackie said.

The boy didn't stand up or speak but he did nod. He reminded Stephen of his own brother Mike. Fourteen or fifteen years old, starting to look a little scruffy and more concerned with his own pursuits than anything else

Jackie let go of Stephen's hand and said, "I've got to go help Mother. Y'all get to know one another," and she went out.

"Have a seat, Steve," Jackie's father said indicating the couch. "We're just watching the UT-Alabama Game." He sat back down in the big chair.

Stephen went to the couch where Johnny was sitting and sat himself on the front twelve inches of it. He hated football and had since playing in high school. *A cop watching football,* he thought. *I'm in hell. At least I don't have to talk to him.*

A commercial break came up, and Mr. Bookman said, "Jackie tells me you go to Mason."

"Yes, sir."

"Pretty good school from what I hear. Their basketball team usually puts up a good fight."

"Yes, sir," he said with a little grin. "UT Martin hates to see us coming,"

"You play? You're tall enough."

"No, sir. I played in high school, but I'm not coordinated enough to be much good at it."

Johnny glanced over at Stephen then did a double take. "You were on TV, weren't you?" the kid asked.

Stephen shook his head. "No."

Johnny looked Stephen's face over closely then turned back to the TV, shaking his head. "I could have sworn," he said, but let it go.

The ballgame came back on and Stephen let out a relieved sigh. *Come on dinner,* he thought.

As if his thought were a genie-granted wish, Jackie came out of the dining room and said, "Come on you men, time to eat."

Stephen rose, as did Johnny, but Mr. Bookman was a little slower, still watching the TV. "Come on, Daddy, it's dinner time," Jackie said.

"It's the last quarter and less than five minutes to go," Mr. Bookman said.

Jackie's mother came out and said, "With five minutes to go you can come and eat cause it'll take them an hour to be done."

"Ahhh," Mr. Bookman growled, but he stood up.

"Turn that thing off," Mrs. Bookman commanded, eliciting another growl from her husband, but he did as he was told, then lifted a hand toward the dining room indicating that they all should precede him.

The table was beautifully set with fine china and what looked like real silver silverware. The service ware matched, even the large platter upon which the turkey rested. Glassware gleamed, water glasses already filled, wine glasses at the ready. A bottle of white wine, already uncorked, lay in a chilled server.

Mr. Bookman went to the far end of the table, near the turkey and stood behind his chair.

"Mr. Mitchell, I understand you are a Divinity student. Would you be so kind as to offer up a Thanksgiving prayer?"

It caught Stephen a little off guard, but he had prayed aloud with an audience many times so he bowed his head and began.

"Father God, we thank you this day for the feast that is set before us, and for the hands that have prepared it. May your blessings and your peace shine down upon us now and forever more. We pray in the name of Jesus our Savior, Amen."

"Amens," answered from around the table, and all save Mr. Bookman sat. He picked up the carving set and began working on the turkey. "Light or dark, Steve?" He asked.

"A bit of both, if you please."

"Integrated turkey coming up," Bookman quipped with no thought.

Estelle extended her hand toward her son and he gave her his plate. She began scooping on mashed potatoes and gravy and green bean casserole. Jackie took the plate designated for Stephen and began dishing up for him.

"They taught you well over at the church kitchen," her father said.

"Yes, sir. We served a lot of kids."

"Always sad for students stuck so far away from home at Thanksgiving," Estelle said. "Good that the church did that for them. Makes it easier."

"Yes, ma'am," Stephen said.

"That's the Cumberland Church, right?" Mr. Bookman asked.

"Yes sir. My uncle is the pastor there."

"Mason is a Cumberland college isn't it?" Estelle asked, handing Jackie a filled plate. "Put that over for your father," she added.

"Yes, ma'am," Stephen answered.

Mr. Bookman, finished with his carving chore, sat down. "Y'all had some trouble up yonder last year, didn't you?"

The acid drip into Stephen's stomach which had slowed down suddenly increased. "Yes sir. Some students were killed in a fire bombing of a church."

"That's where I know you from," Johnny said with satisfaction. "They interviewed you on TV."

Stephen took a deep breath and said, "Not exactly interviewed. They asked me a couple of questions."

"How come?" Mr. Bookman asked.

"My roommate was one of the kids killed."

A distinct silence came over the table. "All of 'em that got killed were nigras weren't they?" Mrs. Bookman asked.

"Yes, ma'am."

The next obvious question in all the Bookman's mouths was, "What were you doing rooming with a nigra?" but they didn't ask it.

After a bit Mr. Bookman asked, "Did they catch them that did it?"

"No, sir. They probably won't. Everybody knows it was the KKK that did it, and the Sherriff is a member so he didn't look too hard. No one cooperated with the FBI when they were investigating. It'll never be solved." Stephen's voice broke a little, but he cleared his throat and regained control.

Bookman heard the catch in Stephen's voice and after a moment said, "Sorry to have brought it up."

Stephen looked over at him and said, "Robert was my friend. I liked him. He taught me a lot about being black in the south, and about what it costs to be a Civil Rights warrior. I pray every day that he didn't die in vain."

The meal was very quiet after that.

When they finished eating Stephen turned to Jackie and whispered, "Can we get out of here?"

She looked from her father to her mother, nodded and said "Okay."

All stood, and Stephen said, with all the courtesy he could muster, "Thank you for dinner. I must be going as I promised to help my Uncle Paul clean up the Church Hall."

"Thank you for coming, Mr. Mitchell," Jackie's mother said and offered her hand. Stephen took it gently and quickly let go of it.

Mr. Bookman extended his hand across the table and Stephen took it. "I hope they get them that killed your friend, Steve," Bookman said.

"Yes sir. Me too. Thank you."

Jackie drove Stephen to Uncle Paul's house. Their talk was all "Turn right, turn left, go straight," though it was unneeded, until they pulled into Paul and Esther's driveway. She put the car in Park, turned off the engine, and scooted over closer to Stephen.

"I'm sorry," she whispered. "I didn't know."

"Yeah, I didn't think. Your dad's a cop. I shoulda backed out as soon as you said it." Stephen shook his head. *At least he didn't black my eyes,* he thought.

"He's not like so many of the other cops," she said. "He doesn't go out of his way to hurt people, and he doesn't let his men do it either."

Stephen looked at her in the dark and thought about saying, *You don't really know that. You don't know how he treats people when he's got his badge on,* but he didn't, just unlocked the door preparing to get out.

Jackie pulled him tighter to her and kissed him. "I am truly sorry, Steve," she said still holding him close. "I hope you don't hate me for what my father does."

"I don't, Jackie. I don't." He pushed the car door open and pulled away from her grasp. "Good night," he said.

"Good night," she answered. "Call me when you come back to Memphis," she said.

Stephen nodded, said, "Good night," once more and closed the door.

It wasn't late, but the house was dark and quiet. Stephen was glad. He didn't feel up to talking to anyone right then. He felt his way to his bedroom, got undressed and climbed into bed. He didn't turn on the light to read.

Thoughts and memories rolled around in his mind. Robert, Miss Connie, marching to honor the four who died, being told his heart was keeping him out of the Marines...listening to Jackie cry in the dark of the observation car on the train. *I shoulda gone to the Pope's house for Thanksgiving,* he thought and suddenly he was crying.

~ * ~

Paul and Esther got up early but not too early the next day. They didn't know what time Stephen came in so they let him sleep a while before Paul went and knocked on the door.

"Breakfast, Steve," he said, "then we'll go fold tables."

"Okay, Uncle Paul. Be right there," he said trying to sound chipper, but his heart was still heavy. He rolled out of bed and pulled on his clothes.

At the breakfast table he was quiet, Paul and Esther seemed to sense his troubled heart. "How'd it go with Jackie?" Paul asked.

"All right, I guess." he said, but didn't volunteer anything more.

"She seemed like a nice girl," Esther said. "Very pretty."

"Beautiful," Paul added.

"Could I have some more coffee, Aunt Esther?" Stephen said hoping it would bring an end to the Jackie talk.

She poured and he sipped.

"Shouldn't take long to pick up the tables and chairs," Paul said.

"Maybe an hour or so. Two if we sweep the place down, if we get at it," Stephen said taking a deep breath and standing with the coffee cup still in his hand.

"Here let me have that," Esther said. "I'll pour some into a thermos. You're going to need it, I think. It's cold and looks like it's gonna rain."

"Hope it doesn't turn into snow," Paul said. "That'll make the trip back to Mason tough."

"Well, Paul, why don't I help you pick up, then you can just put me on the bus this afternoon. Save you a trip."

Paul hesitated a moment, clearly considering it.

"No need for that," Aunt Esther said. "I'm not even sure there's a bus going to Mason this afternoon."

"Well, whatever," Stephen said. "Let's go get this done."

The kitchen and church hall still smelled of Thanksgiving. There were ladies cleaning up the stoves and serving counters. "Hope this rain doesn't turn into snow," one of them said.

"Ah, I wouldn't mind a little snow," another said. "We haven't had snow in a couple of years."

"God be thanked," the first lady said and both went back to

wiping stoves.

Stephen's estimate was right. They picked up and folded the tables and put the chairs on the racks, then swept the place in a little over two hours. The rain was still falling when they were finished and it seemed colder.

"You sure you don't wanna just put me on the Greyhound, Paul?"

His uncle studied him for a moment then said, "No. I got a feeling you need to stay here for a little longer. You look—I don't know—bereft somehow. I think you need to come play with the girls and watch TV. Rest. Connect with family again. Help us eat some of this leftover turkey."

Stephen laughed. "I guess I could stand a turkey sandwich or two."

Paul grinned. "It's one of the good and bad things about being the preacher. You get the leftovers, but you get the leftovers, if you know what I mean."

Stephen laughed again, feeling less morose. He smiled. "I'll help with your burden of turkey."

Stephen did indeed spend the rest of the day playing Chutes and Ladders with Paul and Esther's daughters and watching mindless afternoon cartoon TV shows, followed by the promised leftover Thanksgiving dinner. It was still delicious the second time around, made more so by Esther's addition of buttermilk biscuits. They ate until they could hardly stand then spent the evening half asleep in front of the television.

When the Carson show rolled around Stephen was the only one still awake. He yawned and decided it was bedtime. He lay down to read a few pages and suddenly it was Saturday morning.

Rain was still falling which disappointed him. He had been thinking about hitching a ride over to Beale Street to hear some blues, but he wasn't convinced enough to go in the rain. Music might be magic, but not magic enough to overcome cold drizzle, at least not today, so he spent the morning watching Saturday morning cartoons with the girls and reading the rest of the science-fiction book he'd brought. It felt pretty good to simply veg out. Thoughts of the past couple of days rolled around in his head, but he determinedly pushed them away. All thoughts of Jackie led to depression so he especially pushed those away.

Dinner was again a rerun of Thanksgiving. It was still good, but Stephen could see how it might become boring after another day or two. With it resting comfortably the family again parked in front of the TV. The girls were not much interested in the news so they went to play dolls or something while the adults watched reports from Vietnam. There was sporadic fighting but it seemed to have slowed some.

About eight thirty the phone rang, and Paul answered it.

"Oh, hello Morton. How was your Thanksgiving?" Paul listened for a moment then said, "Oh my. What happened?"

Esther turned down the TV sound and she and Stephen began paying more attention to the phone call.

Paul continued listening more than talking, only adding the occasional, "Oh my." After a few moments he shook his head and said, "Lord, Lord. What is the world coming to?"

He listened a few more moments then said, "We'll be coming up there tomorrow afternoon. I'll talk to you some more then." He hung up the phone, and turned to Stephen and Esther with a stunned look.

"What happened?" Esther asked.

"Arthur Marchant is dead," he said.

Stephen shook his head as if to clear his mind, or perhaps un-hear what he just heard.

"Lord, Lord," Esther said in echo of her husband. "What on earth happened? A heart attack?"

"He was killed. He went to see his mother in Nashville for Thanksgiving, and it appears when he returned to Mason, he interrupted someone burglarizing his house and they killed him," Paul said.

IX

Paul mentioned Marchant's death from the pulpit the next morning, but did not dwell on it, asking that everyone pray that Marchant's family be given strength to carry on with all that must be done to bury and honor their brother. "We Christians must remember that the Lord allows things for His own purposes and that none of us are promised tomorrow."

Stephen could only sit in stunned silence.

Paul's message was the same basic message he had given last Thanksgiving. I Corinthians 13. "Love is patient, love is kind..."

Stephen found he was not feeling too kindly toward God. He had a suspicion there was more to the story than a burglary gone wrong. He remembered hearing Fester insult and belittle Dr. Marchant. He thought he even remembered Fester threatening to do Dr. Marchant hurt because he was homosexual and hostile to Kappas.

Paul's voice came through to him about Christian love, which brought to mind that Jesus said to love your enemies, and pray for those who despitefully use you. Stephen wasn't feeling particularly Christian at the moment, and his prayers tended more toward David's cry in Psalms for the Lord to destroy his enemies.

Lunch was again turkey leftovers and after the meal was through Aunt Esther fixed up a brown bag full of Thanksgiving wrapped in wax paper for Stephen to take along. "For the Sunday evening meal," she said.

Stephen looked at the bag. He wasn't at all hungry, and didn't relish what was in it, but he took it, because Esther made it for him. *Might look better this evening,* he thought. Goodbyes were short. Quick kisses to the children and to Aunt Esther.

Rain was still falling by spells, first misty then pounding. The temperature was hovering in the low forties.

"Depending on the weather, I may stay in Mason tonight," Paul said as he kissed his wife and daughters.

"Fine," Esther said. "Don't hurry home if the roads are slick."

Stephen and Paul got into the car and started just as the sky opened up with a deluge.

"We may have to row," Paul said with a chuckle.

"You shoulda just put me on the bus yesterday." Stephen said.

"Naw. A little jaunt in the rain is no problem." He had no more than said it when the rain turned into snow. Huge flakes that floated down like feathers. "Take about three of those to cover us up if we were sitting still," Paul said.

Stephen just grunted, not feeling very talky at the moment. Dr. Marchant was going around and around in his mind, mixing with all the other depressing thoughts of the last couple of days.

"Shame about Arthur," Paul said, as if reading Stephen's mind. "I really liked him when I had him for English."

Stephen glanced over at his uncle. "I didn't realize he had been teaching that long," he said.

"Pretty close to twenty years I think," Paul said. "Not that it was so long ago for me." Stephen blinked, noticing for the first time that Paul was not so much older than himself.

"Paul, I don't think Dr. Marchant surprised a burglar. "

Paul glanced over, but didn't take his eyes off the road for more than a second. "Whatdaya mean?"

"There are some people on campus who were very hostile to him. Really hated him."

"Oh yeah? Who?"

"A lot of the Kappas. They were pissed that he was the one started making them take off their caps. Lot of 'em called him faggot, under their breaths."

"Nothing new about that. Kappas and other frat guys used to call him faggot when I was in school. Just macho nonsense."

"I don't know. Elgin Fester, the new president of the Kappas, made it pretty clear to me he would like to do something more than just call names. I had to face him down a couple of times because I was in the Poetry group, and he threatened Leroy Parker with a beating right in the cafeteria."

"Parker homosexual too?"

"No, no, black and a lady's man. Fester accused him of eyeing white girls. I'm pretty sure that was a lie, but Fester just needed to have an excuse to threaten him."

"Has it really gotten that bad on campus?"

"Yeah. Black girls have taken to traveling in pairs, on and off campus. Most of the guys try not to be alone with any of the Kappas around. Seems like it has gotten worse since they have been on probation."

They drove in silence, watching the snow pile up on the road. "I think maybe you better keep this to yourself, Steve. A rumor like that might end up being self-fulfilling." After a moment he said, "Looks like I am gonna be spending the night with Morton tonight so I'll mention it to him."

"Good. Of course, if it was the Kappas nothing is gonna happen legally. Sherriff is Klan and he isn't going to do a thing about it. Might even be part of it."

"That really is dangerous talk, Steve."

"It's true," Stephen said. "That's why nobody has ever been arrested for Robert's murder."

"True or not, I wouldn't be noising it around."

"Yeah, yeah, I know. It's in God's hands," he said with a cynical little twist in his voice.

"It is indeed. It is all in God's hands and His purposes too."

"He sure uses up his creatures pretty wantonly," Stephen said

"Not Him, us. God gets blamed for a lot of things he has

nothing to do with, but He takes what is given and uses it as best He can."

Stephen grunted and fell silent. He stayed that way the rest of the way to Mason.

Paul let Stephen off at the street side door of Lorring Home, making sure he took his bag of Thanksgiving reruns with him. It was almost dark and the snow was still falling. "Feel better Steve," Paul said.

"I'll try, Paul. Thanks for the ride. You going to Uncle Morton's?"

"Yeah. Not gonna try to drive home in this. The roads will be cleared tomorrow."

Stephen nodded. "Be careful all the same."

"You too," Paul said, but Stephen had a feeling he wasn't talking about the slippery road conditions.

He nodded, watched Paul pulled away, crunching through the snow that was already becoming ice, and started up the steps. Charlie Horse was shoveling, scrapping and salting the entry way.

With a cynical twist Stephen said, "You don't get paid enough, Charlie."

"Right you are, Stevie," Charlie said with a chuckle. "I may have to reconsider my choice of jobs if this keeps up."

"Did you hear about Dr. Marchant?"

"No, what about him?"

Stephen had the thought to say *They killed him,* but modified it to, "He's dead."

Charlie straightened up and leaned on his snow shovel. "Dead? What happened? Heart attack or something?"

Again, the thought *They killed him,* ran through Stephen's mind, but he said. "Looks like he surprised a burglar and paid for it."

"Burglar? What the hell? You don't usually hear about burglars in little towns like Mason. Did they catch the guy?"

"I don't know. I don't know anything else."

Charlie shook his head. "Sorry to hear that. I kinda liked the old queer."

The word queer stabbed Stephen and caused his temper to flare a little, but he tamped it down and said, "Yeah. Me too. Okay, get back to your shoveling. I'm going in. It's cold out here."

He turned and pushed in the door to the common room. The TV was on, but there was no one watching.

Elgin Fester came from the Kappa tower hall and stopped. Stephen felt a welling of anger at Fester, but kept it down. He expected some nasty crack from Fester, but got nothing save a glare. *Probably doesn't know Marchant is dead or he would have said something about it,* Stephen thought, but kept his mouth shut and turned up his own hall then up the stairs to his tower.

Stephen found the door unlocked. Drew Bankuski was inside. "Hey Steve. How was your Thanksgiving?"

"Decide for yourself." Stephen held up the brown bag now showing signs of grease soaking through.

"Oh boy," Bankuski said and put down the book he was reading. "I didn't think I was going to get any leftovers."

Stephen handed him the bag. "The food was good, but I been eating it since Thursday so I'm a little tired of it."

"Well, I'll help you out so you don't have to eat any more of it," he said opening the bag and sticking his nose into it. "Smells good."

"Was. Enjoy. I got a part of a loaf of bread up in the closet. You can make a sandwich."

"I got some sardines and crackers up there that I was gonna eat. You can have 'em if you want."

Stephen hadn't quite made up his mind on sardines and crackers. He had eaten them a few times and they weren't bad, but still. "I don't know. Maybe later," he said.

"Whatever," Bankuski said. He set the bag on the desk and went back to his reading.

"Did you hear about Dr. Marchant?" Stephen asked.

Bankuski looked up. "No, what about him?"

"Somebody killed him."

Bankuski's mouth fell open. "Really? Who did it?"

"Nobody knows, I guess. They say he surprised a burglar when he came back from Nashville."

"Wonder what that's gonna do to his classes? I was doing pretty well in his English Lit class."

The sound of raised voices came up the stairs and Stephen and Drew both pricked up their ears.

"What the hell?" Bankuski said.

Then Stephen recognized Bill Thinning's voice. "Maybe I better go see what's up," he said. and went out the door, Bankuski close behind him

Down in the TV room Stephen found Bill Thinning facing down a half dozen Kappas, Fester among them.

Oh shit, here we go, he thought and went to Thinning's side. Bankuski stayed back by the staircase.

"What's going on Bill?" Stephen asked.

"Dr. Marchant got killed," Thinning said, not taking his eyes off the Kappas.

"I know. I heard last night."

"Yeah, somebody did for that ol' faggot," one of the Kappas said.

"Probably picked up a nigger to suck his cock and the nigger killed him," Fester said with a nasty laugh.

Thinning shifted his weight to his toes, ready to start forward, but Stephen grabbed him. "There's a half dozen of 'em, Bill, they'll kill us both."

Fester lifted his hands and gestured *Come on* with his fingers. "Bring it, Thinning, unless you're chicken-shit."

That was almost enough for Thinning and Stephen, but as they moved forward Ma Brigman, carrying her mallet, opened her door and stepped out. "That's enough," she said. "Everybody, calm down. Now what's going on?"

"Dr. Marchant got killed," Stephen said.

"And I betcha Fester and this gang of Kluxers are the ones that killed him," Thinning said.

"That ain't so, Thinning," Fester said. "We didn't have anything to do with it."

"Yeah, sure," Thinning said. "I've heard you saying how you hate queers, how they oughta be castrated or killed."

"They should be, but I didn't do it. We didn't do it."

Ma Brigman looked from Thinning and Stephen to the gang of red hats. "Now y'all stop this nonsense and go back to your rooms. Don't make me use this," she said and threatened with her mallet. "I already called the sheriff, and if y'all aren't back in your rooms peacefully by the time he gets here you'll spend the night in jail, I promise. Now get."

"Come on, Bill," Stephen said. "Come up to my room."

The Kappas looked as though they weren't gonna do as Brigman told them, but when Thinning and Stephen turned toward the stairs the heat seemed to go out of the confrontation.

In Stephen and Drew's room, Stephen turned to Thinning, "What the hell were you thinking? Saying that to a gang of those assholes? They coulda killed you."

"Yeah, yeah, but Fester said something about me sucking Marchant's dick, and that was too much."

"Shit," Stephen said. "You know he was just trying to get to you."

"Yeah, yeah, I know. I just couldn't help it, especially since I'd bet my last buck they did have something to do with it."

Stephen drew in a deep breath and let it out. "That's the first thing I thought when I heard what happened. They really hated the doc. I heard Fester threaten to do him harm after the hats thing."

"You really think so?" Bankuski asked.

"Yeah. What's worse is they'll never pay for it," Thinning said.

"Why not?" Bankuski asked.

"Cause they are Klan and so is Sherriff Cruz and the rest of the local law too," Thinning said.

"Are they really that strong, the Klan? To be able to get away with murder?" Bankuski asked doubtfully.

"Ain't you been watching the news, Bankuski? They've been getting away with murder down here since the end of the Civil War," Thinning said. "They been lynching, flogging and shooting black folks and any white folks that have anything to do with black folks for the last hundred years."

"It's the truth, Drew. Lots of places down here the Klan is stronger than the government," Stephen said.

"Lot of places the Klan *is* the government," Thinning said.

"Well, why doesn't someone do something about it?"

"Couple of reasons," Thinning said, falling into the professorial mode he used to explain things to the ignorant. "First one being that people like the power. No one willingly gives up power over his fellow men. Them as don't like it are scared to rock the boat. Of course, the black population is scared and mostly powerless. There are some now that are working at it. My Dad and me, some other white people that think when the constitution says *All men are created equal* it really means ALL men, are working at getting voting rights for everyone and doing away with segregation. Mason College is working at it, but you can see, it ain't easy."

"It isn't just here in the south either," Stephen said. "I don't know about New Jersey, but California is pretty prejudiced, too. It's less overt, but it's still there. We don't have active Klan that I know of, but there is plenty of discrimination goes on, and not just for blacks. I got a lot of Mexican friends that are treated pretty much the same way."

"Lot of it is plain ignorance," Thinning went on. "Up north and out in California white and black mostly just don't mix so the discrimination doesn't get noticed."

"That's true," Stephen said. "Until I came to Mason, I didn't know but one black person, and I didn't know him much. Didn't even know his last name."

They heard Ma Brigman clomping up the stairs followed by a terse knock on the door.

"Come in," Stephen called.

Ma Brigman, still carrying her mallet, opened and came in.

She looked the three of them over before she said, "I'm not gonna ask what happened down there, I'm just gonna warn you, if there's any more trouble I'm gonna go to the housing committee and ask that you all be evicted from this dorm."

The three all gasped and Bill Thinning said, "You can't do that! We weren't the ones that started the trouble."

"I can do it," Brigman said, "and I will. I don't want any law trouble in my dorm."

"Tell those Kappa bastards to keep their mouths shut," Thinning said.

"Yeah," Stephen added. "We didn't say anything to them until they started acting hostile."

"You tellin' the Kappas the same thing?" Thinning asked.

Brigman flushed a little at that, which Stephen took to indicate that she had not said anything to Fester or the others.

"Why are you including me in this?" Bankuski asked. "I haven't had any trouble with anybody. I was an innocent bystander."

Stephen looked from Bankuski to Brigman. "If you don't threaten the Kappas with eviction as well as us I will go to my uncle and the Dean. The red hats are the problem and you are letting them get away with it in *Your Dorm* just because they are Kluxers. The disciplinary board has already put them on probation and you can betcha they'll put them off campus if this comes before them."

"Your Kappa pets would love that, wouldn't they?" Thinning said.

"You can bet we will inform them why they got thrown off campus," Stephen said.

Ma Brigman looked back and forth at the three, clearly judging whether they were bluffing.

"I'm going to the Kappa side right now, but I'll have no more trouble in my dorm," she finished, turned and went out.

The three could only sit with their mouths open for a couple of minutes before the self-questioning began.

Can she really do it? Will she really do it? Will she really talk to the Kappas?

"I don't really want to talk to the Pope about this. Makes me feel like I'm tattling on Fester, but there may not be a choice." Stephen said.

"I don't think she'll do it," Thinning said. "I think she is in enough trouble with segregating this dorm."

"I don't wanna get tossed out of here," Bankuski said. "Especially since I didn't do anything."

"Yeah. Sorry to get you into this, Drew." Stephen said.

"Yeah, me and my mouth," Thinning said. "Push come to shove, we'll tell 'em you had nothing to do with any of it."

Bankuski didn't look satisfied with that, but said, "Thanks, I think. I wouldn't be in this if I had just stayed here reading my history like a good boy. Speaking of which, why don't you go home, Thinning? Or at least go someplace else so I can get back to studying."

Stephen stood up. "Come on Bill, let's see what's shaking over at the Student Union."

Thinning stood and turned to Bankuski. "Stay outa trouble now, Drew," he said in his snippiest smart-ass tone.

Bankuski lifted the history book as though he was going to throw it at Thinning.

X

It felt strange and wrong to be going to English Lit knowing Dr. Marchant was dead, *but pain, death, tears, or whatever, school must go on,* Stephen thought.

The class was subdued when Stephen stepped in and sat down. Even the red hats seemed dejected. There was certainly no attempt to leave their caps on. Stephen wondered if that was out of respect or habit, leaning toward habit.

Professor Daily came into the room, went to the desk and put his books down. He was a tall gray-haired, scholarly looking man who commanded attention like Dr. Marchant had. Stephen didn't know him much, having never had him for any class.

"Good Morning, ladies and gentlemen," Daily said in a mellow baritone. "I will be your professor for the rest of the quarter. Of course, that won't be long. Finals and Christmas break are coming up in a couple of weeks. Dr. Marchant left lesson plans so I will be going by them. Mostly they are talking about Chaucer and the classical poetry of his time so you can guess that the final will be about that. We will be talking about the poetry between now and the final so go to pages one hundred twenty through two hundred and read them thoroughly. I know there are also papers due the beginning of next week so today I am going to dismiss this class early so as to give both you and I time to catch our breath after this blow. Any questions?"

Several hands went up, including Stephen's. Prof. Daily called on Cathy Powell who asked the same question Stephen was going to ask. "Are you going to take over as advisor to the poetry round table sir?"

"I'm not sure, Miss Powell. That will depend on how much time I have. My class load just doubled with Dr. Marchant's death. I'm sure someone will take over the round table, but I don't know if it will be me." He looked around the room. "Any other questions?"

There were a few others concerning papers, but after a couple of minutes, Daily cut them off with, "Rather than take up any more time with these kinds of questions, those of you with questions on your specific subjects, please see me during my office hours. They are posted."

He glanced over the class again and said, "Very well, you are dismissed. I'll see you Wednesday morning."

When evening came Stephen didn't know quite what to do. Was the Round Table going to meet? Was it worth his risking a meeting with the Kappas to find out? Was it worth anything?

Stephen had never felt so down in his life. It seemed that all thoughts for the future were marred and snake bit. *Everything I cared for has gone down in flames. Maybe it's God trying to tell me something.*

With that the decision was made. After supper and dishes, he trudged through the melting snow and mud toward the Round Table meeting. He went around the building and came in the back door and up the back stairs to make sure he avoided Fester and his Kappa gang. When he opened the door of what he had begun thinking of as the Round Table room he almost turned around and left. There were only a couple of people waiting there and the one he saw first was Cathy Powell—another of the things that had not worked for him. He swallowed hard and went on in, hoping others of the group would show up pretty soon.

"You look awful, Steve," Cathy said. "So sad."

Stephen glared at her. "A friend of mine just died," he said. "You know how that feels, right?"

He was instantly sorry to have said that. He knew Cathy had taken Ethan's suicide hard. He was still angry with her for everything, but the remark felt like kicking a crippled dog. To get out of the conversation, he lit a cigarette.

The door opened just as Stephen blew out his first puff of smoke. Sara Phillips and Ed Allen came in. They were carrying folders full of papers which they put down on the table as they sat.

Without preamble Ed Allen said, "Professor Daily has taken over as advisor for the book, but he is very busy under the circumstances so he has handed control over to Sara and me. If you have any problem with this, please go to Professor Daily. We intend to carry on just as Dr. Marchant began. We will put a sign on the contribution box to tell writers we are still accepting work until the last day of this quarter. Sara and I, since we both live here in Mason, will go through the material during Christmas break."

Janice Reed's hand shot up. "Does that mean that you two are going to do all the picking?"

Sara said, "No. We are going to separate what we think is acceptable from what is obviously not, but we will bring both piles back to the first meeting of the Round Table after the start of the new quarter. We will pass the piles around for the opinions of the members, and go from there. Around the end of January, we, all of us, will make final decisions about what to include."

"Sounds complicated," Cathy said.

"Yes, it is. Clumsy. But Dr. Marchant's death left us no real alternative, if we want to go ahead and bring the book out," Ed said.

"Of course, we could just dissolve the group and forget the whole thing," Sara said.

That caused Stephen's heart to sink. He hadn't realized how important this had become to him. It added just one more depressing stone to the load of depression he was carrying, but as he recognized that, he also recognized that he had an opinion. "I think we should go on with it," he said, "and I think we should dedicate it to Dr. Marchant."

"Yeah," Janice said. "Good idea, Steve."

Sara and Ed nodded. "We had thought of that as well," Sara said.

"It's gonna be a lot of work," Ed said. "But I think we can

do it."

They sat silently for a few moments looking at one another then Ed said, "I don't have anything else. We have one more meeting before finals so if you have anything to submit or to say concerning the Round Table, now would be the time." He glanced around and repeated, "Anybody got anything more?" He waited a moment and hearing no objections he said, "Okay, then. We're done. See you next week."

They all stood, and began putting on coats. Cathy grabbed Stephen's arm. "Come on with me to the BSU, Steve. I'll make you some hot chocolate."

For a moment he seriously considered it, remembering he had felt happy and fulfilled with the BSU. *Maybe I can get back with Cathy,* he thought, then remembered all the pain she gave him and pulled his arm away from her grip. "Not gonna happen, Cathy."

She gave him the same look as earlier and he felt just as bad about it. He turned and headed for the door before she could object.

Just outside the door he almost ran into Janice Reed. "Sorry," he said going around her and toward the back stair.

"Steve, can I talk to you a minute?" she asked.

Stephen stopped and turned back to her, noticing what a pretty smile she had. "I guess. I was just heading over to the Student Union."

"Oh, great. Can I come along?"

Somehow that question lifted Stephen's spirits. He felt alone in a cruel world, but Janice's smile lightened that feeling a little. "Fine by me," he said and went on down the stairs.

The Student Union wasn't crowded yet. As finals approached Stephen knew it would begin to be more crowded with people taking a break, grabbing a hamburger, or a cup of coffee just to get away from the books for a few moments, but for now it was fairly empty. The pall of tobacco smoke was still thick, but one could still see through it enough to see who else was in the place. Stephen stood at the door and glanced around. He spotted Jimmy Brodski sitting with his roomie in the back corner and thought to talk with them in a little while, but now he was interested to talk to Janice. He went to the counter, asked for a Coke. Considering his finances, he asked Jan if she would like one.

"Yes."

Stephen stuck his hand back in his pocket for more change.

"I'll buy it." She smiled knowingly and Stephen felt it all the way through his body, especially around his manhood.

"You are a girl after my own heart, Janice," he said grinning.

She grinned back at him with an impishness he had never noticed before. "Good, cause I need to ask you a favor." she said, then asked for a Nehi Strawberry soda.

"Uh Oh. Whatdaya need, someone killed or something?"

"Well, not quite that drastic but pretty close."

They both took their sodas and went to the closest table to sit. Stephen pulled out his Marlboros and offered Jan a smoke, which she refused, before lighting one himself. "So, who do you want killed?" he asked.

"Mark Alberry," she said, her face serious.

Stephen blinked at her. "Mark Alberry?" Stephen knew the guy but not well. They were both tenors in the choir.

"Yes. He has come down with strep throat so he can't sing at the Christmas program. "

Stephen was slated to sing in the choir for that program.

Stephen lifted an eyebrow. "Seems a little harsh to kill the guy just because he can't sing."

Janice reached across the table and slapped Stephen's arm. "I want to know if you will take his place in the quartet we are supposed to do, silly."

"Oh, well, I don't know. Killing him seemed easier. "

"Yes, but you already know the music. We've been practicing it for weeks."

That was true. This quartet was going to be a mixed number with the choir behind it. Stephen was just going to be a part of the choir.

"You can do it, I'm sure," she said. "You got a better voice than Mark anyhow."

Stephen felt the compliment right in his heart. "You really think so?"

"Yeah."

"Well, okay."

"Great!" she said releasing another of those ice melting smiles. "We'll rehearse tomorrow evening at the music building."

"I've got dishes so it will have to be after—like seven?"

"Seven at the music building," she said and popped to her feet. She swigged down the last of her Strawberry Nehi, plopped the bottle back down on the table and went.

Stephen stubbed out his Marlboro and stood intending to go to Jimmy and Dennis's table. There was no need. They were heading out.

"What up, Steve?" Brodski asked. "You look like a bad case of embalming."

"Thanks, I think. You ain't the first one to make that observation."

"Doctor Crow help?"

"Couldn't hurt."

They made their way out of the smoky Student Union into the cold. Their breaths fogged as though they were smoking.

The White House was only a few steps down the street and Stephen was glad. The cold seemed extra bitter tonight.

Inside Brodski and Grant's room Jimmy dug the pint bottle of Old Crow out of his underwear drawer while Dennis brought the three stolen glasses down from the top of the medicine cabinet.

Jimmy poured judiciously, then held up the bottle and looked through it, measuring how much was left. "Gonna have to get some more pretty soon," he said, shrugged then split the remaining bourbon between the glasses. "Maybe I'll make a run to Kentucky this weekend," he said. "You wanna go?"

"Well, yeah. Mind if I noise the trip abroad in the dorm? I'm sure there'll be some orders."

"Yeah, fine. If I'm gonna be a bootlegger, might as well do

it right." He lifted his glass, waited for the other two to do the same then said, "Broken hearts." They all drank.

The toast hit Stephen hard. He lifted his glass again and waited for the other two. When they were ready, he said, "Doc Marchant," and slugged down the last of the liquor, as did Jimmy and Dennis.

"Shame what happened," Brodski said.

Stephen shook his head. "More than just a shame Jimmy. It was murder."

"Well yeah, he came home to a burglary." Dennis began.

"Bullshit," Stephen said. "It was the Klan, sure as hell."

"How do you know, Steve?" Brodski asked.

Stephen looked down at his shoes and said, "I don't really. I mean I got no proof, but I got a feeling. The Kappas hated him for being queer and for being a stand-up anti-segregationist."

"Just because they are miserable excuses for humans doesn't mean they killed the Doc," Dennis said.

"I heard Fester making threats under his breath a bunch of times," Stephen said.

Jimmy grimaced and shook his head. "It might have been the Klan, but it wasn't Fester. He doesn't have the guts."

"Guts? What guts does it take to kill a harmless old queer professor?"

Brodski took a deep breath and looked hard at Stephen. "It is a lot harder to kill a man than you might think, Steve."

Stephen took in the look, recognizing that Jimmy seemed to know what he was talking about. Had Brodski ever killed anyone? In Vietnam maybe? The urge to dispute what his friend said came and went with that thought. After a little he said, "Well anyway, whichever of the Klan assholes did it, he'll never get caught. Cruz won't even look."

"I'm not so sure of that, Steve. Not good for elections for murder to go unpunished in your county, even one that a lot of folks don't mind," Brodski said. "There'll be somebody arrested for it. Whether it is the real murderer," he shrugged.

Stephen looked at his watch. "I got reading to do before tomorrow."

"Me too," Dennis said. "You ready for finals?"

"Is anybody ever ready for finals?" Stephen said putting his coat back on. "When are we going to Kentucky, Jimmy?"

"0800 Saturday morning?"

"Kinda early isn't it? I got dishes. How about nine?"

"Nine it is."

"I'll noise it around a little and get a list together."

"No COD. Cash up front."

"Yep. Cash up front."

The walk from the White House to the back door of Lorring Home was not long. Even so Stephen's ears were aching cold by the time he entered the TV lounge. He hesitated long enough to see that there were only a couple of people watching TV. He didn't bother to see what they were watching, just headed on up the stairs.

~ * ~

The news broke the next morning that Sherriff Cruz had arrested a suspect in Dr. Marchant's murder; a local black man name of Emanuel Jefferson who was known to have done yard work and other handyman chores for Marchant. The situation turned chaotic the instant Jefferson was picked up. A mob of Kappas and other KKK adjuncts gathered in front of the county lock up moments after Cruz brought his prisoner in. There were noosed ropes in evidence, which caused the Sherriff to call for help from the state police. Klan sympathizer or not he knew it would not look good for him to allow a lynching without at least an attempt to prevent it. The mob broke up pretty quickly when the first vanload of state police in riot gear arrived

On campus, sparks flew between the Black Student Union and the Kappas. There were several near riots in the halls between classes which brought state police to the campus like an occupying army.

"You know he didn't do it, right?" Charlie Horse said to Stephen who was eating breakfast before washing morning dishes and going to his sociology class.

"Of course not. Cruz just found someone in close proximity," Bill Thinning who was also sitting at breakfast began.

"Someone *black* in close proximity," Charlie interrupted.

"Yeah."

"We are organizing a march on the courthouse for this afternoon," Charlie said.

"That was fast," Stephen said.

"With the way things have been going on campus and in town the BSU put together an emergency action committee." Charlie said.

"Where's it gonna start?" Thinning asked.

"Town Square, here."

"Long way from here to the county seat," Thinning said.

"We got some cars. Gonna drive to the edge of the county seat and start the actual walk from there. You gonna go?" he said, not aiming the question at either of the white boys but letting the question fall on the table.

Bill Thinning, without hesitation said, "Yeah, I'll be there."

Charlie nodded.

Stephen found himself hesitating. "I got classes I really shouldn't cut this afternoon. I'm kinda hanging by a thread in Greek, so I guess I'll stay here, but I really wish…"

Charlie continued to nod, but there seemed to be a change in it somehow, as though he was saying, "Yeah, sure, Stevie."

"I really would like to go with you guys," Stephen continued then trailed off. He stood, picked up his breakfast tray, said, "I gotta go wash dishes," and made his exit, feeling like a rat abandoning ship.

The dishes were already stacked high, when he tied on his rubber apron and took a deep preparatory breath. Gary Mamoni jokingly said, "Bout time you showed up, Hollywood."

Stephen glanced at the little New Jersey guy. "Shut up,

Mamoni," he said. "I'm in no mood."

Mamoni looked over at him. "Scuse me all to hell! Didn't mean to insult yer lordship," he said.

Instantly Stephen felt bad about being so snippy. "I'm sorry, Gary. Just ain't been a great morning."

"Yeah, yeah. I know. Between the honkies and the niggers I barely made it in here this morning. Be glad to get out of here and back to New Jersey where the gunfire is usually personal not just general like down here."

Stephen smiled at Mamoni's wry humor. "You want me to drag or rack?"

"As you want to, I'm out of here. Jules is supposed to be in any time now."

Stephen looked around, and began stacking plates in the wash rack next for the washer since there weren't many trays coming in at the moment. Breakfast was a fairly easy meal for the dish crew. The only real problem was having to get up early. After he'd loaded two racks and started one through the washer he moved into position beside the window and pulled in the three trays that had been shoved in since Mamoni left. He glanced out and say Mary Ann sitting alone at a front table. She often sat there, right in front of the dish room window. *It's like she parks there just to remind me she is still here,* he thought.

After a little Mary Ann brought her tray up and stuck it in the window, holding it up until Stephen was forced to take it from her.

"Choir is practicing over at the BSU this evening, Steve." she said. "Billie Jo said to ask you if you were coming."

"No. I'm not."

"You sure? We could go out onto the back porch."

It was an invitation that really was tempting, but he said, "No," taking the tray and sliding the dishes off onto the counter before tossing the tray into the stack to his left. "It's too cold anyhow," he added.

Mary Ann didn't say anything, just stared at him for a

moment before turning away.

~ * ~

After classes all day Stephen thought he should have just gone with Thinning and the others since his thoughts were so spun by the situation and by memories of Mary Ann and the Danjo plot. He couldn't keep his mind on anything. Walking back to the dorm he heard a couple of the state cops talking, He thought he heard them say something about a shooting at the courthouse. He stopped instantly and turned back to the cops.

"Excuse me, officer," he said. "Did you say there was a shooting at the courthouse?"

"Yeah."

"What happened?"

"Gang of nigra kids, tried to break that guy Jefferson out," he said.

Stephen knew that was crap, but he let it slide.

"Somebody get shot?" Stephen asked.

"I don't think so. I believe they just fired in the air to scare 'em."

"Waste of bullets," the other state cop said. "Shoulda fired into the crowd."

"Yeah, that woulda taught 'em a lesson. They oughta start shooting into the crowds at them Vietnam demonstrations too," the other cop said, forgetting about Stephen.

"Did anyone get arrested?" Stephen interrupted.

"Probably," the first cop said.

Stephen drew in a deep breath waiting for more but no more was forthcoming so he walked on after a moment, thinking he had done well not to go with the group protesting.

About eight o'clock as Stephen and Drew were studying, or at least pretending to, they heard someone come up the stairs and to Charlie's door. Stephen popped up and opened the door to see Charlie just unlocking his door.

"What are you doing here?" Stephen asked.

"Going in my room, what's it look like?"

"Yeah, but I thought you were in jail or something."

"Naw, they herded us all up and handcuffed some of us," He flashed his grin, "They quit that cause they didn't have enough chains, so they just herded us up in a bunch there on Main Street and left a couple of deputies to watch us. After a couple hours they took our names and addresses and cut us loose."

"I heard there were some shots fired," Bankuski said.

Charlie's eye brows drew down. "Must have been at some other demonstration, cause this one was pretty peaceful. Couple of cops got a little wild with their night sticks but that was mostly poking and prodding. No shots."

"Damn," Stephen said. "Can't even trust the state cops to get it right. I heard a couple of them talking about how they should be firing into the crowd instead of over their heads."

Charlie shrugged. "Can't trust cops at the best of times, and they are gonna start shooting into crowds any day now. I mean, there was plenty of shooting at Pettus Bridge. They just ain't started shooting white people yet."

XI

Finals did not go well for Stephen. He had been steady with his work all quarter, but when finals came the world was too much with him. He was sure he busted a couple of tests. It worried him, thinking of how much trouble he was going to get from his folks when the probation notice came with his grades this time, and this time he had no defense that it was his money. This time it was most all from the folks. The money he had earned at Hardwick had been used for plane tickets, clothes and gas for the car. There was some left in his account which would pay for his bus and plane ticket, maybe a couple of Christmas presents, but the basket was pretty empty. His work-ship money went back to the school in the form of a meal ticket with a little left over for smokes. He had made sure there was a little left over to get a bottle of Old Crow to pay Jimmy back, but the bootlegging trip got canceled because no one wanted to order anything. Too close to finals and to going home for Christmas.

The one thing that went right, or at least right-ish, was the choir concert and his singing with the quartet. He hit every note right, and standing beside Janice had been a pleasure. The choir, as usual, finished the concert, Christmas or not, with the national anthem, assuring them of a standing ovation, but Stephen had a feeling the ovation was more than having been coerced by the Star-Spangled Banner. When it was over, and the choir broke up, Janice threw her arms around him and kissed him right on the mouth, which he thought was a good sign for next quarter, assuming he was back next quarter.

As he was packing his small bag to get ready to go catch the bus for Memphis a knock came on the door. It was his Uncle Paul.

"Well hello," Stephen said. "What are you doing here?"

"Came to take you to the airport," he said with the infectiously cheery tone in his voice.

"You didn't have to do that. I was just gonna catch the bus," he said.

What he didn't say was he was going to catch the bus in hopes of running into Jackie Bookman. He wasn't entirely sure how that would go after having Thanksgiving dinner with her Memphis cop father, but he remembered the firm feel of her behind in his hand and the sweetness of her kiss. That threw a different light on the Thanksgiving meal.

"It's all right. I've been keeping up with you through Morton and my other spies. They say it has been a pretty rough quarter. Thought you might like to talk on the way home."

"It has been rough, I'll give ya that. I don't know whether to be thankful or resentful that you and Uncle Morton are spying on me," Stephen said with a little chuckle.

"Ah, don't worry about it. No interference or influence, just watching out for ya cause you're family,"

"And you're Big Brother." Stephen picked up his carry-on and guitar case.

Paul said, "Traveling kinda light, aren't you?"

Stephen shrugged. "Change of clothes and my axe, all I need. Worse come to worst I'll start playing in the airport to scrounge up ticket money to come back after Christmas."

"Times that hard?" Paul asked.

Stephen shrugged. "Might not be a problem, if I busted something besides that Greek test."

Paul studied his nephew for a moment trying to decide if he was joking or not, but couldn't come to any conclusion.

"All right, Big Brother, if we're going let's get on with it."

The car was parked along the street behind Lorring Home where Paul had let him off after Thanksgiving. That snow was gone and the weather had warmed some, but it was still chilly. Stephen threw his carry-on suitcase and the black cardboard guitar case in the back seat and climbed into the shotgun seat.

They started out going past the Baptist Student Union. Cathy Powell was just outside the gate, on her way somewhere. Seeing her, Stephen still felt a little of the stab of betrayal she brought him, but at the same time he felt the stab of duplicity for what he did to Mary Ann Younger. That one came home doubly as they turned past the Methodist Church cemetery.

"Campus seemed pretty tense," Paul said. "Never expected to see so many state police at Mason."

"Ever since Cruz picked up 'Manuel Jefferson. Things have been dicey. The Klan was waiting for them at the jail. They had a lynch party all set up and ready to go."

"I heard that."

"What better way to railroad a man than to make him too dead to protest," Stephen said cynically.

Paul glanced over at his nephew. "You really think that was what was going on."

"Yeah. I got no proof, but sure as shit that's what was up."

"You don't think this Jefferson did it?"

"I'd bet my last buck he didn't have anything to do with it. And my other last buck that it wasn't a robbery gone wrong. But no matter. Cruz needed something to make him look like he was doing his job so 'Manuel was elected."

"NAACP is saying no."

"They can say no all they want, but when the Black Student Union got a group together to protest, they almost all got arrested."

"Really?"

"Not really. I mean they went and the cops herded them up, took their names and threatened 'em but didn't really arrest them. It could have been a lot worse."

"Um," Paul grunted.

"They asked me to go with them, but I chickened out. Said I had to study and go to class instead, for all the good that did. I shoulda gone with 'em."

"Um," Paul grunted again.

"You know, I heard a couple of state cops talking about shooting into crowds of black and Vietnam protesters," Stephen said.

"I don't think you should take that too seriously."

"As Charlie Horse said, there was plenty of shooting at Pettus Bridge. They just haven't started shooting white people yet."

"Pretty cynical for a college kid," Paul said.

"Cynical maybe, but not wrong. I've seen why right here at Mason. White privilege is a real thing even among the Liberals."

"Sounds like you've gotten a little cynical too."

"More than a little. Seems like pretty much everything I have touched since Thanksgiving has…" —*the thought flashed through his mind to say has turned to shit, but even though Paul had been more like a friend than an uncle Stephen still moderated what he said to him*—"collapsed in smoldering ruins."

Paul chuckled, but cut it short when he glanced over and saw Stephen wasn't even smiling.

The Memphis Airport was pandemonium. It seemed that everyone and their uncle was trying to get on a plane to somewhere else. Stephen noticed there were even more uniforms than there had been when he landed back in August. He realized he had hardly thought of the war in the whole last quarter. It didn't seem to matter much to him since his heart was going to keep him out of it, but the reality of it came home to him with all the uniforms in the airport. "Hope you don't mind that I spend Christmas with you guys, Paul," he said looking around.

"You're more than welcome, but I got a feeling you're gonna make it out, if not today then tomorrow," Paul said.

"Your lips to God's ears," Stephen answered and got in the ticket line.

The line moved pretty fast and the ticket lady didn't seem too harassed. "Lot of stand-by today," she said. "Lot of Californias."

"Yes, ma'am," he answered. "What are my odds?"

She shrugged and smiled. "Can't ever tell."

"Okay, thanks," Stephen said, setting his guitar case on the scale.

The attendant swept it away without a word, and it disappeared down the conveyer and through the curtain. *It'll probably get to LA before I do,* he thought.

When he got to the gate to register for Student Stand-by the Stewardess didn't seem quite so chipper. "We'll know in half an hour. Stay close around. I'm gonna call the names once and if you don't answer up, you're done."

He elbowed his way back through the crowd to Paul and said, "Don't know. She wasn't all that hopeful. Said I should stay close."

"No place to sit," Paul said.

"Yeah, does look a little sardine-y. Guess I'll just stand."

"I'll hang with you until you get on," Paul said.

"Or until we go to your house and I call the folks." Stephen gave half a grin to that.

"Naw, you're gonna make it."

"If you say so."

"Sure are a lot of soldiers," Paul said.

"I was just thinking that same thing. Guess they are all headed for Vietnam."

"Probably. Every time I turn around, I hear about how they are increasing the number of troops over there. They say we are winning but I'm not so sure. Still hearing about a lot of casualties," Paul said. "There's a coffee bar back there. You want some coffee?"

"I do, but I got a feeling I should stay around here pretty close." He looked at his watch. "They are gonna start boarding in a couple minutes and then comes the stand-bys so maybe I'll just stay here."

Paul nodded. "I'll go get a couple of cups and bring you back one."

"Great."

"If you're lucky I'll have to drink them both because you'll be on the plane."

That actually struck Stephen as funny and he smiled at Paul's retreating back.

The coffee bar must have been as jammed as everything else because Paul didn't get back before the first boarding call was announced. The first-class passengers shuffled past the desk and down the loading tunnel. Stephen gripped his carryon bag tighter and let a prayer run through his mind, *"Please Lord let me get on this plane."*

Paul was still not back when the coach passengers were called and Stephen gripped his bag handle even tighter and prayed even more fervently. When all the coach passengers were aboard and the attendant began calling the stand-by names he suddenly thought, *What do I care? I'm just gonna catch hell when my pro notice comes in. It might well be better to just stay here for Christmas."*

"MITCHELL," the attendant called.

Stephen stuck his arm up and shouted, "Here! I'm here," as he began elbowing his way toward the front. At the desk the attendant said, "Stephen Mitchell?"

"Yes, ma'am, that's me." He held out his ticket. The attendant took it, ripped out one section and handed it back.

"Have a good flight," she said.

"Yes, ma'am," he answered and moved on down the boarding tunnel, thinking about Paul having to drink both cups of coffee and chuckling. *Maybe my luck has started to turn,* he thought.

Stephen didn't realize how tired he was. He slept on the plane, which was not normal. He usually didn't sleep in moving conveyances.

When he got to LA, he still felt like he had a shovelful of sand in each eye. He went down to the baggage claim and was relieved to see the cardboard guitar case. It might only contain a beat up Silvertone guitar, but it was precious to him. He found an empty phone booth and called home.

"I'm here," he told Mike. "I'll be in front of the American

Airlines terminal."

He sat down on one of the concrete benches in front of the terminal with the guitar case standing between his knees and watched the traffic.

"Steve," his brother Mike said, putting his hand on Stephen's shoulder.

Stephen came up fighting, but Mike managed to duck and holler, "Steve, it's me. It's me, Mike."

He had fallen asleep sitting on the bench outside the American Airlines terminal. Completely awake, Stephen said, "Sorry. Did I get you?"

"Naw. What you so jumpy about? You came up like you were fighting off wolves."

Stephen said, "Hmm. More like Ku Kluxers."

Mike's eyebrows went up and he looked at his brother questioningly, but didn't say anything about it. As they walked into the parking garage he said, "Well, at least your eyes aren't blacked this year."

"Thank God for small favors," Stephen answered. "Where's Mom?"

"Waiting in the car. She doesn't feel good."

At the car Stephen threw his carry-on and guitar into the back seat with Mike, and slid into the shotgun seat. He leaned over to kiss his mother on the cheek, but she turned away. "You don't want to get too close, Steve. I'm sick with a cold. That's why I stayed in the car. Didn't need to be out in the wind. How are you?"

"I'm okay. Beat, but okay," he said, settling into the passenger seat.

"No black eyes this time?"

"Yeah," he yawned. "I decided I didn't care whether any of the fraternities wanted to pledge me or not so I didn't play any football," he said, sticking with the story he had given them about how he got black eyes last year.

Stephen was awakened by his mother calling his name. "Steve, wake up. We're home."

He opened his eyes to find that they were in the garage at home. He didn't remember so much as getting on the freeway. *Guess I really am beat,* he thought. He dumped his stuff on the top bunk in his bedroom and went to the kitchen. His mother was making biscuits to go with the roast which was already in the oven and beginning to smell heavenly.

"I'm gonna make me a sandwich," he said and opened the refrigerator.

He found ham, cheese, mustard and mayo. He pulled a couple of slices of bread out of the bread drawer.

"Dinner's gonna be ready in a little bit," she said.

"That's fine. I'll still eat it." He took his first bite leaning against the counter beside the fridge. His mother glanced over at him. "You've put on some weight," she said.

"Little bit, I guess."

"You're gonna have to watch that. My family always tended toward heavy."

"Aw, I'm not gonna worry about that. I got enough troubles without worrying about my weight."

"What kind of troubles?" she asked casually but with a small taste of worry mixed in.

He hesitated a moment thinking of the expected probation notice that was surely on its way, but he said, "Just the world. I mean the mess in Vietnam and the mess in the south. It's all around me, picking at me all the time."

"Well, at least you don't have to worry about Vietnam anymore," she said.

Stephen drew in a deep breath around a mouthful of ham sandwich and let his mother's comment go. She had not been happy with his decision to go to the Marines, and had clearly been glad when they turned him down.

He turned, pulled a glass out of the cupboard beside the fridge then poured himself a glass of milk.

"So, how is school going?" She asked.

Again, Stephen hesitated and decided not to burn that

particularly bridge until he actually came to it so he said, "All right, I guess. It's hard what with washing dishes and stuff, but I manage."

"I wish we could afford to just give you an allowance so you didn't have to work."

"Naw, it's fine. I really don't mind." He grinned crookedly. "The Jell-O volleyball makes it all worth it."

"Jell-O volleyball?"

"Yeah, Miss Connie serves institutional Jell-O in various flavors, and a lot of the time it comes in the dish window uneaten, so some of the dish room guys have been known to use it to play catch with. It is so thick and hard you can bat it around for several minutes before it goes to mush and has to go down the garbage," he said, laughing.

"That's barbaric," his mother said, but she was laughing when she said it.

"Making up for all the years mothers have been saying 'Don't play with your food'."

His mother laughed louder. "I'm glad to have you home, Stevie. You always make me laugh."

"That's how I have kept you and Pop from killing me all these years."

His mother was silent for a few moments longer, finishing up the biscuits. "We hear about the civil rights on the news," she said. "I know you and your last year's roommate were close. His getting killed kinda hurt you. Are you still involved with the civil rights?"

"Ma, I never was really involved. I talked with Robert and the other guys from the Black Student Union and went to the march when Robert died, but I was never really very deep into it. If Robert had lived, I don't know. I might have gotten more into it. Lord knows it isn't any better now than it was last year. In fact, it's kinda worse. There are a bunch of Ku Kluxers on campus that are constantly giving the black students grief, and I'd bet my last buck that if they didn't actually do it, they know who did kill Dr. Marchant."

"That's your English professor?"

"Was."

"I thought I heard on the news that they found the one who killed him."

"The Sherriff arrested someone but that's bu..." He thought better before he said bullshit, and said "...Bunk. They just grabbed up a convenient black guy and slammed him in jail, but he didn't do it any more than I did."

"Well, if he didn't do it...

"Come on, Ma, you're from the south, you know how that's gonna work. Doesn't matter if Manny Jefferson is guilty or not, he's going to jail, if he's lucky. The Kluxers already tried to lynch him. Tried to take him right out of the Sherriff's hands. Might have, too, if the world hadn't been watching."

His mother sighed and looked over at him. "I know it isn't right, but you stay away from that mess as much as you can. People get killed."

Stephen thought about having stayed at school when Charlie Horse and the others marched to the county jail. He thought about Charlie saying they weren't shooting white people yet. At the back of his mind he wondered if the real reason he hadn't gone was that he was afraid. He didn't think so, but it was something to be considered.

"People get killed in Vietnam too," he said. "I don't see much difference between there and here. In fact, I think marching and fighting here is more right than marching and fighting there. Here, if we march, we are standing up for equal rights and justice."

"I suppose," his mother said. "Just don't get yourself killed, please."

Stephen slugged down the last of his glass of milk. "How long till dinner?"

"My Lord, you just finished a sandwich, you can't still be hungry."

Stephen shrugged. "I'm a growing boy," he said and got out of the kitchen.

Outside he sat down on the curb, half hoping one of the Turros brothers would come by, but not really expecting it to happen. He lit up a Marlboro and blew the smoke into the air. *I wonder what Sherry's doing right now?* he thought. She had written him a couple more letters after the first "I told ya I'd write," and he had written her back. He hadn't said more than a little about what was going on at school, keeping it light and tickly. He didn't want to write anything too heavy because he didn't know but what her folks were censoring her mail, especially from him. *Maybe I oughta give her a call,* he thought, then thought about the extreme thinness of his wallet. *Maybe I could borrow some from Mike? Or maybe the old man would spot me some, for the sake of romance.* He drew in a puff from his cigarette and let it out slowly, remembering that his father had bought him a pack of smokes before. But a pack of smokes was thirty-five cents. Stephen figured he would need at least a twenty to take Sherry out to a movie or to eat, but with the thought of Sherry came the thought of Mary Ann, which twisted his heart, and his manhood.

It had not started out good to begin with. He had hit on Mary Ann because he had been angry with Cathy Powell and the whole Baptist Student Union. He hadn't thought anything much would come of it, maybe a little petting and kissing like with Sherry, but things had not gone that way. He hadn't realized how vulnerable she had been.

After that first time it was as though she became addicted to him. She was always around and always willing. Stephen thought that was great—at first. But Mary Ann was a woman of parts. She pushed and pulled and shoved him toward the BSU again, after he had sworn he would not do that again. He had spent a great deal of time with the Baptists in his first quarter last year, and it had cost him a probation notice because he spent time away from class traveling with them. He started because he wanted to get closer to Cathy Powell, and he had for a while, but he discovered she was just the bait in the monkey trap, as Jimmy Brodski said. She had no real feelings for him and threw him away when she thought he was thoroughly caught. Now Mary Ann was trying to do the same thing, lure him back to the BSU.

Still, she was not like Cathy Powell. She was more vulnerable and, in her way sweeter, which made Stephen feel like shit because he just didn't want her any more. The thought of not going back to school was tempting. Having a couple thousand miles between Mary Ann and himself sounded good. *Maybe I don't want to go back,* he thought. *Maybe I should just stay here and get a real job. Maybe do some part-time school at Valley State.* But that didn't really appeal to him either. He knew he could get a job as a hod carrier or some of the other building trade jobs, but his lower back twinged at the thought of spending the day shoveling sand and gravel.

He sat quietly for a while just looking at the day and remembering how cold Thanksgiving had been. A kid on a bicycle rode by. He threw a folded paper into the Echiveria's yard next door.

I can maybe get a job writing for one of the throwaway newspapers, he thought. He had delivered the Green Sheet advertiser when he was ten, but that was not a particularly pleasant memory. Getting up in the wee hours to fold papers then going out in the cold on his bike to deliver them. The job wouldn't have lasted long if it hadn't been for his folks getting up with him to help him fold papers and load the bike bags. He kept at it for more than two years until he started working at Hardtwick.

This time he wouldn't be delivering, he would be writing for it. Pictures of receiving a Pulitzer Prize danced through his head and were gone with the same wind that blew away his cigarette smoke.

I wouldn't have to deal with any of it. No Mary Ann, no Kappas, no Ma Brigman. But almost as soon as he thought it, he let it go. Despite all the troubles and pressures, he still felt like a free man at Mason. He liked feeling free.

XII

Christmas Eve. The rattle of the postman opening the porch mail box was soft but Stephen's ears had been sharpened since his first day home so he heard it over the babble of the TV. He shot up from the couch like he was on springs and went to the front door. His mother was there ahead of him, already pulling the mail out of the box. She shuffled through the letters, Christmas cards, and junk mail then handed Stephen an envelope with his name on it with hardly a hesitation.

Stephen looked at the envelope for a moment, thinking *Merry Christmas from Mason College,* then tapped the contents down to one end of the envelope and tore a thin strip off the other end. He fished the contents out, expecting one page to be pink. Probation slips were pink, he remembered from last year, but there was no pink sheet. He pressed the envelope more open again and blew into it then looked closely to assure himself the bad news wasn't still stuck inside.

"Well, what's it say, Stephen?" his mother asked impatiently.

Stephen flipped the sheet down and held the bottom. It was one sheet. He read the top which said, "Mason College Grade report, Fall 1967." Glancing down, he noticed that there were no red marks anywhere on the sheet.

"Says I passed everything," he said with relief in his voice.

His mother threw her arms around him. "Hooray!" she said as she hugged him and kissed his cheek, quickly backing away, as she remembered her cold which was nearly gone.

"Was there some doubt?" she asked.

"Yeah, there was," he looked down the grid of the sheet. "I'm amazed. I even passed Greek and that was pretty iffy," he laughed. "It's a C—a low one I'm pretty sure—but I'll take it."

"Well okay," his mother said.

He blew out a breath. "I'm glad that's behind me now. Makes Christmas feel more Christmassy."

It was with a much lighter heart Stephen rode in the back seat when the family went off to midnight church. He sorta felt as though he had something to be thankful for, but then again not. He could go back to school and pick up where he left off with Mary Ann, the Kappas and the subterranean feeling of threat, but also with the budding experience of participating in music, and, though there was a sad vibe about it, participating in the creation of the Round Table anthology. All in all, the good seemed to outweigh the bad so he put it all aside to celebrate Christmas.

Christmas Eve church was not such a big deal with the Valley Bible Church—the church from which Hardtwick Academy had sprung. It was more a party topped off with a straight reading of the Christmas story from the King James Bible. People dressed in their finest clothes stood in groups drinking fruit punch and nibbling snacks brought by some of the ladies of the church

The church hall was already full of people when the Mitchell family arrived. Stephen hoped the Kinert family would be there, but more especially that Sherry Kinert would be there. He checked his tie when he got out of the car.

"How's that, Mike?" he asked. "Straight?"

"Yep," Mike answered.

"Turn around here," his father said, so Stephen did. His father checked the tie, pulling the knot itself tighter. "Looks pretty good," he said.

"Just like ya taught me," Stephen said.

They both remembered that day. It had not been an easy father and son day. James Mitchell was not a wonderfully patient man, especially as Stephen grew toward manhood. There was something of the "Old bull/Young bull syndrome." Stephen's father quickly ran out of patience trying to teach Stephen how to tie a double Windsor knot. It would have been easier to show him a four-in-hand knot which was just flipping the wide part of the tie around the thin part then shoving the wide part down the loop left by the wrap, but James was not satisfied with that kind of tie knot. *"They are always crooked, and look raggedy."* So he always used the double Windsor. Stephen didn't get it at first so the knot always ended fat with the ends of the tie not matching.

"Good Lord, boy, how hard is this?" James had said, raising his voice.

"Sorry," Stephen had said.

But it hadn't been enough. The simple father-son instruction time turned into a shouting match with both of them shaking with rage by the end. Ultimately, Stephen learned to tie the double Windsor by standing in front of his bedroom room mirror tying and undoing the knot over and over until he got it down to a beautifully compact V-shaped thing that fit perfectly between the wings of the shirt collar.

"Very handsome," Stephen's mother said. "Both of you. Now let's go in, these cookies are heavy."

They went in.

The hall was built like a chapel with exposed beam cathedral ceiling and gothic arched windows, but no pews, only a wide-open floor where there were a few tables and folding chairs set up. At the front, on the right, by the wall between the kitchen and the open floor sat a line of tables with snacks and drinks lined up. Christmas music was softly playing.

Stephen looked around to see who was there. The hall was dimly lit with strings of mixed color Christmas lights. He managed to pick out a few friends, before his eyes fell on Sherry Kinert. Without another thought, he crossed the room to her. She was chatting with two other girls. All were wearing Christmassy dresses, but Stephen only noticed Sherry. She wore a puffy-sleeved white blouse with a red felt vest over it and a dark green skirt with a

Christmas tree appliquéd on it where the poodle should have been. It was an old-fashioned costume, but it suited Sherry perfectly.

Memory of having wanted to kiss Sherry the day before he left for Mason at the end of last summer, crossed his mind.

"You look like Christmas," Stephen said, butting into the conversation.

Sherry turned and looked him over. "Not bad," she said. "You clean up pretty good."

"I should have brought some classroom green paint for your nose," he said.

"I would have to kill you then," she said, smiling.

"So violent," Stephen said. "What are they teaching you at Valley State?"

"Might ask you the same thing," Melissa, one of the other girls on whom he had butted in asked.

Stephen turned to her and said, "What?"

"Valley State hasn't been in the news for students getting murdered or churches getting burned to the ground," she said.

The statement hit Stephen like a punch to the stomach. "That was last year," he said.

"All kinds of trouble stirring back there with Martin Luther King and all the blacks rioting," Melissa said.

Stephen's temper rose a little. Then he remembered that Melissa was the daughter of one of the most outspoken racists in the Valley Bible congregation.

"Dr. King doesn't stir up riots," Stephen said. "He asks for peaceful protests, like Gandhi."

"Yeah, right. Peaceful protests that always turn into riots," she said.

"Only because the cops come in with dogs, night sticks and fire hoses. And guns now."

Stephen felt Sherry's hand take hold of his and begin pulling him away. Stephen was ready to go on with the argument, but he let Sherry lead him away.

"That bitch doesn't know what she is talking about," he said.

"She's just spouting her father's nastiness," Sherry said. "Just ignore her. I do most of the time."

The two moved away from everyone else and went to stand in a shadowy niche beneath one of the gothic windows.

"I should be used to it, I guess. It's the same crap the Kappas put out," Stephen said

"Is it really as bad as you said? Fire hoses and guns?"

"Yeah, it is that bad. I have friends, white friends as well as black, that have been hosed, jailed and beaten. Those folks that were killed in the church last year were my friends. One of them was my roommate."

"I didn't know that."

"Lot of stuff I didn't talk about. I don't talk about because it tears me up inside." He shrugged. "They never caught the bastards that did it."

"Really?"

Stephen shook his head. "They aren't even looking."

"They're not looking? Why not?"

"Because it was some of the local KKK that did it, and the Sherriff is KKK."

"That's terrible!" Sherry said

"Robert was a great guy. Patient with a big honky dumb-shit like me," Stephen said with a bitter half grin. "Showed me how stupid and petty racism can be, when this white Kluxer wouldn't even let us in a laundromat together."

"Really? I thought that kind of thing was illegal now."

"It is, same as the 'White only' waiting rooms in the railroad and bus stations but they haven't heard about that in places in Tennessee and Alabama."

"Have you been involved in marches and things?" she asked.

"I wish I could say I had been, but I haven't really. When the Black Student Union and a lot of people from the Mason Black community marched to honor Robert and the others, I was there, but there wasn't any trouble. I had a chance to be involved when the BSU organized a march on the county jail because Sherriff Cruz arrested a clearly innocent man for the murder of Dr. Marchant, but I chickened out. I had some iffy grades going into finals and a couple cuts might have..." he trailed off. "I should have gone even if it put me on probation again. It was the right thing to do and I didn't do it."

"What happened with the march?" Sherry asked.

"Nothing much really. We ended up with state cops all over the campus. The people that marched got roughed up a little, but not too bad. They got rounded up and questioned, but they weren't officially arrested. A lot worse might have happened if the world hadn't been watching. A bunch of Kluxers got their own march together. They met the Sherriff as he brought Manny in. They were gonna take him right out of Cruz's custody and lynch him, but Cruz stopped them. "

"That was good, wasn't it?"

"Yeah, at least for Manny Jefferson. If the world hadn't been watching pretty close Cruz would have let them hang him right there in the town square."

Sherry shook her head. "Why do you go there, Steve? Why not just stay here and go to Valley with me?"

Stephen looked into her beautiful face and said, "I keep asking myself that same question, but I can't come up with an answer that satisfies me. Trouble notwithstanding, I really like Mason. I feel free there and I like feeling free."

The church bell rang through the PA system, taking the place of the Christmas music. It sounded like a proper church bell but it was a recording as there was no real church bell in the steeple. After a few moments of recorded bell peals, an organ began playing the hymn "O Come All Ye Faithful." After one complete verse of the hymn the voice of Pastor Wilson came over the music. "Oh, come all ye faithful, to hear the story of the coming of the Savior."

Sherry took Stephen's hand again. "Sit with me, Steve?" she asked.

"Your folks won't mind?"

She smiled her most impish smile. "I don't care. I'm a big

girl now and I hang out with whoever I want."

Stephen smiled at that, and a flash of memory passed through his mind and tingled a moment in his manhood. *I gotta take her out again,* he thought, then remembered his financial condition. The thought evaporated, but her warm soft hand was still in his as they went into the sanctuary.

After the service Stephen and Sherry parted. Stephen thought, *I gotta get some money from somewhere to take her out again.*

~ * ~

Apparently, Santa Claus was listening to Stephen's thoughts because on Christmas morning, along with a couple of new sweaters and a pair of gloves there was a wad of twenty-dollar bills in an envelope with his name on it, marked as "From Santa."

"Thank you, Santa," Stephen said.

He wanted to run right out and call Sherry, but he restrained himself, figuring that the timing would have been wrong, but on Boxing Day he called.

"Movies and dinner?" he asked.

"When?"

"Tonight?"

"Um, I gotta ask my mom," she said.

Stephen laughed. "What happened to that rebellious girl from Christmas Eve?"

Sherry laughed, too. "She gets chicken when push comes to shove."

That caused Stephen to frown. He wondered if that was a shot at him because of what they'd talked about, but let it go after a moment. "So, go ask 'em already," he said

She covered the receiver and Stephen heard a muffled "Mom, can I go to the movies with Steve Mitchell?" He couldn't hear what the answer was but a moment later she turned back to him. "What time?"

"Be there at six. Flick at the Chinese starts at seven, dinner after."

He could hear the smile through the phone. "Great. I'll see you at six."

Stephen washed the old Rambler, made it shine like new, then paid extra close attention to his shave and shower. He put on just a little "stinkum" aftershave lotion then stood in front of his closet door, considering. December in California could be chilly, but this Christmas had been fairly warm. After some thought he put on a collared polo shirt, slacks and his sport jacket against the December chill.

"You need a haircut," his father said.

"Look like the shaggy dog," his mother said.

"I'll get one before I go back to school, but," he looked at his watch, "Not right now."

"You be a gentleman," his father said.

"Yes, sir, I will be," he said, thinking of the rubber in his pocket.

He didn't intend to use it. He and Sherry had been intimate before, but not that intimate. He didn't want to screw up this feeling they had between them at the moment, but it never hurt to be prepared.

"You got plenty of gas?" his father asked him.

"Yes, sir, and thanks to Santa Claus I even got money to buy more if I need it." He laughed.

His father laughed and nodded. "Just see you keep a hand on that Santa Money. It can disappear pretty fast."

"Don't I know it," Stephen said. He looked at his watch again then said, "I'm gone."

"Don't be too late," his, mother said.

"Couldn't if I wanted to," he said grinning. "Sherry's folks got a pretty tight curfew on her."

Stephen tuned the radio to KRLA as he pulled out of the driveway. The rock 'n roll brought visions of Sherry dancing through his head as he drove toward her house in the thickening dusk. In a back part of his mind the thought occurred to him, *I might love Sherry.* He put the thought aside, remembering the pain of Cathy Powell. He was not going to throw his heart into anything else that quickly ever again. It hurt too much when it fell apart.

Another part of his mind whispered *Mary Ann,* and that whisper took some of the anticipated joy out of this date.

Stephen parked his car at the curb in front of the Kinerts' lawn and walked up the drive to the front door. The porch light was on. He rang the bell and the door popped open so quick it surprised him. It was as though Sherry's father had been waiting for him to ring.

Mr. Kinert, blocking the door, looked Stephen over as though considering whether or not to let him in the house. After a moment he seemed to make up his mind and stepped out of the way. "Sherry," he called. "Steve's here." After a moment he asked, "What movie are you taking my daughter to see?" He didn't exactly sound hostile, but he didn't sound pleased either.

"*Oliver*, sir. The story of Oliver Twist," Stephen began.

"Um hum."

"Yes, sir, it's a musical, like *The Sound of Music*, but no Nazis."

Mr. Kinert smiled at that. "No Nazis, eh? That's good."

Sherry chose that moment to come into the living room, and Stephen's mouth fell open. Sherry was wearing a bright yellow dress that looked more like spring than winter. and reminded him of the dress Billy Jo had been wearing that first night back with Mary Ann. It absolutely reflected every spark of light in the room, making her glow like a Christmas light. Her long hair was brushed smooth and the light gave back reddish sparks from it.

"Wow," Stephen said. "You are beautiful!"

Sherry smiled and blushed. "Thank you," she said going to the hall closet and taking out a black sweater, which she hung over her forearm.

Mr. Kinert looked from Stephen to Sherry and back. "Midnight," he said.

"Aw, Daddy," Sherry began, but Stephen cut her off with, "Yes, sir," as he stepped over beside her to put a directing arm around her back as they headed out the door.

They went across the lighted porch, and down the drive. Stephen, remembering his chivalry, opened the car door for Sherry, handed her into the seat, then went round and climbed in himself. He started the car, pulled on the headlights, but didn't pull away from the curb.

It was darker now and Stephen was glad. "Sherry," he began, "I've been thinking about this since last summer,"

"What?" she said, looking at him.

Stephen leaned across the seat and kissed her.

She didn't resist, but when the kiss was through, she pulled back and looked at him. "You think of me?"

"Oh yeah. A lot," he said, looking into her golden eyes.

After a moment he put the car in gear and pulled away from the curb.

Sherry blinked a couple of times then scooted over closer to Stephen. "I think of you, too, Steve."

"A lot?"

"Not a lot, but some. I pray for you."

Stephen glanced over at her. "That's more than thinking of me."

"I guess it is."

"Must be your prayers that have kept me out of trouble this year," he said, thinking of all the confrontations between Fester and the other Kappas that might have ended with bloodshed.

"Glad I could help," she said. "Pull over."

"What's the matter?"

"Just pull over, will you."

Stephen eased through the traffic to the curb and put the car in park, not knowing what to expect. He looked questioningly over at Sherry who leaned in and kissed him more thoroughly than he kissed her before. It half stole his breath.

When he gathered himself, he said, "You better watch that

stuff, Sherry. It might just make me wanna tear your clothes off right here on Hollywood Way."

She smiled. "Maybe later."

~ * ~

The flick wasn't bad, but Stephen had trouble following it because his mind was more on Sherry sitting beside him. The seats at the Chinese didn't lend themselves to cuddling or putting arms around so Stephen and Sherry were satisfied just to exchange a kiss or two and hold hands, but that touch was enough to make Stephen's mind whirl. He remembered the last time he had actually been out with Sherry and their time overlooking the lights of Hollywood from Mulholland drive. Those memories caused his manhood to stir.

The excitement died down some when they went to Bob's Big Boy after the movie, but not too much.

They were seated in a booth across from one another, and Stephen could not look away from Sherry's golden eyes. The waitress dropped menus on the table and brought water. She said something that Stephen didn't catch and went away.

"You have pretty eyes, Stephen. Kinda green, but kinda gold."

The spell broke with that and he looked away. "Your eyes are gold," he said. "I never saw anyone with golden eyes."

"What color eyes do you usually look into?" she said teasing as she opened her menu.

"Red," he said.

"Red?"

"Yeah, usually my own bloodshot ones when I shave."

"Silly, I meant other girl's eyes? Do you have a girlfriend back east?"

"Not exactly," he said.

Memory pictures of Mary Ann sitting up on the Danjo tomb stone caused an uncomfortable little twist in his middle. "I mean, I have gone around with a couple of girls, but one of them broke my heart so I mostly avoid women. Anyway, I don't have time or money back there."

"Broke your heart?"

"Yes. I thought she loved me. I sure loved her. Came to find out she was just bait to shill guys into the Baptist Student Union. When she thought she had me she went back to this other guy. Left me hanging," he said, looking down at his menu and taking a sip of water, obviously bothered by telling the story.

Sherry said, "Sorry. I didn't mean to pry."

"It's all right. It's past. I do my best to avoid her now." He looked up at her and smiled. "How about you? You got a boyfriend I'm gonna have to fight for your affections?"

"Affections?"

"Sure. You know, hand holding and kissing and stuff."

"Oh, *stuff*. No, nobody except my dad. You probably won't have to fight him so long as you bring me home before midnight in more or less the same condition as when we left."

Stephen lifted an eye brow at her wit. "I'm amazed that there aren't dozens of guys buzzing around you. You're beautiful and smart."

Her mouth went to a sort of crooked line. "Smart doesn't help. Most of the guys I know like their girls dumb as bricks so long as they are willing to play at *stuff*."

The waitress showed up and they ordered.

Stephen took a deep breath. "Yeah, I guess *stuff* is pretty important."

"For you, too?"

"Again, not so much," he lied. "But I know a lot of guys that are like that. They'll tell any lie and do anything just for the sake of *stuff*."

They sat looking into each other for another few moments. "If I was here for more than Christmas, I would sure be around you," he said.

"For *stuff*?" she asked with an impish smile.

Stephen hesitated then turned the moment. "Yeah, but for

more than that. I thought the other day that it wouldn't be too hard to love you, Sherry."

Sherry hesitated. "That's a pretty serious thing to say Steve."

"Sorry, it's just... I don't know why but sometimes serious just falls out of my mouth without my knowledge. Besides which it is true. Like I said before, I think about you a lot."

The food came and cut off the discussion for a little while. But when the Big Boys were more than half gone, Sherry said, "Do you think of me because of what we did last year?"

"Yes, some."

"Me too."

They finished their meal looking at one another in silence. When it was done Sherry took Stephen's hand as they left the restaurant.

She scooted over tight against him as they drove up Laurel Canyon.

Stephen's thoughts and conscience were in a whirling, grappling battle about what should come next. He knew Sherry had something in mind to which he might not wish to be a party. He was caught between desire—love. He wanted to make love to Sherry so much that he could almost feel the act. His memory brought up the soft silkiness of the insides of her thighs, the rich sweetness of her kisses, the breathy sighs of her increasing arousal. He was prepared for all that, and for the next part which had not happened before. The Trojan in his pocket seemed to burn with wanting. At the same time, memory of Mary Ann seemed to stand off at the edge of his thoughts looking both angry and pitiful.

Stephen had used Mary Ann to satisfy his anger at Cathy Powell and at the BSU. That was his sole intention at the beginning, but in the using he found himself *loving* her. Not in the true sense, but in a sense that his soul found both satisfying and objectionable. He pitied her for the loss of her father, and because she was not as beautiful as Cathy nor indeed as beautiful as Sherry, but she was kind, pliant and sexually hungry, but she was also as true a bitch as Cathy had been, trying to lure him back to the BSU.

Stephen turned left onto Mulholland at the top of Laurel Canyon and they were soon away from most of the street lights. The Sunset Basin below them had more twinkling stars than the sky and when Stephen saw a wide pull out on the left side of the road, he turned in. There were a couple more cars parked there which probably meant that the cops would be along presently. Under other circumstances Stephen would have gone on a bit farther hoping for more privacy, but he had decided something in the last few minutes of the ride.

He shut down the engine and lowered the radio. Sherry kissed him and he kissed her back, then he pulled away.

"We can't do this, Sherry," he said.

She blinked at him for a moment before moving in for another kiss, but Stephen said, "No."

"I don't understand," Sherry said. "You wanted me last time. What happened?"

"I want you this time too, but I just can't."

"Can't?"

"I don't want to hurt you or make you feel bad or obligated."

She squinted at him in the darkness and didn't say anything for a long time, before she asked, "Is it because of the Baptist girl that broke your heart?"

Stephen hadn't really thought of that. His guilty conscience had nothing to do with Cathy or so he believed, but Sherry's having brought it up gave him an unexpected out. Romantic broken heart was less embarrassing and much easier to explain and understand than, *I was fucking this girl and I broke it off with her and maybe broke her heart which I feel bad about.* He lowered his head without a word.

"She really hurt you, didn't she?"

"Yeah, I guess." He looked up wishing he could look deep into Sherry's golden eyes but also glad he couldn't because he wasn't sure he could pull off the lie actually looking at her. "I'm sorry," he said. "I might love you in a little while, but I think I need to heal some more. Please don't be hurt or angry."

She stroked his cheek then leaned in and kissed him. "Poor Steve," she said then moved away from him clearly saying *Take me home,* without words.

They drove silently down the back side of Laurel Canyon and up into the Burbank Hills to the Kinert house. Stephen opened the door for her, walked her up onto the lighted porch. Before he let her go in, he said. "I really am sorry, Sherry. I hope you don't hate me."

She looked up into his face then lifted her face for a kiss, which Stephen gave her. "I couldn't hate you, Steve. I might love you too," she said and went into the house.

XIII

LAX was a zoo. It seemed like everybody in Los Angeles wanted to be somewhere else so they were all at the airport. Stephen went through the ritual of buying the stand-by ticket and wasn't surprised when the clerk said, "Hope you ain't in a hurry. Pretty much everything flying is flying full."

Stephen wasn't sure whether or not that was bad. A couple more days at home, that is, near Sherry, wouldn't be bad, but he was short on money and was going to need some when he got back to Mason, so he let the idea go. *If the Lord wants me to stay, I won't get a seat,* he thought as he pushed his way up to the gate to get his name on the list. The clerk wrote "Mitchell" on a clipboard list and Stephen asked her, "How's chances?"

She shrugged. "Hope you got somewhere to spend the night.
"

He took a deep breath and let it out. "Thanks."

"Boarding starts in about ten minutes," she said.

He elbowed his way back to where his father was waiting, leaning against a pillar.

"Not looking good, Pop," Stephen said.

His father didn't say anything, just took out a can of Velvet Tobacco and a package of OCB rolling papers and began to build himself a cigarette. Stephen watched closely as he had been watching since he was a child. When the cigarette was rolled and lit, it looked like a tailor made.

"I need to learn to do that," Stephen said.

"You need to quit," his father answered. "Nasty habit, and

152

expensive."

"Yes, sir, I know."

"You got plenty of smokes?"

"Yes, sir."

They looked over the crowd again. Stephen didn't consciously know it but he was hoping to see Sherry in the mess, come to see him off, but of course, she hadn't. "Lot of Army around," James Mitchell said. "Looks like an invasion."

"Yeah," Stephen said. "Most of them going toward Vietnam. Probably where I'd be if my heart hadn't crapped out on me."

James looked at his son and said, "Don't feel bad about that, Steve. Just means you have some other job to do."

"You went," Stephen said plaintively.

"Different time, different war. That one was because Hitler and Tojo and them really did want to take over the world."

"That's what they say this is all about too. Domino effect and all that."

"I ain't convinced," the older man said. "I got a feeling this whole mess is just cooked up to keep some generals happy. Don't really have much to do with world domination."

Stephen squinted at his father, having never heard such talk come out of him before. Stephen always thought his father was an "America Right or Wrong," kind of guy, but here he was talking anti-war.

"I figured you'd be all for sending me off to war." Stephen said.

"Nobody hates war more than a man who has been in one. I lost a lot of friends in that war." He took a drag and let the smoke trickle out. "I was proud when you signed up for the Marines, but I gotta tell you, my heart felt much lighter when they found that murmur in your heart. I would have kept my mouth shut and waved you off with pride had you gone, but I am just as glad you didn't."

Stephen thought about that for a couple of heat beats. "What if I had decided to go off to Canada?"

"I would have been ashamed of you and probably stopped

calling you my son."

"But you were just talking about being glad I didn't have to go."

"There's a difference between not going for physical reasons beyond your control and going to Canada. That would have been cowardice. This is just what I said. God has some other work for you to do and in the Marines wouldn't have been the place to accomplish it."

The PA system came alive. "Passengers holding first class tickets for flight 6820 to Memphis, Tennessee, please prepare to board."

"Here goes," Stephen said.

He stuck out his hand to his father and James took it, then pulled him into a hug. The Mitchells were not usually a huggy kind family but it felt good to be in the embrace of a man who cared for him. He pulled away after a moment and his father said, "I'll wait right here. If you get on give me a wave, but if I don't get a high sign, I'll just wait right here till you get back to me."

Stephen found that his voice was a little choky so he just nodded.

He elbowed his way through the crowd toward the desk, knowing he would still have to wait for the coach passengers to be called but not wanting to have to fight the crowd just in case he did get called.

First Class went through in an orderly fashion and coach began to line up. When the ramp was clear the clerk announced "Coach passengers for flight 6820, to Memphis." She unhooked the rope and people began to move forward. Stephen wondered if he could just slide into the moving line and go ahead, but clerks looked at boarding passes as people went by so sneaking aboard was out of the question.

After the coach passengers cleared, the clerk at the desk began calling names. They were called in the order they had been put on the list, and as that call list got longer Stephen had a feeling his name was not going to be on it.

"Mitchell. Stephen Mitchell," the clerk said and Stephen almost couldn't believe it.

"Yes, here," he said.

The clerk gave him a boarding pass. He clutched it, turned around and stuck the hand with the pass in it up in the air and waved it. His father stuck up an arm in acknowledgement. Stephen turned around and marched down the boarding tunnel. He spent most of the flight running memories through his mental playback. Memories of the women of his past, Cathy Powell, Mary Ann Younger, Jackie Bookman, and Sherry Kinert. The memories were not just mental. The remembrance caused a reaction below which began to cause him some pain. After a while he went to the bathroom to relieve himself and resolved to stop thinking about women.

Three out of the four had ended badly, if indeed they had ended. He had a feeling Mary Ann and perhaps Cathy were still going to be trying to hook him back into the Baptist Student Union where he was determined not to go. Sherry was going to be three thousand miles away. These thoughts eased the wanting he felt in his loins. It looked like it was going to be a sort of a lonely winter.

As the flight neared its end Stephen's resolve slipped. He dug out his wallet and counted the money in it. *Thin,* he thought, but enough for a bus ticket back to Mason, on the off chance of running into Jackie again, though that had probably ended, too. But he would never know if Uncle Paul showed up to welcome him back.

When the flight landed in the drizzling rain and he came down the ramp into the waiting area, there were the ever-faithful Paul, Esther, and the girls waiting for him.

"Shouldn't you be home working on a sermon, Paul?"

He laughed. "Already got it. Just wait until tomorrow. It's a real hellfire and brimstone scorcher."

Stephen laughed a little at that. He had never heard Paul preach any way but softly.

"How was the flight?" Esther asked.

"It was fine. Smooth as silk."

"You're not so tan this time," she said with what might have been disappointment.

"Nope. No working outside and it was kinda cold for the beach."

"News made it sound like it was warm and sunny," Darlene, his eldest cousin, eight years old, said doubtfully.

"Clear and sunny, but kinda chilly. They said it was raining here as we landed. I couldn't tell."

"Yeah, it has been drizzling for days. Welcome back to Memphis," Paul said with irony.

They headed down to the baggage claim where Stephen picked up his guitar and the extra suitcase he had been forced to bring in order to get his new sweaters back to school.

They headed to the parking lot. The rain had reduced to mist, more like fog than rain. Stephen threw his luggage into the trunk and climbed into the shotgun seat without thought. The girls went to the back seat.

"Have you heard anything from Mason?" Stephen asked.

"Not much. Apparently, someone put up bail for Manny Jefferson."

"Really? I figured he would be behind bars the rest of his life. Who put up the money?"

"That's the trouble, no one is sure who did and the Sherriff isn't saying. Some of the more cynical amongst us think it might have been a ploy by the KKK to get him out of jail so they could get at him easier."

"Yeah. If I was him, I'd certainly stay out of sight."

"I understand he has sorta gone underground over in Black Mason. Some of the churches are hiding him."

Tension and anger fountained in Stephen's chest. He had managed to keep it mostly at bay when he was home, but here it was too close. It almost made him want to turn around, get on a plane going back to LA and to hell with it all. But a whisper came into his mind, *the only thing evil requires is that good men do nothing.*

"Why can't they just leave Manny alone? Everyone knows he didn't do this."

"They need a scapegoat. Someone killed Dr. Marchant and they can't acknowledge it was the KKK, so just like all down through history, they pulled a black man in to be a sacrifice that covers them," Paul said. "I'm surprised you don't recognize the story, Steve. It's old as the hills—Golgotha to be exact. Blood being spilled to cover the sins of others."

Stephen looked at his uncle, unable to believe Paul was likening the possible lynching of Manny Jefferson to the crucifixion, but then thinking, while it wasn't exactly parallel, it did have its comparisons.

"You've come around to thinking it was a KKK murder, huh?" Stephen said.

"Yeah. It's hard not to with all the noise around it."

They rode in silence for a while. "That friend of yours has come to church a couple of times," Paul said

Stephen had a suspicion he knew who Paul was talking about but he decided to play dumb. "Who's that?" he asked.

"The girl that helped serve at Thanksgiving," Esther chimed in.

"Jackie, I think her name is," Paul said.

"Jackie Bookman," Stephen said.

"Yes, right," Paul said.

"What a beautiful girl," Esther said.

"She is that," Stephen agreed.

"Where did you meet her?" Esther asked. "She's a Memphis girl, isn't she?"

"Yes, ma'am. She's from Memphis. Her family lives over in Sherwood Forest. She is like the bad penny that keeps turning up."

"Bad penny?"

"Well, not really bad, just," Stephen shrugged. "Every time I turn around, I seem to run into her. I first met her on the train from L.A. last year. Then I ran into her on the bus going home last year."

"Oh yes, her mother was picking her up when I was picking you up," Paul said.

"Right. Then I met her on the bus again as I was coming to

your house for Thanksgiving this year, and here we are."

"She has come over here to church a couple of times since Thanksgiving and she asked about you."

"Probably wanting to tell me her dad is hunting me," Stephen said with a bitter chuckle.

"Hunting you? What for?"

"He's a Memphis cop and I sorta messed up his Thanksgiving dinner with my presence."

"How's that?"

"Somebody mentioned that I didn't have black eyes this year, and Jackie wanted to know what that was all about so I told her about driving while black and my little dance with the Memphis cops. That's when she informed me that her father was a Memphis cop."

"Oh. Uh oh," Esther said.

"Yeah, then her little brother remembered seeing me on TV when Robert was killed so I had to explain all that. The whole mess kinda took all the joy out of Thanksgiving. I figured that would be the last of her I would ever see, but, like that bad penny, now she has turned up here."

"Might not be a bad penny," Aunt Esther said. "Might be the dime you find just as you need to make a phone call."

"If she shows up tomorrow, you can ask if she's a penny or a dime," Paul said with a laugh.

The thought Jackie might show up tomorrow made a little twist come into Stephen's stomach and a little warmth to begin somewhat lower.

Next morning Stephen was glad he had thrown a tie into his suitcase. He dressed in his long-sleeved white shirt and tie with a sweater over it for church. He admired his reflection in the dresser mirror. His haircut looked good, though he would have skipped it if his father hadn't insisted. He would have liked to look more Beatle than PFC, but peace was better than Beatle hair so he got it cut. *Wonder if I should try growing a beard,* he thought. Beards had become very popular at Mason, but Stephen wasn't sure he had enough hair on his face to actually sprout one. Truth be told he could go several days without shaving and not look too scruffy.

Aunt Esther gave him her approval. "You shine up nice," she said.

"Yeah, like an old pair of shoes." He laughed.

The weather was cloudy and cold but the rain had stopped. "Gonna start again in a couple of hours," Paul said. "Probably be sleet."

"Gonna make the trip up to Mason tough," Stephen said.

"Ah, not so bad. I hope," he said with a smile.

They went to the church early enough for Sunday School. Stephen didn't know any of the people from the collegiate youth group, but he sat in on their class anyway. It was less Bible class and more school talk which suited him fine. There was talk of the growing restlessness among the black population of Memphis. "It's like they were still slaves," one girl said. "The garbage men get paid almost nothing. They have to haul out the cans and put them back in the backyard."

"They oughta strike," opined a fellow who was going to school at Memphis State.

"Won't accomplish anything," another said. "If they do the cops will intervene and start locking them up. They won't get a raise. It'll probably start a riot, and the garbage still won't get picked up."

Stephen listened quietly. He had opinions on this crisis but he still managed to keep his mouth shut.

"At least things are quieter in 'Nam," another young man said.

"How do you know?" a girl asked sharply.

Stephen happened to know she had a brother overseas.

"News says the body counts are way down," the young man said. "That means the increase in American troops has settled the Viet Cong down and maybe kept the NVA regulars north of the DMZ."

"Hope you're right. Would be nice to have this mess over before any more of us get drafted."

There was universal agreement to that.

At church time Stephen came into the sanctuary, looked around and let out a grateful sigh that Jackie wasn't present. He wasn't sure how he would have handled it if she had been. He sat toward the back looking through the program and was surprised to find that the hymns, which were usually more toward Presbyterian, were more toward the Baptist today. Less "Morning has Broken" and more "Power in the Blood." It made him think about what Paul said in the car yesterday. *Maybe he* is *gonna preach some fire and brimstone,* Stephen thought.

As they sang the opening hymn, "Nothing but the Blood of Jesus," Stephen began to think of the revival meetings he had been involved with in the Baptist Student Union. Those were both good times and bad. There was power in those services, but there had been so much beneath the surface of the BSU which had finally leaked out and destroyed that powerful feeling for him.

Stephen felt someone step into the pew beside him and put a hand on the hymnal he was holding. It was Jackie. When he turned to look, she was smiling that heart-melting smile. She mouthed, "Hello," then turned back to singing. Stephen caught his breath and went back to singing as well.

When they sat down to listen to Paul, Jackie sat close against him, which was distracting, but he still managed to hear what Paul was saying. He was reading the Christmas story again, though it was a couple of weeks past.

"I know you have all heard this same piece of scripture a lot in the last few weeks, but I think now when Epiphany is so close past and Easter so near in the future, we need to remember the true purpose of that lovely story of the baby Jesus. Remember, he lay in that manger and was celebrated by those angels because he had been sent to die. As his mother held him to her breast, he was slated to be the sacrificial blood that washed away the sins of humanity.

"Blood sacrifice has always been seen as the means to connect men with God. The ancient Hebrews built a great temple in Jerusalem to celebrate the spilling of sacrificial blood. The blood they spilled was animal blood symbolic of the blood painted on the door posts of their houses in Egypt so that the angel of death would pass their houses in his task. But they were not the only ones to use blood as the connection to a God. Here in the Americas, the Aztecs, the Mayas, and the Incas all used blood as the lubricant between human and divine. Their blood sacrifice was human blood, a practice stopped by the Christian missionaries that came from Spain, but not before there had been a great deal more blood spilled by the conquistadors.

"When baby Jesus came as a God-sent sacrifice, his was intended to be the blood spilled to save humanity, spilled that humans might never again have to spill blood to atone for their sins. But, as always, we humans failed to learn that lesson and have continued to spill human blood even since that great day when Jesus said, 'Father forgive them,' and on that greater day when He arose from the darkness of the grave.

"Spilled blood was all that was needed to start the process of salvation, but for us to be servants of that same sweet child who grew into that splendidly brave man we must do more. Not because it needs to be done for salvation, but because we are grateful for what has been done for us. We must sacrifice for others because of the sacrifice committed for us all those years ago. We must remember the teachings of Jesus from the sermon on the mount and love one another. We must help one another, and we must remember that 'What thou doest for the least of these, thou doest for me.'

"I don't usually do an altar call on Sunday morning, but today if you feel that you need some extra communication with God, or some extra help from God, please come down to the mourner's bench in front," Paul concluded. Stepping away from the pulpit he walked down from the dais and knelt at the front bench as the organist struck up "Just As I Am," a song Stephen remembered from having sung it a hundred times at Baptist meetings. This time he felt it tugging at him like never before. Halfway through the second verse he stepped around Jackie and out into the aisle, then walked down to the front and knelt beside Paul.

Stephen had made his confession of faith in Jesus when he was in junior high school in a service at the Valley Bible Church, but this was not the same thing. This was more because of his confusion and depression with the way the world was than a personal confession. This was basically a cry out to God for guidance and protection. *Oh Lord, I am lost and confused. Please guide me in the way I should go,* he prayed with tears in his eyes.

After a little while the music stopped. Paul stood and went back to the pulpit, leaving a half dozen people still kneeling. He lifted his open hand, palm out and said, "May the Lord be with you always. Go in peace to love and serve the Lord."

A subdued and thoughtful congregation answered him, "And peace be with you also," as they turned up the aisles to leave.

Stephen, feeling somewhat sheepish stood and looked around. Jackie was still standing at the pew where he had been, waiting for him.

Paul clapped him on the shoulder. "Maybe she is the dime," he said.

"Yeah, maybe."

"You gonna bring her to my house for lunch?"

Stephen looked at him for a moment. "Aunt Esther won't mind?"

"Naw, she won't, but if you have other plans that's okay too, just remember we have to leave here at four o'clock to get you back to Mason."

"Let me go talk to Jackie and I'll let you know," he said.

"Fine, just let me know."

"I will," he said and started up the aisle toward Jackie.

"What are you doing here, Jackie? I thought you were Methodist."

She shrugged. "We're not much of anything really. Christmas and Easter, we go to the Methodist Church, but we're not really members."

"Well, okay, but what are you doing here?"

"Besides hoping to see you again, I like this church. I like

Reverend Paul. He's nice and his sermons always tell me something."

"All right then. Would you like to come have lunch with Paul and Esther and the girls?"

She looked at her watch, and said, "Well, I would like too but I can't today. I got a lunch date with someone."

A slightly jealous sting went through Stephen's heart. "Boyfriend?"

She lifted one eyebrow and said, "Could be." She turned and stepped out of the pew into the aisle. "One more thing," she said. "My daddy would like to see you again. Says he needs some more information on your friend that died."

Stephen was surprised. "How come? I mean I don't really know much more about it than it told in the newspaper, and I don't have time today. Gotta be back at school tomorrow. My first class is at nine."

"Daddy is a policeman right to his heart and he hates to see a crime unpunished. He has started looking into your friend's death."

"Really?"

"Yes. He is fascinated by the puzzle of it."

"Well, tell him thanks for me and the one thing we are all pretty sure of was that it was the KKK who bombed the church. While he is looking at that, he might also look into the murder of Dr. Arthur Marchant."

Jackie opened her purse and pulled out a small notebook. "How do you spell Marchant?" she asked. Stephen spelled it for her, then she asked, "is this connected with your friend's death?"

"Well yeah, sorta. Dr. Marchant was killed at Thanksgiving. Supposedly he came home to a burglary in progress, but most of us think it was really the KKK who killed him because he was a homosexual."

Jackie wrote those details in her little notebook. "Here's Dad's address and phone number," then wrote on another sheet. "Here's my address and phone at school. The number is the dorm, but you can probably get me. Write me or call me if you think of anything specific about either case," she said, glancing at her wristwatch again. "Oooh, I gotta go." She turned and left.

Stephen watched her bottom sway as she walked out the door and thought, *Maybe, she is the dime.*

XIV

Paul's weather prediction turned out to be wrong. The clouds broke and some sun, albeit weak sun, showed through. It made the ride to Mason almost enjoyable.

"Please forgive my being nosey, but what were you and Jackie talking about back there?" Paul asked.

"Murder," Stephen said.

Paul glanced over at his nephew then back at the road. "Murder? Whose?"

"Robert's and maybe Dr. Marchant's. See, her father is a Memphis cop. Detective I guess, and Jackie says he is going to look into Robert's murder, and I said as long as he's looking, he might look into the Doc's as well."

"Hum," Paul said. "Interesting."

They rode along quietly for a time until Stephen asked, "You think he is really going do that?"

Paul shrugged. "Don't know, but why say so if he isn't going to?"

"Yeah, I guess, but even if he does, how much good can a Memphis cop do investigating murders that happened clear over in Mason?"

Paul shrugged again. "I'd think he could do a little anyway. Get the records and talk with the Sherriff and the FBI."

"I don't think he'll get anything out of Cruz. Him and his Klan buddies have kept pretty tight lipped about all this. I'm not sure the FBI were ever anything more than window dressing."

"Maybe so, but if he is really going to look into it further, I'd think a Memphis cop is more likely to be able to wheedle information out of a county Sherriff than even the FBI. They'll be speaking more or less the same language, I'd think."

"Yeah, I guess."

"You don't sound convinced."

"Yeah. That's because I'm not. I don't much trust cops anymore. I mean, when they first arrested Manny Jefferson, Cruz almost let his Klan buddies take Manny away to lynch him. Only reason he didn't is he knew the whole world including the FBI was watching. I'd bet my last cent that the only reason Manny got out on bail is because the Kluxers figured they could get him more easily out of the public eye. When the state police came onto the campus, I heard a couple of them talking about how the cops should just fire into the crowds. That cops and National Guard oughta be firing into protest crowds. "

"I doubt if they meant it, Steve. They were just talking."

"I don't know, I heard some of that kind of talk in California too. Like the song says, 'There are lines being drawn'."

"That's true enough. There is a kind of us against them mindset, but I don't think it's gonna come to that."

"Charlie Horse said there were plenty of shots fired in Selma, and the reason we haven't heard much about it is because they haven't started killing white people yet."

Paul let out a breath and said, "Hope he's wrong."

Paul pulled up at the usual place behind Lorring Home and let Stephen out. "You going over to Uncle Morton's house?" Stephen asked.

"Yeah, for a little while at least. May stay overnight. I'm pretty tired."

"You shoulda just let me ride the bus."

"Naw, couldn't do that. Wouldn't have satisfied my curiosity," he said with a grin.

Stephen grinned back at him. "All right then, thanks for the ride. Tell Aunt Esther thanks for the dinner."

"Will do. Good luck," he said, as Stephen closed the door.

Stephen threw his heavy coat over his shoulders, picked up his suitcase, his guitar case, his carryon bag and tramped up the steps.

Brad Stringer, one of the dorm monitors, was in the TV room and seeing that Stephen's hands were full, popped up from the chair to open the door for him.

"Thanks, Brad."

"No problem. Good Christmas?" the other asked.

Stephen smiled a half smile and said, "Yeah, pretty good."

"Your roomie came in this morning."

"Good. I'll let him open the door upstairs for me."

Stringer laughed.

Stephen turned up the hall, and clomped up the steps to his room. He thought about just kicking the door in lieu of a knock but decided to put down the suitcase to get out his key. He was glad he hadn't kicked the door because Bankuski was napping on his bed fully dressed except for his shoes.

Stephen quietly put his suitcase and guitar on his bed then went to hang his coat in the closet. As he was doing that, he noticed that there were two quart bottles of liquor sitting on the top shelf beside the stack of sardine tins. A bottle of Four Roses and one of Seagram's Seven.

"No need for a trip to Kentucky now," Bankuski said.

"Oh, you're awake. Sorry, didn't mean to disturb you."

"I wasn't really asleep. So how was California? Did you get laid?"

Stephen looked at Drew. He had never asked that before and Stephen wondered why he had now. Stephen felt that was no one's business but his and the lady's so he didn't answer, just said, "How about you?"

"Yeah, as a matter of fact." Drew said, popping up from the bed and reaching toward his hip pocket to pull out his wallet. He flipped it open as he came across the room.

Stephen looked at the picture. The girl was pretty in a sort of a plain way. Her hair was long and straight and blonde.

"Not bad," he said. "What'd you do, get her drunk?" he joked.

"No," Bankuski said, taking offense. "I knew her from school. I took her over to New York City for a show."

Stephen lifted his hands in surrender. "Sorry. Just joking. She anything special or just a casual roll in the hay?"

Now it was Bankuski's turn to just look and not answer for a moment. "Well, it's more than casual, but not too serious, I think. We'll see if she writes."

Stephen laughed. "I know that feeling. If she really cares she'll write—or not. So how was your Christmas otherwise?"

Bankuski's face sobered. "All right, I guess. My brother got orders. His unit is heading for Vietnam."

"Brother? I didn't know you had a brother, Drew."

"Yeah, he's two years younger than me. Came out of high school last May and got drafted. Just as well, I guess. He didn't do much in school but play football. He had no desire to go to college unless he could get a football scholarship. He didn't." Bankuski smiled at that. "I sorta tried to talk him into coming down here, but the draft board got him first."

Stephen had the feeling from Drew's tone that there was not a lot of love lost between the Bankuski brothers. "Well, maybe the army will be good for him, settle him down, give him time to think what he wants to do next."

"Yeah. Right. All he wants to do is play football and raise hell."

"Well, if he's on his way to Vietnam he'll get plenty of the raising hell part."

"Yeah. I guess.

"I take it your grades did okay. Not on Pro or anything?"

"Naw. Got A's in Math and Physics, and C's in English and Sociology."

"Um. Just the opposite for me. Barely scraped by in Math and Biology and got B's in Lit and Psych. Almost failed Greek, but I squeaked through."

"Greek. How come you take Greek, not Spanish or French?"

Stephen shrugged. "Comes with being a Divinity Student. Gotta be able to read the Greek New Testament."

Bankuski pulled his eyebrows down in thought. "You studying to be a priest? I didn't know that."

"In Protestant churches we don't call them priests mostly. Episcopalians do, I think, but usually it is just minister."

"Whatever, you gonna be a minister?"

Stephen didn't answer for a moment then said, "I don't know, Drew. I sorta thought pretty seriously about it last year when I was running around with the BSU and I had declared my intention, but now I'm not so sure. Lot of stuff has happened and I'm not sure anymore."

"Here I ask an almost minister if he got laid," Bankuski said, shaking his head. "Bet I'm going to hell for that."

Stephen laughed. "Save me a seat when you get there." He glanced back at the liquor bottles in the closet. "I usually drink Old Crow. That's what Jimmy Brodski got me drunk on the first time."

Bankuski shrugged. "They were the cheapest I could buy."

"You brought them from Jersey?"

"Where else?"

"Jeez, that makes you a big-time bootlegger. Didn't you worry about getting caught?"

"Naw. I had 'em wrapped up tight in my clothes in my suitcase. They would have had to unpack the whole thing to find 'em and even if they did, they would probably have just confiscated 'em. You want a drink? Celebrate being back at dear ol' Mason," he said with a little twist of sarcasm in his voice.

"Sure."

Bankuski picked up his coffee cup, squinted at it and said, "Good enough," and poured a dollop of Four Roses into it. Stephen held out his cup as well and got his dollop of Four Roses. "Guess we're gonna have to swipe some glasses out of the cafeteria to be proper," Stephen said.

Bankuski shrugged. "Just so's we're not drinking out of the

bottle I think we're okay." He lifted up the coffee cup and said, "Past the teeth and over the gums, look out, stomach, here it comes," and took a slug.

Stephen lifted his cup in answer and thought of the first toast he and Jimmy Brodski had ever made, *Broken hearts,* then took a drink. Four Roses tasted different than Old Crow, but it still burned going down.

~ * ~

Sandy-eyed and yawning, Stephen was up at six AM to report to the cafeteria. Miss Connie was cooking but when she saw Stephen she said, "I knew I could count on you, Steve. How ya doing?"

"I'm tired," he answered.

"Too much Christmas?"

"I guess. What's to do? Nothing in the dish room yet."

"Go make toast," Miss Connie said.

Stephen nodded his understanding and went to the table where there was a stack of flat baking pans, some loaves of bread and a pot of melted butter. He threw bread slices onto a flat pan swirled the butter around with a pastry brush and began painting the slices. When all of them had gotten a swipe of butter he turned, pulled open an oven set to broil, then shoved the pan in. He turned back to the next flat pan and began the routine again. He had just finished laying out the slices when he turned back to the broiler, picked up two pot holders and pulled the first flat pan out of the stove. The toast was browned but not too browned so he dumped the toasted bread into a high-sided hotel pan then turned back to buttering the next load. He repeated the process four times then carried the hotel pan out to the serving line. Though it was still only six thirty there were a lot of students in line for breakfast.

"Just in time," Maggie Fuller, another work-ship student, said.

"Hey Maggie, how's by you? Good Christmas?"

"Good enough I guess," she said taking the nearly empty toast pan out of the steam table and replacing it with the one Stephen brought. She dumped the few toast slices left into the new pan. "How 'bout you?"

"All right, I guess. I made it back and I'm not on Pro so I got nothing to gripe about."

Maggie laughed and turned back to handing out toast.

Stephen took the empty hotel pan and went back to the kitchen. He looked into the dish room, saw that there were trays stacking up in the window so he stepped in and began pulling and stacking plates and trays, and putting glasses in their racks. It didn't take long until he stepped back into the kitchen and began making toast again.

When the hotel pan was full once more, he took it out to the line again, and did the swap. Many students were still filing through. Later into the quarter the breakfast line would be much sparser. Most would just be coming through for coffee, maybe toast or a sweet roll, but this morning scrambled eggs, potatoes and toast were moving right along. Stephen glanced at the line for a moment, and spotted Charlie Horse and Leroy. "Hey guys, how's it going?"

"Steve," they both answered.

Stephen had a feeling he had come down a notch in their esteem when he hadn't gone with them to protest Manny Jefferson's arrest, but it might have just been his own regret.

At seven AM, Big Julie Ryan came in and went straight to the dish room. Stephen looked in. The window was pretty stacked up again. "I stacked 'em once, Jules, but Connie had me making toast, too."

Jules said, "Come help me run a load or two then you can go back to your toast."

Stephen stepped into the dish room beside Jules and began racking glasses as fast as Jules could get them separated from their trays. The moment the rack was full, Stephen shoved them into the maw of the washer and closed the door.

"How was Christmas, Jules?"

"Great. I got a new car."

"Really?"

"Well, it isn't new, but it is new to me. A Chevy Nova. I drove it down here. No more walking for Big Julie." He laughed.

Trays came steadily through the window for the next hour. Stephen stepped in and out a couple of times to keep up with the toast. He had a chance to greet several friends coming through the food line and was glad to see that people like Bill Thinning and Jimmy Brodski were back. There were several BSU people back as well. Cathy Powell, David Hall, and finally Mary Ann Younger. Stephen didn't speak to them but Mary Ann gave him a cheery, "Hello Steve," which he answered with a lifted hand as he went back into the kitchen.

"Line's slowing down, Miss Connie. I don't think we need any more toast and Jules has a handle on the dish room."

"Okay," she said. "Did you get some breakfast?"

Miss Connie was like a mother to all the students who worked in the kitchen. Stephen remembered how crushed she was when the Sherriff told her that her son had been killed in the church bombing last year.

"No, ma'am."

"You want some?"

Stephen thought about it for a moment then said, "Yes, ma'am."

"Couple eggs with they eyes open and some bacon and taters?"

"Yes, ma'am," Stephen agreed, stepping out to get a glass of OJ and some coffee.

Elgin Fester, wearing his red Kappa hat, was standing in the breakfast line. Stephen looked him over and wished Fester had not come back to school. Fester glared back at him and an evil grin came over his face. *This is gonna be trouble,* Stephen thought and turned back to the kitchen.

The plate of bacon and eggs and potatoes sat on the work table beside where he had been making toast. He sat down on a stool, picked up the fork and discovered that Fester had robbed him of his appetite.

At quarter of nine Stephen picked up his sociology book and notebook and headed for the admin building where his first class of the new quarter was going to take place.

Stephen clomped up the stairs but hesitated at the top. The classroom was down the hall a few steps and standing right in front of the door was Fester with four more red hats. Other students were having to force their way past the blockage, and when a couple of black girls tried to ignore them and push on through, the Kappas made sure that they had to squeeze through in such a way that all the red hats rubbed hard against them, and their behinds were grabbed.

Clearly Fester and the others were trying to stir up trouble. Stephen, still feeling regrets for not having gone with Charlie and the others, stepped up and said, "Why don't you leave the ladies alone, Fester?"

"What ladies? I don't see no ladies. Any of y'all see any ladies anywhere?" he answered.

The red hats laughed and shook their heads no.

"You are a complete asshole, Fester. Just trying to stir up trouble."

"Well, Hollywood, what you gonna do about it?"

Stephen looked over the five red hats and said, "I ain't gonna fight the gang of you."

"Ah, what's the matter, Hollywood, no guts? I'm surprised you even came back seein' as how you're such a chicken shit."

That would have been enough, but a hand fell on his shoulder and Bill Thinning said, "Ain't worth it, Steve. They're five to one. They'll beat you, you'll get suspended, or maybe they'll get their Kluxer buddy Sherriff Cruz to lock you up for disturbing the peace."

The class bell rang and the red hats, Stephen and Bill broke up and went into class. The Kappas sat in a knot toward the back of the classroom. Stephen and Bill went more toward the front and sat down side by side.

"This feels worse than it was before Christmas," Stephen

said.

"Yeah, they are trying to stir up enough trouble so they can find out where Manny Jefferson is hiding out."

"Seems counterproductive to rile people up. Seems like making people mad will just make 'em shut up tighter."

"Yeah, but whoever gave a thought to Fester and the Klan having the brains to figure that out?"

Dr. William Archmeyer, tall, well-built and remarkably young to be a full professor said, "Good morning. I will be passing a sign-in sheet around accompanied by a classroom diagram. Please sign in and indicate where you are sitting as per the diagram.

"I noticed that there was some difficulty at the back door this morning. That will not happen again, will it, Mr. Fester?"

Fester looked defiant, as if saying, "*I didn't do nothing.*"

"If it does, my next stop will be the disciplinary committee. Am I making myself understood? And take off those caps. At least try to maintain some semblance of civilized decorum."

The red caps came off but not without some grumbling.

Prof. Archmeyer laid notes on the lectern beside the desk and began his lecture.

Stephen's head went down and he began scribbling notes as fast as he could, shoving the door incident to the side.

At noon Stephen and Thinning sat in the Student Union over coffee and smokes.

"Yeah," Thinning said. "Since Manny got out on bail the Kappas and the Kluxers have been going nuts. There's a group of them running up and down the street over in black Mason honking, shooting in the air, throwing rocks. They figure if they make enough noise Manny is gonna try to run and they'll catch him then."

Stephen thoughtfully tapped the ash off his cigarette and said, "That's the same reason an owl hoots. He hopes the prey will get scared by the hoot and try to run. When the prey moves the owl spots the movement and is on him like a shot."

Thinning studied Stephen for a moment. "Where'd you hear that?" Thinning said, doubtfully.

"Boy Scouts, a long time ago."

"Boy Scouts, huh?" Then he said, "People ain't owls and if Manny is in black Mason he ain't moving. I'm not convinced is still in this county anyway. I think he's down in Memphis. Easier to get lost in a million people than in a few thousand."

Stephen lifted his eye brows at that. "Well, maybe we got a little something else working for us on that," he said, taking a drag off his Marlboro.

"What's that?"

"I met this girl down in Memphis and her daddy is a Memphis cop, detective, I think. He's interested in Bobby's murder and I put a bug in his ear about Doc Marchant too, and how they might be connected through the Kluxers."

Thinning looked even more doubtful. "White cop, outa Memphis?"

Stephen shrugged. "I don't know. He seemed pretty sincere, or rather Jackie did. Maybe something will come of it. If not, we're no worse off."

"I reckon," Thinning said. "This babe good looking?"

"Bill, she is a walking wet dream," Stephen said.

"Hum. Nice. She got a sister?"

"No. Nosey little brother."

"Hum," Thinning said pushing back from the table and standing up. "Uh, I don't think I'd tell Charlie Horse or any of the Black Student Union about your tame Memphis cop."

Stephen considered it for a moment. "They'd probably laugh in my face."

"Can't blame 'em really. White cop really giving a damn? No way they're gonna believe that."

"Yeah. Where you going next?"

"U.S. History."

"I'm going to bonehead math. If I can manage to get through this quarter, I will never have to commit another equation in my life, and I ain't sad about that."

"Gonna have to remember how to add to put all that money you're gonna make writing books in the bank."

"Your lips to God's ears, Thinning."

XV

Racial tension continued on Mason's campus. The Kappas kept going out of their way to cause trouble. There were several face-to-face confrontations between the Black Student Union and the red hats, mostly concerned with the way the Kappas treated black female students. The men of the Black Student Union began accompanying women students to class and making sure the doorways were clear of "red trash," as they started calling the Kappas.

There were some pushing and shoving and a few punches thrown, but not *serious* trouble, meaning no large-scale brawls.

The disciplinary committee held open hearings where both groups were heard. Ultimately, the committee threatened to put both organizations off campus. The Black Student Union protested mightily, claiming they had always been good Mason citizens and never caused any difficulty until the "red trash" began making threats and manhandling black female students.

"The Kappas were already warned last quarter if there was any more trouble out of them, they would be banned from campus," Leroy Parker said to the committee. "It is our opinion the threat should be carried out and the Kappas should be banned from the campus."

There was general agreement among the attending students, but there were still a significant number of anti-integrationists among the student body that were not directly connected with the Kappas who disagreed. The assembly turned into a roaring mob and a near brawl.

In the end, for the sake of peace in the assembly, the committee left it at a warning for both organizations with a little extra snap for the Kappas, which didn't satisfy the BSU, nor did it stop the Kappas from their program of insulting and molesting the female black students, though it did slow them down somewhat.

"Bastards are afraid some of the guys are gonna start cutting them away from their herd and teaching them manners," Charlie Horse said.

Bill Thinning thought that might be a good idea. "Maybe if someone raises a couple of knots on Fester's head, he'll get the hint."

"You really think that will help?" Stephen asked. "I think the only thing that will finally convince him is the inside of a coffin. He's just too stupid and stubborn to walk away to let this all simmer down."

Adding to the tension was the mess in Vietnam. At the end of January, the lull that had been around through the Christmas holidays broke.

Tet, the Oriental new year, was always a time of renewal and beginning. The Viet Cong and the NVA regulars had apparently been saving up spit. At the end of January, they threw all they had into attacking American and South Vietnamese outposts.

Vietnam didn't much worry Stephen at first, since he was in no danger of going there, but it worried Drew Bankuski.

Stephen had not gotten as close to Bankuski as he had to Robert. That was partly on purpose, remembering the pain of loss when Robert was killed, but it was partly accident as well. Between dish room and classes, they hardly crossed paths during the day, and evening was study and sleep time so they mostly said hello, goodbye in passing. If they happened to find themselves trying to sleep at the same time, they occasionally talked laying in the dark.

"My brother Stan got there just in time for all this," Drew said, one evening

"Oh yeah," Stephen said. "He was going over, wasn't he? Have you heard from him?"

"Naw. He wouldn't write me anyhow. My mom, maybe, but not me."

"Too bad. Are you worried about him? I would be if it was my brother."

"Not really. He has always been able to take care of himself. With my luck he'll get himself killed in some heroic battle and I'll never hear the end of it from my folks."

"Doesn't sound too good," Stephen said. "You guys don't get along?"

"No. We get on each other's nerves and my father would just as soon Stan had been an only child."

"Damn Drew, that *really* doesn't sound good. What'd you do to piss 'em off?"

"I got born."

"Seems like a kinda strange reaction since your folks had something to do with that, unless biology classes have been lying to me all these years."

"Well, ya see. Most babies take two people and about nine months to get born. Me it took three people and six months."

"Ooookayyyy," Stephen said drawing out the words. "That's interesting."

"Story of my life. Complicated. "

"Oh." Stephen said, curious but not wanting to pry. Bankuski was wound up now and kept talking.

"See, my brother is really only my half-brother. Same mother, different father and my father has always resented me for that."

"Resented you? Why's that? Not like you had anything to do with it," Stephen said.

"He doesn't see it that way. And the fact I look like my real father doesn't help."

"Your real father?"

"Yeah. My father's brother. My mom was going to marry my father's brother, so she got pregnant with me, then my real father went out, got drunk and killed himself in a car accident, which left my mother three months along with no husband and no prospects, so my uncle, who I now call my father, married her."

"Whoa," Stephen said.

"See, complicated. I told ya. To add insult to injury my brother Stan came out looking just like my father/uncle so every time the old man looks at him then looks at me, he's reminded I'm not really his."

"Shit," Stephen said. "No wonder you came all the way down here."

"Yeah, and I'm beginning to have second thoughts about that as well. With all the racial trouble and now Vietnam heating up. My kind of luck, I might as well go home and wait for the draft board."

"Your grades were good, weren't they?"

"They were all right."

"Then Uncle Sam ain't gonna get cha."

"Sez you. That ain't the way my luck runs."

"Yeah, I know about luck. But sometimes you can't tell good from bad. I thought I was having bad luck when I couldn't get in the Marines. My dad said it was probably because the Lord had some other job for me to do here, and with the way things are going, I might have been right in the middle of the mess in Vietnam if my Marine plans had worked out. We really are in God's hands, like it or not."

"I guess. You really sound like a priest," Bankuski said.

"Not a priest, I told ya. And I'm not exactly sure about that either. I'm having my doubts."

"Oh yeah? How come?"

Stephen was silent and thought about that question for a moment. Did he know? Did he want to spill the whole mess to this near stranger?

"Beginning of last year, I was convinced. I ran around with the Baptist Student Union. Sang with their choir, traveled all over Tennessee doing revivals, but as things went along, I guess you might say I became disillusioned. I saw and heard preachers that were all talk. They preached the gospel, then didn't even try to live up to it. For a lot of them it was more about Baptist than Christian. These guys were in a position to guide people, to teach people about what Jesus said but they weren't doing it. They were putting their own spin on what Christ said, and people were believing them. Even the KKK claims to be Christian, but they aren't. So, I'm no longer convinced my future lies with the pulpit. I don't want people lined up to go to hell because of something I said."

"You think that is what's happening in Protestant churches?" Bankuski asked with a yawn.

Stephen answered with a yawn of his own. "Not all of 'em, I don't think. My Uncle Paul's church, or at least the church he pastors, seems to be working hard at being truly Christian, but there's an awful lot of others that aren't. There's a lot of others preaching hate and death rather than love and life."

"So, you gonna change your fields?"

"Naw, not now. For right now my classes are all pretty much general Liberal Arts classes everyone has to take. When I get up to where I have to start taking more divinity type classes, I'll probably make some changes, but for now, as my dad would say, I ain't gonna mess with a working system." Stephen yawned again. "I gotta wash dishes at breakfast so I'm going to sleep. Good night."

"Yeah, good night."

~ * ~

Sunday morning Stephen got up, did his shift in the dish room, grabbed some breakfast and headed for the Mason Cumberland Church. He sat with his aunt, uncle and two cousins. Various other Mason students also went to Mason Cumberland Church, including Bill Thinning and Jimmy Brodski. Thinning was absent today, however, which made Stephen wonder where he was.

After church he went back to the cafeteria, for lunch. He also picked up several slices of bread from the line and some slices of ham. Those were for dinner. Mason's cafeteria did not serve on Sunday night so students were expected to find their own dinner.

The Student Union grill was always busy on Sunday evening as were the local fast food places, Tasty Freeze, Fosters, and Big Burger. The sit-down restaurant downtown and the diner out at the crossroads were busy too.

Sunday evening Stephen ate his ham sandwiches but decided he needed something further than just bread and meat so he and Drew, who had eaten sardines and crackers for supper, went out the back door of Lorring Home and across the street to the Student Union in search of French fries and sodas.

The Student Union was as crowded as they expected. Still they got their large order of French fries fairly fast and sat down at one of the round tables near the grill counter. As they shared the fries Bill Thinning came over bringing his hamburger, fries and soda with him. He sat down without a word and began eating.

"Must be nice to be rich, Thinning," Stephen said.

"Yeah, I didn't get back in time to hit the cafeteria, so I gotta buy. At least my dad gave me money."

"Where were you?" Stephen asked.

"Cold Water Cumberland, over on the road to Nashville."

"What were you all the way over there for?"

"My dad and some of the elders are gonna try to get the Kappas put off campus for the trouble they have been causing."

Jimmy Brodski stepped up to the table with his fish sandwich and Seven Up and sat. "Sounds like a good idea to me," he said. "But I don't think it's gonna happen. Too many paying students involved in the red hats to just toss them off."

"You don't think that's really a consideration, do you, Jim?" Stephen asked.

Brodski shrugged and took a bite of his sandwich.

"I think they are trying to do like Neville Chamberlain did before World War II. 'Peace in our time' and like that," Bankuski said.

"Yeah. Remember how well that worked out," Stephen said.

Thinning nodded at that. "I think the administration is worried about some of the Cumberland sponsors of Mason deciding these problems are not what they have invested their money in so they are gonna pull out if the trouble doesn't stop. "

"Besides which," Brodski began, "there are still a lot of Cumberland churches that are anti-integration no matter what the official policy statement says. It is still a southern church."

Stephen hadn't actually thought of that. The Cumberland churches he was familiar with, Uncle Paul's church, the Mason Cumberland Church, were all liberal concerning race. That there were still Confederate sympathizers among the Cumberlands somehow offended him.

"Well, well, well. If it ain't Hollywood and the nigger lovers. Sounds like a band, don't it? You out all alone without your niggers to protect you?"

Stephen and the others looked up to find Fester standing beside the table. For once he was alone. No gang of red hats accompanied him.

"Why don't you just keep traveling," Bill Thinning said. "before you say something that might get you killed."

"You ain't got the balls, Thinning," Fester sneered.

Thinning, always a hot head, popped to his feet and sprang over the table reaching for Fester, who backed up a step then came forward swinging. He clipped Thinning, who was off balance, on the ear with his right then brought a swinging left around but connected only with Jim Brodski's arm which stopped the blow from landing.

The Student Union had been roaring with talk, until the trouble started. The place fell silent, turned to the table to watch what was happening.

Stephen stood when Thinning tried to jump the table and he caught his friend when Fester's right knocked him back. Stephen held him tight.

Brodski pulled Fester's arm down as he stepped behind him and held him tight as well. "Pollock son of a bitch" Fester said struggling to get loose.

"You better watch who you're calling a Pollock son of

bitch," Bankuski said standing up. "Some of us don't take kindly to redneck assholes."

He pulled back his fist and threw a punch that would have mashed Fester's nose all over his face had Bankuski not stopped before actually hitting him.

Fester flinched as though he had been hit and Bankuski flicked Fester's nose and laughed.

Brodski spun Fester around. "I think you better travel, Fester, before you say something else stupid."

Bill Thinning was still struggling a little against Stephen's hold, but when Fester walked away, he stopped.

Stephen and the others looked at Fester's retreating back. The roar of talk began again inside the Student union.

"Déjà vu," Stephen said, releasing his hold on Thinning. "I saved Fester's ass from you again."

Thinning said, "Yeah. See? If you'd let me throw him down the stairs last year, we wouldn't be having this trouble right now."

"And *it is* gonna be trouble," Brodski said, returning to the last of his sandwich and Seven Up. "He'll never go anywhere alone again, you can bet. I'm betting he's gonna gather a gang of red hats to come back over here in a little bit." He shoved the last of the sandwich into his mouth, picked up the Seven Up can, emptied it, then crushed it. "I am not gonna be here when he gets back."

"Probably a good idea" Bankuski said, turning to go. Stephen followed him, leaving Bill Thinning standing by the table.

Stephen turned back. "You gonna stand there and wait on 'em, Bill?" Half seriously, he said, "You want me to hang around? We'll probably get our asses kicked but I'll stay if you want."

Thinning looked as though he were considering the offer, but finally said, "Naw, I don't feel up to a fight or a beating. I'm gone." He flapped his hand toward the door, and headed out with Stephen and Drew in his wake.

"Good night, Thinning," Stephen said.

"Yeah, yeah, g' night yourself."

Stephen and Drew crossed the street to Lorring Home. No

one was in the TV room which made Stephen give a sigh of relief since the TV room was right at the edge of Kappa country. They turned up the hall then up the stairs.

Charlie Horse and Snatch's door was open. Charlie was sitting at the desk, chair tipped back on two legs with his feet up on the desk, reading. Parker was sitting up in bed with the reading light on doing the same thing.

Stephen glanced in and said, "Ain't they collegiate?"

Charlie turned to see the two white guys standing at his door. "What's up?" he said.

"Nothin' much," Stephen said. "Just had red hat troubles over at the Student Union."

Charlie took his feet off his desk and let the legs of his chair down. "Now what?" he asked with something more than idle curiosity

"Just Fester being his usual asshole self. Tried to start a fight, but since he was the only one interested it didn't come off too well."

Bankuski chuckled. "I think he peed himself when I drew back on him."

"He might have at that," Stephen said with a chuckle.

"Something is gonna have to be done about him and the damn red hats." Charlie said shaking his head.

Stephen shrugged. "Bout all we can do is keep reporting the trouble they cause to the disciplinary committee till they finally decide to act."

"Well, there are some of us who've had enough. We're thinking we can't wait a lot longer so we're gonna catch a red hat away from the gang and maybe teach him a lesson," Charlie Horse said.

Stephen blinked at that. "I don't necessarily disagree with you. Someone should probably teach Fester and the Kappas some manners, but I'd be afraid it might go too far if you got a red hat and a bunch of BSU in a mob. No offense meant, but that sounds like it could turn into a lynching pretty easily. I would think that would be the farthest thought from your mind, Charlie, but mobs can get out of hand pretty quick."

"I been trying to tell them that," Parker said, closing his book with a finger to hold his place, "but they want to make someone pay attention."

"I'll grant ya that nobody deserves to hang more than Fester, but I don't think Dr. King would agree with you, Charlie. He's a man of peace and from what I hear he's urging everyone to stay peaceful, no matter what."

Charlie jumped to his feet and came to face off with Stephen. "Don't you be telling me about lynching and what Dr. King is saying, white boy. I know what he is saying, but he ain't here right now and we got honky problems that need to be handled."

Stephen lifted his hands palm out. "Like I said, no offense meant."

"Take it easy, Charlie," Parker said getting up from the bed, his book still in his hand. "He's talking sense."

Charlie spun and glared at his roommate, but then walked back to his chair by the desk and flopped down.

Parker took a deep breath and said, "Maybe y'all better go away for right now. Let Charlie cool off."

"Yeah, yeah. Sorry to have stirred things up," Stephen said and turned to unlock his own door.

Inside with the door closed, Bankuski said, "Touchy ain't he."

"With reason, I'd say. He keeps his temper pretty well most of the time. I've seen Fester and the boys just torture him and Parker for no reason at all. I would have lost my temper, started swinging but Charlie and Snatch keep it pretty cool."

"Sounds like it isn't gonna stay cool much longer," Drew said, going over to the closet and pulling down the bottle of Four Roses. He held it up toward Stephen but Stephen shook his head.

Bankuski looked at the bottle then poured a splash into one of the glasses stolen from the cafeteria. He lifted it and said, "To Pollocks," and slugged it down.

XVI

February turned cold and gray, but no snow. A bitter wind curled around Stephen as he walked to the music building with his knitted hat pulled down tight and his coat collar pulled up tight. For some reason Stephen found himself anxiously waiting for something, but he could not put his finger on it. Could have been mail. He hadn't had much, though he had gotten a couple from Sherry. They weren't much satisfying though. It was nice that she was thinking of him enough to write, but the letters had been strictly what was happening at school and church and family. She did sign them "Love," but Stephen thought that might just be formality. Still, he lived in hope and kept waiting for something more. He answered the letters in short order but he did the same thing Sherry did, except he thought his were more interesting since his everyday life always included trouble with the Kappas and fending off the Baptists. He even told her more about Cathy Powell, how she had broken his heart, how it still hurt to see her. He mentioned Mary Ann but only in passing. No reference to the physical relationship. He was tempted to tell Sherry more, hoping to level the field with her, but he had long since learned that there were times to talk and times to keep one's flap shut. The crooked part of his soul told him this was one of the times to keep quiet.

Stephen was certain that one thing he was waiting for was some word from Jackie Bookman. He really expected to hear something from her, that is, from her father via her, about his investigation, but as the days ticked on without any word, he began to call himself a dozen kinds of a fool for ever expecting anything about this investigation. It was wishful thinking at its worst. *But if it was all just a lie,* he thought, *why did she bother to come over to Paul's church just to talk to me?*

He finally wrote Paul a letter and asked if Jackie was still coming to church. He could have called just as easily, but writing somehow seemed more concrete than a telephone call. He guessed he probably liked it more because the actual answer would take longer to arrive.

Stephen plodded up the steps to the music building and in the door. The cloak room was jammed with coats. All the hooks had more than one coat hanging on them. There was a pile of coats on a bench under the hangers. If the weather had been wet or snowy boots and overshoes would be stacked under the bench. He started offloading his clothes in the vestibule, not noticing that Mary Ann was doing the same thing. Stephen was so enmeshed in his own thoughts he didn't notice her. She was paying more attention to him than to her own undressing.

"You all right, Steve?" she asked.

Her voice startled him.

"Sorry," she said. "Didn't mean to scare ya. You just looked like the weight of the world was on you."

"I'm okay. Just thinking about something."

"Oh yeah, what?"

Stephen looked at her for a moment then said, "Thinking about who killed Dr. Marchant. Wishing there was a real investigation of it going on."

"They got the guy who did it, didn't they?" Mary Ann said.

"You know better than that. Cruz grabbed up the first black guy that came to hand and said he did it. It's bullshit. The Kluxers did it sure as hell, and that is gonna be the last people ever get charged with it."

"You sure about that?" she asked, not really contradicting him but not agreeing either. The sound of her voice pinked him and turned his incipient bitterness to acid.

"You white Baptist—you white Southern Baptists, would

188

believe anything another white Baptist said, wouldn't you?" Stephen snapped.

Mary Ann looked as though he had slapped her, "I didn't mean—I meant that they had to have some kind of proof to bring anybody in, don't they?"

"They needed someone to blame no matter what, proof or no proof. That's the way this county runs. Maybe the way all of Tennessee runs," he said and tossed his coat onto the pile.

"I'm sorry," Mary Ann said on the edge of tears.

Stephen didn't know if she was apologizing for her remarks, the Southern Baptists, the county Sherriff or the state of Tennessee, but he hated that he hurt her. *She didn't deserve that,* he thought. *You're turning into an asshole, Steve.* Thinking he should apologize he looked at her for a moment then turned and went into the auditorium.

The class was the large concert choir rehearsal. Most were already in place in the choir area, but there were still some students moving around. One was Janice Reed. She spotted Stephen and came to meet him.

"Hi, Steve."

"'Lo. What up?"

"A galley proof of the book is coming out. We're gonna have copies for the next meeting. I wanted to make sure you got one since your poem is in it."

Stephen snorted. "Isn't much of a poem," he said. "Four lines of doggerel."

Janice grinned. "Yeah, four lines that apply to everyone who ever put pen to paper, 'Mouse prints on the sands of time, a stolen line from a stolen line, that haunts not all my hours but many, with worries of not leaving any'."

Stephen looked at her. She was quite pretty with her long blonde hair, green eyes and killer smile. "You really think it is that good?" he said.

She shrugged. "Good enough that all four editors voted for it."

"Humm. I never really expected to get anything in."

"Well, ya did. Make sure you come to the meeting to get your proof copy."

"Yeah, I will. For sure."

"Choir, take your places please," Dr. Scripps said, tapping her baton on her music stand.

Stephen went to his usual place and sat. Snatch Parker usually sat beside him but he was not here today. It wasn't like Parker to cut choir, but Stephen didn't think much about it, too preoccupied with thoughts of Janice Reed having memorized his poem. It was only four lines of doggerel but she'd memorized it. Flattering. It shoved all the dark thoughts out of his mind, for a little while at least.

The weather hadn't gotten any better when Stephen started the walk to the cafeteria. The thought of the dish room would have ordinarily bummed him out, but he was still riding the high of Janice Reed and having a poem in the Mason Anthology. He hardly noticed when Mary Ann came up beside him.

"You're looking much less troubled than before, Steve," she said, her warm breath puffs of steam.

He glanced down at her. A flash of memory streaked through his mind of her sitting up on the Danjo headstone, knees open, waiting for him, then it was gone. A delicious memory added to the news about his poem made him feel light on his feet. "Yeah, I guess," he said, his breath steaming as well.

"You shouldn't let stuff like death creep into your mind. If it sticks in there it might cause you harm, like with Ethan."

Stephen glanced at her again then said, "Where's Billy Jo and them? Don't you usually have a ride?"

She hesitated. "Yes, I usually do, but I decided I wanted to walk with you today."

"What the hell for? Ain't like it's a nice day or anything." *And it isn't like I been so nice to you,* he thought with a twinge of guilt.

"When I saw you before class it reminded me of how bad I

felt when my dad died last year, and how much you helped me. I just wanted to say thanks and to help you if I could."

Oh crap, Stephen thought feeling like a complete rat. His helping her had been coincidental to his trying to hurt Cathy Powell and the Baptist Student Union. He set out to seduce her, not with any hope of success. Stephen didn't know that Mary Ann's father had just died and she was vulnerable because of it. Mary Ann had not known his more nefarious reasons so she thought he was attracted to her and knew she needed someone to lean on.

"I didn't do anything, Mary Ann," he protested.

"Yes, you did. I was feeling so alone, so separated from everything. You were there when I needed someone."

Feeling guilty irked Stephen so he sneered a little. "Why didn't you go to some of your Baptist friends?"

"None of them volunteered," she said, with a touch of bitterness. "They all knew, but none of them even said they were sorry for my loss, or anything."

"I didn't even know about it, Mary Ann. Not until you told me that night."

"When I told you, you pulled me to you and held me for a long time. I really needed that."

Snow started to flurry down on the cold wind.

Stephen took a breath of the cold air and said, "I'm glad I could help," but wasn't sure he meant it.

She reached up and grabbed his sleeve. They stopped in the middle of the sidewalk. Mary Ann swung around still holding on to his sleeve and hugged him, pinning his arms so he could not lift them. She laid her head against his chest. "I love you, Steve," she said.

It took a moment for Stephen to register what was happening, but when it came home to him, he began struggling to get loose. When he did, he held her at arm's length, hands on her shoulders. "No," he said. "No, you don't. You can't. I don't love you, I'm no good for you. I don't want to hurt you so please, please, stop it!"

"Steve," she began.

Stephen let go of her, turned and walked away quickly leaving her standing in the increasing snowfall.

Oh shit, oh shit, oh shit, he thought, his ebullient mood vanishing like the steam of his breath.

Dirty dishes were stacked as high as Stephen could reach in the dish room, and there was nobody on the work list but him. Mixed with all the other troubles on his mind he felt like just walking away, maybe throwing dishes against the wall like one guy had done last year, but after a moment he drew in a breath filled with the stink of food scraps, tamped down his frustration and anger, began racking plates to go into the washer. He tried to turn his mind off, or at least divert it from Mary Ann. He tried bringing back the joy and pride of Janice Reed and the anthology, but it wouldn't come. Mary Ann seemed to swallow everything. He remembered all the times he'd made love to her, how great it seemed at the time, then cursed himself for being so stupid as not to remember "there are always consequences." You always have to pay one way or another. *God or the Universe or Karma always gets you in the end,* he thought.

He racked another load, pulled the last load out of the washer, shoved the new load in and began stacking the still hot clean plates, before turning back to the window where tray loads of dishes continued to come in from the late lunch crowd.

Miss Connie stuck her head in and asked, "You all by yerself?"

"Yes, ma'am. I'm it until two o'clock when Mamoni and Jules come in," he said, still pulling trays and stacking dishes.

"Umm umm," she said.

Stephen heard something in her voice that made him turn around. "You all right, Miss Connie?"

"The Sherriff got Leroy Parker," she said.

"Well, shit," he said then quickly back tracked from the crudity saying, "Sorry, Miss Connie."

"'T's all right,"

"Why did they pick Leroy up?"

Miss Connie shrugged avoiding the obvious answer: *Because he was black and they needed someone to blame something on.*

"What is he supposed to have done?" Stephen asked.

"S'posed to have molested some white girl downtown."

"Aw, that's bu..." he edited himself to say, "Baloney. Leroy would never do anything like that."

"Course not, but I know he's a friend of yours so I thought you oughta know."

"Yes ma'am. Thank you for telling me. Do you know if they got him in the county jail or is he still in the local lock up?"

"I don't know. It happened early this morning so they probably got him in county jail, but I don't know."

Stephen remembered standing with Miss Connie when the Sherriff brought her news her son had been killed. She was a strong woman, but even strong people could only take so much beating. Miss Connie looked as though she were at the end of her rope. He stepped across the dish room and put his arm around her shoulders. "Lord protect Leroy," he said, not knowing he was praying. "Give us the strength to deal with this."

Miss Connie put one arm around Stephen's waist and said, "Amen."

"Have you said anything to Dr. Connors or any of the disciplinary committee?" Stephen asked.

"Not yet."

Stephen said, "I'll go talk to Dr. Connors when Mamoni and Jules come in."

"You don't have to do that, Steve. I'll give him a call. I don't know what he can do about it, but it's probably a good idea to let him know."

"Yes, ma'am. He and the committee have some suction in town so it couldn't hurt. I'll go see him too."

"Fine. I'll let you go back to your dishes," she said.

"Yes, ma'am," Stephen answered and turned back to the window where trays continued to come in. He began sorting through the mess, but his mind was not really on it. It whirled and bounced on what he had just been told. *Why did they bust Snatch? They know he didn't do that. Black man would be crazy to do anything like that. I bet it was fuckin' Fester. Probably had that girl Sandy make the complaint. She hangs around the red hats all the time.*

Then his mind went in another direction within the same groove. *I wonder if Cruz thinks Leroy knows where Manny Washington is? The Kluxers been running up and down the road for days hunting him and Snatch has been pretty vocal in school assemblies.*

The acid churned in Stephen's stomach and as his rage grew so did the burning in his gut.

"How you doing, Hollywood?" Gary Mamoni said stepping into the dish room. He was a few minutes early. Mamoni was the one who started that nickname for Stephen. At first it had been a laugh, but when Fester and the Kappas picked up on it, it stopped being funny.

"Shut up, Mamoni!" Stephen snapped.

"Whoa, 'scuse me all to hell there, Mr. Mitchell," he said in his finest New York accent.

"Sorry, Gary. Just the damn Kappas have picked up on it and it ain't funny anymore. "

"Yeah, yeah," he answered not sounding mollified. He stepped in beside Stephen and began wracking the dirty plates.

"I'm gonna take off in a few minutes," Stephen said.

"And leave me here alone?"

"I been here alone since twelve thirty. I don't wanna hear it. Big Julie is gonna be in pretty soon. I'll wait till he's here before I go."

"That's real white of ya, Hollywood,"

Stephen turned on Mamoni with almost enough rage to have punched him, but the other turned up ready to fight so Stephen thought better of it. Stephen was a head taller and twenty pounds heavier than Mamoni. *I could probably take him,* Stephen said to himself, *but what the hell good would that do?*

194

"That's it. I'm outta here. Ta hell with ya," he said as he untied the rubber apron he was wearing.

Mamoni turned back to racking and running, clearly not happy with the outcome, but unwilling to push it further.

Outside the snow had stopped, but the wind was still bitter cold. Stephen didn't have another class until three so he headed for the Pope's office, not knowing if his Uncle Morton was in office or between classes but he figured the office was the place to start.

He crossed the quad toward the concrete steps leading into the administration building, noticing there seemed to be a crowd on the landing outside the main door, so he hustled up a little more thinking, *This isn't good. Crowds mean trouble lately.* He could see there were several Kappas in the bunch. They all seemed to be facing the door but not moving forward through them.

Stephen got to the back of the group. He could hear what sounded like Charlie Horse yelling. "You did it, you honky asshole! You know damn well Leroy wouldn't ever do anything like that."

Stephen worked his way around the crowd to the place he could see Charlie, Reg, and Stan blocking the door, facing the crowd which was made up of red hats and other students. They were facing Fester and a couple of his big henchmen, as others just stood watching.

"We didn't do nothin', nigger. Sherriff picked him up right off the street," Fester said. "We didn't have anything to do with it, but we warned that nigger to keep his eyes off white girls."

Stephen saw Charlie reach the boiling point and knew this was going to turn uglier in a few seconds. He understood Charlie's anger, felt some of it himself but there was enough cool left in him that he knew a fight would do more harm than good so he stepped into the middle and grabbed Charlie Horse as that one stepped forward. Stephen blocked him from moving forward and put his hands on Charlie's shoulders.

"Get your hands offa me, Mitchell," Charlie hollered trying to get around Stephen.

Stephen answered, "You don't wanna do this Charlie.

There's enough rednecks to kill all four of us if you go ahead, and even if they don't kill us, it'll get us, or at least you three tossed out of school and fuckin' Fester wins, so let's just back up."

Reg and Stanley who had been on the edge of the boil but not quite as hot as Charlie, saw the sense of what Stephen was saying so they each put a hand on Charlie's shoulders. Reg said, "Maybe he's right, Charlie." Charlie resisted but they held on.

Stephen said, "I'm on my way to talk to Dr. Connors about Leroy, so just take it kinda easy, at least until we find out what's what. If we find out these red hat assholes had anything to do with it, I'll come with you to hunt Fester down."

Fester saw things slipping out of his control so he said, "Shut the hell up, Hollywood. Get outta the way, let him come at me."

Stephen turned around and said, "Fester, I shoulda let Thinning throw you down the stairs last year. I have saved your ass twice in the last couple of years. I'm not gonna do it again. Walk the fuck away while you still can." He turned his back on Fester and said, "Come on guys, let's go see Dr. Connors."

Reg, Charlie and Stan hesitated a moment before they turned and pushed through the door ahead of Stephen, leaving the crowd rustling behind them.

They made their way to the Pope's office and by purest chance found him at his desk. He was on the telephone listening.

Though Morton Connors was his uncle, in non-family situations Stephen kept it formal. "Doctor Connors," he said softly. "Can we talk with you for a moment?" Stephen asked.

Connors looked up with a sort of blank look, not recognizing who Stephen was for a moment. In a blink his mind came back. "Certainly, certainly. Let me," his attention suddenly went back to the telephone. "I will come and see him," Connors said, then listened for a moment. "Of course I trust you Sherriff, but the disciplinary committee will need a report so as to know what needs to be done," he said, listened and finally said, "I'll be there within the next hour." He listened a moment more then hung up the phone and turned to the four. "What can I do for you fellas?"

Stephen nudged Charlie to go ahead. "Dr. Connors," he began, "the Sherriff picked up Leroy Parker this morning, supposedly for molesting a white girl."

Connors nodded at the information. "I know. They called me shortly after. That was the Sherriff's office I was talking too."

"He didn't do anything, Dr. Connors," Reg said.

The other three all agreed.

"They just picked him up for meanness sake."

"I believe," Stephen began, "they think he knows where Manny Washington is and they figure to put some pressure on him by locking him up."

Charlie, Reg, and Stanley all looked at Stephen. They had not thought of that particular idea, and they all tried to talk at once.

Connors held up his hand, "No need to start with the conspiracy theories. Doesn't matter. I'm on my way over to Sherriff Cruz's office to have words with him. Leroy will be coming home with me."

The boys all stood with their mouths open. They knew Connors had pull in Mason. They didn't know he could just walk up and take a prisoner away from the jail. Again, they all tried to talk at once, mentioning bail and money, but again Connors held up his hand. "That won't be necessary," he said. "What is going to happen is that I will take Leroy into my custody as though he were still in jail. I long ago applied for a deputy's badge for just such problems as this. Technically, Leroy will still be 'in jail' but he will be free to go to classes and the cafeteria and about his regular business, but he will come to my house when his day is done. He will stay with me, in my custody other than in the daytime."

"Are they really going to do that?" Stephen said.

Connors shrugged. "They have released students into my custody before."

Charlie Horse and the others looked skeptical. "I don't think that's gonna happen this time, sir. This is not some Mason student that got drunk and caused trouble. This is a lot bigger," Charlie said.

"You may be right, but I am gonna try all the same. If nothing else just to see that Leroy is all right."

XVII

The Pope wouldn't let the four accompany him to the Sherriff. "Just go to my house and when this is done, I'll bring Leroy there."

Charlie and the other Black Student Union members protested but Connors held firm. "Go on now, we'll be along directly," he said as he was leaving.

The four went to Charlie's car and Stephen directed them to his uncle's house. Mason was not a large town but Charlie and the others had never been to the Connors' residence. It was still Mason, Tennessee where whites and blacks mostly did not mix. As they drove, they noticed that any white residents who happened to be out in the cold took particular notice of a car load of black men driving through the neighborhood. *No doubt some of them are calling the Sherriff as soon as we are out of sight,* Stephen thought.

The house was a faux-plantation-style house with a white columned veranda across the front. Charlie pulled off the street to park in front of the lawn. "Why don't you go ahead and park in the drive, Charlie?" Stephen asked.

All of a sudden Charlie, usually sure of himself and blustery enough to take on white society, became much meeker. "You really think so Steve?"

Stephen looked at his friend with a puzzled look, not understanding the hesitation. "Yeah, go on, there's room for you and for Uncle Morton when he comes." It dawned on Stephen what was bothering Charlie. "If you pull into the drive, I think it's less likely that the cops or anyone else will bother it."

Charlie still didn't look convinced but he pulled into the driveway and the four of them got out. Stephen headed for the front door, but the three black students hesitated. Blacks, even modern Black Student Union blacks, went to the back door, not the front. Still when Stephen pushed the doorbell button, he motioned them up onto the veranda and they went, albeit with some hesitation.

Aunt Jean Connors, looking very much like a TV housewife with her white blouse and gingham skirt, opened the door.

"Stephen," she said questioningly, glancing at Charlie and the others. "What's happening?"

"Uncle Morton sent us to wait for him here," Stephen said.

"Ah, very well," she said, stepping back and opening the door wide.

The four entered and, for a moment, stood in the foyer.

Stephen said, "I don't know if you are acquainted with these guys, Aunt Jean. This is Charlie Horse, Reg, and Stan from the Black Student Union."

She extended her hand to each of them. "Nice to meet y'all. Go ahead and have a seat." she said, and perfect hostess that she was asked, "Would you like some coffee? I'd offer iced tea but it is a little chilly for that," she laughed.

Stephen answered with a small laugh. "Yes, ma'am, that would be wonderful."

"Then you can tell me what prompted this visit?" she said headed toward the kitchen.

Stephen went toward the conversation area where there was a long couch with the coffee table before it on one side, and a couple of wingback chairs across the table from it. The four sat on the couch. It was rather crowded but no one volunteered to sit in one of the wingback chairs.

Stephen noticed that the others were all rather closed up and contained, didn't seem comfortable sitting in the living room of Dr. Connors' house, much less being served by his wife.

"Relax you guys," he said. "Remember, the first black student at Mason stayed here for months. Everything is fine."

In a few moments Aunt Jean was back with coffee pot, cups and saucers, spoons, cream pitcher and sugar bowl. There was also a plate of biscuits and a small jar of jam on the tray. She set the tray on the coffee table and inquired with a look who wanted coffee.

"Yes, please," Stephen said prompting Charlie, Reg, and Stan to all agree.

Aunt Jean poured, asking, "What's going on, Steve?"

"Well," Stephen began "The Sherriff scooped up Leroy Parker this morning on some trumped-up charge. Uncle Morton has gone to see what is what about all this."

Aunt Jean shook her head. "I do not understand that. What is the matter with these people? Haven't we Southerners caused the Negro race enough trouble with slavery, reconstruction and now Jim Crow? It would be so much easier on everyone, black and white, if we would just treat each other like common human beings."

"Yes, ma'am," Stephen answered and the three black students nodded their agreement.

Time passed. Aunt Jean talked with her guests for a bit. When her children came bursting into the house when school was out. Jean looked at her watch and said, "I'm sorry to leave you to your own devices, boys, but I must start dinner." She stood, and the boys stood also. "No, no, she said. "You fellows just stay put. Have some more coffee. I'm sure Morton will be home soon, and you are all invited to supper. "

Stephen looked at his watch. It was after three o'clock. *Guess I cut class,* he thought, and began counting how many cuts he had made in the past.

Half an hour later they heard a car pull into the drive. The front door opened and Dr. Connors, looking tired and defeated, came in.

"Sorry it took so long fellas," Connors apologized, "but they had taken him on to the County facility and the Sherriff wouldn't release him into my custody, even after I threatened him with the FBI. Cruz said, FBI or anyone else he was not going to release Leroy until after the arraignment, and maybe not then."

"When is that going to be Dr. Connors?" Reg asked.

"Arraignments are usually held once a week on Fridays unless the crime is considered major," Connors said. "I can't see this as being major enough to rate any change. I'll keep a check on it and show up Friday morning."

"He's gonna need an attorney, isn't he?" Stephen said.

"NAACP will provide one, I'm sure," Connors said. "I'll give them a call after supper."

Aunt Jean came to the kitchen door and said, "A little early, but dinner is served."

All stood and trooped into the dining room where a huge platter of spaghetti sat in the midst of the table.

"That smells great, Aunt Jean," Stephen said.

She smiled and looked a little embarrassed. "Glad you think so. My sauce is pretty good, especially when I mix it with jar sauce, and spaghetti feeds a lot of folks so..." she indicated the heaped plate. "Have a seat, y'all."

They sat. Uncle Morton, Aunt Jean, and the children in their usual places with Stephen between them and the black students on the other side of the table, unconsciously segregating themselves. Aunt Jean bowed her head as did everyone at the table. She said, "For what we are about to receive Lord make us truly thankful," and began dipping noodles into Charlie's plate. "Say when," she said. He did. "Extra sauce right there," she said giving a quick point with her dipping fork, before turning to Stan. She filled each plate comfortably and in the end the serving platter was empty.

After the first bites had been tasted, table conversation went to the subject on everyone's mind.

"Did you actually get to see him, Dr. Connors?" Reg asked.

"Yes, I did. They didn't want me to and I figured it was because they'd roughed him up but they finally let me go back and see him for a minute."

"How was he? Beat up?"

"No, he wasn't bad actually except for being in a holding cell. He said they had been pretty gentle with him."

"What was it all about?" Aunt Jean asked.

"He was supposed to have made an improper remark to a white girl down by the drug store."

"Just an excuse to harass him, I'd bet," Stephen said. "He's been pretty outspoken in assemblies lately and the squeaky wheel gets the grease, ya know?"

"I don't think so, Steve," Charlie said. "I mean there was that too, never pass up a chance to give a nigger a hard time," he glanced at the others regarding his use of the N-word, "but after Steve mentioned them picking him up to ask about Manny Washington I started thinking that is what it was really about."

Dr. Connors stopped a forkful of spaghetti half way to his mouth. "He said they asked him a half a dozen times about that, threatened him."

"He didn't tell them anything, did he?" Reg asked.

"Said he didn't know anything to tell them," Connors said.

They finished their spaghetti mostly in silence.

"Can we go to the arraignment, Dr. Connors?" Charlie asked.

"It is supposed to be open to the public," Connors answered. "But I don't know if it would be such a good idea for a bunch of black students to show up down there. The police are pretty jumpy so it might cause trouble."

"We *can* go," Reg said, more as a statement than a question.

Connors looked from man to man for a moment then said, "Yes, you can go if you must."

Snow began falling in earnest as Charlie drove back to the campus. The ride was pretty quiet. All were full of spaghetti, but there was also a pall over them because of the situation. Still, none of them said anything about it. Charlie turned on the radio, more to break the silence than for the music. WMCA Memphis, "The Night and Day Giant of the Mid-South," was the only station that would come in and Charlie turned on just in time to hear the bad news from Vietnam. The announcer was spinning the story to make it sound like good news, but no one in the car was buying it. The Tet offensive was still going on and though the Americans and the ARVN troops had been caught sleeping, they had stood up to the attacks. The NVA regulars and the VC lost many men, or so the news report said: a hundred to one. But even if it were true no one cared about the hundred Vietnamese. Everyone cared about the one American.

Stephen reached up and turned the news off. No one protested.

Stephen and Charlie climbed the stairs of Lorring Home together. The pall seemed to have extended to the whole campus. *Maybe it's just the snow,* Stephen thought, but when the two came into the TV lobby they found several people, including Fester, staring at the television which was nattering on about Vietnam. *Strange,* Stephen thought. *No matter what our other problems are, we are all concerned about the war.* Stephen was more and more glad that he was not going to have to worry about going off to fight in the jungles of Southeast Asia.

The door to Stephen's room was open. Drew Bankuski was sitting on his bed beneath the reading light with a history book in his hands. He looked up when Stephen came in.

"Hey, where ya been, Steve?" he asked.

"Here and there," Stephen answered. "Had dinner with my aunt and uncle,"

"Well, you better make sure you avoid Big Julie. He got tapped to do your dishes tonight, and he said he was gonna kick your ass."

"Yeah, I'll apologize to him and take one of his early morning shifts, he'll forgive me."

"I don't know, he was pretty pissed."

Stephen glanced at the desk and saw two envelopes there. His heart skipped, as he grabbed the letters, one from Sherry, one from Jackie Bookman. That one surprised and excited him. He packed the letter from Jackie down and tore the opposite edge off, blew into the envelope to widen the opening, fished out the letter. It was rather thick, five notebook pages, written in blue ballpoint in a readable cursive hand.

> *Dear Steve,*
> *I just wanted to write to let you know that I—that we—hadn't forgotten you or Robert. My dad has gotten copies of everything concerning that night including the FBI files. That was apparently a lot harder to do than it sounds but he got copies of all of it. He has come up to Mason a couple of times to question some people. He says he believes you were right in saying it was the local KKK who did it. There is a place that they meet, a pool hall. Daddy went in there pretending to look for bootleg whisky, then stayed to play pool and listen to the talk. He said he didn't ask many questions. He just wanted them to forget he was there and start talking...*

Stephen knew the place she was talking about. He had stepped into it last year when he was seeking Old Crow to replace what he had drunk of Jim Brodsik's, but he took one look over the swinging saloon doors and decided he wouldn't take anything from that place even if they were giving it away. The place was owned and operated by old man Claxton, with whom Stephen's first run in had been when Robert was demonstrating Jim Crow. Claxton owned the Mason laundromat, the pool hall, and the Slide Inn Bar in Henry County. He was known to be the Grand Wizard of the local KKK, a member of Mason First Baptist, and strong supporter of prohibition, which allowed him to bootleg whisky at outrageous prices. No black person had ever set foot in any of his businesses.

The pool hall was really just a wide-open room with a dozen tables set in two rows. Each table had a light hung over it so the tables were well lit despite the fog of tobacco smoke that hung from the ceiling. The walls were hung with cue racks, triangular ball racks hanging underneath. There were blackboards and counting wires, plus a couple of billiard posters. In the left-hand back corner, there was a urinal blocked from full view of the door by a screen wall. The desk was at the back, with a huge Stars and Bars Confederate flag hung above it.

Jackie's letter went on "... *They didn't say much at first with a stranger around, but they did talk some. He said they weren't very specific, but he is gonna keep going back.*

The second time he went up and played pool with them they were a little more forthcoming. He said they talked about how that killing and burning the church last year scared a lot of civil rights crap out of the local coloreds.

He said to tell you he's sorry this is taking so long, but he has to go carefully, make sure it doesn't come out that he's a Memphis cop.

Daddy also said when he nosed around about the professor who was killed, he didn't find much except the basic facts. He had the Memphis police request the complete file on the case so maybe something more will come of that but for right now, nothing.

That was all there was about the investigation but Jackie went on to say she had continued going to Uncle Paul's church and liked it a lot.

He and your aunt are so nice, and I like that he doesn't preach hellfire like so many do. I am even thinking about joining the choir. It'll be kinda hard though since I'm driving from Jackson every Sunday. I miss you. When are you coming back to Memphis?

She signed the letter *Love Jackie,* and put two X's beneath then a PS under that. Stephen read those last lines several times, confused by them. He thought his connection with Jackie had ended at Thanksgiving, but apparently that was not true. As he thought of Jackie and all they had been through together—some things that Jackie didn't even know they had been through together. *I think I just don't understand women,* he thought.

After a moment he looked back at the letter and re-read the PS.

I just talked to Daddy and he says some piece of jewelry from the Professor's house has turned up in a pawn shop here in Memphis. Don't know what that means but thought you would like to know.

A piece of jewelry? he thought. *In a Memphis pawn shop? What could that mean?*

Stephen glanced up from the letter and out the window. Heavier snow was falling, putting halos around the street lights. *I really love this place,* he thought, but the thought had no more than crossed his mind until he saw Mary Ann step out the door of the Student Union. She stood in the snow glowing halo of light for a moment then began walking up the street toward the BSU.

All thoughts of loving Mason crumbled. This place had been torture, in many ways. A place of learning, but mostly learning through pain and disappointment.

XVIII

Stephen went to work the next morning and squared things with Big Julie. He, Stephen, was going to take tomorrow morning's shift to make up for crapping out last night. Other than that, everyone was too busy and not much in the mood for talk. Stephen had to hustle to get to his first class, but he made it and settled in to a day of education, trying to keep Snatch and the others off his mind.

After supper dishes Stephen trudged, head down, through the worsening weather, across the quad and up the stairs toward the anthology meeting. The members had stopped calling it the Poetry Society when they began concentrating more on the anthology publication.

At the top of the stairs the usual knot of red hats stood smoking on the halfway break of their class. They stared at Stephen as he came up the stairs. There was hate in their eyes, but there seemed to be something else as well. *After the face off yesterday afternoon perhaps they're a little more respectful than before, or maybe they just don't feel like giving me grief,* Stephen thought as he glanced up at them. He wasn't sure if he wanted to just pass them or if he wanted them to say something to him so he could take exception, perhaps slug one of them. *Yeah, and get myself stomped,* he thought. He passed without a word said, though several of them watched closely as he continued down the hall.

Stephen was last into the meeting. The others were already seated around the table, but they stood when he came in. He stopped and looked them over. All seemed more than half surprised to see him.

"What's this, a welcoming committee?" he said. He held up his hand and said, "No autographs, please." The joke fell flat. "So, what's up?"

"What's up, he says," Ed Allen, editor of the school newspaper, *The Mason Brick*, said. "The whole campus is buzzing about you, and you say what's up?"

"Me? What'd I do?"

"Stood up to half the membership of the Kappas," Allen said.

Janice Reed said, "Kept a riot from breaking out," with what sounded like admiration.

Stephen looked from face to face, then said, "Oh shit, I guess I'm lucky to have gotten past that wad of red hats at the other end of the hall. They looked even less pleased with me than usual."

"Probably scared of you," Allen said.

"Scared of me? There were ten of them. They could have pounded me in the ground like a peg. Gives me the shakes just thinking about it."

"Still," Allen said, "it would have turned into a brawl if you hadn't stepped in. What made you do that?"

Stephen shrugged. "I don't like fights, never have, and it wouldn't have done any good. Wouldn't have helped Parker or anyone else. Besides, '*Blessed are the peacemakers,*' or so they keep telling me in church."

The whole group stood looking at one another for a few moments then Janice said, "Can we get on with this please? I got pages to read for Dr. Potts."

"I want to talk to you more about this later."

"Ah come on, Ed," Stephen said. "I really don't have anything to say on the subject."

"Not what I heard."

They sorted themselves out and sat down around the big table. There were a half dozen paperback books with white covers in the center of the table.

Allen began, "If you have a piece in the book, please take a proof copy. Read through it, especially your own stuff. See that it is all right. Proofread it. Meanwhile..." he opened the folder in front of him and began sorting through the stack of papers. "These are proposed covers. Look them over and let's hear some discussion."

After the meeting Stephen grabbed his copy of the proof and headed for the door, but Ed Allen caught up to him before he could get away.

"Ed, I got nothing more to say, so just let me go. I got pages to read."

"What really happened? Why did you and those colored boys stand up against all those Kappas?"

Stephen gave Allen an up and down look that should have withered him, but Allen didn't recognize the disdain in the look.

"Charlie and the others accused Fester of having something to do with Snatch Parker getting picked up by the Sherriff. They were going to pound him for it."

"Leroy Parker got picked up?"

Stephen shook his head in disbelief. "Some reporter you are. That's what you should be looking into. Cruz scooped up Leroy on a false charge thinking to make him tell where Manny Washington is, but Snatch doesn't know. They scooped him up and I'm pretty sure that girl, Sandy, that hangs around with Fester and the red hats had something to do with that. Go talk to her and to Fester, maybe to some of those other redneck assholes."

Stephen tried to push past Allen but the other grabbed his arm. A flash of remembrance of Mary Ann grabbing his arm came and went making him even more uncomfortable than he already was.

"Just answer me one more question, Steve."

Seeing that he was not going to get away easily he said, "Okay, okay. So go ahead and ask it."

Allen blinked at him a moment then said, "Tell me why you care about any of this? You're a California boy; really got nothing to do with any of this racial mess here, so why?"

The question pinked Stephen and caused his anger to begin simmering. "Yeah, I'm a California boy, but since so many of you

Tennessee boys don't seem to recognize how bad the black race is treated in the south, hell in the whole country, somebody gotta do something and that's why. Jim Crow laws were evil but more than that they were stupid. How does it help the country or humanity to keep black people from washing their clothes in the same laundromat as whites? How does it help the country or the white race to keep black people from buying groceries at any damn store, so long as their money is green? Besides, these 'Colored Boys' as you call 'em are my friends. They are fighting for the right to be able to walk down the street going about their rightful business without being hassled by anybody, to be considered just another human being subject to the same laws and considerations as everyone else. That's what Dr. King is all about. Just simply to be left alone to go about their daily business."

"Yeah, but you guys weren't being peaceful standing up against the red hats," Allen said with a not quite sneer.

"Peaceful resistance is what Dr. King is aiming for, but not everyone has his patience. And when the offense is so clearly evil sometimes people who have been pushed too far lose their tempers. That's what happened with Charlie, Stan and Reg. They had just had enough. Same thing that happened in Watts and Detroit. People just had enough and tried to fight back."

"But you got in the middle of it."

"Yeah."

"Why?"

Stephen paused for a moment seeing that Allen had not understood anything that he had said, "Blessed are the Peacemakers," Stephen said. "Also, I don't like bullies." He pushed past the other and went out the door.

~ * ~

Friday morning dawned bright, clear and blood-freezing cold. Stephen went to do dishes and get some breakfast. He came back to the dorm at eight o'clock. He didn't have class until eleven so he was going to review some history pages he had skimmed over last night. At the top of the stairs he ran into Charlie clearly on his way out. "Where you off to?"

"Courthouse. Parker's arraignment is today."

That news gave Stephen a twist of shame in his belly. He had actually forgotten Leroy's problem. He looked over Charlie's face. It was set hard and unreadable which Stephen knew meant the other was boiling inside. "You gonna be all right?

"Yeah."

"Not gonna do something silly like the other day?"

Now it was Charlie's turn to scan Stephen's face. "You making fun of me, Mitchell?"

Stephen put up his hands, palms out. "Not me. I just don't want you doing anything that might get you locked up or maybe killed."

Charlie blinked at that and looked a little shame-faced. "Just going to observe, Steve, and maybe give Snatch a ride when he gets out, now get out of my way."

"The Pope is gonna be there for that. You sure this is a good idea?"

Charlie hesitated only a moment before saying, "Yeah it's a good idea, now get outa my way."

Stephen still didn't move. "Maybe I better go along just for the sake of keeping the peace."

"Come if you want, but whatever you're gonna do get out of my way. I want to get there early enough to get inside."

Stephen had a feeling this whole thing could turn into a mess. He glanced down at his watch, gave up on the page review and turned back down the stairs. "Let's go," he said.

The courthouse was in the county seat but it was only a short drive from Mason.

There was quite a crowd in front of the courthouse—all white it seemed. "Go by slowly Charlie," Stephen said. "Let's do a little recon on this before we go jumping into it."

Charlie nodded and eased past the crowd on the steps. It

looked like a hundred or so people all pushing up the steps toward the front door. Puffs of steam rose from their breaths.

"Doesn't look like they are letting anyone in," Stephen said.

He studied the mob more closely as they passed. "I think I see Uncle Morton up at the front by the doors. There're cops blocking the door. Can't tell if they are county or state."

The parking slots in front of the courthouse were full or marked off with crime scene tape. "Just keep going, Charlie. That looks like trouble waiting to happen."

"I'm gonna get in there if I can," Charlie said.

Stephen glanced over at his friend and the idea of trying to talk him out of that faded fast. Stephen let out a sigh of inevitability and said, "We can park up here away from the courthouse."

Charlie turned right down one of the narrow streets and rolled to the curb in front of an office face with a sign that said, Attorneys at Law. No one was on the street in the cold except the mob at the front of the courthouse. Stephen and Charlie got out of the car and began walking back toward the crowd. "You still think this is a good idea?" Stephen said and shivered, not sure if it was fear or excitement or the cold. "Geez, I'd have thought this cold would keep people away," he said.

They edged up to the back of the crowd. The cold air carried the sound to them, and they could clearly hear Dr. Connors voice over the soft roar of the crowd. "I am the representative of the college and I *will* be allowed into the courtroom for the arraignment of one of my students."

The Pope didn't sound like the soft-spoken theology professor now.

The cop, a county deputy, that was standing in the doorway didn't quite seem to know what to do with this clearly exercised professor, so he stood still, legs akimbo and ignored Connors. After a few more moments the Pope had had enough and stepped forward, shouldering the cop out of the way. The cop resisted but not too much. He recognized that Dr. Connors was a man of some power in the county so he decided not to try too hard to stop him.

The crowd noise increased when the Pope was in the door. "Hey, if he can get in why can't we...? Yeah... We wanna make sure that nigger gets what's coming to him."

That caused a little fire of outrage to ignite in Stephen's chest. "He didn't do anything," a voice came from somewhere and in a moment, Stephen realized it was his own. *Me and my mouth!*

The crowd including Charlie all seemed to turn at once to look at Stephen.

"What'd you say, nigger?" one of the men standing close to the two of them said.

Stephen thought, *Oh, shit, here we go.* "He didn't say anything," Stephen answered. "It was me. I said Parker didn't do anything. It was just a Kappa set up to hassle him." He turned to look at Charlie. "Can we get out of here now?" he asked.

Charlie gave a half nod and turned. The white crowd didn't think this was over. Several hands reached out of the crowd to grab the boys. "Maybe we better have a little talk with you two," a large man said as he held each of them.

Stephen could smell the alcohol on his breath. Stephen began squirming and fighting in a moment, assuming Charlie was doing the same, but when he looked Charlie was standing still, locked in the hands of several of the crowd.

Stephen started throwing his elbows and kicking any shin or crotch that came to hand. The crowd got in its own way and Stephen got a couple of good shots in, found himself free. He charged into the men holding Charlie and started throwing punches at any white face he saw. A couple of the men were so surprised they let go of Charlie's arms. He twisted in the grip of the others and began to fight back like Stephen had. Between the two of them punching, kneeing and elbowing they got free.

"Let's go," Stephen shouted and the two started to run toward the car.

The crowd was still recovering from its surprise and was still in its own way, torn between wanting to kill the two kids and wanting to get into the courtroom, so they let the two boys get a good start on them before pursuing.

Charlie and Stephen rounded the corner, puffing steam, and reached the car before the mob reached the turn. Stephen was glad Charlie had not locked the car when they slid in and Charlie turned the starter switch. The car was cold so it took three turns for it to crank over. The crowd was around the car by then, but Charlie didn't even look at them, just tread on it, squealing tires as he pulled out.

"Hope to hell this ain't a dead end," Stephen said.

Charlie groaned but didn't look over, just kept going. In another block the street butted into a cross street. Charlie turned hard right, heading in the general direction of the college. There was no sign of the mob now which allowed Stephen's heart to go back into his chest from where it had lodged in his throat.

"Hope we didn't make any more trouble for Snatch than he already had," Charlie said shaking his head.

Stephen thought bitterly, *I asked you if this was a good idea, didn't I?* but he didn't say anything, thinking further, *My mouth has already gotten me in enough trouble today.*

"Hope the cops don't send anyone after us," Charlie said.

"Yeah, I hope. You think anyone recognized us?"

Stephen shook his head. "Probably not, but if they put two and two together, they are gonna send a deputy to school to ask around."

"Shit."

"Yeah, shit."

They were actually out of town now and headed down the county road toward Mason. Snow was falling again. "Is it slick?" Stephen asked. "Maybe you oughta slow up some. Don't wanna get sideways in this mess." He laughed a little. "Not good to fetch up in a ditch with the cops in pursuit."

Charlie glanced over then laughed a little as well.

They drove the rest of the way in silence. When Charlie pulled into his usual parking place Stephen looked at his watch. Nine-thirty. The whole affair from the ride over to the ride back had taken a little over an hour. *Felt like a day at least,* Stephen thought, and continued in his own thoughts. *Wonder what happened when the Pope pushed on in there? I'll go ask him this afternoon.* Then he thought better of that. "Maybe we oughta just keep this little adventure all to ourselves, Charlie. If they should happen to come asking around, probably better that nobody can send 'em our direction."

Charlie hesitated a moment then nodded. "Yeah. At least not until we see what happened in there."

Stephen nodded his agreement and headed into the dorm.

With good intention he grabbed the history book he had intended to read before the whole adventure started and sat down on his bed. In a few moments the warm after the cold, and the relief after the adrenalin wrapped him in comfort and he dozed.

A noise caused him to jerk awake. He got up and went to the door. In the room across the hall was Snatch Parker, gathering up books. Stephen hurried across the hall and right to Parker's side. He wanted to hug him just to see that he was real, but didn't. "Boy, am I glad to see you!" he said.

Parker lifted an ironic eyebrow and said, "Hey, watch that *Boy* stuff. I've had about all the *Boy* I can stand in the last couple of days."

Stephen blushed with shame. "Sorry Leroy, I didn't think."

"Well, at least ya didn't call me Snatch," he said with a twisted grin.

"Ah shit. You're just giving me grief, ain't cha?"

"Yeah," he laughed. Stephen was amazed he could laugh after all he had been through.

"They let you go?"

"Hell no. I mean yeah, but no. I'm out on bail. Wouldn't be out at all if it wasn't for the Pope. That's a hell of an uncle you got there, Boy. Stood up to that judge like in the movies. Told 'em his next phone call was gonna be to the FBI if they didn't release me into his custody."

"So, they did?"

"Judge didn't like that so they slapped a half-million-dollar bail bond on me thinking that would stop me getting out I guess, but the Pope said, Okay. I went back to jail for a couple of hours till they came around and said I had been bailed out."

"Wow. Where did he get the money?"

"Don't know. You'll have to ask him."

Stephen took a deep breath and let it out. "Glad you're free anyway, Leroy."

"Like I said, I am and I ain't. I'm still in the Pope's custody. That's why I'm here gathering books and stuff. He's waiting for me in the car."

"Oh, well. Can I help you with some of this?"

"Yeah here." Parker held out the stack of books he had been holding. Stephen took it, as Parker scooped up another pile and some notebooks and they headed out the door.

Downstairs in the TV lobby, Dr. Connors, looking more like his Clyde Crashcup self in his long overcoat and hat waited for them. "Hi Steve," he said.

"Uncle Morton. How are you?"

"Just fine." He looked at his wristwatch. "I have a Philosophy class to teach in a half hour."

"Yes, sir, I'm in it," Parker said.

"Me too," Stephen added.

"Oh yes, that's right. Well, if you don't mind, we'll go on to class then go home?"

Parker said, "Yes, sir, that sounds fine."

Connors turned and headed for the door.

The Pope's car was parked at the curb at the bottom of the steps. He opened the back door and said, "Put your stuff in there, Mr. Parker. "

Snatch did as he was told then turned to Stephen, took a book and a notebook from the top of the stack then stepped out of the way so Stephen could put his load in the backseat as well.

When Connors drove away Stephen could only stand and watch. Uncle Morton might look like Clyde Crashcup, but he was a hero all the same.

XIX

No one seemed to have recognized Stephen or Charlie from the courthouse, or at least no one who cared. Life settled down to *work, eat, sleep,* and do it all again tomorrow.

The world wagged on in the same usual bloody routine. The Tet offensive came and went in Vietnam with hundreds killed on either side but after a while even that horrible affair became a barely mentioned footnote.

The civil rights movement continued, with demonstrations, riots and beatings. In Memphis there were rumblings of enlarging the garbage strike. There were protests all through January and into February, but in the middle of February the sanitation workers had had enough. They walked off the job completely and garbage began piling up. NAACP, SCLC, and CORE all supported them, but the white establishment would not budge. Dr. King spoke out about the strike and threatened to come to Memphis to lead a protest march, but the white establishment, having learned nothing from previous times, ignored him.

Stephen paid little attention to any of it. He had his own troubles. He was still in touch with Jackie Bookman and her father, but he was not convinced anything, either in the Dr. Marchant or the Bobbie Gillium investigation was ever going to happen.

Stephen came into the dish room after his Greek New Testament class to do noon dishes. He grabbed a sandwich and went to work. Jules and Gary were already working so the job was not laborious. He began slowly racking and rinsing dirty dishes and shoving them into the washer while Gary Mamoni pulled in trays and raked the garbage off.

"Hey, Hollywood, yer gash is out here looking for ya?" Mamoni said.

"Don't call me Hollywood," Stephen growled. It had gotten to be an automatic response since many people had begun calling him Hollywood since Mamoni started it. Some were just off the cuff like Gary, but some were bitter and twisting like Elgin Fester, who never passed up a chance to gig Stephen.

Stephen leaned over so that he could look out the tray window beside Mamoni. Mary Ann was sitting at the front trestle table facing the dish room window. That was not so odd. She often sat there. Stephen thought she did it just to make him feel bad for having separated himself from her and the Baptist Student Union, and it was succeeding admirably. He felt like hammered shit when he looked at her, and that was mixed with the remembrance of the Methodist graveyard.

Today there was some added misery. Cathy Powell sat beside Mary Ann which caused misery of a different order. Cathy was as beautiful as Mary Ann was plain and Stephen had been smitten with her a large part of his freshman year. She was the reason he had gone to the BSU to begin with. Jimmy Brodski said she was the apple in the monkey trap and that the monkey, Stephen, would never get free so long as he held onto the apple. Stephen knew he was right but letting go and not caring about Cathy was a lot harder than Brodski made it seem. That monkey trap was the reason he ended up with Mary Ann who would make love to him while Cathy Powell would not.

Stephen pulled his head back and returned to his work. "No gash of mine, Mamoni," he said.

Jules turned from pulling the clean dishes out of the washer and looked out the window. "The blonde is a little chunky, but I wouldn't mind gettin' in the other one's pants," he said with a nod.

The comment pinked Stephen right in the belly, and it made his temper begin to rise, but he took hold of himself with the thought, *"No gash of mine,"* and let it go.

After the lunch rush Stephen headed for sociology with Dr. Archmeyer. It was a boring class and he hoped he would be able to stay awake through it. He had gone to sleep a couple of times in the past. *I wonder if Archmeyer knows how dull and monotone he is,* Stephen thought. *Proba'ly not or he would liven it up some.*

Stephen took his seat next to Jimmy Brodski who was looking particularly grim at the moment. He barely acknowledged Stephen's greeting. "What up, Jimmy?"

"Vietnam. I just got a letter from a friend who's still over there. He said it is getting worse. Johnson is talking about upping the number of troops."

"Yeah, I been hearing on the news. Guess that means more draftees."

Drew Bankuski slid into the desk on the other side. "Yeah, I been hearing that too."

"Your brother is over there in it, ain't he?" Brodski asked.

"Yeah, I guess. I haven't heard from him or my folks but last I heard he was on his way. Speakin' of mail, you got a couple of letters, Hollywood."

Stephen glared at his roomie. "Don't call me Hollywood, or I might have to do something about it."

Bankuski put up his hands. "Sorry, sorry. I didn't know you were so touchy about it. Anyway, the letters are on the desk."

Dr. Archmeyer came in and the soft roar of talk ceased. Archmeyer began his lecture without even checking the roll, and Stephen felt his eyelids getting heavy. He put his left elbow up on the side of the desk and leaned his head on it leaving his right hand on his notebook as though he were taking notes.

The passing bell woke him. He sat up, gathered his stuff and stood.

"I'm going over to the student union to get a cup of coffee," Brodski said. "Looks like you could use one too, Steve."

"Yeah. I got history down the hall, but I'll sleep through that one too so I might as well cut it and get some coffee. She probably won't take roll anyhow."

The Student Union wasn't as crowded or smoky as usual, it being mid-afternoon, so Brodski, Mitchell, and Bankuski had no trouble finding seats. They all drew coffee from the urn, tossed a dime apiece into the cup beside it and made their way toward the back of the room.

Brodski, thinking aloud said, "Wonder how long this has been sitting there?"

"Probably since this morning." Stephen said. "We shoulda just taken it without paying for it."

"They don't start giving it away until after four," Bordski said with a laugh.

Stephen took a sip of the coffee, made a face and said, "Well, it's bitter enough to sharpen your teeth. Guess it'll keep me awake through the Pope's class."

"Just make sure you chew it up good before you try to swallow it," Bankuski said with a laugh.

Stephen looked toward the door. Mary Ann and Cathy were just coming in the swinging door.

"Oh shit," Stephen said.

Brodski looked at him and said, "What?"

"Mary Ann and Cathy. Just who I didn't want to see."

"You messing with the Baptists again?" Brodski asked with a bit of disgust in his voice. "Thought you had learned better."

"Not messing with them at all. They seem to be following me around though."

Bankuski shrugged. "Small campus. Be odd if you didn't see 'em."

"Yeah, but this ain't like that. Ever since I broke it off with Mary Ann, they been putting the stink eye on me everywhere I go. Noon they were sitting just glaring at the dish room window."

"No greater fury than a woman scorned, according to Shakespeare or somebody," Brodski said with a chuckle.

"Not funny, Jimmy. I mean I broke it off with Mary Ann, when she started with the love talk. When it was just a casual fuck in the graveyard it was one thing, but all of a sudden, she was at me all the time...

"And after you to come back to the BSU," Brodski finished for him.

"Yeah, that too." Stephen sipped at the thick coffee thoughtfully for a moment then said, "I feel bad about the way I used her, for sure, but not bad enough to get back into that mess over there. Cathy has started hanging out with her adding to the stink eye. She's giving it to me when I go to poetry meetings as well. I don't know what that's all about. I mean she screwed me, not the other way around."

Bankuski frowned at Stephen over the rim of his coffee cup. "You were screwing Cathy Powell?" he asked with a little admiration in his voice.

"No, no. I used to hang around over at the BSU just to be around her. I thought things were going fine, until I caught her giving another guy a blow job when she wouldn't even let me get a feel. That pretty well ended that. "

"What does that have to do with Mary Ann?" Bankuski asked.

Stephen lowered his head and a tingle of guilt ran through him. "Her I *was* screwing, and I shouldn't have been. She's a nice girl that never did anything bad to me. Since I broke it off with her, she's been hanging around just to make sure I know she's pissed."

"You broke her heart." Brodski said, "and she's gonna make you pay for it."

"Yeah, I guess. What am I gonna do about it, Jimmy?"

Brodski shrugged. "Not much to do but wait it out. Time heals and like that."

"Geez, your life is complicated," Bankuski said. "I don't hardly speak to girls. Maybe I oughta go over to the BSU and see about getting laid."

Both Stephen and Jimmy hurriedly said, "No! Don't do that. It's a monkey trap."

Bankuski frowned. "Monkey trap?"

"Yeah," Brodski said and explained the monkey trap.

Bankuski looked from Brodski to Stephen, thinking about the story. "And the girls are the apples in the trap?"

Brodski grinned and said, "You may be a dumb Pollack but you're getting it."

"Yeah, I'm getting it, but I ain't getting IT if ya know what I mean."

"Believe me, it ain't worth it," Stephen said and looked at his watch. "I gotta go to the Pope's philosophy class." He slugged down the rest of the now lukewarm coffee with a grimace. "I oughta be able to stay awake after that. Probably won't sleep for a month."

Stephen didn't have any trouble staying awake in Uncle Morton's class. He never did. The class was always interesting especially since the Pope always encouraged the class to argue with him. The verbal fencing was always amusing and there had been a few times when Stephen turned one of the Pope's arguments inside out and beaten him. Stephen was proud of those times, but that wasn't what was in his mind today as he sat in the class. Mary Ann, Cathy Powell, Ethan Patrick and the whole BSU were going around in his head to the exclusion of philosophy, always coming back to the ultimate guilt—*You're supposed to be a Christian, Hollywood! And you aren't living up to the ideals, not even close.*

All this kept going round and round in his head during the class and as he walked back to the dorm. He clomped up the stairs and just about ran into Charlie coming out of his room. They had seldom seen one another since their adventure at the courthouse.

Stephen said, "You heard anything about our dust up at the courthouse?"

"Naw. I haven't heard anything. You?"

"No." Stephen cocked his head to the side. "Let's just keep it to ourselves, what'd ya say?"

"Yeah. I suppose. I really kinda want to tell Snatch we were there..."

"I don't think that's a good idea, Charlie, what with him living in the Pope's house and all. Too easy for it to slip out in conversations, ya know?"

"Yeah, I guess," Charlie said and headed on down the stairs.

Stephen unlocked his door and went in. As Drew had said there were two envelopes lying on the desk. One from his mom and one from Jackie Bookman.

He picked up the one from Jackie, tore the end off and blew in it to open it up then fished the letter out. It was just a couple of pages written in Jackie's neat, readable cursive. Stephen glanced through it. There was not much news in it, though she did say that another piece of jewelry linked to Dr. Marchant's murder had turned up in another pawn shop. The cops were looking into it, but the pawn shop owner hadn't been forth coming. The cops were questioning everybody concerned but it looked like another dead end. There was a little more, but she signed the letter *Love* and put three little x's under it. Stephen blinked at that. *Love and kisses?* he wondered. That made the thing more interesting for sure. It took his mind off Mary Ann and onto Jackie, with much the same result as the remembrance of seduction. Stephen's mouth had been watering over Jackie since they had met on the train last year, and she had shown some interest in him too with the invitation to Thanksgiving dinner, but her connection to the Memphis Police made that interest cool a good bit.

He left the thought alone and turned to his mom's letter. He glanced through it and found pretty much what he expected. Family news. Mike was doing well in school and probably going to go to Valley State next year. There had been quite a lot of rain and even a few flakes of snow. Dad was growing more and more dissatisfied with the way the Vietnam War was going. He hated to see more young men being sent into what seemed like an endless, pointless war. Beyond that there was not much to say. "... saw Sherry Kinert at church Sunday. She said to say Hi so Hi. She was with Eric Rafton, the youth pastor. They were holding hands so I guess he's a *good friend."*

Stephen went back and read those last couple of lines again, feeling a little jealous. He remembered sitting above the lights on Mulholland drive with the taste of Sherry's lips in his mouth and it caused a stir to replace the one Mary Ann and Jackie caused earlier.

Damnation, boy! Is sex all you ever think about? the little voice he thought of as his conscience sneered at him.

He put the letter back in its envelope and threw it on the desk. He had a couple of hours before he had to go to the dish room so he sat down and pulled the still-neglected history book off the shelf above the desk and opened it. He read a few lines then re-read them again even as he found his hand spinning his mother's letter around on the desk. He gave up the idea of reading, closed the book, put it back on the shelf then pulled his mother's letter out of the envelope again, re-read the whole thing, went back and re-read the part about Sherry. He pulled down a yellow legal pad and pen and began:

Dear Sherry—

He looked at the greeting for a moment then began telling Sherry all about Mary Ann and Cathy and Snatch getting arrested and his going to the courthouse with Charlie and everything: simply everything. He dumped his whole miserable life onto that page, confessing his lusts, desires, needs and love.

...remember when we stood on your porch under the light? Well I am more and more convinced that I really might love you.

By the time he ran out of things to say he had three closely written pages that he could barely read himself. He looked at it for some moments then pulled the pages loose from the pad, tore them into confetti sized pieces and dropped them into the wastebasket.

After a few moments he began again:

Dear Sherry—
Mom said she ran into you at church the other day and she passed on the hello as you told her to. Hello back at you and Pastor Rafton. Hope all is well with you. I was just thinking about that night on your folks' porch before I left, and I was thinking that I still might

love you and hope you might love me too.

He just signed it *Steve.* No love or best or your friend, just *Steve.*

He looked it over thinking how small it looked on the extra-long yellow page. He folded it up, put it in an envelope, put a stamp on it and went to the trouble of walking downstairs to put it in the outgoing mail box.

XX

"She's out there again, Hollywood," Mamoni said looking out the dish room window to the cafeteria. "Been out there morning, noon and night for days."

Stephen glared at him, but didn't say anything. He had given up correcting Gary since it didn't seem to do any good anyway.

"That is one pissed off fat girl," Mamoni went on. "What'd you do to her anyhow?"

Stephen leaned over to look out the window. Mary Ann was sitting alone at her usual table in front where anyone looking out of the dish room couldn't miss her. She had been sitting in the same place since he left her crying on the sidewalk a couple of weeks ago, usually alone, but sometimes Cathy Powell sat with her.

He went back to rinsing and racking. "Why don't you shut your flap, Mamoni," he growled.

Gary looked at him hard for a moment then said, "Excuse the hell outa me."

Truth be told Mary Ann was beginning to worry him in a different way than before. He had heard rumors that she was saying some dangerous things about harming herself. That gave Stephen a chill in his stomach. Better she was screaming hostile with him than this suicide threat—if it was really a threat, not just a malicious rumor. His paranoia grew day by day seeing her at that table and more when Cathy Powell was sitting with her. *Would Cathy start that kind of a rumor just to get back at me?* he wondered, but threw that idea away. Cathy was a lot of things but he didn't think she was a provocateur. *Maybe I'll go try to talk to her,* he thought, but discarded the idea.

When the breakfast shift was over, he sneaked out the kitchen door and headed for his next class, which had been Dr. Marchant's English class. When he came in the door, he noticed there were several red hats still on redneck heads. *Betcha Doc Marchant is spinning in his grave,* Stephen thought. He shook his head in disgust then slipped into his usual seat next to Leroy Parker. "How's it going, Snatch?" he said quietly.

"I'm here ain't I—Hollywood?"

They exchanged looks then grinned. "No more?" Stephen said.

"No more," Leroy said.

"When's your trial date?"

"Early April."

"Damn, they sure put it off long enough. Close to a month, huh? What happened to speedy trial?"

"Yeah, they want to keep the pressure on me to tell 'em where Manny Jefferson is."

"You know where he is?"

"No. I figure he is down in Memphis, but I don't know."

"I can't believe he's still out? I figured his bail time was long gone."

"NAACP got a bail extension on him. And the local KKK don't want a trial on him anyhow. They got no evidence. The press and the FBI are poking around. If they could have grabbed him and lynched him, they would have done it but thanks to your uncle and some others they didn't manage it. They made a mistake grabbing me on a bogus charge thinking I was gonna tell on Manny, but I don't know anything and they got nothing on me except the word of some dubious witnesses."

"They were looking to lynch you too from what I saw at the courthouse." Stephen felt a sudden urge to clap his hand over his mouth for letting that information out.

Leroy gave him a look but didn't say anything about his slip. After a moment he said "Apparently the Pope alerted the FBI to that possibility so the Kluxers are letting it ride, hoping it will all go away."

Professor Daily came in, went to the lectern, and began shuffling his notes. After a moment he glanced up. "Please remove your hats," he said.

They had all known it was coming but when it was actually out there the Kappas grumbled all the same.

Daily listened to the grumbling for a moment before saying, "In civilized western society gentlemen remove their hats indoors, unless they are observant Jews. Any of you boys Jews?"

That caused a rustle and a twitter from the non-Kappas in the room, knowing how the Kappas felt about blacks, Jews, Catholics, and anyone else who wasn't a KKK sympathizer. But the hats came off quickly and the grumbling stopped.

"All right then," Daily said. "Open your text to *The Fairy Queen*."

Stephen and Leroy went down the back stairs and out the back door to avoid any problem with red hats and it was a short cut to their next class, choir. Outside they began taking their time as they strolled toward the music department. Mid-morning was beautiful. The weather had cleared and warmed in the kind of false spring that sometimes comes in March. The month had come in like a lamb and was still calm and beautiful well past the Ides so it would probably turn cold and blowy the last week.

"You going to Memphis to the march?" Stephen asked.

The Black Student Union had passed word that they were going to go down to march with the garbage men around the first of April. There had been rumors that Dr. King might show up in Memphis in support of the garbage men.

"I don't know. I'd like to go but being as how I am out on bail, I don't know how far I can go out of the county. I don't want to cause Dr. Connors any trouble, so I don't know. You gonna go?"

"I don't know either. I got dish room shifts and I'm pretty sure there are gonna be tests around the first of April. I'd like to go, but I'll have to wait before I make up my mind."

"Yeah, always something ain't it?"

"Ain't like I'm burning up the dean's list." He laughed. "I'm in no danger of being on Pro again, but if I was to bust a couple of tests it might come up again if ya know what I mean?"

Leroy laughed. "Yeah, like I said, always something."

They reached the steps of the music building and went in.

Stephen always liked choir. He had been singing in choirs since he was a child and had sung in the church choir since his voice began to change from soprano to alto then on to tenor.

Dr. Scripts was already at her lectern with her baton in her hand when Stephen and Leroy slid into the tenor section.

"All right, choir. The Spring Quarter concert is less than a month away so we need to get this material rehearsed. In two weeks, we are going to go out to the high school to try out the program."

Stephen, standing in the back row, looked at the back of Mary Ann's head. A group of women from the BSU were in the choir: Cathy Powell, Billie Jo Patrick, Linda Wong. All had been part of the traveling BSU choir from last year.

When rehearsal broke up, Stephen got out the door as quick as he could so as not to have to deal with Mary Ann or the others. Billie Jo said "Hi," but that was all. Stephen thought she was looking a bit stressed.

Billie Jo Patrick had taken over leadership of the BSU after Ethan's suicide, and it had not been an easy takeover. There was the suicide itself, but all the homosexual scandal that swirled around it had made it more difficult. Stephen wondered that the Southern Baptist Convention let her step into the position, but they had. He also wondered why Billie Jo wanted the job in the first place. At the best of times the BSU was a swirling snake pit. It might be church related but there was an awful lot of un-church like things that went on. It had been more like a cult when Ethan ran it. *It might still be for all I know,* Stephen thought. He had carefully avoided any contact with them except for his contact with Mary Ann. That was done now, or at least he hoped so.

Stephen walked into the Student Union, bought a pack of

Marlboros and took a cup of coffee from the urn. It was free, sort of. It was a dime a cup in the morning, but by late afternoon it had been sitting there since early morning no one would willingly pay for it since it was even more like road tar than it had been earlier that afternoon, so after four the management let anyone who could stand it have a cup for free.

Stephen shook the change from the smokes in his hand remembering he was running a little short. *I need to learn how to roll my own,* he thought. *Way cheaper than tailormade.* He remembered how his father rolled Velvet tobacco in OCB cigarette papers. He made it look easy, but when Stephen tried it his smoke looked more like a snake that swallowed a whole rat than a cigarette.

Bill Thinning came into the Union, took a cup of the awful coffee then looked around. After a moment, he came and sat down beside Stephen.

"Hey bud, how's it going?" Stephen said. "Haven't seen much of you lately. You keeping out of trouble?"

Thinning shrugged. "Can I bum one of those?" Thinning said bobbing his chin at the cigarette pack.

Stephen hesitated a moment, remembering his dwindling bank, but shoved the pack over.

Thinning took one, stuck it in his mouth then said, "Got a match?"

"All you got is the habit, huh?"

Thinning shrugged again.

Stephen struck a match from the book and held it to Thinning's cigarette. "Want me to stomp on your chest to get you started?"

"Naw, I'll be all right. Where you been? I haven't seen you around either."

"I'm here. I go to class and do dishes and homework. That's about all."

"Yeah. Work, eat, sleep, do it again tomorrow. You going to Memphis to see Dr. King?"

"I don't know. Have to wait and see. Are you sure he is

gonna come?"

"My dad says so. "

"Is he gonna be there too, your dad I mean? I'd like to see him again."

"There's a big denominational meeting scheduled for around April the tenth so I doubt it."

Stephen, who had his back to the door, saw Thinning suddenly tense. "What up, Bill?" he asked.

"Fester and a half dozen red hats," Thinning said.

Stephen turned to look over his shoulder. The gang of Kappas made his stomach sour but he turned back. "Just keep your flap shut, Thinning. Let 'em do their business and get on out of here" he said

"Yeah, yeah—don't buy trouble, I know, but there is just something about Fester's mug that makes me want to stick a fist in it."

Stephen nodded. "He could piss off an iron saint for sure, but we don't need any trouble with him right now. Let 'em clear the door and we'll get outa here. I got a class anyhow."

The red hats didn't seem to notice Stephen and Bill. They ordered food and drinks at the counter and stood around waiting. Fester turned and leaned his back to the counter, his eyes sweeping the room. Stephen saw the sweep stop at him. "Hey Hollywood, where's the fat girl?"

Thinning popped up. Stephen stood up. "Come on, Bill, ignore 'em. Let's get outa here."

He gripped Thinning's upper arm and headed for the door dragging his friend along.

"Hey Hollywood, you quit going out with girls? Even fat girls?" Fester hollered and all the red hats with him laughed. Fester turned to his audience and said, "Ah, him and Thinning been queer for each other since last year."

Thinning tried to turn back but Stephen kept him moving out the door. "Forget it, Bill. He's just a redneck asshole. Not worth the trouble."

Thinning, breathing heavily. "Someday somebody is gonna shoot that son of a bitch."

"So long as it ain't you. "

Thinning looked at Stephen. "Hope I'm there to see it all the same," he said, then grinned.

Stephen finished his late class, surprising himself at not having fallen asleep. He went back to the dorm to dump books and get ready for his dinner shift. Drew Bankuski was sitting at the desk doing math. He looked up when Stephen came in.

"Message for you," Bankuski said indicating a sheet of paper lying on the desk. "Something about calling a cop or something? You in trouble?"

Stephen grabbed the note, read it and blew out a sigh of relief. It said, *Please contact Capt. Bookman, Memphis Metro police.* He read it again. He hadn't known Jackie's father was a police captain. "It's Jackie's father," he said.

"She's that girl you met on the train, right?"

Stephen was surprised that Bankuski knew about that. He didn't remember having told him about Jackie but apparently, he must have. Drew shook his head. "You are a big ugly fuck. How do you managed to meet so many good-looking women?"

"How ya know she's good looking?" Stephen asked. "She might be a woofer."

"You were going out with Cathy Powell, and she's no woofer. Even Mary Ann is cute as hell, if a little heavy. So, this Jackie gotta be a beauty."

Stephen bobbed his head and said, "Yeah, she is pretty, but her dad is a cop, and my history with Memphis cops ain't all that great."

He looked at his watch. More than an hour till dishes. He wasn't sure he wanted to call the number on the paper, and it was rather late in the afternoon—

That's just an excuse, Steve. Call 'em. He wadded the page up and headed for the pay phone down stairs. He dug out a dime and dropped it in the slot, then dialed the number on the paper. Operator came on and said, "twenty-five cents for three minutes." He dropped the quarter in the slot, got his thank you and listened to the buzz that told him the phone was ringing.

"Memphis Metro," a very southern voice answered.

"Yeah, hi, uh, may I speak with Capt. Bookman, please?"

"Hang on," the voice said then there was a click and the buzz of another phone.

"Captain Bookman," said the baritone voice Stephen remembered.

"Capt. Bookman, this is Stephen Mitchell. I got a message to call you."

"Oh yes, Mr. Mitchell. I figured you might like to know that we have arrested someone in connection with the death of Arthur Marchant."

"Really? Who is it?"

"I can't tell you that since the case is still open, but I have the impression you didn't think the case was very high priority since it wasn't a Memphis case."

Stephen didn't quite know what to do with that. "Yes, sir, I understand. I'm glad you arrested someone."

"Jackie told me you would want to know that we really are pursuing this case."

"Yes, sir. Thank you, sir. Uh..."

"Was there something else?"

"You probably can't talk about it, but I was wondering how your investigation into Bobbie's death was going."

"Well, you're right I can't really talk about it, but it is ongoing."

"Yes, sir. I understand. If I can do anything to help on either case please let me know."

"I will do that, Mr. Mitchell. Thank you."

"Thank you for the information. G'bye." Stephen hung up the phone.

Down in his heart he had his doubts that Jackie's dad was really doing much investigating of Robert's murder since it concerned the KKK and, though he didn't seem like a Kluxer, Stephen had learned that most southerners, while perhaps not active Kluxers, wanted to simply leave anything concerning them alone. Let sleeping dogs lie was the prevailing idea.

Stephen looked at his watch then toward the stairs back to his room. He decided to just go on to the cafeteria even though it was early.

He went out the quad door. A gentle rain was falling.

There were a few people seated in the dining room already. Stephen gave the room a look over and saw Charlie and Leroy in their usual places. He went through the buffet line and went to sit with them.

"I just heard from the Memphis cops that they picked up somebody connected with Dr, Marchant's murder."

"Oh shit," Charlie said. "It wasn't Mannie was it?"

That thought hadn't occurred to Stephen. But when he turned it over in his mind, he shook his head. "They wouldn't take Manny in even if they knew where he was. He's out on bail."

"Yeah, bullshit. The cops will do whatever they want." Leroy said.

"Well, anyhow, I don't think it was Manny, unless he really did it, cause they have traced some of the loot from the robbery to a couple of pawn shops in Memphis so I'm betting the arrest is connected to that."

"Yeah, maybe," Leroy said.

Stephen ate quietly for a few moments before saying, "When are you supposed to go to court, Leroy?"

"Fourth of April."

"Couple of weeks more. They sure have drug this out." Stephen said.

"Means you aren't gonna go to Memphis to see Dr. King," Charlie said.

"I'm not sure I should anyway even if it wasn't for court. I don't want to get Dr. Connors in any trouble."

Charlie nodded. "Yeah." Then he looked at Stephen. "You

gonna go?"

"I don't know, Charlie. I got tests and it ain't like I can afford to cut any more classes. I'd like to go, but I don't know."

"Well, just let me know. The car is filling up fast."

"I'll let you know," Stephen said finishing the last bite of his dinner.

He stood up and headed for the dish room window. There was no one inside yet and there was already a stack of dirty dishes piled up. He put his on top of the stack and went around and into the kitchen.

"I'm gonna get started, Ms. Connie." he said.

"All right, Steve. That'll get you an extra hour."

"Yes, ma'am. I need every hour I can get," he said with a laugh.

In the dish room he pulled and organized all the trays and dirty dishes and started to rack the plates for the dishwasher. Sometime later Gary Mamoni came in with a "Hey Hollywood, how's it going?"

"It's going, I reckon," Stephen answered.

Mamoni slid into the window and began pulling trays and racking plates. The stack hadn't diminished much since Stephen started nor did it now that there were two of them. It seemed as though everyone who came in to have supper was finished at once so the stack suddenly grew higher.

"She's out there again, Hollywood."

"Figures."

XXI

The next couple of weeks were strange. Stephen didn't have any trouble with classes or red hats or work. He managed to stay awake in most of his classes, even the boring ones. He continued working with the anthology group and continued to talk with Jan Reed who somehow seemed smitten with him because of his poem. He remembered Drew Bankuski's observation about how he always seemed to meet beautiful women and shook his head over that. He also took it as a caution so, though he enjoyed Jan's company and thought her beautiful, he made no move toward her.

Mary Ann seemed to have calmed down, though she still was sitting at the same table in the cafeteria and glaring at him when she put eyes on him. He got used to that, but he had a feeling in the pit of his stomach that was like a knot. It pulled tighter and tighter every day. He didn't know what it concerned, but it had a Damocloid feeling. The sword was over his head and about to fall.

That was partly the reason he told Charlie he was not going to go with the Black Student Union to Memphis in support of the garbage workers, even if it did mean seeing Dr. King in person. There was more to the feeling but it escaped him. *Just keep your head down and move forward,* he thought. *Just keep moving forward,* which was what he did. One foot in front of the other and repeat.

As he trudged toward the cafeteria for his supper shift in the dish room, he heard a siren. The sound stopped him in his tracks. He had never heard a siren anywhere near Mason. *What the hell?* He listened for a moment and the siren shut off. It sounded like it was over toward the BSU. After another moment of waiting he shook his head and went on to the cafeteria.

In the dish room he took position in the window to pull and rake the plates. He ran his eyes over the dining room and realized that Mary Ann and Cathy were not in their usual places glaring at him. Their absence was both good and bad. Stephen was glad not to have the two of them putting the stink eye on him, but it also made him wonder why they weren't there putting the stink eye on him like they had been doing every meal for weeks.

Suddenly Billie Jo was there in the window with Cathy Powell standing behind her. "Stephen, you have to come with us." Billie Jo said with urgency and a sob in her voice.

"What? I can't leave now. I got another hour in my shift."

"You have to come, Steve," Cathy said. "Mary Ann cut her wrists."

"What?" Stephen was sure he had mis-heard. "Cut her wrists?"

"She went in the downstairs bathroom at the BSU and cut her wrists," Billie Jo said. "She was in there so long I knocked on the door. She didn't answer and the door was locked so David Hall kicked it in. She was sitting on the toilet staring at her wrists. Blood all over the place."

"Oh shit!" Stephen said, and the sword dropped on him. "What does that have to do with me?" he asked.

Cathy's face became sarcastic. "Please? You know what! It was over you. She cut her wrists because of you."

Stephen felt like he had been slapped. "Me?"

"Come on," Billie Jo said. "They took her to the hospital at Jackson. We're going there and you are coming with us."

She sounded commanding. Stephen had never heard her sound so strong.

Big Julie, who had been pulling clean dishes out of the washer, heard what was going on and went into the kitchen to tell Miss Connie, who came into the dish room.

She listened for a moment then said, "Go on, Steve. Sounds

like the girl needs you,"

"But..." Stephen began sputtering, then gave up, rinsed his hands under the sprayer, untied his apron and went out to the cafeteria front doors. Billie Jo and Cathy were waiting.

In the car, the same car Ethan Patrick drove last year, Stephen folded his long legs into the back seat. He was glad both the women were sitting in front so he didn't have to see their faces.

What the hell is going on? Stephen thought. This whole thing had just been a pain in the ass, but suddenly the pain was much more real. Memories of Ethan's suicide passed through his mind. *These Baptists sure seem to have a tendency to overreact,* he thought.

The hospital was not large. About a block square. Two stories. The three parked and went in the emergency entrance. At the first desk they stopped and Billie Jo asked, "Mary Ann Younger? She came in a little while ago in an ambulance."

The nurse nodded, then said, "Have a seat. I'll call the doctor."

They sat on the edges of the bent pipe and plastic chairs in the waiting room. It seemed like an hour but it was just a few moments.

A young doctor wearing a white lab coat came through the swinging doors that lead deeper into the hospital. "You the ones asking about Mary Ann?" he asked, serious, but not grave. His accent was not Tennessee: more northern.

They all stood up. Billy Jo said, "Yes. How is she?"

"She's fine. Sleeping. I gave her a mild sedative."

"How are her wrists?" Stephen asked.

The doctor smiled. "They are fine. They weren't cut deep. Very little actual damage done."

"There was so much blood," Billie Jo said.

"Probably looked a lot worse than it actually was. The bleeding had pretty well stopped before she got here. Coagulation had set in. Most who cut their wrists don't really know how to do it."

"Can we see her?" Cathy asked.

"She's asleep now. Maybe in a couple of hours. I'd wait until morning."

Billie Jo asked, "Can we take her home tomorrow then?"

Now the doctor turned a bit more serious. "I don't think that would be a very good idea. We have to evaluate her to see if she is still a danger to herself. This wasn't a successful attempt, but many times if there is a second attempt it is successful. She can go home in a couple of days probably."

After a moment Billie Jo said, "Thank you, doctor."

Stephen and Cathy looked at one another then back at the doctor.

"Will you be here tomorrow morning, doctor?" Billie Jo asked.

"No, I'll be off. My shift ends at midnight, but I'll leave a message for the duty nurse that you will be in." He smiled again and said, "You don't have to worry about your friend. She's in good hands." He turned and headed back through the swinging doors.

Billie Jo, Cathy and Stephen stood looking after the doctor and at one another. After a few moments Billie Jo said, "I guess we might as well go home."

All the way home Stephen thought about Mary Ann. Her suicide attempt, though botched, reminded him of Ethan. He wondered if the same thoughts were running through Billie Jo and Cathy's minds. As with the trip to the hospital there was no conversation on the way home until they reached the back door of Lorring Home. He opened the car door and stepped out. Cathy rolled down her window and Billie Jo said, "We'll be here at eight o'clock."

Stephen started to protest that he had breakfast dishes and an eight o'clock class, but finally he just nodded and climbed the dorm steps. He thought about making himself scarce the next morning; not going back to the hospital, but decided he would feel like a total rat if he didn't at least try to apologize, until he began thinking, *What the hell should I apologize for. She cut her own wrists—because of me.* He climbed the steps to his room and went in to find Drew already sleeping. With that he turned around and went back down to the TV room to watch Carson.

~ * ~

Stephen came awake to Mamoni shaking him by the shoulder. He had fallen asleep in the TV room. "Hey Hollywood, wake up. Where were you? You were supposed to have breakfast shift."

Stephen sat up, looked at his watch and said, "Not today, Mamoni. I'm going back to the hospital in Jackson."

Mamoni did not look pleased at that. "What for? You sick?"

"No. Mary Ann cut her wrists."

"The fat girl?" he asked.

"She isn't really fat, Gary."

The other shrugged. "Too fat for me."

"I'll probably be back in time for lunch shift, but for sure in time for dinner."

"Damn Steve, what did you do to this babe anyhow?"

"I don't know exactly. Just my usual asshole self, I reckon."

A car horn tooted. Stephen stood and looked out. Billie Jo's car was right where she had let him out the night before. He pushed out the door and went down the steps. The day was quite beautiful. Coming on to spring with clear sky and gentle breeze. Cathy was sitting in the shotgun seat so he opened the rear door and got into the back seat. The women both turned to look back at him with ice in their glare, but they didn't say anything—no hello, go to hell, or anything else, just those ice daggers before they turned back.

The ride to Jackson gave him plenty of time to resent being dragged into this then to feel guilty about being the cause of all this. He also wondered if this could all be part of the monkey trap. He didn't see how, but he admitted to himself he didn't understand women at all, at least not these women. He had enough faith left to believe Sherry back home was good and trustworthy and that Jackie was also, at least to some degree, though he remembered her crying on the train. That memory made him re-think, and Sherry holding hands with the youth pastor, that gave him more to think about.

There were many more cars in the parking lot of the hospital than there had been last night. Billie Jo had to park much farther away. The three got out and marched toward the emergency entrance. Stephen held back a little. The women walked shoulder to shoulder and in step. He watched the sway of their behinds in the skirts they were wearing, pencil style, below the knee. Nothing mini on either of them.

They stopped at the first nurses' desk again. "Mary Ann Younger?" Billie Jo asked.

The nurse, an older woman, looked up at the clock. Below it was a sign that said "Visiting hours nine to twelve." The time was a quarter of nine. She looked the three of them over and apparently decided the time was close enough. "You're a little early, but rounds are through." She lifted a clip board that was hanging on a hook. "213," she said. "Turn right as you come out of the elevator."

Billie Jo and Cathy turned and marched down the hall toward the swinging door. Stephen held back a moment and said, "Thank you." The nurse glanced up and smiled but turned instantly back to the papers she had been shuffling when they walked up. He turned and followed the other two through the swinging doors.

The elevator ride was short, only one floor. They stepped out and turned right to room 213. Stephen continued to hang back a little. Billie Jo and Cathy went into the room. It was a multi-person room with four beds which could be separated with curtains, but all were pulled back now. Mary Ann was the only one there.

Billie Jo said, "Can we come in?" as she walked in.

Mary Ann was sitting up in bed. Her hair was a mess where she had been lying on it. She was dressed in a pale green hospital gown. The sheet was pulled up to her breast. Her wrists were bandaged with white tape.

The TV was on talking about the war. Mary Ann looked toward the three and after a moment she began to cry. Billie Jo and Cathy went on. Stephen followed them but when they reached the bed she said, "Go way. Go way. I don't wanna see you."

Cathy and Billie Jo looked hurt but they turned and started out past Stephen. "No!" Mary Ann shouted. "Not you two. Just Steve."

Stephen, feeling as though he had been caught with his pants around his ankles, stood for a moment before he turned and got out. He went to the elevator, pushed the button then turned down the stairs instead. He didn't really know where he was going or what was happening. He only knew that he needed to get out of there right now. At the bottom of the stairs he turned down the hall toward the waiting area but he didn't stop. He kept going out the double emergency doors and off the dock into the parking lot. When he reached Billie Jo's car he stopped. His mind caught up with him then. *What the fuck are you doing idiot? You gonna steal the car? Walk home?* He turned and leaned against the car then pulled his smokes out of his pocket. The pack was a ragged mess, squashed flat with only a few cigarettes in it. He pulled one out and lit it, remembering he was short on money to buy another pack. He drew in a large breath of smoke and let it waver out to calm himself down.

What the hell did I do to deserve this? he thought, then remembered the Methodist graveyard, the blanket in the grass, the necking in the dark of the girl's dormitory. *Be sure your sins will find you out,* he thought. Maybe that was what was happening right now. He was paying for his sins, *but how can my sins cause Mary Ann to want to kill herself?* He had always been very careful not to tell her he loved her before all this and he distinctly remembered telling her he didn't love her when she attacked him in the quad. Without thinking he pulled out another smoke and lit it from the butt of the last one. He looked toward the emergency room doors hoping Billie Jo and Cathy would be out soon at the same time praying they would not. As he waited, he ran through everything that happened, attempting to justify himself and not succeeding.

A long while later Stephen began wondering how he might get back to Mason without having to ride with the women. He was not above hitch-hiking, but he wasn't quite to the point of sticking out his thumb when Cathy and Billie Jo appeared.

"What happened?" he asked. "You made me come to apologize, but she didn't even want to see me. What the hell?"

Both women glared at him and Billie Jo said, "For some reason she is ashamed to let you see her like that, even though it is your fault."

"Whoa! How is this my fault? I never said I loved her. I never wanted to make us a permanent thing, and I sure as hell didn't cut her wrists!"

"You made love to her though, didn't you?" Cathy said with a bitter edge. "Then cut her off."

Stephen narrowed his eyes at her and said, "At least I didn't cheat on her. It was all aboveboard with no promises made."

Cathy had the conscience to blush and look down.

"It was mutual," Stephen said. "I didn't rape her."

Billie Jo went to the driver's side and got in. Stephen didn't even think about trying to get into the shotgun seat, just folded into the back seat, remembering how he had been so glad to sit back there last year when Cathy would sit jammed beside him as they traveled to different churches. He also remembered David Hall and the memory was both painful and a balm to the pain he was feeling over Mary Ann.

They got back to Mason just in time for Stephen to go for his lunch shift. He jumped out of the car without a word and ran to the cafeteria, and went to work, trying to just concentrate on the task at hand, but his mind wouldn't allow that. It was whirling with everything that had happened. Mary Ann's weeping face would not go away, nor would the whispery accusation from his conscience. The accusation continued to make him angry. He fought against it but the anger only made him tired. He tried to just clear his mind—concentrate on dishes, but they always gave way to guilt.

When the shift was finished, he rinsed his hands and took off his apron. He had a class at two but he didn't feel much like going to it, knowing Cathy would be there. Besides which, he was sure the news of Mary Ann was already all over the campus, so he decided one more cut class wouldn't do much harm and went back to the dorm. He was dragging-ass tired as he climbed the stairs.

He was surprised to run into Leroy Parker coming out of what used to be his room.

"What are you doing here, Leroy? This is the fourth isn't it? Ain't you supposed to be in court?"

Leroy smiled. "Been there already. I'm officially free again."

"Really? What happened?"

"No plaintiff showed up to accuse me."

"After all this no one showed up?"

"My lawyer moved to have the case dismissed since no one showed up to accuse me."

"And they let you go?"

"Judge wasn't happy about it, nor the rednecks, but with reporters in the court room he couldn't do anything else. There were KKK in the court room that made a lot of noise when the case was dismissed. Judge gaveled 'em down but they weren't happy about it."

"Well damn! But you're back here, uh?"

"Not exactly. The Pope thought it might be better if I stayed at his house a little while longer until all this KKK noise quiets down."

"Probably a good idea."

"I got a class," Parker said.

"Yeah, me too, but I'm not going. I'm beat."

"What's up with you?"

"Oh, you haven't heard, I guess. Mary Ann tried to kill herself. Blames me. I been over at the hospital in Jackson the last couple of days."

"Damn, Steve. Is she all right?"

"Yeah. She's fine. Didn't do much of a job of cutting her wrists. Doctor said she wasn't even bleeding anymore when she got to the hospital."

Drew Bankuski came out their door, on his way to a class.

"Hey guys, what's up? You look like shit, Steve. You all right?"

Leroy Parker glanced at his watch and said, "I gotta go, but you gotta tell me more about this when I get back.

"Yeah, yeah. Just keep an eye out, Leroy. There are red hats out there."

Leroy's grin was wide. "Fuck 'em," he said.

"Yeah, fuck 'em."

Drew asked, "You going to class?"

"No, I'm gonna take a nap if I can."

"Okay, I'll see ya later," Drew said and went.

In the room Stephen flopped on his bed still fully dressed with shoes on and was asleep in moments.

Stephen woke with a start. Glanced at his watch. Six fifteen. *Oh shit! I'm late. Mamoni is gonna kill me!*

He burst out his door and ran down the hall headed for the cafeteria, but at the bottom of the stairs a voice from the TV room caught his ear and he stopped. The six o'clock news was on and turned up. There were a half dozen men, mostly black, standing, eyes glued to the TV.

"Repeating," the announcer said. "It has been reported that Dr. Martin Luther King Jr. has been shot in Memphis Tennessee. We have no confirmation as yet."

Oh shit! Dr. King. Charlie and them are down there. He thought, stunned, and threw a quick prayer toward a God he could no longer quite believe in. He stood for a moment more before heading off for the dish room.

The dusk of the day was still beautiful. People were still moving around the quad and heading toward the cafeteria as though nothing momentous had just been announced on TV. *They probably don't know yet,* he thought, hurrying in the back door to the kitchen. Everything there was moving along as though it was an average Thursday. Stephen's eyes fell on Miss Connie, who was sitting at her desk doing paperwork. *God, I don't want to tell her,* but he knew he needed to. "Miss Connie..." he began.

Without looking up, she said, "It's all right, honey, you

aren't late enough to worry about."

"Yes, ma'am, but something else. Dr. King has been shot."

She turned and looked up. Her mouth fell open but after a moment she closed it. "How do you know?"

"It was on the news as I was running out."

"Oh Lord no. Please no. Is he alive?"

"I don't know, they didn't say."

There was a transistor radio sitting on the desk. She reached up and turned it on. WMCA rock and roll music came up. Ms. Connie turned the dial until she got a news broadcast and the two of them listened. "...Was shot standing on the balcony of the Lorraine Motel. Jesse Jackson calmed the crowd as someone called an ambulance...This just in. It is confirmed that Dr. King has been shot and has died." Miss Connie broke down.

All movement in the kitchen had stopped when the radio came on and now there was talk spreading the news person to person. Stephen stepped forward and put his hand on Miss Connie's shoulder. "I'm so sorry," he said.

"Why did it have to be Dr. King?" she said.

XXII

Stephen, though stunned by the news from Memphis, finished out his dish room shift with Mamoni and Big Julie, but the room was strangely silent, with none of the joking, shouting or talk that usually accompanied a dish room shift.

When the cafeteria was almost empty, only two or three more trays to come in, Mamoni said, "Screw 'em, we'll get the last of them tomorrow morning."

Big Julie and Stephen took off their aprons, rinsed their hands under the sprayer and went out. Stephen crossed the quad headed for Lorring Home, but he did it out of habit. His foot hit the first step of the staircase before it dawned on him he didn't want to go to his room. He stopped, thought a moment then went up through the TV lounge, which was full of people, mostly black, watching continuing coverage of the assassination, and out the back door, headed for the Student Union. He was hoping to see Jim Brodski or Bill Thinning or anybody else who could help him make sense of what happened.

He stepped in the door and swept his eyes over the room. The place was in an uproar and an even thicker layer of tobacco smoke hung below the ceiling. There were a lot of red hats which made the knot in his stomach tighten. Mid-way toward the back of the room he saw Thinning, Brodski, and Dennis Grant sitting at one of the small cafe tables. Stephen made his way to them and looked around for a chair, but there wasn't one.

Dennis said, "Ain't that something? Every chair in the joint has an ass in it."

"Yeah," Stephen said, "Most of 'em redneck asses it looks like."

Bill Thinning's face twisted as though he smelled something foul.

Jim Brodski said, "Everybody gotta be someplace I guess."

There was a sudden burst of laughter from one of the tables filled with Kappas. The sound of it stabbed Stephen it the chest, and the pain doubled when he saw that it was Elgin Fester. At that moment Fester looked up and right into Stephen's eyes. The mocking grin came onto Fester's face. He stood up and began pushing through the crowd toward Stephen.

Jim Brodski noticed and said, "Oh shit, here we go."

As Fester came up to them, he said, "Hey Hollywood, where's all yer niggers?"

Bill Thinning was on his feet in a moment.

"Why don't you shut up, Fester?" Dennis Grant said.

"About time somebody shot that nigger," Fester sneered.

Without even a thought of all the times he had been a peacemaker, Stephen threw a hard right that snapped Fester's head around and sent him to the floor.

The room erupted. Red hats began shouting. Stephen threw the small table out of the way so that he could reach Fester lying stunned on the floor. Stephen straddled Fester and hit him again with a right then a left before seizing his throat to choke the life out of him.

Thinning and Brodski grabbed Stephen's shoulders, tried to pull him off Fester's chest, but Stephen's grip was tight. In a moment a bunch of red hats were on the two. They didn't pull Thinning and Brodski, instead they punched and kicked, then began bashing Stephen's head and kidneys while others took him around the throat to pull him off the still-stunned Fester. Just because they pulled the two apart, they didn't stop beating Stephen. A few more punches and he was on the floor covering his head, being kicked and stomped by red hats.

Brodski, Thinning, and Grant piled into those hurting

Stephen, managing to push them back a little.

From somewhere, Brad Stringer and Bill Hartley, the dorm monitors from Lorring Home, joined the melee, trying to break it up. They managed to push the red hats back enough so that Dennis Grant could help Stephen to his feet.

Stephen was bleeding from nose and mouth. Bruises were already beginning to rise under his eyes, but once back on his feet he was ready to continue the fight. Bill Thinning threw his arms around his friend pinning Stephen's arms to his sides and began dragging him toward the door. Jim and Dennis began backing up as a kind of rear guard.

There was still a lot of shouting coming from the Student Union but they ignored it.

"Bring him down to our room, Bill," Brodski said.

"You ready to quit, Steve?" Thinning asked.

Stephen stopped struggling. "Yeah, yeah."

Thinning eased his grip but didn't let go completely. He could still feel Stephen's muscles clenching and his heart beating wildly so he didn't completely trust that Stephen was really done.

At last Bill completely released him and with the support gone Stephen almost collapsed. Bill grabbed him, pulling his left arm across his shoulder. Dennis stepped into the other side and pulled Stephen's right arm over his shoulder. Jim turned back a little. "You all right, Steve?" he asked.

"I think so. Wobbly and my back hurts."

"Come on, you guys," he commanded. The four went off down the street, Stephen being more carried than walking.

In the room, Brodski, indicating a desk chair, said, "Sit him down there."

They did so while Jim got out a big first-aid kit "Put your head down between your knees for a bit, Steve." It seemed counterintuitive to put his head down rather than back, but he did as he was told.

After a few moments, Jim squatted in front and examined Stephen. "Your nose quit bleeding yet?" he asked, but got no answer. He pushed Stephen upright in the chair. "You in there, Steve? Open your eyes, buddy."

Stephen did so. Jim snapped a smelling salt vial and passed it under Stephen's nose, which made him jolt upright. "Better? You know where you are, Steve?"

"I'm in your room in the white house."

"Right. Your back still hurt?"

Stephen shifted his hips left and right a little, wincing. "A little."

Brodski dug into the kit and came out with a flat tin like a travel pack of aspirin. He popped it open, took two tablets out, and handed them to Stephen. "These are super-strength pain pills," he said. "Bring him a drink of water, Dennis."

Grant did as he was told and handed the glass to Stephen. "Go ahead and take 'em, Steve."

"What are they?"

"Just super strength acetaminophen and aspirin. Technically they should only be given by prescription but I got a friend that supplies them for my first-aid kit."

Stephen took the pills and washed them down with the water. "You coulda mitigated that water with a little Old Crow, ya know," he said.

Brodski laughed. "You coulda just come by and asked for a shot. Ya didn't have to go get the shit beat out of ya."

Stephen laughed a little but it hurt so he stopped.

"Way you were getting kicked, you'll probably be pissing blood for the next couple days," Brodski said. "Not really anything much to worry about, but if the pain increases it'll be time for a doctor to have a look at ya."

Stephen nodded and winced.

Dennis wet a wash cloth and handed it to Stephen who began wiping his face with the cool cloth.

"Whatever possessed you to go off on Fester like that?" Thinning asked. "I mean he had it coming but he's had it coming for long time."

"It was the crack about shooting Dr. King. I just couldn't let it pass."

Thinning shook his head. "You'd think that even a bigoted asshole like Fester would know to keep quiet about it just out of self-preservation."

Brodski said, "When your prejudice outweighs your mental capacity your mouth tends to run over time."

"This is gonna turn into a riot when the shock wears off," Stephen said. "The Black Student Union is all sitting in the TV room in Lorring Home, and when Charlie and them that went to Memphis get home the place is gonna explode."

"Maybe," Brodski said. "I'd bet the Dean and the Pope have already called the state police. Mason is gonna look like an occupied city again by tomorrow morning. "

"Not that happy about that," Bill Thinning said, "But maybe they can keep the lid on. I hope."

Stephen shook his head. "The irony of it is that Dr. King preached peaceful protest and his death is gonna bring an end to that. Stokely Carmichael and Malcolm X are gonna start saying, see there, we been telling you all along that war is the only way we'll ever get equal rights."

"I'd say we all better just stay indoors for the next couple of days," Brodski said. "And hope this blows over."

"Yeah, I guess," they all agreed.

Stephen made his way back to his room without help, though about halfway up the back steps, he thought maybe he should have asked Thinning or Brodski to come along.

When he opened the door to his room Drew who was sitting at the desk turned and looked at him.

"Jesus God, Steve! What happened to you?"

Stephen explained all about the riot.

"Really? I didn't even know about the shooting," Drew said. "I been here at this desk since this afternoon."

"You're probably as well off. Just see that if ya go out you keep an eye open. There is gonna be trouble and it won't matter who you are. It'll be black on white and nobody will notice who is who."

"You really think so?"

Stephen waved his hand up and down himself as if to say look what has already happened.

"What are you gonna do?" Bankuski asked.

"Hunker down right here in my little ol' room and not stick my head out for a couple of days until this blows over."

~ * ~

It didn't blow over. It turned into a real storm. It was as though the dust up between Stephen and Fester were the lighting of a fuse. Shortly after Charlie and the others who had gone to Memphis got back some Kappa echoed Fester's stupidity and a riot broke out in Lorring Home, and elsewhere on campus as well. The state police showed up just in time to keep the "unrest," as they called it, from spreading into the town of Mason and perhaps over the whole county.

Stephen kept his head down, didn't even try to go to any of the few classes that still held sessions, or to the dish room, figuring his bruised face and swollen lip would cause more problems than he could handle, but hiding out didn't help. Tuesday morning the knock on the door came. Ma Brigman. She did not look happy about knocking on Stephen's door.

"You are to report to the Dean's office," she said, sounding more Georgia than usual.

"Now?" Stephen, who was still in pajamas, asked.

"Now," she said.

"Okay," he said and closed the door though she was still standing there. He wondered if he had time to take a quick shower, but decided that *now* meant NOW, so he slipped on some jeans and a t-shirt.

"Good luck," Drew said.

"Thanks, Bankuski. Gonna need it, I'm sure."

The quad was empty as he walked across and that was

strange. There were usually several students crossing, going to class or just standing around in the shade, but today the place was a ghost town. He expected to at least see some state cops like in the past, but there were none to be found.

In the admin building, he walked down the hall toward the offices. There was a red hat standing in front of the Dean's door. It was Fester. Stephen was somewhat heartened by the fact Fester looked as beat up as he did. Black eyes, busted lip, swollen ears. Stephen didn't acknowledge the other's presence, nor did Fester. They stood side by side for a moment before the door opened and they were motioned in. Dr. Wesley, the Dean, Dr. Conners, Stephen's uncle and advisor, and James Salinder, Mason's President, waited, looking like a tribunal.

The two stood before the Dean's big desk. Stephen swallowed hard. This was obviously going to be bad if both the Dean and President Salinder were involved.

"Remove your cap, Mr. Fester," Dean Wesley said.

Fester, having obviously forgotten he still had the red baseball cap on, quickly snatched it off.

After a moment of looking the two over the Dean said, "Gentlemen—and I use that term loosely—the brawl you set off in the Student Union Thursday night cannot be ignored."

"He started it," Fester said.

"I did not! You came up to the table where we were and said, *It's about time somebody shot that...*"

"You hit me!"

"Gentlemen! Enough," Wesley snapped. "We don't care who started what, or why. A brawl grew out of it that did damage to the Student Union and to many of those who were there, and stirred up more trouble on campus, so there must be consequences. Mr. Mitchell, you are hereby expelled from Mason College..."

Oh shit! Stephen thought. He had never considered that expulsion might be in the mix.

"...and you Mr. Fester, are also expelled, but more, you were warned that any further trouble from the Kappa Fraternity would result in their being expelled from the campus. This brawl constitutes such trouble. Therefore, the Kappa Fraternity is barred from Mason's campus. "

Fester began to sputter. "You can't do that. I paid my tuition and I'm a member of the Cumberland Church—besides he hit me first. It wasn't Kappa trouble. He hit me first! It was a personal matter."

"You had it coming," Stephen shot back, feeling the anger boiling up in him once more. "You been asking for it all year. Just ask anybody on campus. You are a Kluxer and have been trying to stir up racial trouble for as long as I have known you. I have saved you from at least three beatings before, but this time I just couldn't let it go."

"That's enough," Dean Wesley commanded. "You have twenty-four hours to clear out your rooms. That's all."

"I'll sue," Fester said. "You can't do this to me."

Stephen didn't hesitate. He turned toward the door and glanced at the Pope who was looking very hurt by all this trouble. He had been working at integrating Mason and keeping the peace as it happened for years. Now it looked as though integration and peace were all in ruins. Plus, he was no doubt dreading explaining this to his sister, Stephen's mother. Stephen knew this was going to be much harder to explain than being on academic probation. He turned from the desk and headed for the door, his mind on things he had to do before he left Mason forever.

Walking across the campus Stephen felt lighter, as though a weight had been lifted off him. The trouble had come home to roost but now he no longer had to worry about classes, or work or Mary Ann. That one still stabbed him. He knew that somehow, he had to talk with her, to apologize and beg her forgiveness.

Gonna have to be careful about that, boy. She could mistake an apology for wanting to make up and you'll be right back to where you started from.

He decided to go into the cafeteria. He had been eating sardines and crackers for a couple of days and needed some real food, and to pick up his last check. The check was going to be pitifully small but, *Any is better than none,* he thought.

It was a little before the lunch rush so he stepped right into the line and started. It was Tuesday so there was meat loaf, mashed potatoes and hush puppies. He pointed at them and ignored the fact that all the servers in the line were staring at his beat-up face. When he came to the end he wondered if he still had a valid meal ticket since he was no longer a student, but when he presented his meal card, Marilyn punched it. Marilyn Dawson, the usual cashier, looked over the plate then at Stephen's face. "Hope the other guy looks worse," she said.

"Nothing the undertaker can't fix up," Stephen said and tried to smile. It hurt so he let it go and moved on into the dining room. He sat down at the table where Mary Ann had sat glaring at the dish room window. Gary Mamoni was already in the dish room pulling and racking the few trays that had come in. He spotted Stephen and went out the dish room door. Stephen already knew what was about to happen.

"About time you got here, Hollywood. Haven't seen you in days," Mamoni began but cut off quickly. "You look like a bag of hamburger."

"Fester looks worse."

"I heard about your mess in the Student Union. Whatever. Glad to see you all the same."

"I'm not here to do dishes, Gary. I don't work here anymore."

"What?"

"I'm expelled. Twenty-four hours I gotta be out of my room and off campus."

"What the fuck?"

Stephen explained what happened with the Dean. As he did so Mamoni's face got more and more twisted. "So, it's just me and Big Julie now?"

"Miss Connie will have somebody in pretty quick, I'm sure. Just call it payback for you calling me Hollywood."

Mamoni shook his head. "Shit," he said and turned away.

As Stephen watched his retreating back, Charlie Horse and Leroy came up to the table. They looked him over but said nothing about his battle scars.

"Heard you and Fester had a go round," Charlie said.

"Yeah. I finally had enough."

"After all the times you kept us out of trouble," Leroy said shaking his head.

"Bah, it shoulda happened sooner. We would have been rid of the Kappas sooner if I had just let you guys beat the shit out of that asshole."

"Rid of the Kappas?" Charlie asked.

"Yeah. Because of the brawl they are officially expelled from Mason College, never to return, I hope."

"Really?"

"Yeah. Fester and me, but especially the Kappas are out of here."

"Whatdaya mean Fester and you?"

"We're out. Expelled for brawling. Fester says he's gonna sue but I don't think he's gonna get far."

Leroy shook his head in disgust. "Expelled. Damn! What are you gonna do?"

Stephen shrugged. "Go home and explain to my folks how their son got thrown out of school. If I manage to live through that I'll get a job, maybe take some classes at Valley State. Gonna just keep putting one foot in front of the other." He took a bite of his meatloaf, then stabbed at his mashed potatoes, scooping some onto his fork. A thought came to him.

"Did you see it happen, Charlie?"

Charlie blinked at Stephen, took a deep breath and let it out slowly as though to dispel pain. After a moment he said, "Yeah, I saw it. I was down in the crowd in the parking lot. We didn't know what had happened, just that Dr. King had collapsed. Most of us didn't even hear the shot."

"God, I'm sorry Charlie. When I told Miss Connie she said,

Why did it have to be Dr. King? Broke my heart. She has suffered so much. You all have."

"Just another battle to be free," Leroy said. "Dr. King is a casualty in the war for Civil Rights, but this is just one battle."

XXIII

When Stephen got back to Lorring Home, he stopped at the pay phone. He might have been able to use Ma Brigman's phone but he didn't want to chance it. He got out his little address book and dialed.

"Uncle Paul, I don't know if you heard what happened but I'm in need of a place to stay for a couple of days before I head back to LA. Can I crash at your place?"

"Uh, sure. What happened?"

"I don't have enough change to explain on the phone. I'll tell you all about it when I get to Memphis."

"Uh, yes, fine. You need a ride?"

"No, sir. I don't think so. I can bum a ride with Uncle Morton. Or there is always the bus if he doesn't want to be associated with me. "

"What?" Paul said, sounding confused

"I'll explain when I get there. Probably be tomorrow, but maybe tonight depending on what I can scrounge up for a ride."

"Okay, we'll look for you."

"Thanks. I'll see you."

Stephen hung up and looked at the phone for a moment, thinking. *The Pope will probably be back in his office by now.* He picked up the receiver, dropped a dime in and dialed Morton Conners' office number. The phone rang and rang and rang. Stephen thought the Pope must have had a class or gone home. He was in process of hanging up when he heard Connors' voice say, "Yes."

"Uncle Morton, this is Stephen."

"Steve, I was just on my way to see you when the phone rang."

"To see me? What for?"

"I thought you might need a place to stay when you are out of your room."

"Yes, sir. I will. I called Paul and Esther to ask if I could stay with them a couple of days. Paul said yes."

"Well, you can stay here with us for a couple of days if you need to."

"Well, thanks that would be great, but I think I need to be on my way pretty soon. If I could bum a ride to Memphis that would be great."

"Certainly. We can go after supper tonight if you'd like."

"That would be great. I am still packing up. Take me a couple more hours, I guess."

"Fine. I'll see you in a couple of hours. Bye."

Stephen threw his clothes into his suitcases without order. He kept out his jacket. He looked at his books, knew he couldn't take them. That hurt him. He had always been fond of books and these, even though they were school books, were dear to his heart. At last he pulled his Bible, his copy of the anthology that had his poem in it, and the two notebooks that had his journal and some story notes in them, leaving the others sitting on the shelf above the desk. He threw his guitar case onto the bed beside the suitcases and looked it all over again.

"You can have the books, Drew. Maybe the bookstore will buy them back as used, or you can sell 'em individually."

"You sure, Steve? I mean that's a lot of money."

"I can't carry 'em now. Besides, if I start classes at Valley State, they probably won't use the same texts. Better you should have 'em."

"Well, thanks a lot," he said and stuck out his hand. "Nice to have known ya, Steve."

Stephen grinned crookedly. "I wouldn't blame you if you were glad to be rid of me as much trouble as you have had because of me."

"Naw, all probably trouble I would have gotten into anyhow."

Stephen shrugged, shook Bankuski's hand, picked up his suitcases and guitar case and headed out the door.

In the TV lobby, he left his suitcases and guitar standing as he went to knock on Ma Brigman's door. When she answered he didn't say a word, just held out his key to her. She took it with a *good riddance* look.

Like it or not, old woman, your way of life is about to end. Integration is coming no matter what, Stephen thought as he turned away. He sat down in the TV room to wait for the Pope. He didn't have to wait long.

The short ride to the Connors' house was silent. Uncle Morton glanced at Stephen out of the side of his eye but made no move to speak.

It was actually too early for dinner when they arrived. "I'll just leave my suitcases in the back seat," Stephen said.

The Pope nodded and they went in. Aunt Jean was still the perfect Southern hostess, offering greetings and iced tea, but things seemed a little stiffer than usual. Clearly, she knew something was wrong though perhaps not what it was.

Stephen took the glass of iced tea more out of habit than desire. He went to the living room and sat on a corner of the couch.

The Pope disappeared into the kitchen with Aunt Jean and Stephen thought he was going to be left to sit alone. He wondered if he might turn on the TV, but just as he was about to decide to do so Uncle Morton reappeared and sat across from him in the big chair.

"Have you called home with the news yet?" Connors asked.

"No, sir. I don't want to pass that kind of news on the phone. I figure in person is the best way."

"Maybe it would be better on the phone," Connors said. "Give them a chance to cool before you step into it."

"That's a thought. Let me think about that for a bit. You may be right."

"What really happened, Steve? Fester made it sound like you just walked up and slugged him."

"Consider the source Uncle Morton. He lies all the time, so long as it can cause trouble. I was in the Student Union with Jim Brodski, Bill Thinning, and Dennis Grant when Fester and a bunch of red hats came in. Like always they just pushed through, but when Fester saw me, his mind went to evil. He's been trying to bully me all year, but I haven't let it bother me until then. He shoved up to us looked right at me and said, *'About time somebody shot that nigger.'* That was all it took. I've been holding my temper all year and I've stopped some trouble, but that was just more than I could take, so I belted him. When he went down, I climbed on him and started pounding. That's when the half dozen red hats that had been with him decided they didn't like him getting beat on so they went to work on me. Brodski and Thinning tried to pull us all apart but it didn't really work until Stringer and Hartley and I don't know who all else showed up. I don't know what else happened. I was pretty out of it by then. Brodski and Thinning and Grant pulled me out of there, took me down to Brodski's room and patched me up as best they could."

Connors considered what he heard for a moment then said, "Not quite the same story Fester told."

"Like I said, consider the source. You can go ask Jimmy, Bill and Dennis."

"We did. They told basically the same story as you just did which makes me think that you may be able to re-apply next year, but I don't know."

"Fester was talking about lawsuits. Is that gonna happen?"

"I doubt it. Might work for him, but the Kappas are done. They were on the thin edge as it was because of all the trouble they have been involved in."

"That's the one good thing that will have come out of this," Stephen said. "Almost worth getting tossed just to be rid of them."

"Not sure your folks are gonna agree," the Pope said.

"Yeah, things are gonna be kinda dicey for a bit but, I think they'll forgive me—eventually."

"Any idea of what you are gonna do? I mean you had been talking about the ministry,"

"Truth be told, sir, I had about given up that idea. I just hadn't committed to anything else."

Uncle Morton nodded. "I had a feeling you weren't all that convinced before, then with all the Baptist trouble last year..."

"Yeah, I was kinda iffy before all that, but everything that happened over there pretty much convinced me the life of a minister was not for me. As to what I'm gonna do, I really have no idea. End of last year I thought I had my life all laid out, then the Marines wouldn't take me, so I've pretty much just been treading water since that. Wonder if the French Foreign Legion would take me?"

Morton chuckled at that. "Dangerous thought right now, although they have been out of Indo-China for ten years. They still have some fights going on in North Africa."

"Yeah, just a passing thought." Several thoughts passed, including thoughts of Mary Ann lying in the hospital. He wondered if she was still there.

"Uncle Morton, can I use your telephone for a minute?"

"You gonna call home after all?"

"Maybe, but now I need to find out if Mary Ann Younger is still in the hospital?"

"In the hospital? What happened?"

Stephen was surprised the Pope didn't know what had happened. He usually knew every rumor and happenstance on the campus. "That's another situation I'm in. Mary Ann and I were a kind of an item for a while, but when we broke up, she was not happy about it. She cut her wrists."

Connors straightened, surprised.

"Not as bad as it sounds," Stephen hurried to explain. "Doctor said she wasn't ever in any danger, but they kept her in the hospital for observation. I'd just like to know how she is doing."

"Of course, of course. Who are you gonna call?"

"Billie Jo Patrick will know something, I'm sure."

"Ah. Would you like to go into my office? It is a little more private than this phone."

"That would be great," Stephen said, standing.

"You know where it is, right?"

"Yes sir. I'll be quick."

Stephen went up the stairs and into the bedroom the Pope used for a home office. He sat in the desk chair and pulled the phone to him. He got out his little address book and dialed the number of the Baptist Student Union. The phone rang three times before David Hall picked it up.

"Is Billie Jo there, David?"

"Yeah, hang on."

Stephen heard him cover the mouth piece with his hand and shout, "Billie Jo—telephone."

In a few moments Billie Jo said, "Hello."

"Hi, Billie Jo. This is Stephen Mitchell."

"Steve. Been hearing a lot about you in the last couple of days."

"Yeah, yeah, but I just want to know how Mary Ann is; is she still in the hospital?"

"No, they let her go Sunday. We took her home to Memphis and turned her over to her mom."

"Ah. How was she doing?"

"Still torn up emotionally, but at least I think she has moved away from suicidal."

"I'm glad. I would have liked to talk with her, but...well you know how that worked out."

"Maybe you could call her at home."

"I don't have her number," he said.

"You got a pencil?"

"Yeah, give me the number."

She reeled off the number and Stephen wrote it down.

"Call her, but don't be surprised if she doesn't want to talk to you. She was ashamed of the way she reacted so I don't know if she is gonna want to talk to you."

"All I can do is try. Thanks. Bye." After he hung up the phone, he sat looking from the number he had been given to the dial. Finally, he picked up the receiver and dialed Mary Ann's number.

The phone rang twice before a woman answered. Stephen said, "Hi, this is Stephen Mitchell. May I talk with Mary Ann?"

He heard the woman take a couple of breaths then say, "Hang on a moment." She turned from the phone but didn't cover the mouthpiece. "Mary Ann, there is some fellow wants to talk to you."

Stephen couldn't hear the answer but could guess from what came next. The woman said, "It's Stephen Mitchell."

There was a slight delay then the woman said, "Mr. Mitchell, Mary Ann says she doesn't want to talk to you."

"Could you ask her please to just talk with me for a minute?"

She hesitated a moment and Stephen could picture what was happening. No doubt Mary Ann was standing beside her mother who was offering the phone to her, but she was shaking her head. After a moment her mother said, "Mr. Mitchell, she says she doesn't have anything to say to you anymore. Goodbye," and with that the phone went dead. Stephen hung onto the receiver until the dial tone came back then he hung it up.

I'll try again when I get to Memphis, he thought and stood up. *Should I call home and tell them I'm coming?*

He considered the thought a bit longer, looked at his watch and decided if he was going to call, he would wait until later when his father was home and full of dinner. He nodded to himself and went down stairs into the kitchen.

"Can I have some more tea, Aunt Jean?"

"Certainly," she said. "Are you all right?"

"I'm all right, just a little beat up."

She nodded and handed him a new glass of tea. He carried it back to the living room.

Uncle Morton had turned on the TV. He glanced up at Stephen and said, "Trying to get some news on what's happening in Memphis."

With all the personal trouble, Stephen had almost forgotten the Civil Rights world was in mourning. There had been some riots and broken windows in Memphis. Crowds were still gathering in the parking lot of the Lorraine Motel.

TV news didn't have much to say. They reported what most everyone already knew. Dr. King was dead. Dr. Ralph Abernathy was next in line. Stephen remembered him from last year's march to honor Robert and the others. He had been ill then and had not done anything more than shake hands and appear on the platform with Robert's brother. Stephen didn't envy him having to step into Dr. King's shoes.

"I hope this all settles down soon," Connors said. "No progress gets made when things are all ajumble like this. There'll be fools and haters out doing evil. Thank God we got Leroy through that. Jail would not be a good place for any Negro right now."

"I'm glad too," Stephen said remembering the mob outside the courthouse when he and Charlie had gone there. He knew the only thing that kept that mob from turning into a lynch mob was the fact the national news media had eyes firmly focused on west Tennessee in general and Mason in particular.

Aunt Jean came in. "Dinner's ready y'all." She called up the stairs for the children. "Little early, but if you're going to Memphis this evening it's probably a good idea for you to get going." She looked hard at the Pope. "I'd rather you weren't out after dark, Morton. Things are still pretty bad in Memphis."

The two men stood up and all retreated to the kitchen with the children close behind. Jean had prepared a pot of beef stew and corn bread. All sat and clasped hands as Jean said a simple grace. She ended with, "*Please Lord put your hand of peace and protection upon Memphis and on Morton and Stephen as they travel. In Jesus' name, Amen*"

When Stephen and the Pope climbed into the car, the sun was low in the sky. Aunt Jean said, "Stay the night in Memphis if you think it's safer, Morton."

"I think it will be all right Jean, but I'll stay if I have to. I'll call one way or another. There are a couple of men from the church who are gonna keep watch here tonight."

Stephen had not thought that the Pope's house and family might be in danger. They had endured much as the integration of Mason progressed, and now Fester and the red hats had even more reason to visit violence on Dr. Connors. "You sure this is all right, Uncle Morton? I hate to take you away right now when you might be needed here."

Aunt Jean said, "It'll be all right, Stephen. I don't think there will be any trouble, and with the men sitting on the porch, I'm pretty sure there won't be. Just you two be careful. Memphis is still boiling."

Morton didn't bother with the back roads. He went directly to the interstate. As they flew down the highway in the gathering dark, Stephen said, "Lot faster than the back roads."

"I think it's a lot less likely to find trouble than the back roads," Connors said.

Stephen chuckled. "When I rode with Charlie and them that one time, he thought the back roads would be better. He turned out to be wrong. I hope you aren't wrong."

"I don't think so. Traffic is pretty light. Fewer cops."

"I guess we aren't likely to get stopped for driving while black," he said and laughed.

They drove on in quiet, coming into Memphis. The streets were almost empty though it was still early evening. Stephen began to recognize some of the turns, especially when they passed the turn off into Sherwood Forest.

I gotta try and see Jackie before I go, he thought. *Wonder if she's in Memphis or back at school? I'm gonna miss her. Wonder if her dad will tell me anything more about Doctor Marchant's murder?*

When they pulled into Paul and Esther's driveway, the back door opened. They had apparently been watching for them.

Paul looked over Stephen noting the beat-up face but said nothing. Esther on the other hand gasped when she saw Stephen.

"My Lord! What happened? Are you all right?"

"Yes Ma'am, I'm all right. Still hurtin' a little bit. It happened some days ago now so I am kinda healing."

"Well, come on in and tell us about it," Paul commanded and waved them through the back door.

"You have supper yet?" Esther asked

"We ate before we left Mason," Uncle Morton said. "I could use a glass of tea though, if you got it."

"Me too," Stephen agreed, but thought how he could really use a sip of Old Crow instead of iced tea, knowing full well that there was nothing resembling Old Crow in this house.

Paul and Esther's girls were in the living room watching TV. They glanced up when the adults came into room but it seemed as though they noticed nothing about their cousin, as though they expected to see him beat up. They went back to watching the program.

Esther brought the tea and sat down beside Paul. She examined Stephen again then said, "What happened?"

Stephen took a big slug of his tea, said, "Elgin Fester made a crack about Dr. King's assassination so I popped him one. Half a dozen Kappas took exception, and here I am, on my way back to LA."

"Well, there was a little more to it than that," Connors said. "The whole thing turned into a brawl in the Student Union that spilled out onto the campus. Student Union got broken up pretty good and there were several students that got hurt."

Paul shook his head. "I can't feature that. I mean we used to have the occasional fight but they were few and far between, never what you could call a brawl."

"Have you called your mom yet?" Esther asked.

Stephen looked at his watch. "I'm gonna call them in a little while if you don't mind. I wanted to make sure everything was settled at home before I stirred it all up again."

"Your mom called us the other day when Dr. King was killed, just to see how everything was here. I told her everything was fine."

"I've been hearing about riots and mobs all over the place," Stephen said. "I guess Mom and them are worried."

"The one good thing that came out of all this," Connors said, "it gave us a reason to put the Kappas off campus."

"They never were much before this year," Paul said.

"Integration has brought them out, just like all over the South. All these vocal KKK sympathizers and the ongoing violence everywhere," Connors said. "George Wallace standing in the door of University of Alabama, defying the courts and the president. It's the extension of the Civil War that should have been dealt with during Reconstruction."

"If we knew then what we know now," Paul said.

After a bit Stephen looked at his watch and decided he couldn't put off calling home any longer.

"Paul, can I use the telephone in your office to call home?"

"Yes, sure."

"I'll try to keep it short since it is long distance."

"Don't worry about it. Take as long as you need to."

Stephen went to the office and closed the door. As he had in the Pope's office, he sat in the desk chair and pulled the phone to him. He stared at it for a few moments, not really wanting to make this phone call, but he knew it was better to do it this way than wait until he got back to LA. He picked up the receiver, took a deep breath and let it out before he dialed.

The home phone rang, then rang again. Stephen thought maybe there was no one home, but it was a school night so...Third ring and his father answered. "Hello."

"Hi Dad, it's Stephen."

"Oh, what's up, Steve?"

"Well, I'm just calling to tell you all that I'm coming home."

"Coming home? What happened? Are you all right? You sick?"

"No, sir, I'm fine, I guess. No, I got expelled." Stephen half expected an explosion though his father was not the kind to explode at a moment's notice.

There had been times when father and son had almost come to blows, but that had not happened for a long time."

"What'd you do to get expelled?" his father asked, his voice tight and controlled.

"There's this guy who has been asking for it for a couple of years. I finally had all I could stand from him so I belted him. Then his buddies piled in and my friends piled in to help me. It turned into a whole Magilla. Broke up the Student Center and ..."

His dad cut him off. "Did he really have it coming? What did he do?"

"It was right after Dr. King was killed. Him and his red hat buddies were celebrating Dr. King's death. He came up to me and said, *About time somebody shot that nigger,* so I popped him."

Stephen and his father had talked a great deal about the Civil Rights movement during the summer. Stephen even told him about his run in with the Memphis Police. His father didn't exactly understand why he, a white boy, had enmeshed himself in the movement. He knew Stephen had roomed with a black student and they had become friends. He knew Robert had been killed and he understood how it felt to lose friends to violence from his time in the Marines. He also understood honor and that sometimes honor had to be defended with violence.

"So did this other guy get booted out, too?" Stephen's father asked.

"Yeah, him and all his red hat buddies. All in all, it was a win for the good guys,"

"Sounds like BS to me. Sounds like there aren't any good guys in this mess."

Stephen raised his voice a little and said, "Yes there are! I promise these assholes all had it coming."

"Nice talk."

"Yes, sir. Sorry. Just thinking about Fester and his Ku Klux buddies makes me mad enough to cuss."

Stephen listened as his father took a deep breath. "When you gonna be here?"

"Couple of days. I have some things to take care of here before I head for LA," Stephen answered.

"You got money for a plane ticket?"

"I think so. I got my last dishwashing check. It's pretty slim but I think I got enough."

"Where are you?"

"Paul and Esther's house. They said I could stay a couple of days."

"Okay. Maybe I'll wire you some money."

"If you want to that would be good, but I think I got enough."

"We gonna have to talk about this whole mess some more when you get home."

"Yes, sir, I know."

"Let us know when you get into LA."

"Yes, sir, I will," Stephen said.

His father said, "Bye," and Stephen heard the sound of the phone being hung up.

Stephen looked at the receiver still in his hand and could not believe the call had been as easy as it had been. *I'm gonna catch hell when I get home,* he thought, but at least for the next couple of days he could tend to other business.

XXIV

Everyone, even the children, seemed to be waiting with bated breath when Stephen came back from calling home. He looked at them and couldn't help but smile a little. All these people cared enough to be worried about him.

"Well," Stephen began with a laugh, "He didn't crawl through the phone to strangle me. I am gonna need to stay here a couple of days until my place in Mexico is ready though." There was weak laughter in answer.

Stephen looked at them. "It's all right. Dad was remarkably easy with it. Course, after he has had a couple of days to stew over it that may change. I'm actually more worried about Mom than him."

"You are welcome to stay as long as you think you need to" Aunt Esther said.

"Thanks. I won't stay more than a couple of days. I have some things to tie up before I leave."

"Jackie know about this yet?" Paul asked.

"That's one of the loose ends I need to tie up. She still come down for church?"

Paul nodded.

The Pope stood up. "I'm gonna head for home," he said.

"You're welcome to stay, Morton," Esther protested.

"Naw, I better get on home. I have classes tomorrow."

Stephen stood up and went to his uncle. He stuck out his hand and said, "I'm sorry about all this, Uncle Morton. I know it is going to scramble things on campus for a while."

Connors took his nephew's hand, then pulled him into an embrace. The families Connors and Mitchell were usually Ozark-reticent about hugs but when the Pope squeezed Stephen it brought tears to his eyes. "It's okay, Steve. It may be for the best. We got the Kappas off campus and kept Leroy out of jail. I think we did all right. I'll look into the possibility of your re-applying for the fall quarter."

"Well, thank you, Uncle Morton, but I don't think coming back is in my future. The folks are gonna be a lot less inclined to let go of the money to send me back after all this. We'll see, but thanks for looking into it all the same. Please tell everyone thank you for me."

Connors pulled back but kept holding Stephen's hand. "I will do that," he said, and turned away, then turned back. "Oh, I almost forgot. I told Jean I was going to call her one way or another."

"Don't worry about it, Morton. I'll call her," Aunt Esther said. "You just get on before it gets too late."

"Thank you. I'll see you all. Keep your eyes open. Things seem pretty calm but tense, too."

"Yeah, you too," Paul answered.

~ * ~

Stephen rolled over and looked up at the ceiling. He had slept better than he expected to. Esther and Paul had been obviously curious about what happened and what Stephen was going to do in the next couple of days, but they didn't pry.

Before he went to sleep, he formulated a plan. Now in daylight, he was not sure the plan would work. Mostly it depended on whether Mary Ann would see him. *I don't know where she lives,* he thought. *She's here in Memphis but I don't know where.*

He got up got dressed and headed out to the living room. The smell of bacon was in the air. He looked at his watch. Six thirty. If he had been at school, he would be on his way to the dish room.

"Good morning, Aunt Esther," he said, stepping into the kitchen.

Esther was startled.

"Sorry," he said. "I didn't mean to scare you."

"Silly of me to jump. I'm just not used to having anyone come into the kitchen at this hour. Paul is getting the girls ready for school."

"Ah hah. Smells good."

"Breakfast in ten or fifteen minutes. How do you want your eggs?"

Just barely dead, he thought, but said, "Over easy, or however they land is fine. Do you have a phone book stashed somewhere?"

"I think Paul has one in his office."

"Think he'd mind if I used it?"

"Not at all. Go ahead. I think it is in the shelf behind the desk."

Stephen went into Paul's office and once more plopped down in the desk chair. He spun it and examined the book shelf. All utility books. Operation of the heating system, car parts, household repairs, Memphis phone book. He pulled it out and spun back to the desk. He couldn't remember Mary Ann's father's name but he turned to the Youngers and hit a snag. There were pages of Younger's. Stephen ran his finger down one page then sat back thinking before he remembered Billie Jo had given him her number. He dialed it. When Mary Ann's mother answered Stephen said, "Hi, this is Stephen Mitchell again. Could I talk with Mary Ann, please?"

"She doesn't want to talk with you, Mr. Mitchell."

"I understand. But could you pass along a message?"

"What is it?"

"I never meant to hurt her. I'm sorry she ... well, anyway. Please tell her good-bye. I am leaving Mason, and not coming back, so she won't have to see me anymore. I wish her the best."

"You're leaving Mason?" she said. "Because of all this?"

"No, ma'am. Not just because of this. This has something to do with it but there are a lot of reasons. I got expelled so there's no coming back,"

Suddenly, there was another voice on the line. Mary Ann. "Steve, what happened?"

Stephen was stunned for a second but then answered, "Fester and I had a go 'round in the Student Union. Started a brawl that broke the place up so they threw us both out. So, I'm going back to LA."

"I'd like to see you again," she said.

"I tried when you were in the hospital, but you didn't want to see me then."

"Yeah, I know. I was ashamed of being so stupid and I didn't want you to see me feeling so stupid."

"I had been looking for your address in the phone book. I was gonna come over and stand on your porch until you personally told me to go away, but there's lots of Youngers in Memphis."

She was silent for a time. Stephen could hear her breathing. "Would you like to come over?" she asked.

"Yes, I would."

"Where are you?"

"I'm at my Uncle Paul's house here in Memphis. "

"If I give you the address, can you find my house?"

"I'm sure Paul can."

"Can you come for dinner?"

"I guess, if you think you can stand to look at me for that long."

Stephen could hear her rueful smile across the telephone line. "I think I can. How about six o'clock?"

"All right. I'll see you at six."

"Here's the address." She reeled off a street number. "We'll see you at six."

"Okay then. Bye." he said and started to hang up, but held back for a moment listening until he heard the click of Mary Ann hanging up before he put the receiver back in the cradle.

Aunt Esther called, "Breakfast, y'all. Come on."

Paul and the girls came down the hall past the office door

just as Stephen was coming out.

"How you doing this morning, Steve?"

Stephen shrugged. "Don't know exactly. I sort of feel like I am twisting in the wind."

Paul laughed. "So long as you aren't hanging by your neck as you twist."

"Always something to be thankful for, I guess," Stephen answered.

At the table there were eggs, bacon, cottage fries and homemade biscuits. Stephen ate heartily. "I'll do the dishes, Aunt Esther," he said.

"You don't have to Steve," his aunt said.

"It'll make me feel right," Stephen said. "I wash breakfast dishes most days of the week—a lot more of them than we have here."

"All right then. What do you want for supper?" she asked.

"Oh, I'm sorry, I won't be here for supper. I have a date, sort of. That's what I was on the phone about." He turned to Paul. "Can I bum a ride about five thirty this evening?"

"You want to just borrow the car?"

Stephen considered it for a moment then said, "I don't think so Paul. I'm a pretty good driver, but I don't really know my way around Memphis. If you'll just drop me off at Mary Ann's house that'll be great."

Paul said, "That's fine."

"Meantime I need to make a couple more phone calls if you don't mind."

"Sure. No problem," he said.

Stephen stood up. "Thank you, Aunt Esther. That was great. I'll be back to do the dishes in a couple minutes."

"You really don't have to, Steve."

"Be careful, you'll talk me out of it." He laughed and headed back for the office.

He sat down and dialed the number for Jackie's house. Her mother answered.

Stephen said, "Hello Mrs. Bookman, this is Stephen Mitchell. I came to your house for Thanksgiving, remember."

"Of course, Stephen. How can I help you?"

"I was just wondering if you had a phone number for Jackie at school?"

"I have an emergency number but it isn't *for* her. Just to get hold of her if it is an emergency."

"I was afraid of that. I have her dorm phone number but it rings and rings. If someone does answer they are likely to tell me they don't know or just leave the phone hanging. Can you tell me when she is gonna be home again?"

"Well, she usually comes in on Friday night or sometimes Saturday morning."

"Great. Then can you do me a favor, when she comes in? Please tell her that I am in Memphis at Paul's house on my way back to LA. I'd really like to see her before I go."

"All right, Steve, I can do that."

"Thank you very much."

As he hung up the receiver Stephen thought about perhaps calling Jackie's father, but decided against it, knowing Captain Bookman wouldn't give him any information on either of the cases he wanted to know about.

He headed back to the kitchen and found that Aunt Esther had already done the dishes.

In the middle of the afternoon, Stephen was dozing in front of the TV when the phone rang. Paul answered it. "Yes, he's right here. Hang on a sec. Steve, it's Jackie. Wants to talk to you."

Stephen got up from the couch. "I'll be right there," he shouted.

In the office Paul held out the receiver to him and stood up. "I'll leave you alone," he said.

"Thanks, Paul. Won't be long," he said and put the phone to his ear.

"Hello Jackie, I didn't really expect your call."

"I called home to see how things were with Dad. He's deep

into Dr. King's murder case."

"I hadn't thought of that," he said, but clearly it was possible. The man *was* a Memphis police captain.

"Do they know who did it yet?"

"I don't know. He doesn't talk about ongoing cases"

"I know. He was stretching a point to tell me they had someone in custody for Dr. Marchant's murder. Did he tell you anything about that?"

"Not really. Why?"

"Because several of my friends were wondering if the suspect was black? A couple of them are cynical enough to wonder if maybe the guy was Manny Jefferson again."

"Oh. I don't know for sure but I think the guy was white."

"Hope you're right. Where are you? Still at school?"

"Yes. What are you doing in Memphis? Aren't you supposed to be in school?"

"Well, yeah but there is a story that goes along with it. I'm not in school anymore. Got tossed out."

"My God! What did you do?"

"Slugged a guy."

"Is that all?" she asked

"Not exactly. It turned into a brawl that broke up the Student Union and several people in it, including me. When are you coming home? I'd really like to see you before I leave Memphis. I got a feeling it'll be a long time before I get back here."

"Well, it's Wednesday. I usually come home Friday night, so a couple of days."

Stephen was a little disappointed that Jackie didn't just toss everything and run to his side, but after a second, he thought, *It ain't like she is your girlfriend, dummy.* He said "Good enough. I gotta give Paul back his office. I'll be glad to see you. Bye 'til Friday."

"Bye, bye," she said and hung up.

Stephen glanced at his watch. Couple more hours until his dinner with Mary Ann. His stomach didn't feel much like dinner. That well-remembered knot from the last few weeks was back as was that feeling of the sword hanging by the thread.

Trying to ease that feeling, he flipped the phone book over to the yellow pages looking at airlines. He had usually flown American so he dialed their information number.

Paul came back to the office with a glass of tea in his hand. "You all through?" he said.

Stephen nodded, then said, "Through, not to mention done for."

"Done for? What's up, I mean besides all the other?"

"Do you know about Mary Ann Younger?"

"Uh, no. I don't think so. Who is she?"

Stephen looked at his uncle for a moment trying to decide if he wanted to let Paul into the mess. "Well Paul, she is a Baptist Girl I was..." he didn't quite know what to call her. After a slight pause he said, "She tried to kill herself and it was at least partly my fault."

Paul blinked several times and adjusted his glasses, then turned and sat on the corner of his desk. "Tried?" he asked.

"Yeah. She cut her wrists but a doctor told me she didn't really know how to do it properly so she wasn't really in any danger this first time, but another try might be successful."

"What happened? How was this your fault?"

"She and I were a kind of an item for a while, but when I broke it off, she didn't take it well."

"Doesn't sound like enough to cause a suicide attempt."

"Truth is that I was more using her than anything else. I let the fact she was willing to have sex with me influence me more than it should have. I felt kinda bad about it all along, but desire overcame conscience so I did it anyway. Being a good Baptist girl, she took it as a commitment to forever, I guess."

Paul nodded his understanding. "Free love isn't really free."

"They don't tell ya that on the posters."

Paul smiled at that. "True. True. So, what are you gonna do?"

"I'm gonna go to her house and beg her forgiveness for being a heartless son of a bitch, and hope she forgives me."

"Sounds like you got it figured out. It's what Jesus told us to do, and ya can't go wrong following what he says."

"Yeah, I guess, but I am afraid she'll misunderstand—think I want to start up again."

Paul nodded. "You'll just have to make sure she understands."

Stephen nodded.

Paul stood and stepped around the desk. He put his hand on top of Stephen's head and said, "Lord Have Mercy, Christ have Mercy, Lord have Mercy."

Stephen swallowed hard, said, "Amen," then stood up. "Thanks, Paul." He stuck out his hand and Paul took it.

XXV

The Younger house was in a different part of Memphis than Stephen had ever been into. Most places he had been the houses were brick, but the houses in this area were all fronted with gray shingle. They all looked neat and clean with lawns in front, but Stephen had always thought of shingle siding as somehow lower class. There was a car parked in the drive.

Paul pulled to the curb in front of the house. "Want me to wait a minute?"

"And keep the motor running, just in case?" Stephen quipped.

"I don't think that will be necessary."

"Maybe not. Just hang on a minute until I actually get in the door."

"If you get in and the evening goes all right, give me a call, I'll come get you."

"Thanks a lot, Paul. I owe you."

"Naw, nothing to it."

Stephen climbed out and walked up to the house onto the stoop and rang the doorbell.

Mrs. Younger answered the door. She was an older version of her daughter: heavy-set but not really fat, dirty blonde hair, dark blue eyes. She was wearing a dress that made Stephen think of church clothes. Mary Ann, in a blue skirt and light-blue blouse, was standing just off her mother's left shoulder. She gasped when she set eyes on Stephen. He had forgotten his face was still bruised and swollen. "Good Lord, Steve, what happened?"

"Elgin Fester. Doesn't matter. I gave as good as I got and we're both out now so it doesn't matter."

Mrs. Younger stepped back from the door. Stephen took it as an invitation to come in and did so. Mary Ann moved up to him quickly and threw her arms around his neck. No more white bandages. Her wrists had flesh colored Band-Aids on them.

Stephen felt his body react to Mary Ann, and wiggled free of her, hopefully before she noticed, then said, "No. This isn't going to be that kind of call. I'm not here to make up. Everything is going to be the same as it was last week. I am not in love with you and this is strictly an apology visit."

Mary Ann looked disappointed but not as full of rage as she had been.

Mary Ann's mother, a Southern lady with a much thicker accent than her daughter, said, "Mr. Mitchell, would you like some iced tea before we go to the table?"

Stephen looked from mother to daughter. "Yes, ma' am. That would be great."

She turned her eyes onto her daughter, obviously passing a message of some kind, but she said nothing, only walked across the living room toward a kitchen door.

"Come and sit down," Mary Ann said and took his hand to lead him to a couch. Stephen sat, then looked around the room. He had seen this room in other houses: braided rug, two large chairs, high-back couch with a coffee table before it, all slanted in such a way that anyone could see the TV screen on the other side of the room.

Mary Ann didn't let go of his hand when they sat, but Stephen pulled his away. "Mary Ann, I just want to tell you how sorry I am for being a selfish, greedy bastard and using you like I did. It was shameful."

"I needed you so much that first time, after Daddy died, and you were there."

"Just coincidence. I was really trying to use you to hurt Cathy and Ethan. Especially Cathy."

Mary Ann drew her eyebrows down, not understanding. "Cathy?"

"Yes, Cathy. She hurt me bad when I caught her with David Hall. I felt doubly used and abused when she did that. She was a tease, just playing me to get me to the BSU for some reason, then wouldn't...I know it doesn't make sense to a rational person, but it did to me at the time. Everything just started rolling on from there."

"I knew you and Cathy had been a couple sorta and then you weren't."

"When she started sitting with you in the cafeteria that made me just more nuts."

"So, I was just a substitute for Cathy?" she asked with a small break in her voice.

Stephen looked into her eyes and saw they were shining with unshed tears. He hung his head, "Yes, I guess so. I'm sorry. I'm sorry. "

Mrs. Younger came in carrying a tray with two glasses, a sugar bowl and two long-handled teaspoons on it. She looked from her daughter to Stephen then put the tray down on the coffee table. "Supper will be ready in a few minutes," she said, studying Stephen as though he were a zoo specimen. After a moment she turned and went back toward the kitchen.

Stephen returned his attention to Mary Ann. "I'm not going to ask you to forgive me, because I certainly don't deserve it. I just wanted you to know how sorry I am."

She studied his face then wiped her eyes. Stephen glanced at the Band-Aid on her wrist when she wiped her eyes. Mary Ann noticed him noticing and said, "I'm sorry too, for this." She turned her wrists so they could see both the Band-Aids.

Stephen shook his head. "I don't understand why you did that."

Mary Ann shook her head. Tears came back into her voice. "I don't know either, Steve. You wouldn't pay any attention to me and it seemed like the only way to get back at you. Same kind of logic you were using, I guess. Made sense to me at the time, but not now."

"Come to the table, y'all," Mrs. Younger called. "Bring your glasses."

Stephen had not been looking forward to this meal. His stomach knot had been tight but seemed looser now that he'd apologized.

They stood and went to the kitchen. The table was spread with a checkered oilcloth now covered with a platter of fried chicken, a bowl of mashed potatoes, a boat of brown gravy, a bowl of green beans and three sets of dinnerware. There was a pitcher of iced tea and a sugar bowl.

"This smells wonderful," Stephen said sitting down, discovering that, surprisingly, his appetite seemed to have returned.

Before serving began Mrs. Younger bowed her head. There was no hand holding just a quick *Bless this food to our need and nourishment, in Jesus' name Amen.* Stephen said "Amen," then took a sip of tea.

Mary Ann lifted the chicken platter and began serving him. She stabbed a half breast, moved it onto his plate, then took the potatoes from her mother and dipped a large spoonful onto his plate and poured gravy over them. Then came the green beans, cooked with bacon and boiled onions placed on top. She dipped some beans onto his plate. The service rather made Stephen uncomfortable. Made the knot in his stomach pull up a little.

"Dig in, Mr. Mitchell," Mrs. Younger said.

With a glance around Stephen dug into the mashed potatoes and gravy.

"So, you and Fester got into it?" Mary Ann asked.

"Yeah. He made a stupid remark about Dr. King's assassination that I just couldn't take so I hit 'im and we were off. Turned into a whole big riot in the Student Union. They might have let it go if we hadn't broken the place up so much and/or hadn't gotten a couple dozen others involved in it. As it was, they tossed both me and Fester out."

"Tossed you out?" Mrs. Tucker asked.

"Expelled us."

"Oh my," Mary Ann said. "Seems pretty harsh."

"Yeah, kinda, but I understand. The whole campus was on edge after Dr. King was killed. Several fights and near fights. They pitched us out as a warning to anybody else that might consider more fighting. They want to keep the lid on until this all simmers down. They called the state police to put in an appearance just in case. And they chucked the Kappas off campus. No more red hats, so all in all I think getting expelled was worth it."

"So, what are you going to do now?" Mrs. Younger asked.

Stephen shrugged. "Go back to LA and get a job. Go to school part time."

"You have to worry about the draft?" Mary Ann asked.

"Naw. Marines turned me down so I'm guessing I'm through with all that."

"Turned you down?" Mary Ann asked.

"Yeah. Said I had a wonky heart. They don't want anything but physically perfect in the Marines."

"You could stay here in Memphis," Mary Ann said with a somewhat longing look.

"I don't think so, Mary Ann. Too many bad memories," then he thought of what he had said. "No, not you or us or anything like that. I was thinking more about Ethan and Robert, Dr. Marchant, and now Dr. King. There's just too much pain and death connected with Tennessee, so I don't want to hang around to see what's next. "

"That's a pretty dark view of Tennessee, Mr. Mitchell. You didn't find anything good about us?" Mrs. Younger said.

Stephen looked at her and a chill went up his back. This was a trap of some kind for sure. He took another bite of mashed potatoes and a big drink of tea. "Yes, ma'am. I did, but it confuses me in a lot of ways. Southern hospitality is wonderful, but it can turn on a fella in a heartbeat, depending on the color of his skin or his point of view."

Mrs. Younger looked as though she wanted to argue about this, but Stephen caught another look exchange between mother and daughter that ended the older woman's desire.

The rest of the meal was taken up with small talk. Stephen told them about California and about helping to build Hardtwick Academy.

"I'll probably go to work there again when I get home. There's always something that needs doing. I started working there when I was about fourteen. Learned a lot about construction."

"There's a lot of places to get that kind of work here in Memphis," Mary Ann said.

Stephen nodded, "It would still be in Tennessee though, and the same reasons I talked about before still apply."

Eventually, Stephen thought he had stayed long enough and said, "I need to call my uncle Paul and head back to his house. I still have a few things to do before I head for LA."

Mary Ann quickly said, "You don't have to call. I'll take you." Another exchanged look between mother and daughter, that Stephen didn't understand. This was something else that seemed like a trap but he let it pass "You don't have to go to all that trouble, Mary Ann," he said.

"It's no trouble, Steve."

"Well, all right. If you don't mind."

Stephen could not tell, but he had the feeling Mary Ann's mother was not much happy about this ride business. "Be careful out there, Mary Ann," she said.

"Yes, ma'am," she said.

Stephen wasn't so sure this was a good idea the second he got in the car with Mary Ann. There was something about the way she looked over at him, and the smell of her perfume. His maleness began to react and memories of the Methodist cemetery ran through his mind. The taste of desire was at the back of his throat. He took a deep breath and tried to dispel the thoughts.

She seemed to be driving slowly as though unsure of her directions. "You know where you are going?" he asked.

"Yes," she said with a glance at him.

The look was one that shot through him and went right to his rising erection. *Oh shit, please God, not now. I can't, I can't.*

In what seemed like an hour but was only a few minutes Mary Ann finally pulled up to the curb in front of Paul and Esther's house, but rather than just pausing long enough for him to get out she turned off the engine and slid over next to him, and put her hand on his thigh.

"No, Mary Ann. No. Please don't," he said.

"But you want to, I can tell," she said and slid her hand a little higher until she could feel his now fully erect manhood.

"Yes, I want to, but I'm not going to. I was using you and I don't want to do it more. I'm leaving and I don't want anything more to regret. I'm sorry." He pulled the car door latch and it popped open. "Good night, Mary Ann. Please forgive me." He turned his legs out the door and stood.

She didn't say anything, just fixed her eyes on him. "I don't know if I hate you or love you, Steve."

Hanging his head, he said, "Hate me. Please. It's easier than loving me."

He closed the door and turned away. He didn't stop until he opened the front door then he looked back. Mary Ann was still looking at him. He went in and closed the door behind him.

It wasn't late so Paul and Esther were still awake watching TV. The girls had gone to bed.

"So, it looks like you survived," Paul said.

Stephen cleared the last few minutes out of his mind as best he could and said, "Yeah, but it was a near thing, I wanna tell ya."

Paul looked hard at him and didn't know whether to laugh or not. He decided to not.

"For good or ill, it's done," Stephen said. coming into the living room.

"Your dad wired you some money." Esther said. "You'll have to go down to the office to pick it up."

"Tomorrow."

"Jackie Bookman called, too," Aunt Esther said. "Said she was gonna skip Friday and be up here tomorrow morning."

Stephen felt that information in his stomach and thought again of Drew asking how he always managed to meet such beautiful girls. It made him smile. "Great. Thanks."

"Have a seat, we can put this TV anywhere you want," Paul said.

"No, thanks. I think I'll just go to bed. Been a rough couple of days."

"Okay. Good night," they both said.

In the bedroom with the door shut Stephen thought about what just happened, and shook his head. *Lord, I hope she doesn't do anything else foolish.*

Stephen didn't really sleep much. He tossed and turned and was plagued with frustration dreams: dreams where he felt he must reach for something. It was something unknown—out of reach.

Morning finally came with the smell of bacon, eggs and coffee. He got up and climbed into the same jeans and t-shirt he had been wearing. He closed the bedroom door firmly and purposely made some noise coming down the hall, remembering how he startled Aunt Esther before.

"My, my, you're up early?" Esther said.

"Force of habit, I guess, and the smell of bacon and coffee."

"Have a seat," she said, and indicated where by pouring him a cup of coffee. "You timed it pretty well." She set a large bowl of scrambled eggs in front of him and a plate of bacon beside it. "Dig in. Paul and the girls will be here in a minute or two."

The words were no more than out of her mouth when Paul and the two children came to the table. Paul quickly bowed his head and repeated the same prayer Mrs. Younger said over the dinner last night. Stephen almost burst out laughing when a Boy Scout camping prayer came to his mind, *Rub-a-dub dub, thanks for the grub. Yeah, God.*

As Paul was serving the children, Stephen asked, "I hate to be a pain, but could I bum a ride to the Western Union office, wherever that is, so I can pick up the money Dad sent?"

"Sure," Paul said.

The doorbell rang. "Who could that be?" Esther said, going to answer it. She returned with Jackie Bookman in tow.

Stephen stood up. "You must have left before sun up," he said.

"What happened to your face, Steve?" she asked.

"Walked into a door," he said with a crooked smile. "You should have seen me a couple days ago."

"Not more Memphis cops?" she asked, half joking.

"No, not this time."

"Have a seat," Esther said.

"No thanks, I'm fine."

"Well, at least have some coffee, and let me finish my breakfast," Stephen said.

"Sure," she answered, and pulled out a chair. "We going somewhere?"

"Going to save Paul a trip to the Western Union office," Stephen said.

"Oh, okay," Jackie said and sat down. "Maybe you'll tell me what really happened to you."

Esther poured coffee.

"Rednecks," Stephen said.

"You'll have to be more specific. Lots of rednecks around."

"Yeah. Remember I told you about Elgin Fester and his red hat buddies?"

She nodded.

"Well, after Dr. King was killed, he made a crude remark about it. I just couldn't take it anymore so I belted him. There were a dozen or so of his red hat buddies who piled on in his defense, so here I am." He flipped his hand up and down in front of his face. "What time does the Western Union office open, Paul? You know?"

Paul shrugged. "Probably at nine. That's when most non-food businesses open."

Stephen looked at his watch. "Hour and a half. Guess I'll have another cup of coffee, Aunt Esther."

"How about you, Jackie?" Esther asked.

"Sure."

Jackie knew exactly where the Western Union office was so it only took a few minutes for Stephen to pick up the money. His father had sent him two hundred fifty dollars, which seemed excessive to him, but he folded the cash and put it in his pocket. Back in the car he said, "I really don't want to go back to Paul and Esther's."

"Well, you got any particular place you wanna go?" she asked.

"Nothing open on Beale Street now, I guess."

"They are *Night Clubs,*" she said.

"Some place we can talk for a while?"

"How about Overton Park?"

Stephen smiled at that. "Yeah, that'd be great. My folks used to bring me to the zoo there when we would come to visit Grandma in the summer."

As they drove Stephen split his time between looking out the windows to take in all of Memphis he could, and looking at Jackie. He remembered the first time he met her, last year on the train from California. She was as beautiful then as now and he thought how much he envied the guy who had made love to her in the darkened dome car that first night. The fool had screwed her and abandoned her, leaving her to cry alone in the dark. *That dumb ass,* he thought, *I would never have left her like that.*

Jackie pulled into an almost empty parking lot beside a wide swath of green. She parked then turned to Stephen. "You wanna get out and walk?" she asked.

Stephen shook his head. "I just want to sit here and talk to you. I'm really gonna miss you, Jackie," he said. "I hope you'll remember me when I'm gone."

"Geeze, sounds like you're dying." She looked over at him. "You aren't dying, are you?"

Stephen shrugged. "Probably not, but ya can't ever tell. I just meant that I'm not gonna be back in Memphis for a long, long time, if ever."

"What? Why not?"

"Lot of reasons. Dr. Marchant's death, Robert's, Ethan Patrick's, now Dr. King's death. Mary Ann Younger. Lot of bad memories here."

"Mary Ann Younger?" she asked.

"It's a whole big mess. I was going out with her, kinda. She got the wrong idea and ended up getting hurt. It was my fault. Like I said, bad memories." Stephen looked away from Jackie's face and down at his feet.

"I'm not one of them, am I?"

Stephen looked at her for a long quiet moment then said, "God, no. You are one of the few reasons I might ever consider staying."

"Thank you. I'd like you to stay." She reached across the car and took his hand in hers.

Her touch gave him a tingle that ran up his arm. He let his hand linger in her grip for a few moments then pulled away.

"Probably not a good idea, considering. Besides, I can't."

"Why not?"

"Oh yeah, you didn't hear the rest of the story, did you? I got thrown out of school for inciting to riot. I'm on my way back to LA to try and pull my life together again."

"Inciting to riot?"

"Yeah, the punch in Fester's mouth led to a huge brawl in the Student Union and I got pitched, but so did Fester and the whole red hat crew, so all in all I think I won. Course explaining that to my old man is gonna be—interesting, but apparently, I'm still in the will. I mean, he sent me money to get home on."

"How can you joke about it? You got expelled from school. That's pretty bad," she said with real concern in her voice.

"Yeah, I guess, but it makes me feel a little better that I got pitched because I was defending Dr. King's honor." A bolt of regret shot through Stephen's heart and he fell silent.

"What are you gonna do?"

"Truth is, I don't know. I intend to get a job and go to school

1

part time. We got great state colleges in California, a lot cheaper than Mason, but truth be told, I don't know. If I have learned anything in the last couple of years it is that if you wanna make God laugh, tell him your plans. Right now, all I want to do is sit here and look at you. God being willing, I'll memorize your face so I can remember it anytime I want."

Jackie blushed a little at that. "I'll have to remember you, too," she said. "You're the closest thing to an interesting man I have known outside my father."

Stephen frowned at that. "Thanks—I think."

"If we'd had more actual time together there might have been more, but truth is I barely know you."

"Yeah, I guess that's true." *Some ways I know you better than you know me,* Stephen thought. "Speaking of your father, how's his investigation into Dr. Marchant's murder coming?"

"All right, I guess. He won't talk much about open cases but I know they picked up some guy who was pawning some of Marchant's missing jewelry."

"Yeah, but that doesn't tell me much."

"That's about all I know. Oh, the guy is white, I asked after you asked me before."

Stephen nodded. "Really was just a burglar, I guess."

"I guess."

"You know anything more about what's happening with Robert's murder?"

"He talks more about that one since it is a cold case, but there isn't much to tell. He is still working at getting into the KKK up in Mason, but they apparently aren't a real trusting bunch. He'll keep working on it, I'm sure."

"Please keep in touch about that."

She nodded. After a moment she asked, "When are you actually leaving?"

"I don't exactly know. American has a flight going to LAX every day, some in the morning and some in the evening. I coulda gone yesterday, but I wanted to hang around long enough to see you again. Say goodbye, ya know."

They sat quietly looking at one another for a little then Stephen glanced at his watch and said, "I guess I need to go back to Paul and Esther's. I think there is a flight this afternoon that I can get."

Jackie looked down and Stephen thought she was going to cry, but after a couple moments she looked up with no tears. She turned and started the car.

Back at Paul and Esther's Stephen asked, "You wanna come in for a little bit? Let me check on the flight time."

"Might as well," she said. "Mom doesn't even know I'm home. Doesn't expect me till tomorrow so I can hang around a bit longer."

They climbed out of the car and as they walked toward the front door side by side, their hands brushed. Jackie took hold of Stephen's hand. He hesitated to let her continue but her hand felt so good in his that he didn't let go.

"Hello," Stephen called out as they came in.

"Oh, hi, y'all," Esther said, looking up from the sewing she had in her lap.

"Paul in his office?" Stephen asked.

"No. He's at the church," Esther said.

"Good. Can I use the phone?"

"Of course," she said.

He pulled his hand loose from Jackie's grasp and headed back to the office. He dialed the American Airlines number from memory.

Back to the living room. He plopped down beside Jackie. "There is a flight for LA at eight o'clock tonight," he said. "Could I get you guys to get me over there, Aunt Esther?"

"I suppose," she answered.

"If not," Jackie began, "I can take him."

Esther glanced up, her eyes going from Jackie to Stephen and back. "Thanks Jackie, but I don't think you'll need to do that."

"Is it okay if I go to the airport with you?" she asked.

"Fine by me," Esther said and went back to her sewing.

"How about you, Steve? Can I come see you off?"

Stephen realized how much he wanted her to come to the airport with him. "Yeah, that'd be great."

Jackie and Stephen watched soap operas and afternoon talk shows as Esther sewed then got up to prepare supper. Jackie held Stephen's hand the whole time.

Esther fed them supper early enough so that they could get to the airport and be first in line for Student Stand-by tickets. The airport was not as crowded as Stephen had seen it in the past, but there were still quite a few people moving around. Lots of people in uniform, and they all seemed to be headed west.

Stephen got in line at American and when he reached the clerk, he asked, "How's chances of getting into LA on a Student Stand-by?"

The clerk shrugged. "Maybe. Tomorrow there wouldn't be a chance, but Thursday night, maybe."

"Okay, let me have one," he said.

When the ticket was in his hand he went to the gate and registered. "You are fourth on the list, Mr. Mitchell," the stewardess said.

"Not bad, thanks," he said and went back to Paul, Esther, Jackie and the girls. "I'm fourth in line," he told them, looking around.

There were several people in the waiting area but it wasn't as crowded as he had seen it.

Jackie took his hand again.

"Sure are a lot of soldiers," Esther said.

"All going west on their way to Vietnam," Stephen said.

Paul shook his head. "Johnson was on TV the other day talking about ramping up the number of troops there. I pray every day that it will be over."

"Strange, but since the Marines turned me down, I don't think about it too much," Stephen said.

"That's the way empires work," Paul said. "They go

marching on and the people that are left at home never think about it."

"Empires?" Stephen said. "You think we are becoming an empire?"

"That's the way history usually works. A civilization starts out more or less democratic or at least inclusive but it tends to evolve into a single ruler empire over a period of a couple of centuries."

"We aren't a dictatorship,"

"Not yet. Give it time. One way or another, it is all in God's hands."

The waiting area began to fill up. Stephen looked at his watch. "They're gonna call first class any minute now," he said.

The words were hardly out of his mouth before the desk stewardess called, "All those with first class tickets for Los Angeles International Airport please line up here at the desk."

There was some movement but not too much. In a few more moments coach class lined up. There were considerably more of them and the thought crossed Stephen's mind, *I could probably have afforded a coach ticket. If I don't make it on this one, I may do that tomorrow.* but then the thought was gone. As the coach passengers marched down the loading ramp, he felt Jackie's hand tighten on his.

Stand-by calls started. The clerk called three names and stopped. *Oh shit,* Stephen thought.

"I may be coming back home with you guys tonight," he said. The clerk called "Mitchell, Stephen."

Stephen stuck up his hand, "Here, I'm here." The clerk acknowledged him and crossed his name off the list.

"Guess that's it," Paul said, and stuck out his hand. Stephen took it.

"Thanks again, Paul, and you too, Aunt Esther," he said, giving her a quick hug and a peck on the cheek.

"Hope everything goes all right when you get home." Paul said with a grin.

"We'll see," Stephen said. "Do me a favor and call Mom, will you, Aunt Esther? Tell 'em I'll be in LA about nine o'clock their time." He smiled at his aunt and she answered with a smile.

"I'll do that," she said.

"Maybe smooth things out a little," he said.

Turning toward the gate, he tried to pull his hand out of Jackie's grasp but she was hanging on tight. "I am gonna miss you something awful," she said.

"Me too," he said and bent to kiss her cheek, but she was having none of it.

She threw her arms around his neck and kissed him on the lips with passion. When she pulled back, he said, "I gotta go before they give my seat away."

"Let 'em," she said and kissed him again.

Now there were tears in her eyes. "You better write me, you rat."

"I will. I promise."

XXV

The grind of the cement mixer induced such a feeling of déjà vu that it gave him a chill, though the weather was already hot. This time he was mixing mortar for Vic Sandvig, another Hardtwick teacher working to build the school during the summer break.

Coming home after being expelled had not been easy, but had not been as hard as he expected. Dealing with his mother's wails of *all that money wasted* was more difficult than anything. After a couple of days rest, he began looking for a job but ultimately came back to working at Hardtwick though there were other jobs that paid better.

He looked into starting classes at Valley State but decided that he would wait until the fall semester to really begin. Meantime, he would work, read books, and write letters, stories, and poetry and begin the process of learning how to submit his work to publishing outlets. As he thought back on the last couple of years, he decided that they would probably make pretty good novels.

Sixth of June, with the presidential race ramping up, Bobby Kennedy was killed. Stephen and a large part of the country saw it happen on TV. Somehow Stephen was not surprised. It seemed as though the universe was out to get everyone who espoused equality.

The Hardtwick breakroom was a fuming bomb because of it. There were those who thought, but didn't say, "The liberal SOB had it coming." They still managed to make their positions clear.

Stephen tried desperately to stay out of the arguments and ultimately his reaction stopped the strife. One day when the arguments hit high decibels, he couldn't take it any longer and stood up. "Shut up all of you! Two of the lights of the world have been put out and it is because of people like you Christians. So shut the hell up!" He stormed out of the room leaving stunned silence behind him.

In the end of June 1968, Stephen came home from work, dirty and tired. Coming in the back door into the laundry room he stripped off his clothes and went directly to the shower. In a few moments, refreshed, in clean shorts and t-shirt, he went to the telephone table in the front room to look through the mail. He hoped to find a letter from Jackie Bookman but the only thing he found with his name on it was an official-looking document from the Selective Service. *What the hell? Thought I was through with this.* He opened it and glanced through it. It was a directive telling him to report for a pre-draft physical.

Gotta be a mistake, he thought, but when he called the information number on the notice, they assured him that it was not. They told him to bring all his paperwork from his last physical and his draft card and report to the same place on Van Nuys Boulevard where he had reported before.

It was the same room where he had gone through his Marine physical. Might have been the same examiners for all he could remember. He and a half dozen other young men, mother-naked except for paper shoes, carrying file folders, shuffled along, stopping every few steps and turning to some vaguely medical examiner to be examined. Eyes, ears, open mouth, bend over, spread your buttocks, turn your head and cough. The one at the end was the one Stephen was waiting for. The man with the stethoscope.

Stephen felt as though he had been dropped into a surrealist painting. The déjà vu was so palpable it made him shiver. The feeling was becoming so familiar it no longer surprised him. When he reported to the federal building, he tried to explain this was a mistake, that he had tried to enlist in the Marines, that he already had a physical and failed it, but the sergeant at the desk just nodded his head, stamped the notice Stephen had been sent, pointed to the right.

With a deep breath he went. *I'll just go on like last time until I get to the end. They'll find out it was a waste of time and I'll go home,* he thought. Now here he was again, after being poked prodded and thumped, facing the man with the stethoscope. He held out his folder to the examiner.

"I don't need that yet," the man said.

"You might want to have a look at it before you waste your time," Stephen said.

"Oh yeah? Why's that?"

"Cause I been here before, and they washed me out."

The examiner frowned and took the offered file folder. He looked through it, skip reading. "Heart murmur," he said, then blinked at Stephen a couple of times and handed the folder back. "Okay. But I still gotta check just to make sure the paperwork and the stethoscope agree."

Stephen shrugged. "All right, then." He took a deep breath and held it for a moment.

The action caught the examiner a little off guard, so he said, "I'm not ready yet. Just stand there and breathe regular for a minute."

"Sorry," Stephen said.

The examiner looked him up and down to see if Stephen was being a smart ass, but found just a tall, kinda skinny kid with hazel eyes looking back at him. "Deep breath and hold it." he said.

Stephen did as he was told and the stethoscope was pressed to his chest for a moment.

"Again," the examiner said. Stephen let out the breath and took another.

After a moment the examiner straightened. "I don't hear anything abnormal."

Stephen didn't protest or do anything except raise an eyebrow.

The examiner took the folder back, opened it and skipped through it again, then handed it back. "Tell ya what I'm gonna do. I want you to go through that door right there and have a word with the man you find in there."

"Yes, sir," Stephen said.

He turned and walked the few steps to, then through, the half-glass door that he remembered from last time. Inside was the same empty desk.

A balding older man in a white lab coat with a stethoscope draped around his neck stepped through the door beside the desk. Stephen thought this might be the same doctor as the one who examined him last year, but he couldn't be sure. "Right this way, young man."

Stephen did as he was told and stepped through the door.

The doctor pulled a wide strip of paper from a roll at the head of an examination table to cover it. The déjà vu feeling washed over Stephen again and he shivered.

"Have a seat on the table," the doctor said, and again Stephen did as he was told, laying the brown folder beside him.

The doctor put the stethoscope in his ears and pressed the listening part against Stephen's chest. This one was not pre-warmed like the other one had been. This one was icy cold and it made Stephen pull a short breath and wonder if the thing had been kept in the fridge.

"Slow deep breath, please."

Stephen drew in air and let it out slowly.

The doctor moved the stethoscope a little and said, "Deep breath again and hold it."

Stephen did as he was told and after a moment the doctor said, "Okay." He picked up the folder, opened it, examined the papers then settled the folder on the table again, wrote something on one of the sheets.

"Hum," the doctor said. He turned back to Stephen and said. "Another deep breath and hold it." He pressed the somewhat less cold stethoscope to a couple of places on Stephen's chest, then said, "Okay. Do it again." Stephen did as he was told. This time the doctor pressed the listening device to his back.

When he was done the doctor stepped back and looked at

Stephen, then looked at the folder again.

"I don't find any heart murmur, young man."

"Yes, sir. I tried to tell them last time they were hearing things, but they said I wasn't fit, that I was done. I went to my doctor, had an EKG. No murmur. I came back and tried to tell them, but they didn't want to hear it. I thought I was done. Then a couple of weeks ago I get a draft notice that says I gotta come down here for a physical, so here I am."

"Well, I gotta tell you, your heart seems fine, and everything else does, too." He closed the folder and handed it to Stephen. "I don't know what to tell you, young man," he said offering his hand. The gesture was so familiar it made Stephen shiver again. He shook the offered hand and the doctor said. "You're all well. Welcome to the U.S. Army."

About the Author
ghelm11109@earthlink.net

G. Lloyd Helm is a ne'er-do-well scribbler who has been scratching away for fifty years through the support of his long-suffering wife. He has many books on the market of which this is one. He has traveled the world seeking adventure and has found that most "adventures are cold, hungry, painful things best avoided."

The Design

"Are the gods truly gods or just powerful humans?" The question still echoes through the city of Peshar even six hundred years after the coming of the gods. Garith Balal, a successful scribe and fair witness in the city, is pulled into the resistance to the gods through influence of a slave bought to satisfy his wife's social-climbing desires. Alvis, the slave, a human from another world of the Cadeki empire, has roots in the planet Archlea where he is now a slave. He is a believer in "The Design," the belief that all things in the universe are controlled to an unknown end by the Great Designer who created the universe.

Part I

One

22 (B)efore the (C)oming of the (G)ods

In the seventeenth year of the reign of Whidbis IV over the city of Peshar, Indi Ransis, short, skinny, and green-eyed with an infectious grin, strolled through Tapestry Plaza idly looking at the tapestries displayed there. He was supposed to be hurrying to the far side of the Plaza where the best Houses displayed their work. He was to relieve his sister Atris, who was minding the three tapestries House Ransis was displaying. But somehow Indi's feet would not move faster than a stroll.

The plaza was alive with noise and color and aromas, but not the same as the market squares. Those were alive too, but they were filled with commerce. Tapestry Plaza was filled with—life? With spirit? With…Indi could not say with what else, but he could feel the power and joy of it wash over him like the warm breeze that ruffled his hair as he walked. All of Peshar could feel it, for at one time or another, all of Peshar passed through Tapestry Plaza.

"About time," Atris snapped at her brother. "I'm starving."

"I doubt that," Indi said, smiling at his younger sister.

"I am. And where have you been anyway?"

"Looking around the plaza. Taking in the air," he answered, knowing it would annoy her.

"While I sat here in the hot sun, practically fainting from hunger!" she said, outrage in her voice.

"I am here now, Atris, so why waste time scolding me? You might drop dead from starvation."

"Why…" she sputtered. "I'll tell Papa. I'll tell him you left me sitting out here while you wandered around the plaza."

Atris huffed and fumed and boiled for a few more moments, but Indi ignored her, and when she saw he was not listening, she flounced away and disappeared into the crowd.

Indi was sure she would tell Papa, and he was sure he would catch the sharp edge of the old man's tongue when he got home, but he didn't let it bother him much. He stretched his arms wide and yawned, then settled himself upon the short stool beside the tapestries. He did not glance at them. He already knew them well. One of them he knew far more intimately than he would have liked. He had strung most of the warp thread for it on the medium loom in the Ransis tapestry factory. It was a tedious, eye-straining, patience-trying job at the best of times, and much worse when the workman hated the work to begin with.

Young Ransis tried not to think about the factory. Thoughts of it made his stomach knot, as did thoughts of the dye works, the spinnery, or the sheep and goats on the farms that supplied House Ransis with wool. His stomach knotted with dread when he thought of the life which was planned out for him. He was the eldest son of House Ransis, and as such, was fated to take over as Patriarch when his father decided to retire and begin weaving his *Memoria*. That would not happen for many years, if the Gods were kind. The old man was strong and vigorous. But when the *Memoria* was woven Indi would be expected to bring it here to Tapestry Plaza to display it. That would be his first act as Patriarch of House Ransis.

"A life well planned," which could make Indi's mood bleak if he thought about it for more than a few moments.

He looked around the plaza. The day was beautiful. Blue sky with puffy white clouds slowly drifting by on a warm breeze. Bright golden sun which gave everything it touched a tasty aura of brightness. Small groups of people moved slowly from display, to café, to teahouse, talking and nodding. Everything seemed right to Indi except for a group of people too large to be friends talking. Above the heads of this gathering a single head rose, facing the others.

Young Ransis glanced around, saw that no one was near the House Ransis display, and left his stool to find out what was going on. He pushed up to the outside of the crowd and turned an ear toward the man who was standing on something to raise him above the people so he could be heard.

"All things are in the hands of the Great Designer," the man said.

He was youngish, but not a boy, for he had a considerable growth of beard. Much more than the scraggly fuzz Indi's chin could boast.

"The Designer is like a weaver of tapestries, like these here, only his weaving is the world and all that is in it. We are only threads within the Design, and can no more understand the fullness of it than can one thread in a House Ransis weaving perceive the greatness of the whole work.

"We poor children of this world go through our lives

thinking we control what goes on around us. We think that with enough gold, or land, or herds we will have say over our lives, but it is not so. We prepare our lives and suddenly, without warning, the Great Designer speaks and all we have, all we are, comes to nothing. Our fortunes are lost. Our lives are changed. Our very hearts are pulled out and put back different than ever before. And it happens in the blink of an eye. It happens between one breath and the next. The Designer and Maker of All crooks his finger and a breath of wind comes to stir a puff of dust, which blows into a wagoner's eye and causes him to pull tight upon the reins, which causes his animals to rear up in their harness and, though they be the most gentle of beasts, they paw the air and strike the head of one passing and he dies. Perhaps he is rich. Perhaps he is poor. But rich or poor, high born or low born, he is dead, and all his illusion of controlling his life is gone as fog before sunlight. Or perhaps a blind beggar sleeping in a ruin beside the refuse pit turns in his sleep rolling upon a lump of rock. The beggar pulls the stone from beneath him and casts it away with a curse, but a scavenger child, trying to stay alive upon the garbage of Peshar finds the stone and sees that it is a lump of stone with nodes of gold in it. He rejoices thinking that now he can control his life. He will no more have to dig in the refuse pit. But his control is illusion also. In fact, he has found this gold because the Great Designer wanted him to find it. The Great Designer has a purpose in the scavenger child's finding of the gold, just as there was purpose in the accidental death of the man beneath the hooves of the horses. Just as there was purpose in the curl of wind. All is in the hands of the Great Designer."

"But you can see tomorrow, I suppose," a voice sneered from the crowd, "and you will be more than happy to tell us what our tomorrows will be—for a zari or two."

Many of the crowd laughed and hooted.

The speaker grinned a twisted grin. It was not the shamefaced smile of one caught in a fortune-telling scheme. "Even you, my friend, are moved by the Designer to his purpose."

"No doubt," answered the heckler.

"No doubt," said the speaker. "No, I am no teller of fortunes.

I cannot see tomorrow any more than you can. I only know that I am in His hands, and He will deal with me in some way which will enhance the Design. My life will be a part of the Design and I will be a willing thread."

"I do not understand, oh thread," another voice called. "What would you have us do?"

The speaker turned toward the questioner. "I would have you believe. I would have you leave off your belief in the old gods, and your dedication to their temples as did Macar Holis when the Great Designer spoke to him from the flame. I would have you know in the depths of your heart that everything you do, everything you think, every breath you take, is at the behest of the Great Designer. Believe that you serve a purpose, and submit yourself to that purpose."

"And what will it cost us, oh thread?" the mocking voice asked.

"Nothing, and everything. When you acknowledge the Designer your life suddenly changes, for you no longer have the illusion of control. You find yourself completely at peace, knowing that you are truly a part of the Great Design. A willing thread, playing out your part with joy. Knowing that you have no control of life, but happy that you are controlled by the hand of the mighty Creator of All."

The crowd murmured and shifted, almost ready to turn away and go about their business.

"And suppose, oh thread," the mocking voice spoke, and the crowd calmed again, hoping for more amusement. "Suppose, oh thread that your part of this great weaving is to stain it with your blood, when some servant of the true Gods separates your head from your neck? "

The crowd, half anxious for such an execution to add a little excitement to their dull lives, laughed and leaned forward to hear how the speaker would answer.

"I will not look forward to it," he said. "But, if that is in the Design, that is what will happen. It will serve some purpose though

I will not live to see that purpose worked out."

The crowd broke up after a little more baiting by the heckler. The speaker refused to rise to grow angry or answer spitefully.

Indi noticed that several acolytes from the Temple of Pesh had been among those listening to the Servant of the Design. It did not surprise him. The Temple of Pesh had been assaulted by this cult of the Design before. They did not talk about it, but almost everyone knew that some time back the Macar Holis the preacher had mentioned, who had been a righteous believer in Pesh, had claimed to have received a vision from some other god, telling him that Pesh was not a god. These Designers returned now and then from wherever they hid to preach their god. It almost always ended badly for the preacher.

Young Ransis went back to his stool and parked himself upon it once more. *This Designer sounds like Papa,* Indi thought. *He has all the future planned out and I have no say in it.*

The thought left a bitter taste, but as Indi rolled it around in his mind, he saw that it was probably true. No one truly controlled his own life, even Papa. He was only doing what his own father had set him up to do and would only do what he thought best.

"They are very beautiful," a voice said.

Indi looked up, and then shaded his eyes from the glare of the sun to see who stood before the display racks. It was the Designer cultist.

"They are House Ransis works, are they not?"

"Yes," Indi answered.

"The workmanship is something to be proud of."

"House Ransis is very proud of its work. That is why we have them displayed here in the plaza."

"Yes, of course." He continued to stand before the tapestry for which Indi had strung the warp threads. "This one seems somehow different though," he said.

"Different?"

"Yes. More—pained than the others." He turned to face Indi who had risen and now stood close. "It is your work, is it not, Indi Ransis?"

"Not…" Indi stopped short. "How do you know my name?"

The man smiled his twisted smile. Now that he was close enough, Indi saw that the twist was caused by a scar on the left side of the man's mouth. It was almost hidden by his beard, but not quite.

The man noticed the direction of Indi's eyes. "The Designer decreed that one who listened would be a strong believer in another god, and would demonstrate his belief with a large stone," he said with wry humor.

"How do you know my name?" Indi asked again.

"A dream. Your name and face came to me in a dream."

Indi snorted. "Those in the crowd who jibed were right. You're only a soothsayer and a dreamer of dreams. Go away. Leave me alone. I want nothing to do with your Designer."

"It does not matter. Your wants are of no consequence. The Designer has a special purpose for you, and it will be worked out as surely as the pattern of thread and colors are worked into your tapestry."

The laugh rose bitter as bile from Indi's heart. "Much your Designer knows. I have a part in a Design right enough, and not one of my own making either. I was born eldest son of House Ransis, and nothing I can do, except perhaps die, can change my life from what is set out for me."

The other shrugged, unperturbed. "As you wish. Nevertheless, when the time comes, travel north to Keep Holis. It is not difficult to find. On foot the journey took me a little more than three months. You will know you are near when the mountains called the Three Needles are the last thing touched with the light of evening, and the first thing touched with the light of dawn. Ask for guidance then. You are expected."

Indi could think of no answer for the surety of the man. He could only stare open mouthed as the man turned and disappeared into the crowd.

~ * ~

Design and Designers and what the Servant of the Design had said were never far from Indi's thoughts. He talked with no one about the visit to the display racks, or about anything else. He kept his own counsel and shrugged off the sharp words of his father who told Indi to pay attention to what he was doing, lest he knot the threads or string them backward.

Seven days after Indi had talked with the Servant of the Design he sat at a table outside a tea house in Tapestry Plaza, a cup of tea going cold in his hands and watched ten men in the robes of the Temple of Pesh haul the Designer from the stool which lifted him above the crowd who listened to him. Indi joined the crowd which trailed the priests and their captive to the square at the foot of the broad steps leading up to the colonnade of the Temple of Pesh. A hooded priest dressed all in white came down the temple steps to join them. He carried a heavy bronze sword with shaft long enough to be gripped with two hands.

"By order of Whidbis, Ruler of Peshar, Protector of the Ancient Faith, Chief Worshiper of Mighty Pesh, Father of Gods, you are accused of the crime of blasphemy. Will you answer this charge?"

The Servant of the Design did not smile, but the smile was in his voice when he said, "How can one blaspheme something which does not exist?"

The crowd gasped. This was blasphemy thrown into the very face of Mighty Pesh and his servants.

Indi found a catch in his throat that made him want to cry out, "NO...NO...NO...Do not say that. They will kill you! Do you not see the sword?" But he said nothing, only watched like the rest of the silent crowd.

"By your own mouth you stand condemned," the priest said, cutting off any further words from the Servant of the Design. "Bind him," he commanded.

The priests began winding strips of cloth round the Servant of the Design. They bound him into a cocoon of cloth so that he could not move. The man did not resist or speak.

Indi watched, horrified. He had seen executions before, but

not like this. He could not take his eyes away from the face of the Servant of the Design. It seemed that the other's eyes were locked onto Indi's.

At last the man was bound, leaving only his head and neck exposed. He stood still, held steady by three priests. These knelt in their positions, and the executioner stepped forward. He lifted the sword to the heavens and cried, "Behold, Mighty Pesh, we protect thy temple." He lowered the sword and let it rest broadside upon the left shoulder of the Servant of the Design who still stood upright. The executioner drew the sword back, coiling himself to strike.

In the half heartbeat between the executioner's drawing back his sword and the cut, Indi saw the Servant of the Design draw a deep, calm breath, and he knew the man's last thought was, *All is in the Design.*

The sword swung clean and flat, and the head of the blasphemer leapt to the right and rolled down the back of one of the priests who knelt holding the body. Blood pulsed in a fountain from the severed neck and washed down over all the kneeling priests.

The executioner stepped to the severed head and lifted it by the hair. "Thus, ever Blasphemers," he shouted.

The following morning Indi Ransis told his father that he was going to Keep Holis to study the Design.

~ * ~

All who studied the Design at Keep Holis changed their names. Indi chose to be called Javi, which meant seeker, and added Holis in honor of Macar Holis who had first heard the voice of the Designer.

Javi began his training as did all novices. He cleaned endlessly. Common rooms, yards, gardens, dwelling rooms of the Masters. He also helped in the kitchen and worked in the fields which fed those of the community of the Design. He slept and ate in the common rooms with other novices. He learned to look within himself for privacy, for there was no physical privacy in Keep Holis for novices. In the hours of the day not taken up with work he contemplated the drawings and writings of those who had lived and died in submission to the Design.

The Mandalai were Designs of incredible intricacy. They often took the form of wheels with the artist who had drawn them at the center. The artist's personal perceptions of the Design radiated out from this personal center. Other Mandalai had trees or the sun at their centers. All these were magnetic to Javi the tapestry maker. He could almost feel the stir such designs would make if they were displayed in Tapestry Plaza.

Some of the Mandalai he understood. They were celebrations of family, growing things, the changing of season, but others, called *dark,* he did not understand. He went to his masters to ask what they meant.

"We do not know," Master Aram told him. "That is why they are called the *Dark Mandalai.*"

"But they have meaning, Master Aram," Javi said. "I can feel that."

"Yes. You are not the first to feel that they have meaning, but thus far no one has been given the understanding of them."

"But how did those who drew them know what to draw?" Javi asked.

"How does a mother bird know what she must do to hatch her eggs? How does the egg know that it must become a bird not a turtle?" Master Aram shrugged. "It simply knows. That is the way of the Mandalai, and not just those called *Dark.* The Master of the Design whispered to the makers in their dreams or while they sat quietly listening for his words."

Javi sat a long time, and Master Aram did not disturb his thoughts.

Aram remembered the man who had first told him of the Design. That man had spoken of dreams and voices too, and student Aram had thought that man a fool at first. Now he sat, saying the same things to his student.

At last Javi came back from his contemplation and said, "Master, I think I have heard the voice of the Designer."

Master Aram blinked at this. He could hardly believe such effrontery. "Go on," he said.

"The words are not clear," Javi said. "I cannot see the full meaning of them, but I am sure the Designer has told me something of the power of the Dark Mandalai."

Master Aram did not quite succeed in keeping his doubts out of his voice.

"That is the way of the Designer," he said pulling his cloak tighter around him against the cold. "He knows our needs and our capacities, and gives us only that which he knows we are ready to know." He stretched out his hand and patted Javi on the shoulder. "Wait upon the Designer, Javi. He is preparing something for you. But do not be too quick to declare the whisperings of your own mind to be the voice of the Maker of All."

Javi bowed his head. "Yes, Master Aram. I will be careful."

The old man nodded. "Open your mind to the Designer," he said. "Allow yourself to be his instrument. Understanding will come to you, but do not be in too much of a hurry for it to come. Sometimes understanding brings more pain than satisfaction."

"Yes, Master," he said, and went back to his duties.

~ * ~

Winter's depths closed over the Keep. The already restricted life became even narrower. No fire seemed able to shield against the knife-like cold which hemmed the Servants of the Design into Keep Holis.

It was during one such bout of cold that Javi, with a wry thought, took the Dark Mandala called The Fire, and began to study it. He carried the velum sheet with care to the hearthstone of the common room and sat down to study it. After many hours of contemplation of the Mandala he found himself nodding, heavy with sleep. The fire in the hearth had burned low, and the room was cold.

Javi stood, stretched, rubbed his eyes, and shivered. He thought of his cold pallet at the other side of the room and decided to make a cup of tea to fortify himself against the chill. He shivered yet more as he broke the thick skin of ice which had formed on the water jar near the door. Javi dipped water into the teakettle and hung it on the pot hook above the fire, then punched up the flames with a poker and added a few sticks. When the blaze merrily licked at the bottom of the teakettle, he sat down on the hearth again. His mind wandered back to the Mandala he had been studying. The meaning of it seemed just on the edge of his comprehension, but he could not pull it into the full light of understanding. After a little while he forcibly shoved the thoughts from his mind and leaned over to check the teakettle.

The fire's warming tongue licked up around the teakettle's bottom and thin wisps of steam rose from the spout. The picture it formed stopped Javi as though he had been struck in the face. This was the meaning of the Mandala. It was the fire, whereby the steam of the spirit could be released from the teakettle of the body. The meaning was so clear Javi was astonished and ashamed that he had not understood before.

With his heart pounding in excitement, the young Servant of the Design lay down upon the hearth and closed his eyes. The hiss of the steaming kettle made a soft background which blanked out the sounds of wind and the crackling of ice from outside.

Javi brought the Dark Mandala called The Fire before his mind's eye. It was fire licking up around him, as fire licked the bottom of the kettle. It heated that part of him which was the real Javi Holis. The essence of him.

After a time, the Mandala began to have an effect. Javi felt his spirit warm and bubble—like heated water, and steam began to rise: the conscious steam of his essence, his spirit.

There was lightness to him. He felt himself drift up like steam from the kettle and he wondered if indeed he was rising like steam. He opened his eyes.

Below him, lying on the hearth was the body of a skinny young man with a ragged beard who was wrapped in a battered cloak. At first glance he looked dead, but a moment's observation showed slow, shallow movement of breath.

Javi wondered who the young man was. He did not remember seeing him among the students. There was something familiar about him though. He looked like—he looked like Javi's father. But that couldn't be. Papa was old.

Realization came to him like a slap. The body on the hearth was his own body! The Mandala had done its work He had separated spirit from body through concentration upon the Mandala.

Shock and surprise robbed Javi of control and his essence was drawn back into his body with a snap. In a moment he sat up and rubbed his eyes wondering if what had just happened was only a dream. He had often dreamed of flying like a bird when he was a child, but never so vividly that he could see his body below him.

Suddenly, Javi was shaking, and not with cold. He was sure this had not been a dream. He had separated his essence from the vessel created to contain it and the very thought of it was overwhelming. Frightening.

Javi drew in a deep breath and tried to calm the shaking of his hands and the quivering of his stomach. He set about finishing the tea he had started to make, not because he really wanted it, but because his mind needed the refuge of common things in order to keep sanity.

Sunlight had barely touched the peaks of the Three Needles when Javi presented himself to Master Aram. He explained what had happened.

"Perhaps it was a dream, Javi," the master said doubtfully

"It was no dream, Master Aram," Javi answered positively.

"But have you tried this separation again to be sure?" the old man asked.

"N,o Master. I wanted you to help me in the test. And…I am afraid."

Master studied his student for a moment, looking for the truth of what had happened. If the boy had been dreaming, then the dream might very well have come from the Maker of All. What else had Master been telling the student? Now Master Aram was being put to the test. Did he truly believe what he had been telling young

Javi?

"If this is a real power, then there is reason to be cautious, Javi, just as there is cause for caution when using fire or knives or medicines. But all those things are gifts of the Designer and when they are controlled, they are beneficial. I believe that this power, if it is real, is the same. Controlled, it may be of great benefit. Uncontrolled, it may be very dangerous."

"Then, shall I try to use it again, Master?"

The old man thought a moment. "Yes. I do not think the Master of Design would allow understanding if he did not wish the power used."

"I will go back to the hearth, and when the thing is done, I will come to you in my essence."

Master Aram nodded, and wondered if he had done right as he watched his student go.

Javi returned to the hearth, placed the teakettle upon its pot hook and punched up the fire. When steam was rising thick from the spout, he lay down and brought the Mandala of The Fire before his mind's eye. He was so nervous that he had trouble concentrating. Several times he opened his eyes and drew deep breaths, trying to calm himself. At first, he feared to relax too much, lest sleep, rather than the deep relaxation of meditation, overtake him.

After what seemed hours, he was ready to give up the attempt. He rose from the hearth and went to Master Aram's chamber to confess his inability.

At the closed door of the master's chamber he stopped, and lifted his hand to knock. His hand disappeared through the door.

Javi snatched his hand back and stared at the solid wood of the door. Then he slowly reached out…and put his hand through it.

It was an odd, watery feeling upon his wrist where it remained within the precinct of the door. He pulled his hand back. After a moment Javi drew in a deep breath, then laughed at the incongruity of a man without a body drawing in breath and stepped through the door.

Master Aram sat at his desk studying another of the Dark Mandalai. He looked up toward the door a second after Javi entered as though the entrance of the student's essence had disturbed him.

"Master Aram, I am here," Javi said.

The old man did not react to the voice, but his dark gray eyes seemed to deepen into their bony sockets and his lined face took on a haunted expression, as though something frightening were just on the edge of his vision.

"Javi, I cannot see you, but I feel the truth of your presence. Can you make yourself known somehow?"

Javi hesitated a moment, then moved to the desk and put his hand into the hand of his master.

The old man snatched his hand away as if he had been burned, but after a moment he returned his hand to the position it had been in before and said, "Javi, if it was you who touched me, touch me again."

Javi did as he was told, and again Master Aram snatched his hand away. "Your touch is like ice, and your presence makes my stomach queasy. Please go before I am unable to control myself. Return to me when you are again joined to your body."

Javi found that he was glad to return to his body. He had begun to feel cold and watery all over, almost as the steam rising from the kettle must feel as it was longer and longer away from the source of heat. He hurried back to the hearth and felt the chilly liquidity growing. When he reached the hearth, he had a moment of panic when he realized he did not know how to reunite with his body. He suppressed the fear and lay down on top of his waiting body, hoping this was the way to reunite body and spirit.

Minutes passed and the chill began to dissipate. Javi could feel the warmth of the fire, and knew he was no longer in two parts. With a corner of his mind he could see the Mandala of The Fire and realized that during his separation he had focused on it from time to time. Now he consciously closed that compartment of his mind and opened his eyes to the physical world.

Javi squeezed his eyes shut once more and flexed all his muscles to assure himself that they still worked, then stood and went to Master Aram's quarters. He knocked and entered when the old man called to him.

"Is all well, Javi?" the master asked.

"Yes, Master. I am fully restored."

"It was you who touched me," the old man said, no question in his voice.

"Yes. I spoke also, but you could not hear me."

"The instant you entered I felt your presence. There was a chill, but not from the winter's cold. Deeper, more bone freezing. And there was a sense of…like being at sea in a small boat. I felt sick."

"Yes, I understand."

The old man was in awe of his student. No one until now had understood any of the Dark Mandalai. Now this young man, hardly more than a boy, had been granted understanding by the Master of the Design. "What was it like, Javi? How did it feel?"

Javi tried to explain, but found it impossible. "There is no way to tell you, Master," he said at last. "And I do not know how I did it. I was unable to achieve the separation at first, but when I stopped trying, I suddenly found myself in two parts."

Master looked at student and found himself humbled. All the doubts he had harbored. All the silent laughter he had heaped upon what he thought was a pretentious child. All came back to haunt him now, and he was ashamed.

"Javi," Master Aram began, "The Maker of All truly has a special part of the Design for you to work out. I can only ask your forgiveness for my doubts. You must continue studying the Dark Mandalai. We have known for a long time that they were filled with great power, but we did not know, until now, what that power might be."

Javi, feeling suddenly alone and incompetent, swallowed hard. "Master Aram, I am only a student. I must have your guidance in this."

The old man was silent for a time, then said, "Perhaps I can help you in your studies, Master Javi."

Javi's eyes widened in surprise and he began to protest the title, but Master Aram waved him to silence. After a few moments Javi smiled, shyly. "Then we shall be students together, Master Aram."

Other books by G. Lloyd Helm
at
Rogue Phoenix Press

Serpents and Doves

The title "Serpents and Doves" comes from the warning Jesus gave to his disciples as he sent them out to preach the gospel, knowing the dangers they were going into. He said, "Be wise as serpents and harmless as doves." Stephen Mitchell learns first-hand what that warning means when he goes to a Tennessee church college in the midst of the turbulent sixties. He learns about friendship, war, protest, the sexual revolution, and civil rights.

World Without End

When an author writes a story, creates a world and the creatures in it, does the literary world actually come into being in some parallel universe? Joshua Gordon, creative writing professor and writer of pulp fiction thinks so and is in fact so convinced it is true that when he is diagnosed with a terminal illness, he sets out to find a protégé who he can convince to take over as the creator god of the world. He finds that protégé in the person of John Fisher.

Other Doors

Ben Fordham was a misfit destined to die in the gutters of

L.A. until he found himself in a seedy bar trying to cadge a drink from an odd-looking little fellow who claimed to be the best tattoo artist who ever lived. The next morning Fordham woke up with a beauty of a hangover, a beauty of a tattoo on his left forearm, and a beauty of a problem. He found himself chained to the slimy wall of a torch-lit dungeon with the threatening sound of soldiers' measured tread coming toward him—and his problems were just beginning.

Train Wheels, Flying Saucers and the Ghost of Tiburcio Vasquez

Most of the people in these stories are at least tangentially based on real humans. Big Dave was a fellow I worked with many years ago and his description in the stories is accurate. The reader should also notice that all these stories start and mostly end in a bar somewhere. I don't play adventure games, but I am told that most of them start in bars as well. There are still several Big Dave stories to be told, and I am working on them, but I just couldn't get them done in time to come out in this book. Many elements of these stories are true. The fun and the trick is to figure out what is true and what is fantasy.

Borrowing a Moosehead from Cole Porter

In our time as members of the US Air Force, we had lived in many places and gone through many things. We didn't expect that being stationed at Grissom AFB in Indiana would be the trial it turned out to be. We were leaving Germany, a foreign place, to come to middle America, supposedly home, but Grissom certainly didn't feel like home.

Between the circus that seemed to run the town of Peru, the god-awful weather and the hostile locals we felt like we had moved into a war zone. But, military families make the best of what they are dumped into so we did our best.